Raise the Dead

A Mystery

Jane Rubino

Llumina Press

Other Books by Author

The Cat Austen/Victor Cardenas Series:
Death of a DJ
Fruitcake
Cheat the Devil
Plot Twist
Cake Job (the Deadly Morsels anthology)

The Sherlock Holmes series
Knight Errant: The Singular Adventures of Sherlock Holmes

ISBN: 1-59526-342-X
1-59526-341-1

Printed in the United States of America by Llumina Press

Library of Congress Control Number: 2004091867

"*When one tries to rise above Nature,*
one is liable to fall below it."
Arthur Conan Doyle, The Creeping Man

FOR BILL

PROLOGUE: Three Years Ago

Ray skittered along the rain-slicked asphalt like a sowbug in a skillet. *Sowbug in a skillet*. His mother's phrase wrung out a skeleton smile. Ma. Too damn good for a woman poor as she was. Poverty hadn't made her mean and Ray had never figured out why. She'd taken on hard times like some sort of test, how much one good woman could put up with and stay good. Well, she'd passed, long before she'd passed on, and there had been too long a stretch when there'd been no one to keep Ray good. Maybe if Kathleen'd come along sooner.

Kathleen. Loving him made her either the stupidest woman in the world, or the loneliest. One of those women who just need someone to love. Anyone. And the harder you made it for them, the more stored-up love they doled out, until they almost had you believing you deserved it.

He heard the smooth splash of expensive tread on the wet asphalt, gave himself one last moment of believing that the headaches, the sleeplessness, were just the strain of the money, and losing little Ray and trying to be good when he didn't have it in him. He turned and saw what the headlight beams did to his shadow, split it at the trunk into some inhuman thing. *That's what I look like inside*, Ray thought. Like what had taken root inside Kathleen, then expelled itself dead. Raymond Stites, Junior. *Couldn't even give her a kid. Only thing she ever really came out and said she wanted, couldn't even do that.*

I should've been the one born dead. I'd be better off dead.

The lights died, his misshapen shadow evaporated. Ray got into the car, rested his head, his palms, on leather that smelled like money. He closed his eyes. "So how long do I got?"

"I'm sorry, Raymond."

The five syllables snuffed out his last ember of hope.

"I have your test reports and the X-rays- "

"Forget it. I don't know from that medical junk. A year?"

"Without treatment, a month. Maybe six weeks. With treatment, six to nine months, but they would be expensive months, and..." Pause. "Right now is the best you're going to be. It's downhill fast from here on and...."

"And it won't be a soft landing."

"Pro Patrol doesn't provide much in the way of medical, does it, Raymond? And Kathleen's policy won't cover this. And then there're your unfortunate habits. How much are you in for?"

Raymond opened his eyes. Raindrops slid down the windshield like those quiet tears falling down his mother's cheeks. "Ten. Large."

"I think we can do better than ten, Raymond. I think we can do more like fifty. Large."

Fifty grand. Ray tallied his debts. Even throwing in a grand or so to get him a decent burial, Kathleen'd clear almost forty thousand. But there was only one thing Ray knew how to do that anyone would pay him fifty grand for. "Who do I gotta kill?"

"Three people."

"Jesus." Ray licked his dry lips. "Not for..."

"Fifty? Sixty, then. But it's going to cost you, Raymond. I believe it's a sacrifice you'll be willing to make."

"What sacrifice?"

"Five weeks of your life."

"I don't get it."

"What were you thinking, Raymond? Before I pulled up?"

"That I'd be better off dead."

"Then it shouldn't matter if I ask you to sacrifice five of the six weeks you've got left. I want it done next Saturday. And one of the people I want you to kill is yourself."

Raymond's cynical snort might have been a chuckle in happier times. But this was no laughing matter.

"I don't want anyone left some smart DA can cut a deal with. I want you to do the job and then I want you to take yourself out. No interrogation, no investigation. File closed."

A thirty-eight revolver materialized. Raymond looked at the blue-black metal, felt the cool cylinder of the barrel.

The driver winnowed the barrel through a gap in his buttoned shirt until he felt its cold circle of steel two inches from his heart. "It doesn't hurt, Raymond. Not like the next six weeks would. Not like they'd hurt Kathleen, watching you go slowly. It's quick as hitting a switch."

"How much up front?"

"Twenty."

"Thirty. And the rest the morning of the job. Before."

"*Ray*mond. After."

"There won't be no 'after' for me. Before or find yourself another triggerman."

"Before, then. But there's a little bonus I can throw in, a little something to console Kathy in her grief. And she won't get it if you let me down. You love Kathleen, don't you?"

He did love her, that was the thing. "What bonus?"

The driver told him, and that sealed it. Ray would have taken the fifty with that thrown in, though he didn't say so. "It'll get done." Raymond took the gun, checked the load, slipped it into his pocket. "Who else do you want me to do?"

"One person is a woman. You have a problem with killing a woman, Raymond?"

"No." Ray saw his mother's sorrowful face. He closed his eyes. "Who else?"

"A cop. Named Christopher Austen."

CHAPTER ONE
Three Years Ago

"Can I call your husband, ma'am?"

The dark-haired woman shook her head, winced.

Trooper Austen did not repeat the offer. Stranded on the roadside, alone, no wedding ring; it was likely that there was no husband. "Don't worry about your car, I'll call in a tow. Your first?"

She nodded, her smile tense, the eyes roving. "Yeah. Yeah."

He hoped she wasn't in pain. He remembered when Jane had been born, a difficult pregnancy, a difficult labor. Yet, Cat could not have been more stoic; after everything she had gone through to conceive, she was not about to capitulate to pain. "I've got two. Girl and a boy. Kids are great."

"They say they cost a lot."

"They're worth it."

He offered to let her sit in the car while he got a wheelchair, an orderly, but she said she could walk if he would take her arm. He walked her through the large, automated revolving door, one hand barely touching her waist, the other holding her hand, like a pair of ice-skaters. She wondered what was up, why it was necessary to pull him off the road, get him to the ER. It didn't matter, ten grand was ten grand.

He saw a wheelchair parked against a wall. "Stand here, let me get that for you."

He stepped away from her. He thought he heard her scream,

"Hey! No!" If he'd had five seconds to process it, he would have realized she had cried, "Ray! No!"

But he only had time to hear a single syllable, the last one to echo in his head. Cat!

For Kathy. You love Kathy, don't you? You'd do anything for Kathy, wouldn't you? Anything if it meant Kathy would get what she always wanted?

Raymond rose, one hand stealing into the sling. Take out the cop first, he's armed and his reflexes would be better. Then her, she'd freeze up, be an easy target.

I can't. I can't do it.

Six weeks. Versus sixty grand for Kathy. And the rest.

He waited until the cop moved away from her. For Kathy, he fired, one clean shot. He heard the scream, swung the gun but he'd miscalculated. She didn't freeze, darted behind a couple people and was out the door. He fired wildly, damn it, damn it, damn it! Too late, now.

Finish the job.

He felt a roar vibrate his brain, heard the hammering of his pulse, felt the hands grip him, saw the floor rise, felt himself falling, grasped the weapon in two hands and turned the barrel toward his chest.

I love you, Kathy.

CHAPTER TWO:
Present Day

This is crazy. I can't, can't, CAN'T be doing this!

Cat Austen felt a hot tide swell from her midsection to her hairline. She heard its pulsing in her ears, drowning out the little voice that urged, *Close your eyes until it's over.* Her legs trembled and her joints went liquid. *Close your eyes.* She couldn't. The wonder of it, the mystery, the sheer, forbidden fascination anchored her to consciousness. She had to look.

"First off, haul out your hog heads." 'Head' was *hay*-id, two syllables. The speaker plopped a pair of them, eyeless, snoutless, on the counter, beside the vat on the burner. "These here's already got the brains dug out, an' I popped the eyeballs. Some folks think we put the brains in the scrapple?" His chuckle disparaged such obtuseness, because of course- " –we mostly cook 'em up with eggs for supper the evenin' we have the kill. The snouts, we souse- " He shifted one of the decapitated hog's heads onto the wooden slab and Cat found her gaze riveted to those eyeless sockets. "As for the eyeballs-"

"Is 'souse' a verb?" Ellice whispered. "Would that make the infinitive 'to souse'? I souse, you souse, he, sheeei-"

Cat's stomach did a nimble cartwheel. "Shhhh-"

"-it souses."

"What you want to do now is whomp your *hay*-ids down to chunks'll fit your pot."

Each animated "*hay*-id" set off a costal tremor; Cat stood with arms crossed tightly over her quivering ribs.

"Now I'm almost positive," Ellice declared, "- that 'whomp' is a verb. Today I whomp, yesterday I whamp, last week, I had whump."

"Stop!" Cat hissed.

"You can use your cleaver, or- " The speaker produced a small buzz saw. He yanked the cord, lowered the rubber-rimmed goggles that had been perched on his forehead. The goggles left indentations in the flesh of his brow, two circles that resembled the eyeless sockets of the hog... *hay*-ids.

Dismantling the head sent pink mist raining on the onlookers. Cat heard, in the saw's pulsating whine, Ritchie Landis's bray, "It's the Scrappa*looz*a. It'll be *fun*." She imagined Ritchie Landis's pink-cheeked head on that plank.

"Then you're gonna plop your hacked up hunks of hog *hay*id into your boilin' water. Now here's some already cooked up an' worked off the bone. You skim off the fat, jumble it up good with the liver and the whatnot. The heart, too, if nobody fried it up for lunch already." The rueful chuckle intimated that, on occasion, he had not been so prompt in securing that particular tidbit as he ought to have been.

He tipped a broad ceramic bowl so that the audience could see the lumpy purplish mass that his "jumbling" produced. "Then give it a turn through the grinder and then it's back into your stock pot, to simmer up. Spoon in somma that fat you skimmed up, or I like to add a nice hunk of suet." He lopped an eight-ounce blob from a mound of white paste, plopped it into the mix. "Put in your salt, your celery seed, your sage, give it a good once-around-the-pot, keep up a slow heat. Take up your cornmeal- "

Ellice quoted *Antony and Cleopatra*. "'It is reported thou did eat strange flesh, which some did die to look on'."

Cat gulped down a yelp of laughter and they fled to the shade of a pair of maples whose leafy canopy offered little relief from air that was motionless except above the grills, where it shimmered with heat. Ellice sank onto a picnic bench while Cat hunted up a couple cold drinks at a concession stand.

The Memorial Day Delaware Valley Regional Scrappalooza was a four-day barbecue, cook-off, cookbook sale and flea mart sponsored by various purveyors of the delicacy. The Ocean City Tabernacle grounds, site of non-denominational religious services, the high school baccalaureate and the occasional car wash was taken over by mobile barbecue grills, cotton candy and soft drink vendors, plastic-sheeted picnic tables, a dozen or so flea market stalls and a display table where Mrs. Willie Mae Leitner was signing copies of her cookbook, *A Scrapple a Day: 365 Favorite Scrapple Recipes*.

Cat handed Ellice a dewy can of Diet Pepsi. She squinted at something in bold print on a placard next to the judges' dais, read, "'How Much Do You Love Your Scrapple? Delaware Valley Old Tyme Scrapple and Varietal Meats will award *one hundred thousand dollars* for the best slogan in ten words or less.'"

"That should be 'ten or fewer words'," Ellice observed.

"'Scrapple:'A meeting of the minds. Hearts, spleens, intestines and-' what was that other ingredient? Oh, yeah. 'Whatnot'." Cat dropped onto the bench. "From consultant for a top-rated TV show to covering a scrapple cook-off has to be a Guinness league plunge."

Ellice smiled, her dark skin glowing like fine chocolate in the May sun. "Freddy was saying pretty much the same thing last night. One morning, he's backing up federal marshals going after an armed fugitive, that afternoon he's telling some third grade class why they should wear their seat belts." She took a sip of Pepsi. "So why did you tell Landis you'd take the assignment?"

"The same reason you're attempting to *teach* literature to kids who can't *spell* it."

"Can't spell 'literature' or can't spell 'it'."

Cat chuckled, mirthlessly. "You get ten calls a day to sub. At least you know that every day there's work if you want it. This was all Ritchie offered. Then he tries to flatter me by expressing his confidence in my ability to put some sizzle in it, and every time he flatters me, I translate that as 'I may be a little late with your pay'. And the only thing worse than having my byline above anything with Scrappalooza in the copy, is having it get around that I wrote it for free."

Ritchie Landis, editor of the monthly *South Jersey Magazine* and the weekly *Cape-Atlantic Chronicle* employed Cat Austen to provide the entertainment features that were his publications' main draw. When *CopWatch* had come to Atlantic City to film an episode based upon Cat's ties to a local murder investigation, she had wrung a half dozen features from the location shoot, received minor celebrity status from the fact that she had been the inspiration for the main character, sassy female sleuth, Kate Auletta. But that had been almost two months ago; it was Memorial Day weekend and only the annual Scrappalooza and preparations for the wedding of Ellice to Cat's brother Freddy lay between Cat and idleness.

Cat's gaze trailed from the author, signing copies of *A Scrapple A Day*, down the line of people queuing up to exchange a few words with someone, anyone, who had written a book.

I bet you could write a book.

Cat felt a twinge, blinked back the swift pressure behind her eyelids and closed her notebook. The echo in her head was as distinct as if Chris whispered the words in her ear. Chris, who could dream for both of them, dream with an assurance that saw no shade between her dreams and his reality.

Mrs. Austen? Mrs. Christopher Austen? I know something importan' about why your husban' died. Don' hang up again.

Echoes again, recent, unremitting and anonymous. Each time, Cat had slammed down the phone, chalked the calls up to the onset of summer. To Ocean City's year-round residents, summer meant the influx of seasonal nuisances: the accumulation of litter, traffic, noise, the lawns overrun by unleashed children and unmannerly canines, the time-consuming queues at the bank, the market, the post office, cars idling on raised drawbridges as recreational boaters passed below. Many year-round residents surrendered, rented their homes to vacationers, retreated to a quiet, offshore condo, then returned to the island in mid-September with a tidy profit, minus the wear and tear.

Ellice laid her hand over Cat's briefly. The sun kindled fire in Ellice's engagement ring. "Landis had *better* pay you, or I'll sic Freddy on him. I mean, we feel bad about taking the apartment rent free until the end of the year, especially over summer." Freddy and Ellice planned to move into the ground floor apartment below Cat's beach block home."Joel Kaminsky said he could put you into a nice split level off the island, you could come back September first with eighteen thousand in the bank."

"Well, I think it was in *The House of Mirth*, that line? 'Poverty simplifies book-keeping'? I'm tired of realtors trying to rent my home, my children's home, out from under me."

"Was it one of them who called yesterday evening?"

"Who?"

"A realtor? You yelled, 'what's in it for you', I heard you all the way on the front porch."

"No, it was just some crank call."

Cat Austen? Someone's trying to hook up with you. Why don't you let me put the two of you together, hear her out?

Not the crank, this time. Whitney Rocap, the *NewsLine90* anchor whose last exchange with Cat had been a slurred, "I know where you live, bitch", uttered at Jerry Dudek's funeral.

What's in it for you?

You found Jerry's killer. I figure I owe you. I'm taping down along Mays Landing-Somers Point Road. There's a Twenty-Four/Seven about a quarter mile east of the golf course. Why don't we all meet in the parking lot around nine? I don't have to give you directions, I know you know where I'm talking about.

Cat took her last gulp of Pepsi, the icy carbonation paralyzing her quivering stomach. "Let's go."

"Don't you have to talk to the cookbook author?"

"I'll get her card and do it later."

Ellice chatted with the local bookseller while Cat scheduled the interview. They cruised the flea market tables, then strolled toward Morningside, said polite, "Good afternoons" to people they didn't know, summer renters who were down for the weekend, or the week, or the season, perhaps.

"Nancy's not back yet." Nancy Fortunati, married to Marco, Brother Number Three (Cat had six brothers, all older) had taken her son and his cousins, Mats, Mark and Johnny to pick up their tuxes while Cat's mother had chaperoned her three granddaughters to an afternoon fitting. Freddy and Ellice had chosen the Fortunati nieces and nephews for their attendants. Joey Fortunati, Freddy's immediate senior would be best man, and Cat would be matron of honor.

Ellice examined the fresh layer of mail and packages slowly eclipsing the surface of Cat's dining room table. She sifted through the envelopes with an eagerness that settled into quiet resignation, went up to her room. Still no response from her brother, Cat surmised. Long estranged, Ellice had not even asked for her brother's help when she had fled from a violent relationship. Her letters, informing him where she had settled, that she had planned to marry, had gone unanswered. "Chances are pretty slim that a guy named 'Fortunati's not gonna make the melanin count, and Elon's like my folks were. 'Marry black or don't come back'."

"Well, it beats 'marry Sicilian or we'll have to kill him'," Cat had replied.

Cat flopped on a living room chair, dug the Daytimer out of her tote bag and flipped backward to March like an athlete reliving the glory days. The coveted interview with megastar Tommi Ann Butler; the feature on Cici Bonaker, the star of the *CopWatch* spin-off, *Auletta!* The nuptials of a hit man's daughter, she and Victor, of all people, acting as witnesses. The Scrappalooza. Freddy's and Ellice's upcoming wedding and after that, pages of vacant squares, confronting her like "Hollow-eyed hog's *hay*ids," Cat declared aloud.

Someone's trying to hook up with you.

Cat slammed the Daytimer shut with shaking hands.

Why don't we all meet around nine?

Last night, the phone had rung right after nine. Cat stood with clenched fists while it rang, rang, rang, rang until her machine picked up. No message, only static and a click.

She prepared dinner early enough to have it cleared away before *NewsLine90* at six. Veteran Roland Atkinson, alone at the anchor desk, reeled off the local news. It was not until twenty minutes past the hour when a sleek, polished and sober Whitney appeared in a pre-taped segment. As the camera retreated to reveal Whitney standing in front of a circle of folding chairs, she looked directly into the lens and said. "Infertility." Paused. Cat felt her rib cage constrict. "Dating from Biblical tales of barrenness," Whitney continued, "- the sense of shame, despair, unwomanliness has divided the childless from the childbearing. Here, at the Tri-County Social Services Annex in Atlantic City, an Infertility Support Group, founded by the late Miriam Bender, and carried on by her colleagues in the mental health community - "

A surge of nausea sent Cat lurching into the den's small powder room. She slammed the door just as the scant contents of her stomach dislodged with a force that strained her ribs. She flushed the toilet with a shaking hand and groped for the spigot gulped a palm full of cold water, rinsing her mouth. Her stomach throbbed as though something long digested was trying to reverse its course, tear its way free of her.

There was a knock on the door. "Cat? You okay in there?"

Cat forced herself to inhale, exhale, looked into the mirror. Semblance without substance, not a real woman. That's how she had felt so many years ago, before she had finally gotten pregnant. "I'm okay, Ellice, I just felt a little woozy."

"Don't pass out in there. Open the door."

Cat emerged from the powder room. The program had moved on to a pre-taped segment on the "highly anticipated" Memorial Day traffic congestion. Whitney's change of attire suggested this had been taped at another time, the sepia light indicated late afternoon. "As early as the Wednesday before Memorial Day weekend, even remote back routes like this one will see a steady stream of shore-bound traffic." Her arm swept upward, gesturing toward the two-lane road behind her. "This is Whitney Rocap, NewsLine Ninety, reporting from Mays Landing-Somers Point Road."

Cat's gaze followed Whitney's gesture. In the background, late sunlight raised a glint on window glass flashing between an even row of trees like furtive eyes winking at her, reminding her of a shared secret.

State of the ART.

"Hon, you okay? You're white as a virgin's wedding dress."

"I guess the scrapple did me in. If I go lie down for a couple minutes, could you see that Jane gets to her homework?"

"Sure, no problem. You want me to help you upstairs."

"No, I'm fine."

She felt her pulse settling into its normal rhythm, heard in the wake of its pounding the echo of her own voice.

What if I can never have children? What if I never can?

And then Jane and Mats. And Nicholas-or-Charlotte.

Another fit of chills raised goose bumps on her bare arms. Cat stumbled into her large, walk-in closet and flipped on the light. "Where is it?" she whispered.

She dropped to her knees and groped for a box wedged into a corner, the long skirts of formal dresses she never wore draped over it. Cat upended it on the bedroom floor, began sifting through layers of papers, old bills, reports cards, yellowed newspaper clippings, snapshots: Jane with her first sprout of hair held in place with pink bow; Chris in a chair with an infant Mats in his arms, both asleep; a Christmas tree wreathed with wrapped gifts; touristy shots from their jaunt to New York. Folders, tax forms going seven years back, copies of their wills.

State of the ART.

Cat took a deep breath and began examining the file. Copies of her lab work, Chris's (*Where is it? Where is it*?); instruction sheets for the oocyte retrieval protocol (*Where is it? Where is it*?); miscellaneous forms for cryopreservation options, embryo transfer options (*I can't have lost it, I can't have forgotten about it*!); fee schedules. A brochure, slick and glossy as the day Chris had handed it to her.

Cat sat back on her heels, her fingers running over the State of the ART logo, a fetus curled up in a heart that was pink at the top, bleeding into blue at the bottom.

STATE OF THE A R T

Innovations in Assisted Reproductive Technologies

Randall Hoffman, MD, FACOG and Miriam Bender, MD, PhD, founded State of the ART in order to provide the Delaware Valley with advanced reproductive technology that has only been available in urban or university hospital-based settings. Their comprehensive facility will incorporate state of the art information, counseling, diagnostics, fertility engineering, and cryogenic options in a single, personalized and intimate setting...

Her eyes scanned down to the heading '*Cryogenic Storage Options*'. *All embryos stored in our facility will be subject to a $300 annual, $175 semi-annual or $30 monthly storage fee. Long-term options will be offered for five years or ten years (maximum storage) at the rate of $1,250 for five years and $2,500 for ten years...*

Cat scanned further. *Thirty days prior to expiration of the contract, clients will be advised by certified mail of the expiration date, and forwarded a copy of the initial contract. If the client fails to respond to the notification, embryos will be considered abandoned and will be terminated.*

Abandoned.

Cat began plowing through the papers on the carpet. No copy of the contract, no letter, no envelope with a green and white certified label. She closed her eyes, tried to recall the precise date she and Chris had made the pact. Jane's birthday had been last month, April. Nine months back. Ten years back.

Abandoned...terminated...impossible...

Nothing was impossible. It had been impossible that Chris could be murdered, impossible that life could go on. Time turned yesterday into a month ago, a year ago, three years ago, and the last tiny fragment of her union with Chris had been forgotten.

A sob tore from her throat and Cat stumbled onto the bed, weeping. She had not cried so hard since Freddy had brought her home from the hospital after the miscarriage, when the enormity of what she had lost had ambushed her.

An hour later, when Victor knocked softly on her door, slipped into the room, she had fallen into a dead, barren slumber.

CHAPTER THREE:
Three Years Ago

Raymond looked down at Kathy, taking it in, how peaceful she looked when she slept. Once her eyes opened, the mantle of worry set in and sank the corners of her sweet mouth. He pressed his lips to that mouth, waking her, intending to wake her. "Raymond," she said.

Nobody ever said his name like that, no one ever would again. The two syllables stirred up a fleeting notion of turning down the sixty grand and taking his chances. Then he remembered what sleep had obscured, that those chances had a six-month shelf life at best. He felt Kathy's limbs wrap around him as though she could draw all of him inside her, give birth to him once more, bring him into the world clean.

Chris's hand slid under the oversized T-shirt Cat wore to bed, his palm settling over her abdomen. Cat could not believe that he didn't detect anything in the pulse beneath her flesh. She would tell him tonight, after they put the kids to bed, and tucked away all of the colored eggs. It would be the perfect Easter surprise, and that's what Easter was all about, wasn't it, a new beginning?

A Christmas baby? Nicholas. Or Charlotte.

CHAPTER FOUR:
Present Day

There was a moist patch on her pillow when Cat woke, the residua of a dream that had called up tears. She pushed away her covers, her limbs heavy, tried to remember when she had been conscious enough to put on the pajama bottoms, sleeveless T-shirt she was wearing. A headache pulsed to the cadence of slamming drawers from Jane's room.

She stepped over the litter she had left on the floor, padded downstairs. "Ellice?"

No answer. Ordinarily, Cat would be out on a morning run and Ellice would be preparing breakfast for Jane and Mats, bracing herself for another day of substitute teaching. But Cat found the kitchen vacant, a sheet of note-paper on the table: "Victor came by last night. I had to run. Sorry. E."

No matter. Cat wasn't up to a morning run, anyway. "Jane, hurry up," she called. "You won't have time for breakfast!" She snapped on the radio to morning talk, got a Diet Pepsi from the refrigerator and took a cautious sip. Her stomach didn't revolt.

"Take a trip to hog heaven!" emerged from the radio.

Sonny at Sunrise. Sonny's Arbitrons had been flatlining when the murder of shock jock Jerry Dudek and subsequent cancellation of the Six AM Circus sent talk show addicts into withdrawal. Sonny's education, vocabulary and temper were in short supply, and he didn't have wit enough to convert his ill humor to a sort of wry curmudgeonliness. But his mangled grammar provided some unintentional humor, and his irritability generated some interest in whether and when he would be the next local personality to get himself whacked. He was, in short, marginally better than nothing.

Cat surmised from the "Jowls and bowels" "Nothin' could be swiner" and "Hocks in a crock" that Sonny was coaxing his listeners to offer up their Old Tyme Scrapple slogans.

The phone rang and the response to Cat's "Hello" was her mother declaring, "You write good, come up with something for scrapple. Sonny's running his own contest, you could win a T shirt."

"Gird your loins."

"Don't talk dirty. You tell Victor to come by and eat on Saturday?"

Cat reached over and turned down the radio. "I haven't had a chance to talk to him for a couple days."

"How you gonna get things moving along if you don't get together once in a while?"

"Don't talk dirty."

"You get married by New Year's, it's better on the taxes. It's okay to get on with the rest of your life, you know."

"That's easier said than done, Mama."

"*Figghia mi'*, name me one thing that isn't easier said than done. Lemme tell you, your father and me, we're married forty years. When he died, I didn't know what I'm supposed to do. So you know what I did? I went over to his grave- "

There was a pause and Cat imagined her mother crossing herself.

"- and I asked him. I just said flat out, 'Carlo, *caru*, how long you want me to be in mourning?'"

"What did he say?"

"What do you mean, what did he say? He was dead, he didn't say anything. But you know your father, rest in peace-" Pause for the Sign of the Cross. "- he was never much of a talker."

Cat felt her throat muscles seize in an aborted laugh.

"You go try it, go have a talk with Chris," Jennie advised. "You just say 'Chris, I'm still a young woman, it's hard raising two kids without a father, I found myself a nice man, he's not *sicilian*', but he's a Cath'lic and you can't have everything.' And don't feed the kids any of that scrapple, even if you get some for free, you don't know what winds up in there." This from a woman who had incorporated into her culinary repertoire, a subdivision diplomatically referred to as "organ meats".

Cat called out, "Jane! I'm not driving you if you miss the bus!" (A lie, and Jane knew it), promised her mother she would not feed the kids scrapple, she would think about talking to Chris and she would invite Victor to the barbecue on Saturday.

The phone rang again, and Cat picked up the receiver, heard a shrill, "Cat! Cat! Cat!" before she could put it to her ear.

"Ritchie, what if you dialed a wrong number and yelled 'Cat, Cat' like that?"

"So what's the deal?"

"What's what deal?"

"Whitney Rocap. I thought you hated her guts."

"Ritchie, after nearly two hours at the Scrappalooza yesterday. I hate *all* guts, indiscriminately."

"Two of you sitting on something hot and not telling me?"

"I almost always know when I'm sitting on something hot."

"You see the six o'clock last night? Whitney did some support group thing and then something on traffic?"

Cat wedged the receiver between her ear and her shoulder, chafed the eruption of goose bumps from her arms. "I saw it."

"She shot the first one on Tuesday afternoon, the traffic clip she shot Wednesday after the show. You see how stressed-out Atkinson looked last night? That's because it wasn't supposed to be a solo gig, Rocap never reported for work."

"Maybe she's taking a long weekend."

"Well she didn't tell anyone at NewsLineNinety. Besides, she's made a point of not taking time off since she got the anchor gig, word is she wants higher up. But get this. Tuesday, after she shoots the support group gig? Rocap and Cherry wind up having a drink over Bud 'N' Lou's the cop's bar?"

"I didn't know Cherry was friends with Whitney." Cherry Wein was Ritchie's secretary.

"Maybe Rocap was buyin'. Anyway, they take separate cars, Rocap gets there first, Cherry wheels in, Rocap's chatting up some suits. She's got some three-year-old copy about your husband. Cherry heard her asking them about the investigation."

I know something importan' about why your husban' died.

Mats padded in dressed in shorts and a striped T-shirt, carrying his socks and sneakers.

Cat kissed his unruly hair, slid over so that he could climb into the kitchen booth. "Ritchie. His k-i-l-l-e-r committed s-u-i-c-i-d-e at the scene. There was no one to arrest, nothing to investigate. Whitneys barking up the wrong tree."

Cat Austen? Someone's trying to hook up with you. Why don't you let me put the two of you together, hear her out?

"Jeez, Austen, I always know I struck a nerve when you fall back into the clichés. Be happy to pass your message along to Rocap, but the thing is? Rocap's either holed up with a bottle and not picking up the phone, or she took off without sayin' good-bye. Nobody's seen or heard from her since she shot that segment Wednesday night."

CHAPTER FIVE:
Present Day

Because Mays Landing-Somers Point Road meandered below the north-eastern portion of Cape May County, most people forgot this was Atlantic County, which put its crimes under the jurisdiction of Atlantic County's prosecutor. A single vehicle fatality – moreover, one that occurred at the onset of a busy summer season – would have called for an investigation by the county's Fatal Collision Unit. But Kurt Raab's antennae picked up an aberration in the initial report, and he placed a call to Victor, instead.

Victor was Lieutenant Victor Cardenas, homicide investigator with the county's Major Crimes Bureau. While Victor drove to the scene, Detective Jean Adane navigated, a map spread across her knee. "Right beyond English Creek Road, there's a fork. We should see the eastern road block set up there."

State police cruisers, grille to grille, obstructed a *NewsLine90* van. Victor braked, coasted, holding up his shield. State troopers waved him onto the un-paved shoulder of Mays Landing-Somers Point's narrow two lanes, where another cruiser, the paramedic's vehicle and the medical examiner's white hatchback had queued up.

Victor felt the humid, somewhat brackish air bear down as he went to open Adane's door, offer his hand. She accepted his assistance, accustomed to an inherent courtesy that came as naturally to her lieutenant as coarseness did to many of their colleagues. She noticed that Victor did not surrender to the eighty-five degrees and shed his jacket, nor loosen his tie.

Freddy Fortunati called out to them, approached. "Half an hour into my shift. Not even time for a cup of coffee." Even Freddy's gripes sounded good natured. Perhaps it was the imminent wedding that buoyed his spirits.

Victor's mustache, arched in a resolute frown, relaxed a bit. Freddy was Cat's favorite brother. "Give me a rundown."

Freddy pointed to a five foot swatch of flattened foliage, saplings snapped at the base, the thick undergrowth matted to the earth. "No swerves, no skid marks, she just shot off-road, plowed straight through the brush until she hit. High speed. Two foot dent and some paint sheared off the driver's side, looks like she mighta been sideswiped good and hard."

"ID?"

"Not a visual, that's for sure." He glanced at Adane and his pleasant face clouded. "It's pretty grim. She – her face is gone. We ran the registration. Whitney Rocap, Linwood. That's why we're keeping *NewsLineNinety* in the bleachers."

Victor scanned the road. On the opposite side, a row of tightly aligned American arborvitae eclipsed the open field beyond. In the distance, Victor thought he saw sunlight reflecting off window glass. "What's down the road?"

"Medical clinic. A little past that, there's a Twenty-Four/Seven. Fire department's a half a mile down the other way."

"It seems an unusual place for a medical facility," Adane commented.

"Land's cheap, I guess. Casino migration's been spreading out toward Galloway. Guy who runs the clinic, he used to be Cat's doctor," Freddy added.

"What sort of clinic?" Victor asked.

"'T's called State of the ART. Ob/gyn, sort of."

Victor logged that and cupped his hand under Adane's elbow. "Let's go."

They followed Freddy through the mix of evergreen and deciduous that offered a bit of shade but snuffed out the faint breeze so that the humid air took on a stifling concentration. Flattened brush gave way to a clearing where the ground sloped toward a ribbon of translucent water that ran over a bed of mossy stones and brown sediment. The uneven ground was littered with scraps of rusted metal, a few discarded beer cans, broken glass that sparkled like gemstones embedded in the earth. A cloud bank of gnats hovered above the brown water.

Paramedics, state police, a crime scene trio, the ME and his gangly photographer orbited a small bronze BMW. An amputated tree trunk that rose from the water and leaned inward at a forty-five degree angle had penetrated the windshield, punctured the driver's side air bag, sheared off the face of the driver and the convertible's top. A gull and a couple of blackbirds had settled on the jagged, bloody stump squabbling over bits of decomposing flesh. A few aggressive greenheads had collected at the threads of caked blood had slid from pulp, pooled and dried.

Impaled in an upright position was what appeared to be a manikin dressed in an iris blue linen suit. The purple/black pulp above the neck, the patches of exposed white bone, were all the more horrible because the slim body had escaped relatively unscathed. The white blouse was stained red-black with bloody flesh and brain matter. The arms were thrown out at the side. Victor's gaze turned to the open palm, of her left hand, the flesh darkened but intact, one slender finger still bearing Jerry Dudek's cheap engagement ring. The hushed conversations of the cops and CSU team were underscored by the chirrup of insects that had already gone to work on her.

Freddy introduced Victor to his fellow trooper, Halloran, who had been the first officer on the scene. Victor detected a particular deference in the man's tone. *He knows I'm dating Cat, that she's Freddy's sister, that she'd been married to a state cop. Probably even knew Chris Austen.*

"Gonna be a long summer," Halloran said. His sweat-soaked shirt strained over gym-toned muscles.

"What time did this happen?"

Halloran turned. "Doc? Time?"

The ME shouted over his shoulder, "Eight forty-five."

Halloran shot Victor a wry frown. "*Doc*! Time of *death*!"

"Whadda I look like, Kreskin? Joe Fahrenheit hasn't dipped below seventy since Monday."

"Come on." Victor took Adane's arm once more.

Their approach stirred up the haze of gnats, that pestered a bit, then merged with the larger cluster billowing above the shallow brown water. Victor waited for the ME to coach the young photographer, who fired off a roll of film in under two minutes, stopping only to stow his rolls of film and switch to a handheld digital camera.

Victor stepped in front of Adane. "Doctor? An estimate?"

"She's been here awhile." The ME pointed to beads of glistening black plodding along the ground. "Beetles. What with the damn heat, I'm gonna say more than twenty four, but not quite forty-eight. Late Wednesday, early Thursday?"

"Why is the passenger door open?"

"You askin' me? It was open when I got here."

Victor called out to one of the CSU unit, got another, "It was open when we got here." Another from the first officer.

Victor nodded to Adane and walked around, examined the passenger side of the car from the dry land that bordered the stream. "It doesn't look as though it's been forced open."

One of the criminalists spoke up. "We'll impound the car. Looked like a trace of either lipstick or blood on the passenger air bag. And we found this on the seat, almost missed it because it slipped into a seam in the upholstery." The criminalist held out a small plastic bag with a pair of black bobby pins.

The young photographer cursed, slapped at his bare thighs. "They don't spray for mosquitoes around here?"

"Miss Rocap is blonde," Adane said.

"Can you pop the trunk?" Victor asked.

The ME leaned into the car, pulled the release with a gloved finger. Victor walked around and removed a pen from his pocket, used it to raise the trunk. A small spare and tool kit, a plastic mesh tote with a couple rolled up beach towels and a bottle of sunscreen.

"Anything in the glove compartment."

"License and registration," Halloran replied.

"Women carry purses. Where's hers?"

"We didn't find one," the criminalist said, somewhat defensively. "If we had, it would have been bagged."

"Miss Rocap was a television journalist. I would expect to find a purse, a briefcase, a Daytimer, a cell phone, certainly. And if there was a passenger with black bobby pins in her hair, where's *her* purse? And where is she? Theories, Adane?"

Her grave, "'Data, data, data, I cannot build bricks without clay'," eluded the cops, who were not aware of Victor's affinity for Sherlock Holmes. "However, I don't think it would be incompatible with the available facts to suggest that since only the driver's side collided with the tree, the combination of an air bag and seat belt may have saved a passenger. Perhaps she went for help."

Halloran panned the area. "You get out, you make it up to the road, where you gonna go for help? That medical clinic?"

"If it's open," Freddy replied. "Late Wednesday, early Thursday? It's the Twenty-Four/Seven or the fire department."

Victor circled the car, angled himself so that he could see the driver's panel. "Gloves," he said, quietly.

A box of pop-up Latex gloves was passed to him. Victor tugged out a pair, pulled them over his hands. He edged toward the open driver's door, reached toward the headlight switch. A pale circle of reflected light illuminated the still water in front of the car. Victor turned the headlights off, looked up. "Late Wednesday, early Thursday? She would have had her headlights on. They didn't burn out, they were turned off."

"By who?"

"By whoever ran her off the road and removed the witness. By whoever didn't want the headlights to attract premature investigation."

"You telling me, guy ran her off the road planned for her to have a head-on?"

"No, I'm saying he wanted her dead." Victor's monotone was chilling.

"Damn stupid way to go about it." Halloran slipped a finger into his collar, tugged it. "He think she'd just lay around here and nobody would find her, a TV personality, a road like this with all the shore traffic over Memorial Day?"

"But she did just lie around here," Victor replied imperturbably. "According to the doctor, it's been more than a full day since the crash. So if you get the job done, does it really matter whether you were stupid or smart, or just plain lucky?"

CHAPTER SIX:
Present Day

Victor guided Adane up the embankment. "Put Stan Rice on the post mortem. Arrange interviews with her colleagues and get me a tape of her last program." His gaze focused on fragments of the building visible between the closely-planted wall of arborvitae. "You ever heard of State of the ART, Adane?"

"No, sir."

He could tell by the tenor of her reply that she would know everything about it by tomorrow morning.

"Let's take a walk, shall we?" He pointed west and began walking. Adane adjusted her sunglasses and fell into step.

He glanced at the expanses of open field behind the border of trees. "I don't see any sign of growth."

"It's only May. Or perhaps it's never planted."

Victor nodded, absently. His parents would have found it sinful to allow such a tract to lie barren. There had been a small plot in back of their Atlantic City home, intractable, weedy turf, yet his mother had managed to coax strawberries and tomatoes from it every summer.

The wall of arborvitae ended abruptly in a split rail fence that was dissected by a wide asphalt drive, a security guard's kiosk planted in the middle, a black and white striped barrier lowered across the entrance. Beyond a vacant parking lot was a structure with a two-story concrete core flanked by glass corridors on either side.

The stretch of split rail fence and arborvitae continued for another quarter mile to the bold red-and-white sign of a Twenty-Four Seven mini mart.

Victor opened the door for Adane and felt the surge of the convenience store's air-conditioning. His glance took in the configuration of the aisles, the monitor mounted on the ceiling. He walked to the rear of the store, took two bottled ice teas from the refrigerator case, laid them on the counter.

"Will that be all, sir?" The kid wore a green apron with a plastic badge clipped to the front that read, 'Hi! I'm Jason'.

Victor drew out his billfold, paid the boy, held up his shield. "Who works nights, Jason? Wednesday night."

The kid's Adam's apple bobbed. "Uh – I sort of did. Four 'til midnight."

"Alone?"

"The overnight night manager, Joe? He came in at eleven."

"You see anything out of the ordinary? Hear anything?"

The kid shook his head. "Except I recognized this woman who came in because she's on the news. I think her name's Rocap?"

Victor handed Adane one of the drinks. "What time was this?"

"A little after nine, I think. I didn't see her pull up, she must've parked off to the side. She and this other lady- "

"Other lady?"

The kid nodded. "This other lady was with her."

"Can you describe her?"

"I dunno. She was about the same age as the news lady, but she looked, you know, Hispanic? Dark hair. Kinda pretty. The news lady takes out her cell and punches in, then she goes, like, 'I'm just getting her machine, maybe she's on her way here'. Then the other lady goes, 'What about Kathy?' and the Rocap lady goes, 'I tried, she hung up, she won't talk to me.'"

Victor logged *Kathy*. "Then what?"

"And then the dark haired lady goes to me, 'Where's the nearest mail box around here' and I go, 'it's about twenty yards down the road.'." He pointed to his right, away from the scene of the crash. "And she goes to the reporter, Rocap, 'I'm gonna run drop this because the Boston lady, she's not coming.'"

"Drop what?"

"She had this brown envelope, kinda padded. Thick. So she goes out to mail it and the other lady goes to get some coffee."

Victor nodded, uncapped his bottle and took a drink. "You notice if Miss Rocap was carrying a purse?"

"Uh – yeah. Because it's like she's got the shakes, and she gets her wallet out to pay for the coffee and drops it, and there's change rollin' all over the floor."

"The shakes? As in drunk?"

"Nah, I don't think she was drunk. We get people in here, comin' back from the shore, they're stewed. She didn't look like that. Just sorta nervous."

"Then what?"

"Then the other lady comes back in and the news lady says does she want some coffee and the other lady goes 'No' and then the Rocap lady goes, 'Come on, maybe she's on her way out, we'll wait in the lot.' And the dark-haired lady goes again how the Boston lady's not gonna show, and then they leave. And then, I'm restocking dairy in the back corner? And I hear this engine gun, and I see this little brown Beemer shoot across the front in reverse, and she's at the wheel, the Rocap lady? And she jets, and I see this other car jet after her."

Victor nodded toward the video monitor. "You keep the security tapes?"

The kid shrugged. "You have to check with the manager, he's in back."

Victor turned to Adane. She walked into the back room. "Can you describe the other car?"

"Old. Four door sedan. Dark."

"How many people?"

"Just looked like a guy at the wheel."

Adane emerged, handed Victor a videocassette.

Victor handed the boy his card. "If you remember anything else, call me."

He held the door for Adane and they headed back down the road. Victor related the kid's version of the incident.

"In reverse?" Adane took a sip of her iced tea. "That suggests that someone may have been blocking her."

"And that he took off after her." Victor capped his drink. "So now we know she did have a companion, a dark-haired woman, who mailed something." He glanced down the road, saw the blue mail box at the point where two roads merged, just beyond the police cruiser. "We know that Miss Rocap expected some woman from Boston to meet her at the store, and that another woman named 'Kathy' wouldn't talk to her."

"And that her cell phone wasn't found at the scene," Adane reminded him. "I'll get her cell phone records."

They walked to the guard post at the clinic. Victor approached the sliding glass window and saw a uniformed guard bent over a paperback. Victor knocked on the sliding glass window with his shield.

The man opened the window. He was a fair, sun streaked blonde, the blue eyes with a bit of residual blurriness from alcohol or lack of sleep, perhaps both.

"C'n I do for you?"

"We can start with your name."

"Tony. Gibson."

"Is there someone posted here all the time?"

"Twenty-four seven."

"What's your shift?"

"This week, I'm eight to four, through Sunday. Rodney's on four to midnight and Bobby's the overnight."

"They have last names?"

"Rodney Towers, Bobby Borch."

"Last night, Wednesday night, Rodney relieve you on time?"

The man nodded.

"What about Bobby? He here when you reported Thursday?"

"Yeah."

Victor looked over the kiosk. There was room for a chair, a pair of monitors, one flashed a series of images of the clinic's interior, the other was a television, tuned to a game show.

"Notice anything unusual in the past few days?"

The guy shook his head.

"You're out here the entire shift?"

"Client lets us use their break room for meals, they got a fridge and a microwave. Use the john. But it's mostly out here."

"Client?"

"I'm Pro Patrol Security." The man tapped the emblem on his sleeve. "The clinic's one of their clients."

"There's a need for manned security?"

The guy shrugged. “They got electronic surveillance in the labs, but they’re off the beaten path, plus with those trees you can’t see the building real good from the road. That’s always bait for vandals and the druggies. Whackos.”

“And this is an obstetrical clinic?”

“Fertility clinic,” Tony corrected.

Guy who runs the clinic, he used to be Cat’s doctor.

“Not open today?”

“Nope. They’re taking the long weekend. Won’t be open again ‘til Tuesday morning, nine AM.”

“What about their usual hours of operation.”

“Nine ‘til five or so. Sometimes they’ll do a half-day on Saturday. And Wednesday nights, they hold some kinda show-and-tell information get togethers.”

Victor looked at the building. Below the glowing letters that spelled out State of the ART was a plaque: Randall Hoffman, MD, FACOG, Mark Shoenberg, MD, FACOG, Paul Aquino, MD, PhD. “Who supervises the Wednesday night sessions?”

“Aquino, I think. Him and sweet little Evie.”

“Evie?”

“Eve Bellamy, she’s a nurse.”

“They both show up for work yesterday?”

“Yup.”

Victor handed the man two of his cards. “Leave these for Bobby and Rodney. The state police will probably be in touch but if they think of anything out of the ordinary that occurred last night, or early this morning, I want them to call me.”

The guy took the cards, put them under the small counter.

Victor and Adane were headed toward his car when he heard a reedy voice call out, “Hey! Hey, Lieutenant! Hey, wait up!”

Victor turned and saw the kid from the Twenty-Four/Seven sprinting toward him, his green apron flapping around his knees.

“I just thought of something,” he panted, wiping a sheen of sweat from his forehead with the hem of his apron. “What that dark-haired lady was saying. Now that I come to think of it, I don’t think she was saying ‘Boston’, I think she was saying ‘Austin’. Yeah, ‘Austin’. So,” he added, helpfully, “Maybe who they were waiting for was from Texas, you think?”

CHAPTER SEVEN:
Present Day

"Yesterday, you can't do over. You got today and what comes after. So you can mope about what's gone or make the best of what's left." Cat's Aunt Caterina had said that. She had been making the best of her terminal diagnosis, passed those words of advice to her niece in the last lucid moments before she died.

Cat strolled toward Chris's modest gravesite waiting for the echo of his voice, some whisper telling her to go on and make the best of what was left in his wake. But the echo she heard wasn't Chris.

I know something about why your husban' died.

You call here again and I'll have the police trace it!

There had been crank calls after his death. Even the night of his funeral. Then the insurance company, the reporters and in their wake, the estate planners and real estate sales people and home repair operations that went on for months, scavengers, smelling frailty. *Hang up,* Marco had instructed her. *They keep it up, refer 'em to me, I'll put a stop to it. The cranks, tell 'em you're gonna get a trace. Get an answering machine in the meantime.* They stopped; resumed sporadically when the Dudek murder put her name in print, again after her *CopWatch* stories. Cranks were the price of celebrity, even small-time celebrity.

You got today and what comes after. But yesterday would never be settled until she found out if that fragment of their union still survived or had been...terminated.

If I had been the one who died, would you have forgotten Nicholas or Charlotte? Would you have taken that anonymous phone call? Would you have met up with Whitney? Say something!

Scraps of sunlight trickled through the leaves of the high maple, spattered her like hot rain. The leaves seemed to rustle a gentle, three-note refrain. *Stay a-way. Stay a-way.*

She's got a file with her, some three-year-old copy. About your husband's murder.

Stay a-way. Stay a-way.

SAY something!

A sudden breeze churned the leaves, sent something scuttling over her bare instep. Cat jerked her foot back, looked down. A few withered petals had detached from the three long-stemmed roses nestling at the base of the headstone. She bent down and brushed the petals off of her sandal.

What on earth...?

Cat picked up one of the stalks gingerly, tipped the drooping bud to her nose. A heady, sensual perfume seeped into her nostrils, triggered memory.

She had carried roses on her wedding day. Chris had brought her roses after she had given birth, first swathed in pink tissue, then blue.

She raised her head and looked around. Except for an elderly woman standing over a gravesite, her fingers sliding over the beads of a rosary, the cemetery was deserted. If her mother, one of her family had intended to visit, bring flowers, they would have mentioned it. Charlotte, Chris's sister, was traveling abroad. None of his colleagues would have left roses.

Cat stood and brushed the hem of her sundress. She spied the little brick hut that was the caretaker's office, walked over and knocked on the door. A plaque, fixed to the green-painted wood read: Leon Geller, Groundskeeper. Beneath that was a sign, 'I'm Out. Be Back At- ' below it, a clock face with movable hands read ten-thirty.

Cat checked her watch. It wasn't ten yet. She didn't want to wait around for half an hour.

She pulled one of her business cards out of her purse, scribbled on the back, 'Regarding my husband's site, Christopher Austen, please call.' She penned her phone number below that, her name, wedged the card into the door jamb above the knob.

The leaves rustled. *Stay a-way. Stay a-way.*

Don' hang up again.

Why don't you hear her out?

"Okay, Whitney," Cat said aloud, ignoring inscrutable *Stay a-way, Stay a-way* whispered by the leaves. "I'll hear you out."

CHAPTER EIGHT:
Present Day

Cat scanned Hemlock Drive's door posts and mailboxes for Whitney's address, finally spotted the small house, with its front yard smothered in blue spruce, juniper crawling over the lawn. A weeping willow with an oddly distorted trunk looked like a crippled torso with one leafy arm sheltering the driveway.

Cat turned off the ignition and got out of her car, gave the block a casual appraisal. Older homes, reasonably well-kept, the heavy foliage leaving a confetti of drying leaves and nettles along the street and walkways. Laughter somewhere, the splash of a backyard pool, the hum of air conditioners.

Cat crossed the street, glanced at the dark, older model sedan, parked at the curb in front of the irregular slate walk. *Rocap's either holed up with a bottle and not picking up the phone, or she took off without sayin' good-bye.*

But Whitney drove a small gold BMW. Cat hadn't considered the possibility that Rocap might have company.'

She approached the front door, raised her hand to knock. She heard the cadence of a male voice under the cranked up hip hop from one of the Philly FM stations.

Male company.

I know something...

Cat drew her fingers into an obstinate fist and pounded on the door, waited. No answer. She realized that her knock might not be audible over the amplified music, and decided to try the back door.

She winnowed through the narrow, foliage-choked side yard to the back door. The back yard was an open square of emerald lawn, bordered by a low chain link fence with a flagstone patio outside the glassed-in kitchen nook. Cat cupped her hands to the glass, peered in, saw a little wrought iron table and chairs, a center island, butcher's block, with a stainless steel double sink. On the counter lay an overturned pocketbook, a cell phone, something loosely bundled in a dish towel, a cardboard box filled with papers and folders, and a handgun.

A gun? When had Whitney started carrying a gun?

Cat realized that wall phone's receiver was off the hook, the long cord trailing into the corridor beyond the kitchen, swaying to the thump of the music. A pair of broad shoulders, muscular buttocks encased in tight black jeans, appeared in the doorway, grinding to the music's jumpy cadence, his half of the phone conversation mimicking its rhythm. "...No - just a lit-tle - *bo*-nus - doncha sweat it - they check out - this place - they won't know anything's gone *mis*sing. And her cash, I pinched it – her purse, I pitched it." A pause, then his patter returned to a normal conversational mode. "Nothin' on the air yet, I gotta wait until word breaks, then I'll do my bit over there. Don't worry, I planted..." A pause, a follow up that had the pace of an expletive, a dark laugh. "Forget the paint job, you owe me new wheels. New crib, too, tell Mommy dearest to check around."

Cat was so focused on analyzing the words that she hadn't realized that they had ceased. She looked up and saw a hostile gaze locked on hers. She back-stepped instinctively, spun and pushed through the narrow easement at the side of the house, collided with a torso so heavily muscled that at first she thought she had smacked into the trunk of a tree.

"You lookin' for something?"

"In the movies, your hero keeps 'im talking. In the mix, you wanna minimize the chitchat and get your keester out the door." Marco taught that in his Female Without Fear class. Unfortunately, there were about two hundred twenty pounds of muscle between her keester and her car door. Cat looked up into a pair of hostile dark eyes, heard herself saying, "I'm Cat Austen. I'm a-" *friend*? "- colleague of Whitney's, we're working on an assignment together. I guess she didn't hear my knock."

He seized her, his fingers closing over her upper arm and dragged her to the back door. Cat wondered if she should scream, decided, too late, that it was worth a try. The sound that issued - "Yawp" - was not loud enough to carry across the yard.

He pushed open the back door, flung her into the kitchen. Cat stumbled into the center island's countertop.

"Okay, what's your name, Austen? What assignment?"

Cat raised her chin. "Is Whitney here?"

Something about the way his upper lip flinched, contemptuous of the question, sent ice sliding along her nerve endings.

"You move?" he told her. "I'll wring your neck."

He backed over to the wall, where the receiver dangled by the cord. He had not hung up when he had run out to intercept her. He snatched the receiver, stood with one palm braced against the wall, as if to display the gym-honed pectorals visible beneath the open shirt. A pendant in the shape of a letter 'D' was suspended from a heavy gold chain, circling a neck the diameter of Jane's waist. "Still there?" he asked.

Cat took a covert glance over her shoulder, saw that the cardboard box was half-filled with manila folders, Zip disks, an address book, Daytimer, a stack of papers. Cat's furtive glance took in *As far back as the Biblical tales of barrenness, the sense of shame, despair, unwomanliness divides the childless from the childbearing-* A draft of Whitney's copy for the segment she had taped.

"We got ourselves a little problem," he was saying.

Cat ordered herself to breathe, shifted a bit to see if the movement put him on alert. He was absorbed in his conversation, confident that she wouldn't make a run for it. She braced her forearms against the counter behind her to support her quivering knees, glanced back at the paper again, saw something scribbled in ink at the bottom, underlined. Santucci. She saw the gun.

"Got her nose to the window, says her name's Austen, here to brainstorm with Rocap." Pause. "How do I know?"

Cat probed behind her for the gun. Her pinkie curled around the short barrel and she drew the weapon in, slid it onto her palm, assessing the weight. Marco had said he could determine a weapon's load blindfolded, simply by the feel.

"Nobody's seen me, don't sweat it, it's dead around here." A dark chuckle. "Look, you want, I'll do her right now, because I can't make that other stop before the news hits the air."

Cat gripped the weapon. The movement caught the man's attention. "Gotta go, I think she's gonna try to split."

Cat swung her arm in an arc, aimed the gun at his sternum, holding it in a two-handed grip. "Say goodbye," she ordered.

The man's flat, dark stare sized her up. Cat called up the one thought that would toughen her resolve. *My children.* He repeated, "Gotta go," into the receiver, hung up.

"Okay. Put your hands behind your head, turn around and stand in the archway."

He raised his arms and laced his fingers behind his head. When he turned his back to her, Cat reached toward the counter, flipped a corner of the dishtowel aside, saw a piled of jewelry, pearls, large gold earrings with some golden gemstone, a watch. She looked past him, saw that beyond the archway was a short center hall which lead to the foyer, the front door that he had left ajar when he'd run out to intercept her.

"Look, lady- "

"Shut up. Take a few steps forward."

He walked to the center of the hallway.

Cat advanced to the doorway, saw that the corridor opened to a living area on her right. "Who was on the phone?"

"What, I don't tell you, you're gonna shoot me?"

"You won't be the first." The lie sounded like a line from *Auletta!*. "Back up. Into the living room."

The living room was tastefully decorated, navy upholstery, an Oriental rug over parquet. A small secretary in the corner, the drawers half-open, papers scattered on the floor.

"Who are you?"

"Lady, you don't got what it takes to shoot."

A shudder shook the gun in her hand. He sprang. Cat fired, shattering the leaded glass lamp six inches to his left. *I hope it wasn't genuine Tiffany.*

He jumped back, tried a grin. "Okay, okay, I can explain this."

His smile was more frightening than his scowl. "Move to your right and face the window," she ordered.

He did as he was told.

Cat back-stepped toward the front door, slipped out, walked backward across the front yard, gun in hand. The man stood at the front window, glaring at her.

She backed up several paces, then turned swiftly and sprinted to her car, jumped in and hit the lock.

She tossed the gun on the seat beside her, rested one hand on the horn, ready to lean on it if he appeared. She groped for her key, one handed, inserted it in the ignition with shaking fingers, sped off.

CHAPTER NINE:
Present Day

Victor sent Adane back to the bureau with one of the state cops, instructed her to review the videotape with Stan Rice and Phil Long, start checking out the clinic, the security service, the ERs, to locate Whitney Rocap's next of kin. By the time the crime scene was processed and Victor had interviewed the two canoers who had found the body, the burden of detouring traffic had intensified. People getting a jump on the weekend had converted the sporadic flow to a steady stream, and Victor's commute time back to the Major Crimes bureau in Northfield was tripled.

Victor made his way to the second floor, the stepped-up cadence of conversations signifying the onset of summer.

"- and the jumper's hangin' by one arm off the deck-"

"-rousting the gomers in the Underground Motel before the shoobs come in for a landing-"

"- this guy is hackin' away with a buzz saw- "

"- gash on her neck's bleeding all down her throat and she jumps *me*, don't want him taken in 'cause she loooooves him-"

"- get this, get this, get this, 'the pigger the better'. That sound like a hundred grand to you?"

He found his unit huddled over sandwiches, watching the video Adane had obtained from the store. He gave them the open-handed signal that indicated they were to report to his office in five minutes, went into the office and closed the door on the background noise. He picked up a stack of memos, separated the official (*Raab will call back after two*), from the personal (*Call your mother*). He dialed Cat's number, his mind reverting to the image of Cat lying on her bed, asleep, looking pale and troubled as if some furtive sorrow had ambushed her. Could that sorrow have anything to do with a proposed rendezvous with Whitney Rocap?

Victor heard a knock on his door jamb, saw his detectives standing in the doorway. He hung up on Cat's recorded message, rose and waited until Adane took one of the chairs in front of his desk before he sat.

Stan Rice placed a wrapped sandwich and a can of Nestea on Victor's desk, leaned against the makeshift bookcase. "I checked out the store's tape. Their time log reads nine-fifteen when Rocap and the other woman walked out."

Jean Adane laid two video cassettes on Victor's desk. "These are the store's tape and a tape of Miss Rocap's last broadcast. She anchored the news Wednesday night, then sent a small crew out to Mays Landing-Somers Point Road to shoot a segment on holiday traffic, to be aired Thursday. I spoke to the videographer, he said she didn't accompany them, they got there first and had about a twenty minute wait before she showed up, he was afraid they were going to lose the light. When she arrived, there was a woman in her car who remained in her car for the entire shoot, which only took about fifteen minutes.

Thursday night, Miss Rocap didn't report. Calls placed to her home and cell phone received no response. This tape-"she tapped the top one, "- has the Wednesday night news program and the segment that she shot later that evening. On both occasions, she's wearing the same suit, the same one she was wearing in the store's video."

"So," Victor concluded, "-she never got home to change between the time she anchored the news Wednesday night and the time she was found."

Adane nodded. "There is one discrepancy between the tapes and Miss Rocap's body. On the tapes, you can see that Miss Rocap is wearing a gold watch and a string of pearls. Rather prominent earrings, too, gold with a gold-colored stone, topaz or amber. But the only jewelry she was wearing when she was found was an inexpensive ring."

"Dudek's engagement ring." Victor frowned.

"And your instincts about the purses were correct, sir," Adane added. "In the Twenty-Four/Seven tape? Both women are carrying them, but no purse was found on the scene."

"What time did they finish shooting that traffic segment Wednesday evening?"

"Around seven-fifteen."

"And she walked into the Twenty-Four/Seven at nine PM? That leaves nearly two hours unaccounted for."

"Other than the Twenty-Four/Seven, the clinic is the only public place in the immediate vicinity. On Tuesday night, Miss Rocap taped a segment on an infertility support group, perhaps she had been developing a more comprehensive feature on the topic."

"I'm having the photo lab make me some prints of the Jane Doe on the videotape, they're gonna come up a little grainy, but maybe someone'll recognize her," Stan said. "Rocap's next of kin's a father and new stepmother livin' in Maui, so I'm gonna wait another hour or so before I contact them."

"I called this Pro Patrol, got the numbers of the guards workin' the clinic this week," Phil offered. "Neither one picked up. But," Phil shifted his long legs. "The overnight, that name rang a bell. Borch. Robert J. He used to work in the condo over Margate, one where Tom Hopper lived? You interviewed him 'round the time Jerry Dudek got himself whacked."

Victor ran his thumb along his mustache, recalled the guy, big, hostile. "That guy was on parole."

"Pro Patrol contracts out to malls, offices, apartment buildings. Pay's no more than okay, work's pretty routine. Boring. Uniform junkies without much education makes up most of their applicants. They're not armed, just suit up and strut."

"His arrest record?"

"Two. First time, four years on aggravated assault, second time, it's moving stolen goods. That one set off bells, 'cause the goods he found himself in possession of? Which is how his legal beagle puts it at the arraignment, '...found himself in possession of', like he's standin' around minding his own business and all of a sudden he's hip deep in hard candy."

Victor translated the slang. "Jewelry?"

Long nodded. "Lifted from a pawnshop in AC. Gabors, down Pacific. I had a talk with Mary Grace Keller at the DA's?" He cleared his throat, shifted. There was still a bit of residual discomfort in the wake of the discovery that Keller and Jean Adane were a couple.

"What did Keller say?"

"She said she thought the Gabors slipped Borch the goods to fence. Borch moves the goods and collects on one end, the Gabors report 'em stolen and collect insurance on the other, they split the take. Thing is," Long shrugged. "Keller couldn't make a case on the Gabors and Borch wouldn't roll. But if this guy Borch did time for moving stolen goods, jewelry..." Long shrugged.

"And Rocap's jewelry was missing," Victor concluded. "Have Pro Patrol fax us his application. Go over those tapes again and record a description of the jewelry Miss Rocap was wearing, then check the dailies from all the local pawnshops, with particular attention to these Gabors. If you and Joey Fortunati have any connections on the street, you may want to check in with them as well. Where does Borch live?"

"Somers Point."

"What about Rocap?"

Stan replied. "She got promoted to anchor, she bought a rancher in Linwood. I asked the local PD to check it out."

Victor's mustache arched in a thoughtful frown. "Good. What about the studio, she may have kept personal property there, address books, a laptop, files. Get a warrant for any property she kept at the studio. Phone records would be helpful, too."

Stan would have reminded Victor that it was Memorial Day Friday, that finding a judge to sign a warrant would be difficult; Adane simply said, "Yes, sir."

"Rice, call the Somers Point department for backup and go have a chat with Robert Borch." Victor rose. "Anything else?"

Stan chuckled. "You mean other than the three fatalities on the Parkway, the thirty drunks piled onto a rental unit deck, deck collapses and it goes into the bay, the couple body parts turned up in a dumpster the ME thinks match up with head turned up back in March, Mrs. Finkle's missing husband, she knows he's dead and why aren't we doing anything about it, the jitney collides with a horse and buggy and the horse's gotta be put down, he's not gonna sue 'cause he's Amish-"

"The driver of the buggy," Victor clarified.

"Yeah. Well, technically, I guess the horse is, too. Was. One of the passengers on the jitney, she's here for some animal rights get-together, she starts whackin' out the jitney driver, so he's over the ER getting his head stitched up, the animal rights bunch takes to the streets to make sure Trigger doesn't get hauled over that Scrappalooza, wind up sandwich spread. A shots-fired over Linwood, no injuries reported, I'm waiting to hear from them. And your usual road rage, checkout line rage, drive-through rage, summer weekend altercations. Interested?"

"Were weapons involved in any of these altercations?"

"Does an Italian hoagie with everything count?"

"Only if it's on day-old bread," Victor replied, gravely.

"Two."

CHAPTER TEN:
Present Day

Cat realized she had not been to Steven Delareto's Linwood home since she and Chris had brought him a housewarming gift five years before. It was a small colonial at the end of Country Club Drive, with a golf course for a backdrop. Steve shared Cat's opinion that it was always too cold, too hot, too inclement or too pleasant to waste time on a golf course, but it presented a pleasing view from the large bay window in the kitchen.

Steve greeted her in khaki shorts and a white polo shirt, moccasins. "What're you doin' in the neighborhood?" he smiled.

"I called your office, your service said you were taking the day off." Cat ran a shaky hand through her hair. "And I didn't want to call my brothers and Victor was out of the office and I don't have a cell and I didn't have any more change for the pay phone- "

"Cat. You don't need a reason to drop by."

He led her into the kitchen, pushed aside a pile of folders on the table and poured her a glass of ice tea. "I'm taking the long weekend, the new secretary wanted the day off and I'm at her mercy." He sat opposite her. "Okay, where are the kids?"

"S- school. I guess I'll pick up Mats early since I'm already in Linwood so I don't have to run back to Ocean City for Jane's bus and then drive offshore again. Friday, you know, Memorial Day? The traffic on the bridge- "

Steve reached over, chafed her upper arm, gently. "Where'd you got those marks on your arms?"

"I went to the cemetery this morning."

"You hurt yourself at the cemetery?"

Cat took a deep breath, shook her head. "If I start crying or anything, just let me get it out, and keep going. You don't have to get all sensitive and compassionate."

"No chance. I leave sensitivity and compassion to those TV lawyers. Just tell me what's wrong."

Cat's laugh was shaky, bordering on tears. "It's not exactly going to be chronological, is that okay?"

"You don't get a gold star for chronology. Just get it all in, I'll cut and paste."

Cat sipped her ice tea, took a deep breath. "Let me start over. I've been getting some crank calls. Weird ones."

"'Weird' as in heavy breathing, or Playboy Channel stuff?"

"I don't have the Playboy Channel."

"I just watch it for the hard news."

Cat tried to smile. "No, nothing like that. More like after Chris died. 'I know something about your husband'. You have no idea what sort of deviants scan the obituary pages."

"That what this crank's been saying?"

"She says she knows something about Chris. Something about his murder. That she wanted to meet with me."

"You report it?"

Cat shook her head. "I just hung up. It's been so crazy lately, with the wedding and all."

"And these started...?"

"About three weeks ago. I'd hang up. The last one, I told her I'd call the police. Then I got another call, Wednesday afternoon only this time it was Whitney Rocap. The news anchor?"

He nodded, laid his hand over hers. "Keep going."

"She said she knew someone had been trying to get in touch with me, that I should hear her out, and she wanted to bring us together Wednesday night. I wouldn't talk to her. Yesterday, I was busy enough to keep from thinking about it. Then I watched the news, Whitney was doing a segment taped right around the spot she told me she wanted to meet." Cat swallowed.

"Keep going," Steve prodded, gently.

"And it started me thinking about those calls again. Something I ought to know about Chris's murder. And then this morning, Mama told me if I needed to talk something over, I should go talk to Chris. I know that doesn't make sense- "

"You're not the only one had a mother."

"And then Ritchie Landis called. He said that Whitney had been asking around about the murder investigation. And I just sort of started thinking. If I'd been murdered, and someone told Chris they knew something about it, even if he thought she was a crackpot? Chris would have checked it out. He wouldn't have hung up and – and forgotten. He would have checked it out."

Steve propped his elbows on his knees, pressed his palms together. "Keep going."

"So I decided to confront Whitney. I went over to her house. It's a couple blocks from here, and there was no answer when I knocked but I heard some-one talking inside so I went around back. I saw this guy on the phone, this – *huge* guy and I tried to leave, but he grabbed me and dragged me into the house and said if I moved, he'd wring my neck."

"And that's how you got those marks on your arm?"

Cat nodded. "Then he got back on the phone and he told whoever was on the other end that I was there, asked what he should do with me."

"Where was Rocap?"

"I don't know. But there was a pile of jewelry and a box of Whitney's property on the kitchen counter, like someone had packed it all up."

"What sort of property?"

"Papers and files, some computer disks."

"Burglars usually just cart off the computer, leave the papers. So what happened after the phone call?"

"I managed to get out of there."

"How did you manage?"

Cat pushed a strand of hair behind her ear. "This is where we sort of encounter a complication. Legally speaking."

"Which is where I come in."

Cat nodded. "Beside the jewelry and papers, there was this gun. I managed to get my hands on it while he was on the phone, and I sort of pointed it at him, and when he tried to jump me?"

Steve winced. "You sort of fired?"

"How was I supposed to get out of there? You don't think I won him over with *charm*, do you? Don't look at me like that, he's not dead. He wasn't even hit."

"Where's the gun now?"

"In my car."

Steve pressed his palms together, rested his chin on his fingertips. "Okay, well, we have to report it to the police."

"I've heard better options from those TV lawyers."

"I heard more convincing stories on CopWatch." The words implied sarcasm, but the Linwood detective kept his tone civil. Cat was, after all, "King" Carlo Fortunati's baby sister.

"Where do you have a problem with my client's story?"

Cat perched on a stool beside metal bookshelves overflowing with binders, corkboard walls covered with snapshots, newspaper clippings, wanted posters. A Mister Coffee nestled between stacks of folders, an inch of brown sludge in the glass pot.

The detective sank into one of two desk chairs in the room. Steve stood behind Cat, his hands on her shoulders.

"And you're a writer, right?" the detective asked Cat.

Cat heard the tacit "and this is the best you could come up with?"

"Yes," Steve replied, shortly. "You implying this is a fabrication?"

The cop sighed. "You first saw him, he was on the phone?"

They had gone over this. Twice. Cat glanced at her watch. A half hour until Jane's dismissal from school. "Yes."

"And he's saying?" the detective glanced at a clipboard.

"Something about how if they check out the place, they won't be able to tell that anything's missing. And that he planted something-"

"Planted, like he's trying to incriminate someone? Plant that gun or the jewelry somewhere?"

"I don't know. And then he said he wanted new wheels. And a new crib and that 'Mommy dearest' was to check around."

"For what?"

"Either the new wheels or the new-" she shrugged. "Crib?"

"Place didn't look ransacked?"

"It looked like he'd gone through her desk."

"And the gun, you only fired once?"

"You can verify that yourself, we turned over the weapon."

"'M I gonna turn up some neighbor says she heard more than one shot fired, saw you carrying when you entered the property?"

"No," Steve said.

"Describe that jewelry again, what was it, pearls...?"

"And earrings with a gold stone. Topaz. A gold watch."

"Anything else, bracelets, rings?"

"Not that I saw. But..."

"Something else?"

"On the phone? He also said something about how he couldn't make another stop until something on the news hit the air."

The detective nodded, knowingly. "Anything else."

Cat closed her eyes, concentrated. "There was this box, with a lot of folders, papers, computer disks. On one of the papers, there was a name handwritten in pen. Santucci. Underlined."

"Mean anything to you?" he asked Cat.

"No."

The detective tossed the clipboard aside. "Let's go over this one more time- "

"Look," Steve said, shortly. "My client's been over this three times, her story's not gonna change. She's gotta pick up her kids, you maybe wanna make an appointment with a sketch artist, do it now, because we're outta here."

"You know, I can hold your client-"

"You can hold my keester, Detective, but try to put the squeeze on, you won't be singin' baritone."

Cat felt a ripple of mirth skate over the tension.

"Love to see you in action in the courtroom, Counselor," the detective remarked.

"No you wouldn't."

"Look, we're gonna have to go over this just one more time, start with your client's relationship with Ms. Rocap."

"Why don't you wait until you can turn up Rocap? She gets home, she's certain to report the burglary."

"She's not gonna be contacting us, Counselor. Because right after you called, we got faxed by the county. They hauled what's left of Whitney Rocap outta a dried up stream runs off the Great Egg Harbor River. Ms. Austen, don't you pass out on me."

CHAPTER ELEVEN: Present Day

Only the thought of Mats scrutinizing the hands on the pre-school clock, of Jane sitting impatiently on the porch, locked out, kept Cat from allowing the declaration to unnerve her. She went over her story again, point by point, the questioning did not vary except for a couple additional queries: "Where were you from, say Wednesday night until early this morning?" and "Would you say the relations between Miss Rocap and yourself were what you call, cordial?"

It didn't occur to Cat until she and Mats idled at an open drawbridge that those questions were not questions one would ask about a traffic accident.

She made it home minutes before Jane's school bus rounded the corner, got Mats a box juice and a sprig of seedless grapes and checked her answering machine.

Ritchie's four messages – "Cat!" "Cat!" "Cat, Cat!" and "*CAT*!" told her that he had heard about Whitney's death, perhaps had heard that she had been questioned by the Linwood police.

Jane arrived with a "Can we go to the *beach*?" which told Cat that all the Popular Girls were going to the beach after school that *they* were going to show up on Monday *tan*.

"All right," Cat sighed. "Go tell Mats to get changed."

She dropped into an armchair and picked up the phone, dialed Ritchie's office.

"Cat! Cat! You got mugged snooping around Rocap's place!"

"Who's the mole, Ritchie? Not the Linwood cops."

"Nope. So who's the perp?"

"I don't know."

"What about the cops?"

"I don't think it was the cops."

"Jeez, Austen. You got a way of putting a whole new spin on 'open season'. Think he did Rocap? You heard about her, right?"

"The Linwood police said it was a car accident."

"C'mon, Loverboy didn't call you?"

"By 'Loverboy', I assume you mean Lieutenant Cardenas?"

"Jeez, Austen, you don't call him 'Lieutenant' between the sheets, do you?"

"What would he call me about?"

"About *Rocap*. How come he was at the scene?"

"Major Crimes doesn't investigate traffic fatalities, Ritchie, that's the Fatal Collision Unit."

"That's my *point*, Austen. Word is the cops think she and the other gal were run off the road on purpose."

Cat felt a wave of dizziness. "Wh-what other gal?"

"Rocap and some brunette were hanging around the Twenty-Four/Seven half mile down the road from where they hauled up her car. One of the clerks told one of my moles the cops confiscated their Wednesday night surveillance tapes. Can't you squeeze someone in the PD?"

"Ritchie, right now I'm up to my eyeballs in wedding preparations and knee deep in scrapple. Squeeze yourself."

"You hear Delaware Valley Old Tyme's running a slogan contest? Whad-dayou think of this? 'Get high off the hog'?"

"'I abhor every common-place phrase by which wit is intended'." Cat quoted loftily from *Sense and Sensibility*, omitted that on a page in her notebook, 'Get high *on* the hog' had been scribbled down, crossed out.

"At least ask the cop."

"For a scrapple slogan?"

Jane appeared in the new hot pink bikini with silver mesh inserts over the hip, and the rhinestone-studded sunglasses that her Nonna had bought her. "Are we *going*?"

Cat put her palm over the mouthpiece. "Put something on over your bath-ing suit."

"It's *hot* outside."

"Jane, just do it, please. Ask him what, Ritchie?" she said into the phone.

"Jeez, whaddamy talkin' about? For an ID on the brunette. I mean, you and Loverboy come up for air once in a while, right?"

Mrs. Austen? Mrs. Christopher Austen? I know something importan' about why your husban' died. Don' hang up again.

Cat employed the one foolproof way of ending a conversation with Ritchie. "You still owe me for most of my CopWatch pieces."

Ritchie hung up.

Cat dropped the receiver into the cradle, went upstairs, pulled a cotton shift over her bathing suit, slipped her feet into hemp-soled sandals. She glanced out the window. People were lolling on patio furniture or sunning themselves on decks, skateboarders and bikers cruised the sidewalks, cars coasted a slow circuit, scanning for some curbside parking, shirtless landsca-pers pushed noisy lawnmowers across tiny patches of sod. Strangers. Except for the Nixon ladies across the street, and the rarely-seen Ufflanders down the block, all strangers.

You got a way of putting a whole new spin on open season.

Cat felt a chill scuttle just beneath her flesh. She chafed her upper arms, felt the tenderness set in where that thug had grabbed her.

"Jane, take Mats out back and help him put on some sunscreen, I'll be right out."

"It makes my hands all *greasy*."

"Then take a towel. I'll be out in a minute."

She leaned down and opened the cabinet at the base of her nightstand, unlocked the oblong metal case where she kept her Taurus. She dropped it into one of the large square pockets of her shift, went down to the kitchen and reached for the glass canister on a top shelf, where she kept a supply of rounds, loaded the gun covertly. She didn't have a carry permit. She didn't care.

"It's not open season on me," she vowed, softly.

CHAPTER TWELVE:
Present Day

Victor turned down Delancy, wedged his Jag into the solitary break in the chain of cars parked along the dead end street, got out and heard the drone of humanity and surf, merged, drifting toward him on a current of warm salt air.

Mrs. DiLorenzo lay on a chaise, wearing a bright, full-skirted bathing suit, her brassy hair in pin curls. Nero lay coiled on the sun-baked patch of grass, raised his head at the vibration of Victor's footstep, receded into a torpor once more.

Mrs. DiLorenzo eyed Victor over the rhinestone rims of her sunglasses. "Shoobies," she informed him. "Don't wanna pay for parking. Summer's nothing but troublemakers and crooks."

" 'I depend upon them for my bread and cheese'." Victor suspected that she would not recognize a quote from *A Study in Scarlet*, that it would have been more to the point if he had been able to quote from – he glanced at the cover of the paperback she was reading – *The Scarlet Buccaneer*.

He went inside and hit the 'Play' button on his answering machine, listened to an extensive message from his mother while he sifted through his mail. He dialed Cat's number, got her machine, took a quick shower and changed into dark slacks and a white polo shirt, grabbed a sport jacket.

His cell phone rang on the way into Ocean City. It was Stan Rice. "Okay, I go over this guy Borch's place, he lives in a small rancher on Decatur over Somers Point? Nobody home. I walk around the property, there's a bedroom window off to the side, I can see his closet's open, empty. I see a couple women across the street firin' up the grill, gonna cook out tonight, I'm invited. One of 'em, her name's Rosemary Rienzi, but I can call her 'Ro'? She says an hour, hour and a half ago, Borch pulls up, he's in the house fifteen minutes, comes out with a couple suitcases, throws 'em in the trunk and splits. Which is weird because it's usually in by eight thirty AM, sleep all day. I ask about company, she says nobody, except a couple weeks ago she's putting out the trash, she hears him and someone goin' for the gold. She says he's got the doors and windows closed and you can still hear 'em goin' at it. Ohbaby, ohbaby, ohbaby. So she's watchin' out her window, sees a woman come out, wearin' a parka with a hood, heads down the block toward Bay. I figure we're talking maybe about end of April, the latest, not all that cold, right? So the parka's 'cause she doesn't wanna be ideed."

"Left on foot? She lives within walking distance."

"I'm already on it. May be slow goin', Somers Point can't spare a lotta manpower because of the weekend."

"Okay, keep me posted. I'm on my way over to talk to the administrator at this clinic. Hoffman."

Randall Hoffman was living on a narrow bayside street that threaded along the north end of Ocean City and dead-ended in a fingertip of land that had a lagoon on one side, the bay on the other. The house was situated at the base of this narrow cul-de-sac, a white Moorish structure with roof tiles that were a glossy dark blue. There was a sculpture in the front yard, a slender woman with flowing hair and flowing skirts, treading upon what appeared to be a sea of skulls. A wrought iron gate enclosed the mosaic stonework of the path, a dogwood and a few sculpted evergreens arranged around a tiny gazebo.

Victor knew enough about island real estate to know that this place cost seven figures.

He heard the doorbell echo, a four-note chime. After a moment, a uniformed maid answered the door, and he got a glimpse of a polished parquet oak that extended straight back to a wall of glass overlooking the bay.

He presented his shield to the woman, who invited him in to the foyer and left him to admire the textured walls, lined with diplomas and commendations, candid photographs of a tall, high-browed man wearing a self-satisfied, upturned crescent of a smile. Several featured him at a podium, others with well-known political figures, one with a pair of bona fide celebrities, a chubby toddler lifted between them, and a breezy, 'Never enough thanks!' penned above the autograph in the corner.

Victor turned his attention to the free-standing spiral staircase that rose, like a miraculous beanstalk, to the skylight twenty-eight feet above. The oaken railing, glistening in the overhead light, betrayed no seams. It had been cut from a single piece of timber.

He heard a light step on the stairway above and turned, saw a young woman descending. She was barefoot, wearing translucent white pedal pushers, a bright green silk blouse. Her skin glistened with the first dusting of golden tan, the loose hair, honey blonde. Her eyes were green-blue, like a changeable ocean, her mouth had the sort of bee-stung fullness that cost women collagen and pain, but looked genuine. Seamless perfection, like the railing her slender hand skated, vibrant as the spray of fire from the sizeable diamond she wore on her left ring finger. She appeared to be in her mid to late twenties, but there was a maturity about her; she had shed that complete unconsciousness of the effect of her beauty, realized what power it could wield.

"Lieutenant? I'm Eve Bellamy." Her voice had a liquid huskiness, sliding like honey over the neurons, the glands. The security guard's 'Sweet little Evie'? Living with Hoffman? "Lucia said you wanted to see Randy. I think he's outside."

She gestured with a crooked finger, inviting him to follow as she crossed the polished floor into a room decorated with aquatic greens and blues that contrasted with a carpet of such stark white that Victor hesitated before he stepped onto it.

The wall of window that overlooked the deck and bay was not a sliding door but one twelve by twenty pane so scrupulously clean that one might have mistaken it for an opening in the wall. As the woman approached it, the light sifted through the thin fabric of her pedal pushers, revealing explicit contours, the absence of undergarments. She opened a small door in the corner of the room and Victor saw her re-appear on the deck, walking toward the boat moored at their private dock. After a moment, Hoffman emerged from a lower deck. He sprang down with the calculated vitality older men affect in the presence of a younger woman.

Hoffman planted his battered deck shoes onto the white carpet without hesitation. "You ready to go?" He looked over at Victor. "Oh, didn't know we had company?"

"Randy, this is Lieutenant Cardenas. A police detective." She turned to Victor.

Hoffman offered a firm, brief handshake. "You've met my fiancée."

Victor knew it wasn't an inquiry, it was an announcement that this stunning woman was his property. "I apologize for the intrusion."

"No, we were just going to take the boat across the bay for dinner, they'll hold our table. Sit down, please."

"The lieutenant is investigating Whitney Rocap's automobile accident." She smiled at Victor's cocked eyebrow. "I had the radio on upstairs. It made the top of the hour news."

Victor waited until Eve nestled into the corner of a sea green sofa before he sat. "Did you know Miss Rocap?" he asked.

"Actually, I'd only met her Wednesday night."

"Really?" Victor slipped a notepad and pen out of his pocket. "Where was this?"

"At the clinic. Wednesday evenings we hold our orientations. Apparently, she had registered, the receptionist assumed she was simply a prospective client. When Paul-"

"Doctor Aquino."

"You've been doing your homework, Lieutenant," Eve's smile was gentle, appreciative.

"I've been doing my job, yes. Please continue."

"When Paul and I arrived she introduced herself and said she was thinking about doing a story on the clinic."

"What sort of story?"

"She didn't say. She asked if she could sit in on the orientation session." Eve toyed with a long strand of hair. "I wasn't entirely comfortable with that."

"What made you uncomfortable?"

Hoffman took over for his companion. "People who attend an orientation session need to feel free to ask some rather intimate questions. We've never admitted the press."

"I told Miss Rocap she would have to speak to Randy, that I wasn't able to authorize any interviews with the staff," Eve continued. "She asked if I would mind if she waited around until the session was over, she would outline the specifics of her proposal and I would communicate them to Randy. I told her she could wait in the employee's lounge. When the session was over, I had Paul handle Q and A, and I went to speak with her."

"And she gave you her pitch."

"Yes."

"And how long did that take?"

"Oh...ten minutes. Maybe fifteen. Then she thanked me and left."

"About what time was that?"

"Oh, nine or a little after, I guess. The last people in the session were on their way out."

"And you and Paul Aquino were the last to leave?"

"Yes. Paul left shortly after that, I finished up some paperwork and left a little before ten, I guess."

"The guard was at his post?"

"Yes."

Instinct told him to shift gears. "The guards, I imagine that's because of the site's location?"

Hoffman shrugged. "And to the fact that the facility holds sensitive medical files, as well as being a cryogenic storage facility. Security is crucial."

"Why not choose a less isolated location?"

"Isolation is relative. The site is easily accessible to four counties, and it was undeveloped, so we didn't have to deal with demolition. There's a fire department less than a mile down the road, we're fifteen minutes from Shore Memorial Hospital. Those are all to our advantage."

Victor backtracked. "The purpose of these seminars?"

Hoffman swung into promotional mode. "Well, couples who are having difficulty conceiving need to be made aware of their options, introduced to the specific procedures, our success rates. And the cost involved, because IVF is not an inexpensive procedure," he added. "So that they can decide whether IVF is for them, whether they can afford it. Once they've opted to enter the program, we schedule a follow up interview to address any unanswered issues, give them copies of the consent forms, instruction sheets, a little tour of the facility, discuss fee schedules and the OvaShare option, that sort of thing."

"OvaShare?" Victor heard the question in his mother's voice, *Qué es ésto, OvaShare?*

Hoffman nodded. "When a patient's oocytes – eggs – are extracted for IVF, the procedure will usually yield a dozen. Sometimes fewer, occasionally many more. These are fertilized with partner sperm to produce embryos. In the event that there are excess embryos, beyond what the patient requires to achieve the desired pregnancies, she may opt to donate unused embryos in exchange for reduced fee."

"To whom?"

"To a patient who may not be able to produce ova, or viable ova, who for some reason may not be a candidate for oocyte retrieval, but who is otherwise capable of carrying an implanted embryo to term. How is this relevant to the matter at hand?"

"The accident occurred between late Wednesday night and Thursday morning, less than a half mile from the clinic. Naturally, we're questioning anyone who might have been in the vicinity. And we know that Miss Rocap had taped a segment on the subject of infertility." He turned back to Eve Bellamy. "How many people were present?"

"At the orientation?" Eve's shrug caused the thin layer of silk to outline the unfettered breasts. "Forty."

"Plus you, Doctor Aquino the security guard at the gate."

"Right."

"You were the last to leave, except for the guard at his post. The guard didn't report anything out of the ordinary? Didn't notice a speeding car, hear the crash?"

"No."

"Did you drive directly back to Ocean City?"

"Yes."

"That would have taken you past the accident site. You didn't see anything?"

"No, nothing."

He turned to Hoffman. "How long have you used Pro Patrol?"

Hoffman's shoulders seemed to stiffen; the shrug seemed to be an attempt to shake off tension. "Several years."

Victor sensed that he had grazed a nerve. "You satisfied with their performance?"

"Yes. Though there's a lot of turnover."

"What about the rest of your staff?"

"What about them?" Defensive, now.

"No problems? Tension among the staff, ill feeling that might have caused one of them to start talking to the press?"

"Are you suggesting that Miss Rocap intended to do some sort of exposé?"

"Is there anything potentially damaging to expose?"

"Aren't we getting a little off the subject, Lieutenant?"

It was Eve who patted his arm, soothingly. "I started with Randy when I was a teenager, worked all through nursing school. Almost everyone on the medical and clerical staff has been with Randy since I've been there, except for Doctor Aquino and Doctor Shoenberg, maybe one of the lab techs. The auxiliary services, security, cleaning, disposal, they're contracted, so they're not clinic personnel. If any of the workers has a grudge, it would be with their employers, not State of the ART."

"No recent dismissals among the staff?" Victor inquired.

Hoffman shook his head.

"Unless you count Kathy," Eve said.

Kathy. The clerk at the Twenty-Four/Seven had heard Rocap mention a 'Kathy'. "Who's Kathy?" Victor asked.

Hoffman's eye flicked toward Eve. Victor thought he saw a trace of annoyance. "Kathy Petrone. She was my – well, when she started, you called them secretaries. Now it's 'office manager' or even 'administrative assistant'. A clinic like ours is a many-headed monster. The medical staff. Two labs, one for embryology, andrology and cryo, the other to perform the blood tests, chem. profiles. A clerical staff to handle the paperwork, billing, correspondence, scheduling. That requires a nerve center, someone to coordinate the operation of the separate units."

"And Kathy Petrone was that nerve center?"

Hoffman nodded. "Very competent girl, quick study, hard worker. She left a month ago."

"Why?"

It was Eve Bellamy who answered. "Her son's been quite ill, and she was having difficulty arranging child care. We – Randy – dismissed her so that she could collect unemployment."

"And I agreed to cover some of her medical for the next year," Hoffman added.

Victor nodded. "So there was no rift, no ill feeling?"

"None."

"No threat of whistle blowing?"

"There is no whistle to be blown, Lieutenant."

"Have you heard from her, spoken to her since she left?"

"No."

Victor rose and pocketed his notebook, handed them one of his cards. "If you recall anything else, please call me."

Hoffman became genial once more, extended his hand.

Victor shook it, briefly. *Cat's doctor.*

"I'll show you out, Lieutenant." Eve drew Victor's hand into the crook of her arm. He felt the back of his hand lodged against the outer curve of her breast, only a thin layer of silk between his flesh and hers.

She opened the door, and he took that opportunity to disengage her hand. She walked barefoot, impervious to the heat that the sun had baked into the slate tiles.

"Was Miss Rocap alone?" Victor asked.

"Alone?" Eve seemed puzzled by the question.

"She would have had to drive through the gate. The guard didn't mention that there was someone else in her car?"

"No."

"What's wrong with Mrs. Petrone's child?" he asked.

She hesitated. "I believe Randy said it was leukemia."

"Where's the husband? The child's father?"

She looked away. "I don't know..."

"You're prevaricating, Miss Bellamy."

"The husband wasn't the child's father. He died three years ago, and her little boy is about two, I think." She sighed. "It's just rather messy. Kathy's son *is* ill. But I think quitting may have had more to do with one of the security guards, the overnight guard."

"In what way?"

"I don't know, but I did get the idea that she'd known him for some time. In fact, she provided him with a job reference. She was lonely. A widow. Maybe looking for something permanent."

"And he wasn't?"

Eve shrugged.

"How did the husband die?"

"Suicide." She looked away, combed her fingers through the hair, letting the long strands catch the sunlight before they fell to her shoulders. "I'd heard he was depressed. In debt. Just sort of lost it one day and shot himself. One reason Randy kept Kathy on, I think, was this sort of sympathetic bond they formed after that happened, because, well Miriam? His wife? She died around the same time, and she was a suicide, too."

"The overnight guard? You having any problems with him?"

"With Bobby?" Eve shook her head. "I rarely saw him. He came on duty at midnight and was usually gone before I arrive."

His beeper went off and he checked the read-out. Adane. He slipped on his sunshades, nodded toward the fountain. "Greek or Roman?"

"Greek. Ate, the daughter of Zeus. She is the mistress of delusion, drawing men into folly."

"It's very striking."

"Does it strike you ninety eight hundred dollars worth?"

An eyebrow cocked above his sunshades. His mother would have told him, outraged, how many indigent children could be fed for ninety-eight hundred dollars.

"One of Randy's follies," she smiled.

Victor thanked her for her time, headed for his car, saw her standing with the sun sifting through her light clothes, turning her loose hair to spun gold. He picked up his cell, punched in Adane's extension. "What's up?"

"When I called Linwood for assistance in getting into Miss Rocap's residence, sir? They told me they had just filed a report of an intruder. I went over there and made a cursory examination. It hadn't been ransacked, but other than her file of bills and household statements, I couldn't find any address books, computer files, disks, not even any numbers programmed into her answering machine. And her hard drive had been swept."

"Someone wiped out her personal data. What about her property at the station? Files? Address book? Rolodex?"

"I haven't prepared the affidavit yet," she said, somewhat apologetically. "I was delayed in Linwood. You see..."

"Yes?"

"I've been assured that Mrs. Austen is unharmed, sir."

Victor felt his midsection knot. "What happened?"

"I have a copy of the statement. Mrs. Austen went to visit Miss Rocap this morning. She hadn't heard about the accident. Apparently, she surprised an intruder. A man."

Victor's fingers curled over the steering wheel, the knuckles whitening. "Then what?"

"She was able to distract him and get away. She reported it to her attorney who accompanied her to the department."

"This afternoon, Rice mentioned a shots-fired in Linwood."

"It was only one shot, sir."

"Who fired?"

"Mrs. Austen. The only casualty was a Tiffany lamp, but I don't believe it was genuine."

"She give them a description of the guy?"

"Muscular. Young. I can arrange for a sketch artist."

"Hold off on that. Borch? The overnight guard? Pull his mug shots." He thanked Adane and hung up, shoved his car into gear, tried Adane's trick with his rear view mirror, saw that Eve Bellamy was still watching him as he pulled away.

CHAPTER THIRTEEN: Present Day

Freddy had changed out of his uniform, stretched out on a lawn chair in front of the ground floor apartment. He jumped up when Cat and the kids, shouldering their totes, sandals flapping against the concrete, made their way back from the beach.

Cat shot him a panicked glance. The covert shake of her head did not escape Jane, who demanded, "Did something *happen*?"

"Jane, you and Mats take the towels around back and shake them out at the sandbox, okay?"

She waited for them to go around back. "Cops. Nothing but a lot of lousy snitches."

"We take care of our own. Anyway, it was Dom who told me."

"Who told him?"

"Mary Grace Keller." Mary Grace was an ADA; the Kellers and the Fortunatis had been neighbors, their children, schoolmates. "Steve Delareto reported it to the DA. He suggested that Mary Grace inform the family before Carlo found out on his own, and she volunteered to call Dom. I think she was maybe hoping Maggie would pick up at the rectory, I hear things're sort of cold between them. Ellice with you guys?"

Cat shook her head. "She wasn't here when Jane got home from school. Maybe she had a fitting."

"So what's her dress look like?"

"None of your business."

The kids emerged from the back yard. Freddy turned to them. "You guys wanna walk up the boards, pick up a couple pizzas?"

"Yeah!" Most of the shops had opened for the season and a trinket or a treat could always be coaxed out of Uncle Freddy.

"Jane, you are not to tell Uncle Freddy what Ellice's dress looks like."

"Oh, I took a call, some guy named Geller? Leon? I left the number on the kitchen table."

Cat didn't recognize the name, watched to see that the kids were allowing Freddy to hold their hands.

She went around back, hung her tote bag on a hook inside the enclosed outside shower, threw a clean beach towel over the top of the door and turned on the water, showered off the sand, washed it out of her hair, wrapped herself in a towel and padded up the narrow back stairs to the landing. The phone started to ring. Cat unlocked the door and hurried to grab the receiver from the wall unit. "Hello?"

Carlo. "'Get the inside scoop'. Whaddayou think?"

"About what?" Cat secured the towel, one-handed.

"For a slogan. For that scrapple thing. 'Scrapple – Get the inside scoop.' The fuck happened over Linwood?"

"You're the one with the inside scoop." Cat groped in her tote for a barrette, clipped her wet hair in a loose knot at the top of her head. "As for a slogan, I'm thinking, 'Scrapple. It's not the same old sh- "

"Vinnie already come up with that one. I called earlier, no one answered. You okay, or what?"

"We were at the beach. You want the evening's agenda?"

"I'm just askin'."

Cat heard a slow, deliberate tread on the back stairs, not Freddy, not Ellice. She slipped her hand into the tote bag, tugged the Taurus free from the small towel swaddling it.

"What's the matter?" Carlo's cop instincts were still acute.

Cat wedged the phone between her ear and her shoulder, gripped the gun in her right hand, her left hand cradled underneath. "Nothing, Carlo. Look, I have to free up the phone."

"You there by yourself? Where are the kids?"

"Freddy took them to get a couple pizzas. They'll be back any minute," she added, pitching her voice toward the back door. "Say hi to Annie and Mark." She hung up quickly and resumed her two handed-grip, raised the weapon.

The back screen door flapped and she heard footsteps in the pantry passage. In her haste to answer the phone, she hadn't latched it, closed and locked the door. Summer attitudes, careless and far too relaxed.

Victor stepped into the room, assessed the image of Cat, wrapped in a beach towel, her weapon trained on him. "Is that a pistol you're packing? Or are you glad to see me?"

Cat felt the slow thaw of a blush. "I didn't expect you."

"Considering the mixed visual cues, I don't know whether to be relieved or disappointed. Is that loaded?"

Cat nodded.

Victor approached her, slowly. He had good reason to respect a loaded gun, particularly one aimed at his heart. "I've had my share of receptions, you know. I'm pretty well versed in the protocol. Conventional forms of greeting and so forth. The wrapped-in-a-towel, brandishing-a-loaded-weapon, that I've only seen maybe once or twice in my forty – nearly forty-one years."

"How'd it work out for you?"

Victor detached the gun from her hand, angled it away from them, released the clip. "The first time, if memory serves, it worked out quite nicely."

Cat arched her chin. "And the second?"

"It only worked out nicely for one of us." He walked over to the cabinet, reached for the canister on an upper shelf, dropped the clip in and put it back. "I came by last night, you were out cold. Ellice said you weren't feeling well."

"The Scrappalooza did me in. I tried to get a first draft done on the beach, but I get as far as 'hacked up hogs' *hay*ids', and start to pass from 'feelings of sickness and shudderings of horror and from hot fits of fever to cold'. Mansfield Park. Oh, that reminds me. Mama's barbecuing tomorrow, late afternoon. You're invited."

"I think I'd like something more of a segue between 'hacked up hogs heads'-"

"*Hay*ids."

"- and 'you're invited to dine. Why don't we skip the barbecue and see if I can coax a reservation out of Giacinto?"

"Even dropping Paulie The Apron's name can't get us a table at Giacinto on Memorial Day Saturday."

"Next Friday, then. It's my birthday."

"Oh, Victor, I can't next Friday. The wedding rehearsal. It's been-" she pressed her hand to her forehead, the other hand gripping the knotted towel "-everything's such a mess."

He studied the dark gaze, the trace of misery that hinted at something beyond a hectic week. "Because of the wedding?"

There was a pause. "No. That's the least of it."

"Because of what happened at Whitney Rocap's house?"

Cat's expression was one of wary appraisal, weighing how much trust she should mete out. "That's part of it."

"What was going on between the two of you?"

"What makes you think anything was going on?"

"On Wednesday evening, Whitney Rocap and another woman were hanging around a convenience store, anticipating that someone the companion referred to as the 'Austen woman' might show up?"

"Victor, it's complicated."

"Well, Sherlock Holmes said that the very point which appears to complicate a case is the one which is most likely to elucidate it. And I think if it's not too complicated for you to confide to Delareto, it's not too complicated for me."

Cat laid her hand against his cheek. Her fingers were cold. "And what was it that Sherlock Holmes said about jealousy? That it's a strange transformer of character, *verdad*?"

His mouth turned down in a reluctant smile.

Cat eased into the booth. "Okay. She called me. Whitney."

"Wednesday night?"

"Afternoon. She may have tried Wednesday night, but I didn't pick up."

"Relations between you two were less than amicable. Why did she call you?"

"This is where it starts to get complicated."

"Then, pray. Elucidate."

Cat sighed. "In the past few weeks, I've gotten some crank calls. A woman, saying she knew something about Chris. About his murder. I'd just hang up. Then *Whitney* called Wednesday afternoon and said she knew the woman who was trying to get in touch with me, that I should hear her out, and she wanted to put us together." Cat pressed her hand to her forehead. "I hadn't heard about her accident. I didn't know she was dead when I went over to her house and ran into that guy. And today, after I got home? Ritchie told me that *Tuesday* night, Whitney was at Bud 'N' Lou's, asking around about Chris's murder. It's all just so strange. Frightening."

Victor sat opposite her. "Which is why you're packing heat this afternoon? Do you have a carry permit?"

Cat crossed her arms over her chest. "Victor, even Sherlock *Holmes* did things he knew were not quite legal when he believed they were morally justifiable. Besides, I didn't bring my gun to Whitney's when it was obvious that I needed one. And when I brought it with me this afternoon, I didn't need it. So, logically, the likelihood that I *won't* have to use it is on those occasions when I'm carrying it."

"I remember my sister Remy arguing for personal protection in much the same way."

"She carried a gun?"

"No, I don't think she was referring to a gun."

Cat felt warmth prickle the flesh of her throat. "Ritchie told me that you confiscated the surveillance tapes from the Twenty-Four/Seven. That's where she wanted to meet, but I have no idea why."

Fishing, for more than information. For trust. A confidence for a confidence. "Perhaps because that's where she was. She taped a segment, then went to State of the ART, a family planning clinic. She was there until about nine, from there she went to the Twenty-Four/Seven, was there maybe fifteen minutes. We suspect the crash occurred shortly after she left."

"What was she doing there?"

"At the convenience store?"

"Don't be evasive, Victor." Cat's gaze detached from his. She toyed with a wet strand of hair. Finally, she said, "It's a fertility clinic."

"I know. I spoke to the administrator, Doctor Hoffman, and one of his associates today. They live over on the bay."

"Here in Ocean City?"

"Yes."

"What associate?"

"Eve Bellamy. She's his fiancée as well."

"Eve? Little Eve? She's just a kid!" She bit her lip, realized what her exclamation betrayed.

"Freddy mentioned he'd been your doctor some time ago."

"A lifetime ago."

Another silence. Victor decided to approach the subject from another angle. "Did you know Hoffman's first wife?"

Cat shook her head.

"I understood she had been his co-founder."

"Oh, you mean Miriam. Miriam Bender. She was Doctor Hoffman's *second* wife. I heard that Jackie Wing dated him briefly before he started seeing Miriam, he was divorced." Jackie Wing was a nurse, a close friend of Cat's. "He had to be in his forties when he and Miriam got married."

"You two were friendly, then?"

"Not really, why?"

"Because you call him 'Doctor Hoffman', but you call her 'Miriam'."

"Oh. They had a theory that a first name policy was more stress-free for the patient. Eve. Miriam. Mark. I just could never bring myself to call him 'Randy'."

"Considering he's approaching his third marriage, and to a woman half his age, I should think it highly appropriate."

Cat's laugh hit a minor key, took a discordant track.

"What about a 'Kathy', the office manager?"

"Kathy?" The name sent a rapid palpation below her ribs as memory pulled up a mournful Modigliani face, dark hair, intelligent eyes. It had been Kathy who had gone over the form with her and Chris. *"Thirty days prior to termination, you'll be notified by certified mail."* Kathy had smiled her melancholy smile. *"But I'm sure ten years from now, you won't have embryos left in cryo. You'll probably have a half dozen children."*

"Six," Chris had said.

"Four," Cat had corrected.

"She's been with Doctor Hoffman forever. Why?"

"The woman with Rocap was overheard suggesting that Rocap give 'Kathy' a call. And she doesn't work for Hoffman anymore, she left about a month ago."

"You don't think something's happened to her, do you?"

"I don't have any reason to suspect so."

"But it is Major Crimes that's handling the investigation. That means foul play is suspected."

"I didn't say that."

"You didn't have to. You know, I went over Whitney's because word of her accident hadn't made the news yet. She doesn't need to leave for the studio until around five. Of course, she might have been out shopping or something, but Borch wouldn't *know* that, wouldn't know that he'd have time to comb her place for files and paperwork and chat on the phone, unless he was absolutely sure she wasn't going to show up."

"Or was quite prepared to deal with her if she did."

CHAPTER FOURTEEN: Three Years Ago

Raymond had fixed breakfast. Bacon, eggs, toast, orange juice, coffee. Kathleen's smile radiated a surprised glow whenever anyone did her a kindness, as though she felt she never quite deserved it. She didn't remind Raymond that she rarely ate breakfast, only said, "Raymond, don't make yourself late for work." And he forced the corners of his mouth upward in a frozen smile and replied, "You need to keep up your strength."

He listened to her chatter while she pushed the food around her plate, apologized that she would have to take the car from work because she needed to get to the market to buy their Easter ham, told him how sweet he was not to mind that she'd invited her mother to join them. He didn't mind. Soon, her mother would be all she had to love, for a little while. The smile, chewing, swallowing made his face hurt. He ate breakfast as though it was the last meal of a condemned man. Which it was.

Chris was feeding breakfast to the kids, reading Peter Rabbit, Jane helping out with the hard words. "I made coffee," Chris told Cat.

The scent made her queasy. Nicholas or Charlotte, she thought.

CHAPTER FIFTEEN:
Present Day

Cat pulled the brim low on her baseball cap, zigzagged around bicycles, surreys, strollers, inline skaters, low-flying seagulls, jogging pigeons as she trotted along the boardwalk. She inhaled the sequence of scents; caramel popcorn being mixed in copper tubs, coffee, bacon, salt air, the redolent oil and sugar aroma from a doughnut vat, the whiff of sunscreen. The scents evoked every summer, all the way back to her youth, when the first hot day she and Freddy and Steve Delareto and Trina Morosco would fill a cooler with sodas, grab a few towels spend the day splashing in the ocean, lolling on the sand, coming home exhausted, then showing up in school the following Monday chafing under a layer of sunburn.

Cat descended the north end ramp and cut back to a walk. She entered by way of the back door, pried off her running shoes in the pantry, felt the air conditioning chill her soaking T shirt. "Ellice!"

"In here." Ellice was reading the morning paper. She was dressed in tailored slacks and white silk blouse, white blazer, though it was Saturday.

"What time did you get in last night? Freddy hung around until after nine."

"My fitting ran late. I have a meeting today, sort of an opportunity that came out of the blue. Jennie called, said they won't be eating until five, she wants the kids to sleep over."

Cat nodded, knowingly. "She always wants the kids to sleep over on Saturdays. So she can sneak them into Mass on Sunday."

A car horn honked outside. Ellice grabbed her jacket. "Tell Freddy I'll get a ride to Jennie's after I finish my business."

Cat followed the shrill cackle of a cartoon character to the den where Jane and Mats sat side by side on the couch. Jane had put up tray tables and filled two bowls with Cheerios and milk, gotten a couple box juices, napkins.

"Jane cooked us breakfast," Mats announced to his mother.

Cat nipped back a smile. Jane wavered between the aggravation of looking out for her baby brother and the grudging awareness that he needed *someone* to do it.

"Would you two like to stay over at Nonna's?"

"Yeah!" That from Jane. Nonna let them watch anything they wanted on TV, Nonna let them make brownies without any help, Nonna always turned up a few of those bulky silver dollars that wouldn't fit in her purse and needed to be given away.

Mats looked up, pensively. "Will you be lonely for us, Mommy?"

"I always miss you when you're not here, but I'll be there for the barbecue and we can spend all tomorrow at the beach. I'm going to get a shower and then we'll pack your overnight bags."

Cat stepped into the shower. The smooth flesh of her abdomen under her palms triggered a ten-year-old echo.

What if I can never have children? What if I never can?

She had said it to no one except Chris until she asked it of Randall Hoffman, who had replied with a smile that was too kind to be condescending, "Of course you can have children."

His quiet explanation of his campaign to outwit her wayward biology gave Cat hope. Of course, his use of the term "assisted conception", had triggered a suspiciously mirthful cough from Chris. Cat's discreet kick silenced him while Hoffman went on to outline the protocol, which would involve a series of hormonal injections, monitoring, a trial procedure, the actual retrieval, the implantation. Finally, Chris leaned forward and inquired, gravely, "Doctor Hoffman, these hormonal injections –"

"- are perfectly safe –"

"- don't mean Cat's going to grow a beard, do they?"

Cat waited until they got home before she let him have it.

It had been more difficult than Cat had anticipated. The hormones wrought emotional havoc, and even with their overstimulation, her ovaries yielded only six oocytes, not the expected ten or twelve. "But all viable," Hoffman reported, explained the fertilization procedure, his determination to implant three at most. "The chances of your conceiving," he explained to Cat, "-as well as the chances of multiple conception both increase with the number of implantations, but so do the risks."

"Is there a chance Cat could have triplets?" Chris asked.

"Possible, but not likely. It's more likely that one at most will implant."

Cat felt a moment's twinge, a little tug of conscience for those that would not survive. Hoffman smiled, intuitively. "Not all conceptions survive to term," he reminded her. "It's no different than a pregnancy that ends in miscarriage."

Three days later, three of the embryos were implanted, in a procedure that was painless and relatively quick. Cat walked out of the office wondering, *am I pregnant*?, thinking of the christening gown of satin and antique lace that Aunt Cat, unmarried and childless, had passed to her namesake.

A year later, Jane wore it at her baptism.

Three left, placed in cryogenic storage. Cat and Chris opted to have two of the remaining embryos implanted with the second attempt. Mats. One left; Cat and Chris knew that the odds against a single embryo producing their third child were significant, but Hoffman assured them that with adequate preparation, it was possible, he had done it, and by now, Cat and Chris believed Hoffman could do anything.

Then, while considering when to time their last attempt, there had been a romantic weekend in New York, the aftermath of weariness and nausea and the exhilarating *It can't be.*

And then Chris, coming home that Easter Saturday, stopped to play good Samaritan to a lady in distress, escorted her to the ER, where he was shot and killed.

I know something about why your husban' died.

Cat stepped out of the shower into a cloud of steam, wrapped a towel around her hair. "It's a week before Freddy's wedding. I won't think about this," she said aloud.

She pulled on a loose cotton sundress, slipped her feet into sandals, braided her wet hair, helped Mats pack Mr. Rabbit on top of his folded clothes, assured him that Mr. Rabbit liked getting a ride in the overnight bag, gave Jane a look before Jane could articulate her hope that Mr. Rabbit wouldn't *suffocate* in there before they got to Nonna's.

The drive to her mother's was poorly timed. It had her returning to Ocean City in time to hit the incoming caravan that hadn't been able to get a Thursday night jump on the weekend. She found parking three blocks from the Scrappalooza, pumped coins into a meter and ran to catch the beginning of a panel, moderated by a lesser known TV chef, "To Puree or Not to Puree", which retained it's Shakespearean assonance by virtue of the fact that the moderator pronounced the verb 'pree'. She hunted up the author of *A Scrapple A Day*, and conducted a brief interview, during which she learned that 'souse' was indeed a verb, made a note to mention this to Ellice.

Cat hurried back to her car and headed down Asbury Avenue, cruising a widening orbit around her target location until she could find a parking place reasonably close to Miss Yolanda's Dressmaking and Expert Tailoring. Miss Yolanda hustled her into the gold chiffon gown. "Some detective called for you."

"Lieutenant Cardenas?"

"No, someone from Linwood. He said he's been callin' all over, your Ma, she told him to try here. Why don' you have a cell phone?"

"I guess I take after my father. I'm not much of a talker."

Miss Yolanda helped Cat onto a stool, knelt and began pinning the hem, her expression dour. "I'm sure glad Ellice didn't go for a dozen bridesmaids. These hems gotta be run off by hand. You can take your girl's dress when you go, I finished it up last night, waiting around for Ellice. She cancels once more, she's gonna walk down the aisle stark naked."

"I thought she had a fitting last night."

"Umph." Miss Yolanda muttered "O ih I" (So did I) through pin-filled lips. "So, Jane, she tells me you're gonna be next, *chica*? Some cop? She's a pistol, *tu hijita*. You're lucky she wasn't twins."

She might have been triplets, if the other, frailer embryos had not failed; Jane had been the tenacious one, the one that had held on.

The chimes on the door jangled. A man entered with the tentative wariness of one approaching unfamiliar, possible hostile terrain. Cat recognized the detective who had taken her statement yesterday. Today, he was dressed more casually, in khaki slacks and a white polo shirt his badge clipped to his belt.

"Mrs. Austen?"

Cat gave him a half wave.

Miss Yolanda barked, "Hold still."

"I called around, your mother said I could find you here."

He produced a manila envelope, removed a panel with six mug shots laid out in two rows. "Guy who jumped you yesterday, just tell me if any of them look like him."

Cat's eyes settled on the square face, the hostile gaze."If I confirm that it's one of them, will you tell me who he is?"

"Can you make an identification?"

"Yes."

"Well?"

"You first."

"Mrs. Austen- "

Cat crossed her arms over her chest.

"Put your hands down straight!" Miss Yolanda ordered.

Cat put her hands down at her sides.

"Okay, you can ID the guy, I'll give you a name."

"Number four."

"You sure?"

"Positive," Cat nodded. "What's his name?"

"Borch. Robert J. Recognize it?"

Cat shook her head.

"Okay, I'll notify Major Crimes. Meanwhile- well, you got, what, five brothers in the trade, you know the drill."

"Keep my doors locked, report anything suspicious, don't take candy from strangers."

He grinned and nodded, made his way to the door.

"Okay, that's it. I'll help you get out of this dress," Miss Yolanda said. Your firs' husband, he was a cop, right? Cops," she added. "Too many secrets, you know?"

Mrs. Austen? Mrs. Christopher Austen? You don' know me, but I know something about why your husban' died.

"Yes. Far too many."

CHAPTER SIXTEEN: Present Day

The Fahrenheit was heading toward eighty degrees when Victor, rolled out of bed, pulled on black swim trunks, grabbed a beach towel and strode down the street toward the boardwalk.

The narrow beach was starting to fill. He dropped his towel near the shoreline and walked straight into the water, plunging into a wave when he was thigh deep and swimming toward the horizon. The water was pleasantly cold, its chill driving off his thoughts, focusing on the motion of the water as he worked to match his strokes to the rhythm of the waves, synchronizing himself with the current that ran diagonal to the shore until they were a single rhythm, a fluid union. He wondered if he and Cat would ever fall into that easy rhythm, a natural tempo, not hitting a discordant note as they had last night. Something, some secret, coiled like a riptide beneath a subdued surface, one moment they drew closer, the next moment impossibly distant.

He made his way back to shore and threw the towel around his shoulders, headed home. His relaxed gait and steady gaze betrayed no awareness of the fluttering of curtains across the street. If there was, perhaps, a suggestion of humor in the slight twitch of his mustache, it was far too subtle for Mrs. Ricci across the street to detect from her living room window.

He walked into his office forty-five minutes later, his gray suit and red and silver tie, his aloof, professional air making no concession to the holiday. Phil and Stan were more relaxed, Phil in a burgundy knit pullover and khaki cargo pants, Stan in jeans with a rumpled linen jacket over a polo shirt.

Stan laid a folder and a packet of four-by-six glossies on Victor's desk. "Cat's statement, Linwood faxed it over, and stills of the woman with Rocap, the lab printed off the video. Grainy, but they should be clear enough for an ID. Cat okay?"

"Yes, fine, Sergeant." Victor studied the subject's tense, dark-eyed face, mass of black hair. "We may have another lead." He told them about Cat's anonymous phone calls. "Miss Rocap called Mrs. Austen, implied that she was acting on behalf of this anonymous caller and suggested they all meet at the convenience store Wednesday night. The counter clerk heard this woman-" He held up one of the glossies, "-ask whether Rocap had called the 'Austen' woman."

Stan ran his fingers through his graying hair. "Okay, Jane Doe wants to hook up with Cat. What's with bringing in Rocap as go-between? Rocap and Cat weren't all that friendly."

"Perhaps it was something that Jane Doe also intended to take to the media," Adane suggested.

"Small time news anchor's hardly media," Stan countered.

"She would be if our Jane Doe was new to the area."

Victor gestured for Adane to continue.

"I just meant, if you just moved into the area; 'local media' is likely to be the face on the local news."

Victor nodded. "You turn up anything on the phone records?"

"I was able to get Miss Rocap's. No calls were made from her home phone later than Tuesday. If Mrs. Austen interrupted her attacker in the middle of a phone call on Friday, that call came from outside. Her cell phone record from Wednesday logs calls to three different numbers. One, an Arturo Chavez, West Atlantic City, also showed up on her home phone records, and she called that number twice on Wednesday, once at five PM and again at six thirty-five PM."

"Chavez," Long echoed and started shuffling through the files on his lap. "Chavez..."

"Six thirty-five would have been right after she went off the air." Victor tapped his steepled fingertips against his chin. "The video crew said they went directly to Mays Landing-Somers Point Road after Wednesday's broadcast, but Miss Rocap was late. Had a woman in her car when she showed up."

"She calls the Chavez number, arranges to pick up the Jane Doe at his place, bring her along to meet with Cat. Maybe Jane Doe's his wife? Mom? Daughter?"

"She went to the clinic before she stopped at the Twenty-Four/Seven," Victor recalled. "The nurse who spoke to her said that Miss Rocap was alone." He turned to Adane. "What did you find out about State of the ART?"

Adane slipped a brochure on his desk. "State of the ART. ART stands for 'assisted reproductive technologies'. It was the project of Doctor Randall Hoffman and Doctor Miriam Bender, his wife. They married just before the clinic opened. She was a psychiatrist, had done infertility counseling in free clinics, ran State of the ART's counseling programs, while he acted as medical director. Their success rates match those of any on the East Coast, including urban and university-based settings. Apparently the technology has evolved rapidly in the past few years. Advances in hormonal monitoring, assessing which oocytes – eggs - are optimum prior to fertilization, availability of embryos, due partially to their OvaShare donors, all add up to an impressive live birth rate."

"Donors? What gets donated?" Stan inquired.

"Embryos. Eggs fertilized with partner or donor sperm." She looked at his puzzled expression. "Freshman biology Stanley?"

"Jeannie, I was twelve, I coulda taught freshman biology-"

"Sergeant," said Victor. "Continue, Adane."

"A few years ago, Doctor Hoffman patented what is considered the most reliable fertility monitor on the market. It's so accurate that in many cases, it has eliminated the necessity for any hormonal assistance. The device is called 'The Hoffman', and it's made him a millionaire several times over."

"Now, I get what it means!" Stan slapped his forehead.

Adane looked at him.

"'Tonight's not good, Stan, I'm a ten on the Hoffman'."

Victor sighed, patiently. "Continue."

"The practice draws from all of Southern New Jersey, Northern Delaware and even Philadelphia. Doctor Bender's role has been assumed by Dr. Paul Aquino and Doctor Hoffman shares the medical duties with Dr. Mark Schoenberg. Some of the women opt to use Doctor Hoffman and Doctor Shoenberg as their obstetricians, some go to the clinic for IVF procedures, but have prenatal care and delivery elsewhere. Three nurses, an RN, a nurse anesthetist a licensed nurse practitioner, Miss Bellamy. Three full time lab techs and one assistant in the embryology and cryo labs, the RN and the lab tech in the testing lab. The ultrasound tech is on an on-call basis. Generally, lab work is performed early in the morning, procedures in mid-morning, routine follow-ups in the afternoon. The doctors don't have office hours every day. Orientation sessions on Wednesday evenings. Attendance runs thirty or more."

"What's cryo?" Stan inquired.

"Cryogenic preservation. Unused embryos can be frozen."

"Jeez. For how long?"

"Estimates vary. Generally they place a ten year maximum for embryos in cryo before they're terminated."

"Terminated mean what I think it means?"

"It means destroyed."

"Jeez." Stan ran his hand through his hair. "Time comes, I am bakin' from scratch and no leftovers in the fridge."

Phil, still shuffling papers, chuckled.

Cat's doctor. "What about non-medical staff?" Victor asked.

"Clerical, cleaning, disposal and security. Clerical are clinic employees. The other services are contracted."

"Disposal as in...?"

"Removal of the neutralized embryos. And medical waste, anything that has been in contact with tissue, bodily fluid."

"What's in the main building?"

"Physicians' offices, treatment rooms, file rooms, staff and public restrooms, a staff lunchroom and the reception area."

Victor was beyond being impressed by Adane's ability to assemble such a detailed summary in a day. "You said Miss Rocap called three different numbers on Wednesday. The Chavez one, correct? And we know that she called Mrs. Austen. The third?"

"It's an unlisted number in Somers Point. K. Petrone."

"That's it!" Phil Long snatched a paper from a folder. "Chavez and Petrone! The overnight guard, Borch? Applies to Pro Patrol for work, he's gotta get a physical, do the drug screen, put down three references, right?'I know such and such to be a man of good work habits', etcetera. The three references? One is a *Daria* Chavez." Phil handed the paper to Adane. "Same number?"

She scanned the paper, nodded. “Yes. Arturo Chavez.”

“Get me an address.” Victor recalled what Eve Bellamy had told him. “Another was this K. Petrone?”

“Kathleen. Yup.”

“So who was his third reference?”

“Doctor Randall Hoffman.”

That was something Hoffman and ‘sweet little Evie’ had left out.

CHAPTER SEVENTEEN:
Present Day

Cat winnowed into the heavy stream of traffic on the Ninth Street Bridge. Once out of Ocean City, she diverted toward Mays Landing-Somers Point Road and traffic thinned away. Soon she was the only westbound motorist, the others skimming like gulls, toward the shore. She had not been down this road in years; still, instinct directed her, that and the fact that there had been no encroaching development to transform the landscape. The clinic was still flanked by open tracts of land, just as it had been when she had last seen it, more than five years ago.

Cat pulled up to the guard's kiosk, saw a single car in the lot, small, sporty and brighter red than a car needed to be. Hoffman's mid-life crisis, dating-a-girl-half-my-age car? Or that of the young sun-bleached blonde who pushed open the sliding glass window and greeted her with a "Help you?"

Cat felt a chilly whiff of air conditioning emerge from the kiosk, saw 'Pro Patrol Manned Security' appliquéd on his sleeve.

"Clinic's closed today? I thought they had Saturday hours."

"They're taking the long holiday, won't have office hours again until Tuesday."

The 'long holiday' was relative, Cat reflected. Her father had owned a restaurant and her brothers had been cops. Holidays had been workdays for them, with the toil and aggravation tripled.

"So nobody's around, not even office staff?"

"No."

"I heard there was a pretty horrific car accident down the road. You didn't happen to be around when it happened, did you?"

"We're not supposed to talk to anyone, unless the cops call us in. Hoffman's orders."

Cat glanced inside the hut, saw a paperback lying open face down, the novelization of some action movie. She played her trump card. Fumbling for the press credentials Ritchie had given her, she flashed an apologetic smile. "Fine by me. I don't know why I even got stuck looking into this when I've still got a couple *CopWatch* pieces to turn in."

"You hooked up with *CopWatch*?"

Cat executed a self-deprecating shrug that would have done her mother proud. "I was the one they based the main character on, the one Tommi Ann Butler played?"

The blue eyes flirted. "That was you?"

"That's me."

"I tried to get work on that. As an extra? You get to meet Tommi Ann Butler? What's she like?"

"She's pretty much what she seems on the screen," Cat lied. She had thought that Tommi Ann's secret would have eroded the admiration and awe that her screen image evoked, but it hadn't. Cat found her magic all the more intriguing. "Anyway, the producer told me to keep my eye out for material, just in case."

This was true, though Cat had suspected that it had been extended as Hollywood proposals generally were; insincerely, quickly forgotten. "Like the car accident? I mean, the fact that the victim was a TV personality, and she'd been engaged to Jerry Dudek gives it a certain spin." She smiled. "So, what, do you rotate your schedule, or are you only on days?"

"I don't mind the days, I get off at four, still time to catch some sun. Rod's four to midnight, and I guess they hadda replace Bobby already. Some new guy was on when I clocked in, said Pro Patrol sent him out, Bobby never reported for work."

"Midnight to eight must be boring. Maybe Bobby asked for a transfer, someplace a little more stimulating?" Cat suggested.

"What, like the malls, have some fifteen-year-old snot busting on you? Forget it. Here, you got room to kick back, got TV- " he nodded toward the small set mounted in a corner. "I want, I can take a break, use the microwave in the employees' kitchen, use the johns. We don't have access to the medical wings or the labs, just check 'em through the cams." He nodded toward a video monitor. "Prob'ly cause of the drugs, but I don't think that's what either Rod or Bobby got sent up for."

Sent up? The clinic was hiring ex-cons?

No, they weren't employees of State of the ART, they worked for Pro Patrol. Cat felt the seed of a story take root. *Who's Minding the Store – the Mall, the Clinic and the Warehouse?*

"What else is there you're gonna risk gettin' violated for? The doc's Louis the whateverteenth desk and the fancy artwork?" He shook hishead. "Nah, he's only been workin' here a month, an' I got the idea Bobby asked for this gig because of the hours. Looks like he's been makin' the most of it."

"In what way?"

"You report for work, find two, three used condoms in the wastebasket, I figure it's any which way but Sunday."

"He was meeting a girlfriend, you mean?"

"Maybe he hooked up with the clientele, if you get my meaning?" His wink implied that his meaning was obvious.

"The patients?"

"Maybe they figure they'll try out a new stud service as a last resort, before they plunk down the ten grand to cook up some test tube kid. "

Fourteen grand, Cat thought. "How would he meet the patients if he's only here midnight to eight AM?"

"Maybe he's got himself an inside gal, too."

"It hardly seems an appropriate place for a rendezvous," she commented. *But an excellent place for a murder, come to think of it.* "Thanks for talking to me." She prepared to back out when isolated phrases filtered through the conversation, collided in her consciousness.

Bobby.never reported for work... got sent up...

"Oh," she said, casually. "Just wondering. Bobby's last name wouldn't be 'Borch', would it?"

"Yup, that's him. Robert Borch."

CHAPTER EIGHTEEN: Present Day

The Fortunatis had assembled in Jennie's Richmond Avenue back yard. Joey's wife Sherrie sat on the grass, cross-legged, cradling baby Gio to her breast while Vinnie and his three boys lined up picnic tables. Annie and Nancy, married to Carlo and Marco respectively, bussed paper plates, plastic utensils and buckets of ice. Jane lay sunning on beach towels with her cousins Meryl and Andrea. Meryl was Sherrie's daughter by her first unfortunate marriage, a ten-year-old with a precocious beauty; Andrea was dark-haired like Marco, with Nancy's dimpled, merry expression. Carlo, in a voluminous Hawaiian shirt coached fourteen-year-old Mark in the grilling two dozen saucer-sized burgers, the basting of fat links of Italian sausage. Mark watched with studied disinterest, his expression making clear that he was present under protest.

"Hello, Mark." Cat noted that despite his sullen expression, he wore new khaki shorts, a clean shirt, his hair was neatly combed, looked nothing like the ragged wolf cub she had turned up in an Atlantic City tenement last December.

"Hi."

Carlo gave her a rough kiss on the cheek. "Heard they ideed the schmuck grabbed you, name's Borch. What's in the box?"

Cat opened the top lid to reveal three dozen profiteroles. "Hanky Spanky's Porn Parlor, Pleasure Paraphernalia and Patisserie. Annie told me you had this craving for chocolate and whipped cream, but I forget whether she was talking about pastry or pleasure paraphernalia, I always get those two mixed up."

"Shut up. Where d'you learn to talk like that?"

"I can't imagine. Six older brothers are such a civilizing influence, after all."

Jennie appeared at the back door. "Mark, you wanna come help me finish the salad or stay out there?"

Mark's expression brightened. "I'll help you out, granma."

Carlo watched Mark hurry to the back door, shook his head. "What's she got some kinda voodoo?"

"Everybody winds up doing what Mama wants, Mark's just smart enough to realize it saves time if you do it right off. So how's it going?" Cat asked.

"Slow."

"What about his father, did you hear anything?"

"Other than he's a bum shopped the kid for drug money?"

Cat winced. "Do you think he'll turn up sometime?"

"Let him try. I'll geld the dumb fuck. So, Babe, what's the skinny on this Borch? Victor says he's some kinda rent-a-cop, went AWOL."

"When did you talk to Victor?"

"He called twenty minutes ago, wanted to know if you got here okay, gave me the heads-up on Borch." Carlo checked the underside of a burger."So he ask you to marry him yet, or what?"

"Don't be silly, Carlo, I hardly know Mr. Borch."

"Don't be funny, I'm just askin'."

"You're never 'just askin'."

Cat's brothers became studiously occupied.

"Okay, look, we kinda got this pool going."

"Who's 'we'?"

"A little friendly action."

"Friendly action or fraternal action?" Cat demanded.

Marco wiped his sunglasses on his shirt hem. "I got you down for the ring before Freddy's wedding, married by Christmas. Work with me, I'll cut you in."

"Don't be mad, Cat," Freddy coaxed.

Cat picked up the boxes of pastry. "Why don't I go inside and tell our mother that while she's whipping up her killer sauce, you're out here laying bets like I'm the Pick Six."

"Whadda you gotta tell Mom for, she's in for a C note. An' tell Victor stop sendin' her flowers, he's makin' us look bad."

Cat stalked into the kitchen. She put the pastry in the refrigerator, found Mats asleep on a living room sofa, his cheeks red from sun and exertion. He looked so like Chris when he slept. Solemn and utterly content with his lot. The sight always provoked a tide of love that swelled to proportions that frightened her. How could you love a little being so much?

Mats opened his eyes, rolled upright. "Mom. Jane says if I'm ring bear, I gotta wear a bear suit."

Cat sat beside him, took him onto her lap. "You're going to wear a nice tux, like a grown-up."

"Uncle Carlo says he's gonna take us on the rides tonight."

"You gotta be a good boy and eat first," his grandmother advised. "Look at these nice flowers Victor sent. He told Carlo he's gotta work late, I told him come by whenever he can, you-"

"Still gotta eat." Cat concluded her mother's favorite maxim. "Maybe they should skip the r-i-d-e-s tonight, they'll be too t-i-r-e-d."

"They're kids. They get old like me, they can be tired. That idiot you write for, call him back, he's called her three times already."

She picked up the wooden salad bowl. Mark took it from her, said, "You're not old, granma," balanced it on his hip so that he could hold the door for her again.

Lorraine, Vinnie's wife, came in, fanning herself with a dish towel, gave Mark a dour glance. She wore loose pedal pushers, a sleeveless top, her russet hair was piled on her head. Her pale flesh was pink and moist. "I don't see why we have to eat outside when we got air conditioning. So whaddayou think of Freddy, asking that kid Carlo and Annie took in to be one of his ushers?" Lorraine grumbled. "He's not even family."

"Ellice asked me to be matron of honor and I'm not family."

Lorraine dropped into a chair and shrugged. She knew better than to take on Cat when the subject turned to Ellice.

Nancy and Annie came in, giggling over something. "Cat, don't be mad at the boys, it's just- "

"I know. A little friendly action." She knelt down to tie Mats's sneakers.

"Can't he tie his own shoes yet?" Lorraine asked. "He's starting school in the fall."

Cat saw Mats's troubled expression, made a funny grimace, her back to Lorraine. Mats giggled. "Go outside, baby, I have to make a phone call. Tell Uncle Carlo you can go on the rides."

Cat watched him trot off. *What if I hadn't had them? What would I have done if I'd been left alone with no one to love?*

"So what happened to get you hauled into the police department yesterday? Some guy roughed you up?" Lorraine asked.

Nancy Fortunati hooked one of the stems with her finger, drew the rosebud toward her nose. "It's awful. Marco says a lot of the women in his self-defense class, they don't care about hand to hand combat any more, they're asking about guns."

Cat went into her mother's bedroom, closed the door so that Lorraine couldn't eavesdrop. She settled the phone on her lap and dialed Ritchie's number. "My Mom said you called."

"Cops're checking out pawnshops, they're puttin' the Gabors under the lens, what's up with that?"

"Gabors? As in Zsa Zsa and Eva?"

"As in Dunya and Tibor. Mother and son entrepreneurs. Own some real estate around the county, small rentals mostly, and they run a pawnshop right down the street from the office. I'm thinking, this guy who jumped you? Maybe the cops figure they got him stashed someplace. You know he dropped out, right?"

"Mother and son?" *Tell Mommy dearest to check around.* "I saw that he'd rounded up some of Whitney's jewelry. Maybe they think he's going to try to pawn it."

"You get tipped off that they're gonna hit the pawnshop, give me a heads-up, I can grab my new digital and run down, fire off a few for the *Chronicle*. They got an ID on this guy yet?"

"Yes."

"So?"

"I'll trade it for my ID on a paycheck."

"Jeez, Austen. You know it's a holiday. Next week. And if I win the scrapple contest, I'll throw in a bonus. When do they gotta be postmarked? How's this: 'Scrapple: Pleased to meat you.' M-e-a-t, get it? Whaddayou think?"

"'Those scraps are good deeds past,'" Cat quoted.

"I don't get it."

"It's Shakespeare. Though considering that demonstration I witnessed, his line about 'the fragments, scraps, the bits and greasy relics', would be more fitting. I've got to go, Ritchie."

"So Victor on his way over, or what?" Carlo asked when Cat rejoined the family.

"Hold your wagers, I didn't call Victor. I was talking to Ritchie. He's using me as a sounding board for scrapple slogans." She started helping Annie slice hamburger rolls. "I can't think of a less demeaning way to make money than to come up with a slogan for a meat product – not actual meat, mind you, but meat *residue* – that any sensible person would throw out."

"You kiddin'?" Carlo flipped a burger, caught it on the spatula. "People'd turn granma into meat residue for a hundred grand."

"Half that," Vinnie grunted.

"A hundred thousand." Lorraine multiplied four years of college tuition times three sons. "'Waste not, want not.'"

"'Scrapple," Marco began herding the kids toward the picnic tables. "'For our pork you pine.'"

Carlo started handing down the burgers. Cat wedged herself between Mats and Vinnie at the picnic table. Vinnie worked Burglary, knew all of the pawnshops in Atlantic City. "Vinnie," she inquired, with studied indifference. "Suppose I wanted to turn over some merchandise for cash, how would I go about it?"

"You mean pawn it, or what? You okay? You need a few bucks?"

"It's some background for a piece I'm thinking of doing. Say I just wanted the money, I probably won't redeem it."

"You're in a hurry, or it's hot? Gabors."

"Who are they?" she asked, innocently.

"Down Pacific. Mary Grace Keller tried to make a case against them, had Joey and Phil Long undercover. Phil's all tricked out like street meat, tries to turn over some ice we took in on a drug bust, but like I told Victor, Gabors? They can smell a cop, even with Long in gold satin and fishnets."

Cat called up an image of Victor's slim, mustachioed detective, still could not picture him as his street persona, Phyllis. "Pawnshop transactions are regulated, aren't they?"

"Yeah, when it's on the level."

"Give me an example of off the level?"

"Say I had a bad run at the tables," Vinnie explained, patiently. "I maxed out my house credit, but I got the nice set of emerald cufflinks the wife gave me last Christmas. I don't got time to look up who buys old jewelry, someone, maybe a dealer, tips me off to how XYZ Pawnshop'll gimme two hundred' but Gabors'll gimme three fifty. I don't give a damn about getting' the cufflinks back- "

"Uncle Vinnie, you're not asposed to say bad words in fronta us kids," Mats reminded him.

Vinnie reached over, ruffled Mats hair. "Don't give two hoots about the cufflinks," he amended.

"That's how *you* profit. How do *they* profit?"

"They turn 'em around."

"To who?" Cat asked, ungrammatically.

"Some guy who wants to *buy* cufflinks. He can go to Clevingers and throw down a grand, or you can go to Gabors and pick up ones just as good for five bills, the ones the Gabors paid three fifty for. I get my run at the tables, the buyer gets a good price on the cufflinks. The Gabors, they gotta give a kickback to the referral, they'll still clear a C note. And jewelry, it cleans up like new, travel's light. Break it down, you move the stones here, the weight there. Move it under the table, do the flea marts, even what the boys were tellin' me about, this online site called Cyber Swap. And all under the IRS's radar. That why Victor's askin' about them? He said there looked to be jewelry taken off Rocap."

"The DA must think foul play was involved if he assigned it to Victor's unit." Cat nibbled her burger, thoughtfully. "But you don't run someone off the road for a handful of jewelry."

"I ran into Paul Aquino's wife when I was picking up the rolls," Annie commented. "She said someone from Victor's unit wants to interview him about the accident."

"Who's Paul Aquino?" Vinnie asked.

"He took over for Hoffman's wife at State of the ART, that fertility clinic? Miriam Bender. You know about her, right?"

Cat's brothers nodded, grimly.

"Paul was working Wednesday night, some sort of seminar. He and this young nurse that Randall Hoffman just got engaged to. I got a look at her at the Heart Fund Ball. Mini dress up to here-" Annie patted her hip, "- an you should have seen her on the dance floor. Half his age, if that."

"C'mon, hon," Carlo protested, "-his wife's dead, he's only in his fifties, right? Why shouldn't he get on with his life?"

Annie prodded his top shirt-button, roughly eye-level.

"Don't get any ideas, *carino*. If I kill myself, you're not getting on anywhere, you're staying right where I left you."

"Did they ever figure out why she committed- " Cat glanced at Mats, mouthed 'suicide?'

Annie shrugged. "Paul said once that her interest in the clinic just went lukewarm after a few years."

"What about Doctor Hoffman, did he turn lukewarm, too?" Cat asked.

"He'd have to heat up a few degrees to get to lukewarm," Annie chuckled. "The nurses who dealt with him, back in the day? Before he and Miriam opened the clinic? They used to call him the Indomitable Snowman. Nerves of steel."

"He's the Snowman, he's got nerves of ice," stated Carlo. "Nerves of steel's your Superman. Who's ready for seconds?"

"Superman's *man* of steel," Freddy commented.

"Yeah," Carlo conceded. "But he's your man of steel, then everything he's got's gonna be steel, right? Which means he's got your steel nerves, your steel muscles, your steel prick-"

"Uncle *Car*lo!" exclaimed his trio of ten-year-old nieces.

"Whereas your Iceman's prick's gonna be more of an icicle-"

"Uncle *Carlo*," Cat mimicked.

Mats's curiosity was piqued. "What's Batman got?" he asked.

Carlo's bellowing laugh could be heard a block off.

"I'm just *sayin'*," Carlo continued. "Me, I'd rather be your Steel Man, 'cause say you're your Snowman. Wine, dine, it's lookin' fine, things heat up, your polar icecap's gonna melt, an' there goes the romance."

"I got one!" Marco declared. "'Scrapple: Swine and dine.'"

"How now ground sow," Nancy giggled.

Freddy snapped his fingers. "How about..."

The family looked up.

"'To the victor goes the spoils'?"

Cat wriggled out of her seat at the picnic table, grabbed a pitcher of iced tea and dumped it over his head.

Freddy fell over onto the grass and the family burst out laughing. "Serves you right, you dumb *cetriul*," Carlo chuckled.

Cat headed toward the house to refill the pitcher, saw that even Mark was laughing.

CHAPTER NINETEEN:
Present Day

The *CopWatch* location shoot had given St. Agnes Church a transfusion. The exterior's dark stonework had been brightened with a bit of landscaping, the interior had been revived with some fresh paint, new carpeting, its shattered stained glass window restored, the floor in the bell tower replaced.

Still, rejuvenation had not extended to the congregation. Victor was the youngest of the Saturday evening penitents, the only male. A few of the elderly women offered to let him go to the head of the line as though afraid he might cut and run before securing absolution. Victor, with characteristic politeness, shook his head and sat quietly, waiting his turn.

He knelt, waited, saw Dominic's silhouette behind the screen. "Bless me father, for I have sinned," he began. "My last confession? Before Kevin's funeral Mass, I imagine."

"So what's been goin' on Victor? I heard about the Q and A with Cat over the Linwood PD. What's she mixed up in?"

"I'm not sure. I don't like where it's leading, though."

"Look, you wanna take this outta the box? Unless it's like, you've been lusting after my Cat. Something like that you better take to Monsignor Greg."

"I want to marry your sister. Does that count as lust?"

"You tell me."

"My father used to say that we are what we want."

"Well, the way I see it, you become what you aspire to, there's nothing wrong with that. You become what you covet, it starts to own you. Cat doesn't own you."

"Doesn't she?"

"Well, maybe just enough to make you a little nuts. Join the club. What else you got on the list?"

The list was short. Pride, kept in check with too much effort; envy over that portion of Cat's heart that would always belong to Chris. Impatience with Cat for not trusting him, for the barrier of secrets that separated them.

Victor recited the Act of Contrition and walked up to the bank of votive candles at the side of the railing, knelt and recited his penance, lit a candle for his father.

After Mass, Dominic invited Victor to the rectory for coffee. They walked the long corridor that linked the sanctuary to the rectory kitchen. "Didn't make it over to the barbecue, either? Want some dinner?" Dominic offered. "Maggie's out grocery shopping, but I can make us a sandwich or something."

"No, thanks, coffee's fine. How is Sister Maggie doing?"

Dominic gestured for Victor to sit at the long kitchen table, rooted around in the cupboards for coffee and filters. "Kevin's death hit her where she lived, lemme tell you. She was like their mother, growing up. Mrs. Keller, God forgive her, couldn't protect those kids from the old man." He shook his head. "Two dead. The rest, some did better than others. Not bad odds, what with nine kids." He poured water into the pot, plugged it in. "She's kinda on the outs with Mary Grace. I don't think the two of them talked since the funeral."

"Because of her relationship with Adane."

"We grew up with the Kellers, I thought I knew Mary Grace pretty well, but then, I thought I knew Kevin, too." He shook his head. "Mary Grace didn't get married, I figured it was because she didn't exactly get a rosy picture of holy matrimony from the folks. Now, Louie Cicciolini, I always had pegged. I started takin' ballet class, the only reason the Colucci twins beat me up every other day instead of every day was because on alternate days, they're working Louie over."

"That who worked him over a few months back? I saw his arm was in a sling at Kevin's funeral."

Dominic shrugged. "I'm thinkin' the Colucci's outgrew it, but who knows? One of them's in prison again, I forget which. So what's the deal, Victor, the guy who jumped Cat, Carlo says he's some rent-a-cop. Carlo also mentioned that this guy's still on the loose and Carlo gets a hold of him before you guys round him up, he's gonna pare him down to the giblets." He rose, eased the coffee pot from the burner, filled Victor's mug, filled his own. "I'm omitting the invectives and the modifiers and what-have-you."

"I get the gist."

"So what's the problem, Victor? I'd be willing to bet that you're not here just 'cause you got the urge to come to Saturday evening mass. Is Cat in some kind of trouble?"

Victor took a sip of his coffee. "You know all of your parishioners?"

"Meaning there's few enough to keep them all straight? Don't rub it in."

"You've got quite a few Latinos. You know if any of them are named Chavez? Arturo?"

Dominic nodded. "He and his wife married outside the church because he and his first wife divorced. Came here for years, when they moved out to West AC, they kept coming."

"His wife, is her name Daria?"

"No. I think there's an adult daughter, though. Moved to San Juan, the last I heard."

Victor hesitated. "What about a doctor named Randall Hoffman?"

Dominic looked at him. "You're not asking if he's a parishioner, are you?"

"No." Victor hesitated. "That rent-a-cop was posted to Hoffman's medical facility, works for an outfit called Pro Patrol Security. A Daria Chavez and Randall Hoffman both gave him job references, I'm looking for a connection."

"And?"

Victor's mouth turned down in a rueful smile. "And Freddy mentioned that Hoffman was Cat's doctor."

"And Hoffman's a fertility specialist." Dominic slipped his glasses off, wiped them on a corner of his sleeve. "I've never met him, but I was somewhat acquainted with his wife, Miriam Bender? We did a couple interfaith seminars together, religious and ethical spin on fertility medicine. She never mentioned to me the fact that Cat was a patient, but I suspected that there were some issues Cat and Chris were working through because Chris asked once what the Church's position was, asked if I'd ever heard of Hoffman, what I thought."

"Do you mind my asking what you told him?"

"I told him what the Church's position was, and that I understood if he thought differently because he wasn't a Catholic. And privately, I figured, a good Catholic, Italian girl like Cat, married six years and no children? Either they didn't want them, and what they were doing about it was none of my business, or they wanted them and why they weren't having any was none of my business. I know she and Chris wanted kids. Then along comes Jane." Dominic smiled. "And Jane? She's Cat to the bone at that age, something Cat'll never admit. And Mats is the image of Chris, God rest his soul. Beyond that, I don't know the particulars. Freddy might, he and Cat've always been close as twins. Is this personal or professional, Victor?"

"A little of both. I had to interview Hoffman in connection with that traffic fatality. The case is taking off in a couple disturbing directions." Victor set down his mug. "Not to mention the fact that my mother read a newspaper account, it mentioned how the accident occurred near a fertility clinic. You have to understand, my mother, she's had to make her own way since my father died, she's pretty independent, only fifty-eight. Not a naïve woman. Still, fertility clinic? She didn't know what they were talking about. My sister Remy filled her in."

"I'd like to've been a fly on that wall," Dominic chuckled. His family had met Victor's younger sister, liked her.

"So my mother calls me because Remy told her that you can put your – fill in the euphemism – in a freezer where anyone can get his hands on it, I'd better never think of such a thing, I'll go straight to hell and I am to tell my younger sister the same, because she would be just crazy enough to try it."

Dominic threw his clasped hands behind his head, grinning. "And did she speculate upon what this world is coming to?"

"At least three times in the course of the conversation. *El mundo loco*. I am also to make sure I eat right and get enough sleep and don't overuse the air conditioning."

"It just circulates the dead air," Dominic concluded, and the two of them laughed. "Mothers. What would this world be without them? Carlo and Annie, their twins are grown, he's retired, time for them to kick back, what do they do? They take in a fourteen-year-old street kid. Tells you why people like Hoffman thrive," he said. "It's not about children, it's about family. I guess that's why I get Mary Grace and Adane coming together. Just because you're not, as Dottie Cicciolini puts it, the 'marrying kind', it doesn't mean you don't need family. The saddest people in the world? They're not people who aren't loved. In time, they harden to the point where they don't give a hoot. It's the people who don't have anyone to love. Those are the people I really pity."

CHAPTER TWENTY:
Three Years Ago

Cat stood gripping the counter when Chris came up behind her, pressed his lips to the back of her neck. "You okay?"

Nicholas or Charlotte, Cat thought.

"Da! Da!" Mats raised his arms insistently and Chris laughed, lifted him from the high chair. Jane had decamped to the den to watch Saturday morning cartoons.

They walked Chris to the door. He took his cap and set it on Mats's head, turned him toward the foyer mirror. "Wanna be a state cop like your old man?"

"He does not." Cat took Mats from Chris. "Now say, 'No overtime, Daddy'."

"No o'ti', Da," Mats said obediently.

Chris leaned down and kissed him, kissed Cat.

"Me go, too, Da," Mats insisted.

Chris chucked him under the chin. "We'll go for a car ride tomorrow, okay?"

Tomorrow. With no doubt in his mind that there would be one.

Raymond watched her standing at the sink. The light from the window filtered through her thin robe, revealed the silhouette of her slender figure and he felt his pulse kick in. He came up behind her and drew the folds of her robe above her hips, slid his hands over her flesh, possessively.

"Raymond," she murmured. Amused. "Raymond, I have to get dressed for work."

She never complained about going back to work after the stillbirth, but is must have killed her inside, watching all of those other women getting pregnant. She needed a baby to love. Babies were easy to love. They hadn't screwed up yet, they hadn't done anything you had to forgive them for. You just loved them and they loved you back.

"Kathy, I love you. You know I love you, Kath? That I'd never hurt you?" If there was some way left to avoid it.

She turned and looked at him, her dark eyes searching, probing for the source of his sadness. "I love you, Raymond."

She won't love me tomorrow, he thought.

CHAPTER TWENTY-ONE: Present Day

Victor rose early Sunday morning, pulled on black swim trunks, grabbed a beach towel and strode toward the Boardwalk ramp. When he finished his swim, there were already families staking out a section of beach for the day, working umbrella poles into the sand, laying out blankets, opening beach chairs, lining up coolers, tote bags, belly boards. And where was his family? There had been a few women after Marisol, but nothing had taken root. One of them had found a more affluent companion, one had returned to an ex-husband. And Sheila was dead.

Descending the ramp at the base of Delancy, he saw Cat, sitting on his porch step, her arms wrapping the skirt of her pale sundress around her shins, watching him walk with the quiet detachment of one who is watching a movie.

"You know when you were walking down the sidewalk, I saw three window shades flutter as you passed," she told him.

He sat down on the step beside her. "Really? Did anything else? Flutter?"

"Not that I'm aware," she replied, primly. But the proximity of flesh was unsettling. Cat analyzed it, realized that she had never seen him wear anything more casual than slacks and a sweater. Her gaze settled on an irregular pucker of white against the brown skin beneath his collarbone. She traced it tentatively with her finger "What's that?"

"I was shot."

Shot. Her finger flinched.

"I was working undercover. A gun shipment deal went bad, and Gino Forschetti and I were cornered. He's got a matching scar, incidentally. We were the good guys. And we got lucky."

"The good guys don't always get lucky," she murmured.

I survived it. He didn't say it. He was afraid it might be an affront to Chris Austen, who hadn't gotten lucky, hadn't survived. Hadn't done anything but chaperone a lady in distress into one of those wrong place/wrong time scenarios.

He took her wrist, rose. "Come inside." He unlocked the door. "You can inventory my battle scars."

"I hardly think that would be entertaining."

"Speak for yourself, madam." He drew her inside and closed the door, took her face in his hands and kissed her. His mustache bristled against her lip and she tasted salt.

He took her hand and kissed her palm, her wrist, his lips traveling upward, settled on the bruises that banded her upper arms like bracelets. He looked at them, felt anger infiltrate lust, thought, *I received the sacrament fourteen hours ago.* "Kids over your mother's?"

"They stayed overnight. I'm on my way there to pick them up, and I thought I'd drop by to see why you didn't come over last night. Everyone asked about you. I thought maybe you'd located Robert Borch."

"Isn't that what they call burying the lead? Landis goaded you tapping your law enforcement sources, so you're here to soften me up?"

"Is it working?"

"Quite the opposite."

She gave him the arch glance that said she had lived with six brothers, was not going to put up with any male nonsense. "I'm sure you were told that I identified the photo of Robert Borch as the man who attacked me."

"I was told that you refused to cooperate until you were told the man's name."

"I won't be kept in the dark."

"Ah, *qué lástima*. You're not curious about my battle scars, you don't want to soften me up, and you won't be lured into the dark. It's probably all for the best," Victor conceded, with mock resignation. "After all, I did make my confession last evening, and received the sacrament. It will be interesting to see how long I can keep the state of grace reasonably intact."

"Well, don't pose the question to *fratelli* Fortunati, they'll get a pool going, and before you know it, my mother will be in for a – I believe the expression is a 'C note'." She crossed the room, dropped on the arm of the sofa. "You really went to confession last night? It's funny, you always seem like someone who's able to forgive yourself. Or perhaps it's that you never seem to be afraid of anything."

"Of course I am," he replied. "But there's rational fear and unfounded paranoia."

"And good old-fashioned Catholic guilt. I keep wondering if I'd met Whitney on Wednesday... whether she would be dead now."

"Cat- "

"I just didn't want it coming back."

"Didn't want what coming back? Chris? Or when you were a patient at the clinic?"

"I can't separate the two. It was Chris who found Hoffman, finally persuaded me to see him."

"'Finally'?"

"Well, we'd been married for six years. And they were busy years, what with Aunt Cat leaving us the house, and fixing it up and Chris talking me into going back to school to get my degree. When anyone asked when we were going to start a family, we'd always say 'Later'. And then all of a sudden, it *was* later. And that's when I started be afraid that there was something wrong. I knew Chris wanted children. He was born to be a father. And one day, I asked him..." she bit her lip, shook her head.

"You asked if he wanted a divorce," Victor said, quietly.

Cat looked up, her eyes wet. "How could you know that?"

Victor smiled. "It's the self-sacrificing thing to do and you have just this faintest aura of martyrdom about you."

Cat wiped her eyes with the back of her hand. "That's a Catholic thing, too. Randall Hoffman was more than sympathetic. He had this wonderful confidence, not conceit, just this single-minded certainty that he could fix whatever my problem was."

"And that's not conceit? I'd call it vanity, at very least."

Cat smiled, a bit wistfully. "And you think he's 'indulged in the freaks of a cold-blooded vanity a little too long'?"

"Jane Austen, *verdad*? I'm starting to recognize the rather pithy insights into human frailty. I got the impression he thinks well of himself, yes."

"Well, maybe he does, but I didn't care. I didn't care whether it was ego or vanity or talent because within six months, I was pregnant with Jane."

"And this was in vitro?"

Cat bit her lip, nodded. "The initial preparation was difficult, I had to take hormonal injections and they can make you sort of out of whack."

Victor perched on one of the stools at the counter that separated the living room from the small kitchen. "And how is 'out of whack' discernibly different from when you're in-"

"Lieutenant."

"- whack. So sorry. Idle speculation. Please continue."

"Most extractions-" She covered her face with her hands. "Awful. It sounds like dentistry. Worse, it sounds like that scrapple demo."

"That reminds me, I have a message from Stan Rice. 'Scrapple: It's a minding of the- '"

"Meats. Too late, Joey already came up with that one."

"I didn't mean to interrupt."

"The retrieval only yielded six. Eggs. They're fertilized in vitro and implanted three days later. Doctor Hoffman elected to implant three with the first pregnancy, and the rest were stored in cryo. There were problems. I thought I was going to miscarry, and it was a difficult pregnancy, but Jane was born. With three embryos left, we didn't know what to do. Doctor Hoffman said if we implanted two and kept one in reserve, eventhough the odds are significant against a pregnancy resulting from implanting a single embryo, we would have that option left open to us. And then..."

Tell him. Tell him that you allowed little Nicholas or Charlotte to be discarded.

"Then?"

She detoured the truth. "I got pregnant. I remember not being quite sure if I was really pregnant until I couldn't stand the smell of coffee, couldn't look at food before noon. If you're a Fortunati, that means that you're either pregnant or endstage. I was planning to tell Chris the day..." She pushed herself away from the couch, her arms crossed over her chest. "I never knew if it was better or worse, that he died not knowing. It didn't matter, though, because I lost the baby a week later."

"Never went back to the clinic?"

Cat shook her head. "Not until yesterday. I went out to the clinic to talk to the guard on duty."

The phone began to ring. Victor ignored it. "Haven't we had discussions about interfering in a police investigation?"

"Answer your phone."

"Answer my question."

The machine kicked. Adane. "Lieutenant, there's something I need to discuss with you regarding Mrs. Petrone."

"Who's Mrs. Petrone?" Cat asked.

"What did you and the guard talk about?"

"It must have be something particular if Adane's calling you at home on a Sunday morning?"

"It must have been something significant to draw you out to a place you've avoided for three years," Victor countered.

Cat sighed in mock exasperation. "The guard told me that Borch hadn't reported for work Friday night and that they'd been instructed not to talk to anyone about the accident. He also told me that Robert Borch is an ex-con. Pro Patrol only assigned him to the clinic last month and he had a distinct preference for the overnight shift. It seems that the hour and the isolation provided for a unique opportunity if one was, um, inclined. Romantically, that is."

Victor cocked an eyebrow. "And contrary to the maxim, opportunity knocked more than once, I gather?"

Cat colored faintly. "Sometimes more than once an *evening*."

"Well, then. Sherlock Holmes may have been mistaken when he lamented that audacity and romance seem to have passed forever from the criminal world. And how did you get Tony to disobey Doctor Hoffman's mandate not to talk to anyone?"

"I mentioned that I have ties to CopWatch. Believe me, the phone number of a television producer loosens the tongue a lot more effectively than a badge."

"*Dios me salve*. Listen, I'm going to get dressed. Call your mother and tell her you may be running late."

"Why?"

"There's something we need to talk about." Victor went into his bedroom and closed the door.

Jennie was delighted to hear that Cat was at Victor's. "*La festa di Giovanni diBattist'*. That's when your father gave me a *fedina*." June twenty-fourth was a popular date for engagements. Jennie still had her fedina, a gold promise ring, fastened to a charm bracelet. "I went on the Boardwalk with Annie an' Carlo an' the kids las' night." Jennie lowered her voice. "Annie tells me that doctor, the one marrying some young girl, he's got a clinic where they take your eggs out and freeze them, so you can have them put back later on when you want to get in the family way. Whaddayou think, you think she was pullin' my leg?"

Cat felt her heart knock against her sternum. "No, it's true, Mama."

"Whaddayou think the Pope thinks about that?"

"I think he's pretty much inclined toward a more traditional approach."

"It's all this internet that's doing it."

Cat blinked. "What's the internet have to do with it?"

"People don't have time to get together, all holed up in front of a computer and by the time they get around to meeting a nice Cath'lic boy, all your eggs've gone bad."

She heard Mats in the background, asking if that was his mother. Jennie handed over the receiver.

"Did you have a lot of fun last night?" Cat asked him

"We had *some* fun, but it wore off. This mornin', Nonna took us to see Uncle Dom do his prayers."

"Did you like it?"

"We hadda sit a long time and we couldn't go up to the front, only Nonna could. She said your soul hadda have a steak and grapes, but all they had were some crackers, an' you only got one each. Nonna says if we tell Uncle Dom everything we did wrong we get to go up and get a cracker, but not 'til you're seven. An' then Uncle Dom drank some wine but he didn't give Nonna none of it. Jane says that's 'cause he don't wanna spread the germs."

Victor came out, dressed in dark slacks, a white short sleeve shirt, his jacket over one arm. He stood at a small mirror beside the oak coat rack, knotted his tie.

"Baby, you tell Nonna I'll be there in fifteen or twenty minutes." Cat said good-bye and hung up the phone. "My mother thinks we're going the way of Brave New World because the internet has replaced traditional courtship ritual and nobody can come up with a nice Catholic boy any more."

"I'm a nice Catholic boy, and more than willing to-"

"Victor. What did you want to talk to me about?"

He nodded toward the couch. "Let's sit down for a minute."

Cat sank back onto the couch and Victor perched on the coffee table, took her hands. "You're right. You shouldn't be kept in the dark about matters that concern you. There are aspects to the investigation I can't talk about just yet, but I'll tell you this much. Adane searched Rocap's residence after your report was filed. Apparently, Borch not only took her jewelry, he also cleaned out all of the data, phone numbers, files, notebooks, anything that might indicate whom she had been in contact with, what she was working on. Then he went to NewsLineNinety, conned the receptionist into believing that he was Whitney's brother and made off with all of her personal property. All we were able to get were the phone records. On Wednesday, Whitney Rocap contacted, or attempted to contact three people. You, Kathy Petrone and someone else whose number is listed to an Arturo Chavez in West Atlantic City."

"Kathy Petrone is this Mrs. Petrone that Adane called you about?"

Victor nodded. "Apparently, the clinic took this first-name business to heart. That's the Kathy who was Doctor Hoffman's secretary."

"Victor, you're behind the times. Teachers are educators, insurance salesmen are human services providers, librarians are media specialists and secretaries are administrative assistants. How does this Arturo Chavez figure into Whitney's accident?"

"When Robert Borch applied to Pro Patrol, he had to provide references. One of them was a woman named Daria Chavez." Victor removed an envelope from his jacket pocket, drew out a pair of grainy photographs. "You recognize this woman?"

The photos triggered something too faint and distant to be memory. "Something is familiar. I can't think what."

"Seen her recently?"

Cat shook her head, handed the photos back.

"It was printed from Twenty-Four/Seven's surveillance video. This is the woman who was with Rocap Wednesday night."

Cat's mouth dropped open. "Then she was...the one who was phoning me?"

"I think so. And if the same names that Rocap had attempted to contact were the people who provided Borch with references, maybe she stumbled onto something that would give him a motive for getting her out of the way."

"But what? And..." *Why?* An echo broke through her subconscious. "Why," she whispered. "I didn't think about it before."

"About what, love?"

She looked up at him, her dark eyes dilated as if trying to absorb an impossible speculation. "What she said to me on the phone.'I know something about *why* your husband died'. Victor, there *was* no 'why'. Chris got flagged on his way home by a woman who needed help, a pregnant woman. He took her to the ER. When Chris walked through the door, some maniac with a gun-" Cat swallowed hard. "He started firing. Chris was killed, a couple other people were injured, the man killed himself. *There was no 'why'*? Unless… it wasn't random. Unless there was a reason."

"Could that reason have eluded the witnesses at the hospital? The officers called to the scene? Your own brothers?"

"Maybe it didn't. Maybe everyone has kept it from me. Protected me, the way they always do."

"*Querida*. Is that likely?"

"Do you think Kurt Raab would re-open the investigation?"

"His resources aren't unlimited, Cat."

"Will you ask him?"

Victor looked at her, soberly. "Before you ask that, think. You said you never knew whether or not it was better that Chris died without knowing about the baby. You said you didn't want it coming back. Why bring it back? And are you sure you're strong enough to deal with whatever turns up?"

Cat looked up at him, her dark eyes sober and direct. “Mary Wollstoncraft said that nothing calls forth the faculties so much as being obliged to struggle with the world.”

“I’ll think about it.”

“And if he does, and whatever you find out, no matter how bad it is? Promise you won’t keep it from me?”

“I won’t keep things from you.” He took her hand, threw his coat over his arm. “Come on, I’ll walk you to your car.”

He opened her car door, leaned down to kiss her, wondered if there were curtains fluttering across the street.

Victor took out his cell phone, thumbed Adane’s extension. “What’s the story on Mrs. Petrone?”

“I may have found an explanation for the job reference that Mrs. Petrone gave to Mr. Borch.”

“What is it?” He looked down at Cat who was adjusting her seatbelt.

“Robert Borch and Mrs. Petrone’s husband had been cellmates. After his release, ten years ago, Mrs. Petrone’s husband went to work at the Twenty-Four/Seven down the road from the clinic, some years after that, he was hired by Pro Patrol. As it happens, the three references on his job application are identical to Mr. Borch’s. Chavez, Petrone and Doctor Hoffman.”

“How long did he work for them?”

“Until his death. That was three years ago.” Adane hesitated. “I don’t mean to be personal, sir, but if Mrs. Austen is with you, you may want to be careful not to repeat this aloud. In case she isn’t aware of it.”

Victor stepped back while Cat started her engine, put the car in drive. “You can talk.”

“ ‘Petrone’ is Mrs. Petrone’s maiden name. She went to court to resume it after her husband’s death, I imagine so that her child wouldn’t carry the burden of her married name. Her married name was Mrs. Raymond Stites.”

“Should I know the name?”

Her pause set Victor’s neurons on yellow alert. Vacillating was not Adane’s style and usually preceded something unpleasant. “Raymond Stites is the man who killed Christopher Austen.”

He saw Cat’s arm extend from her open car window, waving.

CHAPTER TWENTY-TWO:
Present Day

Cat and Jackie Wing had placed their beach chairs at the shoreline so they could watch Jane and Mats, and Jackie's son Robbie as they waded in front of the lifeguard's post.

Jackie wore a scant green bikini. "You okay? You look tired."

"It's just the wedding. We're all a little strung out."

"Where are Freddy and Ellice?"

Cat nudged her sunglasses up the bridge of her nose. "Freddy's at work and Ellice is off doing I don't know what. She never made it to the barbecue last night. Ships in the night, forgive the cliché. They haven't seen each other in four days." She watched Mats hunker down then vault the last ripple of a wave as it rolled to shore. "How'd you get the day off?"

"I promised to work a double on the Fourth. Dwight gets Robbie then, anyway."

Cat nodded. Jackie's ex had mounted an expensive custody battle; won primary custody, reducing Jackie to alternate weekends, summers and shared holidays.

"Besides, Stan's on call. All weekend. What's up with that?" Jackie had been dating Stan Rice since Christmas.

"Whitney Rocap's accident. They suspect foul play."

"No kidding!" Jackie stretched her slender legs toward the water's edge, dug her toes into the wet sand. "Is that what you're working on?" She nodded to the notebook on Cat's lap.

"No. I'm trying to write up the interview I did with this cookbook author." She held up her notebook, read, "Mrs. Willie Mae Leitner, a blue ribbon scrapple specialist with five championships under her transverse colon cites the secret of her culinary triumphs. 'Snouts', she affirms. 'Snoutless scrapple is simply sacrilegious.'" Cat slapped her notepad on her lap. "Did I mention she had a lisp?" she declared.

"Is it true, about that slogan contest? A hundred grand?"

Cat nodded. "At twenty five words max, that comes out to four thousand dollars a word. What you get paid for writing is in an inverse proportion to it's merit."

"Well, I've got the perfect one, it's the same axiom I've used for choosing men: 'Make Mine Swine'." Jackie's mouth twisted in a self-deprecating smile. "Stan excepted. Maybe I'll have better luck with scrapple."

Cat adjusted her beach chair. "Jackie, did you really date Randall Hoffman?"

"Yeah, BD. Before Dwight. I worked with him a little when he moved into the area, he was just practicing ob/gyn back then. It didn't last long, my mistake."

"Mistake dating him?"

"No, mistake not landing him. *He's* not diddling around with scrapple slogans. He made a mint off that fertility monitor."

"Why did the two of you go your separate ways?"

Jackie shrugged. "I guess I wasn't partner material. He was dating a lot back then. I got the idea we were all sort of auditioning."

"You know anything about his first wife?"

"Someone mentioned her name once. Henrietta? Harriet? Same old story, she juggles two jobs, a couple kids and the home so he can get his MD, and as soon as the finish line is in view, he dumps her." She ran a finger under the string that secured the scant garment across her hip, studied the pinstripe of untanned flesh. "Why? Are you doing an article about disgruntled exes getting screwed over at the custody hearing? Then interview me."

Cat chafed away the chill that skimmed along her upper arms. That didn't sound like the compassionate Randall Hoffman she had known. "I didn't know he had kids."

"Well, I heard only about the family second-hand, he never mentioned them. He never had to juggle a visitation schedule when we were dating."

"Then she must have gotten custody. If she got screwed over, it would have to be financially."

"I don't know. He never griped about alimony and child support, so I guess he either forked it over and kept his mouth shut or hid the assets and let them fend for themselves."

Cat thought of all of the Rands and Randalls. And Randis, and Randees and Randas. Jane and Mats. *Charlotte or Nicholas.*

"He was a lot older than you are, wasn't he?"

Jackie shrugged. "Eighteen years. Chalk it up to the daddy complex. My dad walked out, too. Just like Hoffman did on his first wife, and just like Dwight. You'd think I would have learned by now. But Randy was a charmer. Still is, I guess."

Cat slipped the straps of her swimsuit off her shoulders. "He didn't walk out on Miriam Bender."

Jackie dropped onto one of the beach towels, rolled onto her stomach, untied the back of her halter top. The suit was a thong bikini. Jackie's narrow back and tiny waist, her taut bottom were exposed to the sun. "Miriam was smarter than he was, maybe he figured out he wouldn't come out on top. Or he needed another six figures to co-sign on the clinic's construction loan. That chick he's engaged to now, have you seen her?"

"Eve Bellamy? She's on his staff."

"I'll bet she is," Jackie said, emphatically, and the two of them were seized by a fit of giggles.

"Do you know Paul Aquino?" Cat asked.

"A little. I remember that Paul was one person who didn't seem at all surprised by Miriam Bender committing suicide. He said something had been eating at her."

Cat had little memory of the incident. She had been so numb from Chris's death, the miscarriage, that Miriam's death had barely registered. "Annie said the same thing."

"Of course, Randy was in total denial. And there was a sister, too, who said Miriam would never kill herself."

"What did her sister think happened?"

"Well, I didn't get the idea she was accusing Randy or anything, but what I heard? Her sister thought Miriam Bender had been murdered."

CHAPTER TWENTY-THREE: Present Day

People lie in two ways. They don't tell the truth, or they tell you only as much of the truth as they want you to know. Either way, it's what they don't say that's important. Me entiendes? Victor's father had said that.

Te comprendo, Victor thought.

Kathy Petrone was Mrs. Raymond Stites. How could Cat not know? Victor realized that he didn't know the surnames of his doctor's staff. They wore engraved pins, 'Ina', 'Joanne', 'Dee'.

But Hoffman had to know, and that altered Victor's agenda. Instead of heading to the Chavez home in West Atlantic City, he drove back to Randall Hoffman's, determined to find out why Hoffman had omitted mentioning that his office manager's husband had killed the husband of one of his patients.

The midday sun bore down on the surface of the blue roof tiles, the bay, the water splashing in the fountain. Nearly ten grand for a hunk of granite better suited to a cemetery.

Victor offered a polite, "*Buenos días*" to the maid, asked, "*El doctor Hoffman está aquí?*"

"*Sí, señor. Pase por aquí.*"

Victor walked into the living room. Through the glass wall overlooking the waterway, he saw a gathering of about twenty people. The men wore khaki shorts, T-shirts and deck shoes, the women were fussier with sundresses, or snug pedal pushers with matchin espadrilles, tailored cotton blouses. Too much jewelry and too much makeup, or perhaps it was the unpretentious beauty of Eve Bellamy, barefoot, her honey-colored hair hanging loose, that made them look glazed and overdone by contrast.

Victor watched as the maid gave Hoffman a timid tap on the arm, nodded toward the house. Hoffman made a visor of his hand, looked through the glass window. He laid his drink on a table spread with hors d'ouevres and a bowl of crushed ice rimmed with cold cooked shrimp, walked into the house.

"Lieutenant." Hoffman offered his hand. He wore a crisp blue shirt, rolled to the elbow, white shorts. "Can I offer you something? Non-alcoholic of course."

"No, thank you."

"Did you want to see Eve, too?"

Victor opted for a direct hit. "I wanted to ask why you failed to mention that Kathy Petrone was Mrs. Raymond Stites."

"Ah." Hoffman walked around the wet bar, took a bottle of club soda from the minifridge, unscrewed the cap, drank.

Stalling, Victor thought. "Or that you provided job references not only for Stites, but for Robert Borch."

Victor heard the door open. Eve Bellamy entered. Her throat and long legs glowed gold against the short white shift.

"Lieutenant." She padded across the white carpet, perched on a stool beside Hoffman. "Still investigating that accident?"

"Who is Robert Borch?" Hoffman inquired.

"Bobby?" Eve asked. "What happened to him?"

"Why do you think something happened?" Victor asked.

"The service called, oh, after midnight Friday. Apparently, Bobby never reported. I told them to contact Pro Patrol and have them send a replacement." She turned to Hoffman. "He's been working the overnight shift."

"Why would you think I gave him a reference?" Hoffman asked.

Victor wanted him kept off guard, sidestepped. "Perhaps because you have a history of providing references to ex-cons," Victor replied. "Which brings us back to Raymond Stites."

"Oh, dear," Eve sighed. "Lieutenant, I should have told you the whole truth, I know- "

Hoffman held up a hand, silencing her. "Look. I was less than forthcoming, but she was Kathy Petrone when we hired her, and she took her name back, what? Almost two years ago? I imagine she didn't want her child to carry the husband's name after what happened."

"Her husband killed a police officer, the husband of one of your patients, and you didn't think that was worth mentioning?"

"What difference it would have made?"

"You know that Stites and Robert Borch were acquainted?"

"How would I know that?"

"Kathy mentioned it to me." Eve crossed one long leg over the other, tugged at the hem of her skirt. "When she told me some friend of her husband's was looking for a couple references on a job application. That's why I always wondered..."

Victor recalled his prior conversation with Eve Bellamy. "Wondered whether Robert Borch is her child's father?"

"It's just that I can't think of any other man Kathy was even casually acquainted with."

"I recall Borch now," Hoffman said. "Big guy, somewhat coarse character was my impression."

"Any sign of a relationship between him and Mrs. Petrone?"

"Kathy's the quiet type. My first instinct would be 'you're joking'. But then, she did marry Raymond Stites. Funny, you think you know people." Hoffman shrugged. "Opposites attract, I guess. And if you say he was a friend of Stites's..."

"Mrs. Petrone ran your office for nearly ten years, isn't that correct, Doctor?"

"That's right."

"Could she have forged your name on Borch's job application?"

"No."

"You're certain?"

Hoffman took a gulp of club soda, seemed to reconsider a too-hasty reply. "I don't know. She certainly was familiar with my signature, the payroll, the paperwork went through her."

"Could Daria Chavez have done it?"

"Who?"

Eve tossed her long hair over her shoulder. "Daria? We haven't seen her for years."

A flash of impatience marred Hoffman's brow. He tried to sound jovial. "Darling, don't you think the usual suspects ought to synchronize their stories? I don't know this Daria Chavez."

Eve turned and gave him the look that wise women reserve for the clueless male. "The home office worker? Remember? She used to do our typing?"

Hoffman palmed his thinning hair. "The one who took off, left us hanging a few years back? I didn't remember her name."

Eve addressed Victor. "She worked at home, so she only came in to pick up and drop off the dictation and to pick up her pay. Of course, she'd see Randy's signature on her paychecks."

"You haven't heard from her recently?"

"From Daria? No."

"She didn't call the clinic, perhaps, leave a message?"

"Not that I'm aware."

"Why are you asking us about her?" Hoffman inquired.

"We have reason to believe Miss Chavez was with Whitney Rocap the evening of Miss Rocap's crash."

"Then perhaps you should be interrogating her." Hoffman's tone was edgy. "Your original question was about Mrs. Petrone. I didn't go into her past because you came here inquiring into that newswoman's car accident. I saw no connection to Raymond. Or to some former typist, or to one of Pro Patrol's security people, for that matter."

"Mrs. Petrone's husband and Robert Borch weren't merely acquaintances. They had been cellmates."

"Cellmates!" Eve cried.

Hoffman glanced anxiously toward the guests as if concerned that they might have overheard Eve's exclamation.

"And two days ago, he attacked a woman. Quite coincidentally the wife of Raymond Stites's victim."

"Wh – what? Mrs. Austen?" Hoffman sputtered.

"Is she all right?" Eve asked.

"Yes. She surprised Borch in the act of ransacking Miss Rocap's house. Shortly afterward, Borch went to Miss Rocap's place of employment, managed to get hold of her personal property. So you see why I would be curious about your name appearing on his job application, Doctor."

"I never gave him a reference," Hoffman maintained. "I did give Raymond a referral, as a favor to Kathy. He was trying to go straight, he and Kathy were getting married, it seemed the decent thing to do. Do I regret it? Of course. I had no idea he was capable of doing what he did. Is there something else, Lieutenant?"

"You keep in touch with Kathy Petrone, Doctor?"

"No, I haven't heard from her since she left." He turned to Eve. "Darling, go tell our guests that dinner's in ten minutes."

Eve slipped off the bar stool, tugged at the hem of her dress. The gesture did nothing to lengthen the garment, only served to draw attention to the long legs. Victor scrupulously kept his eyes on her face. Too beautiful for her own good, that's what his father would have said.

He waited until he heard the door close. "What's your theory, Doctor? About why Stites did what he did?"

Hoffman shrugged. "Raymond had money troubles. Gambling, I believe. A job that didn't pay all that well, he and Kathy lost a baby. Kathy mentioned to me that he was suffering from headaches, insomnia. I was shocked when I heard about what he did. Shocked, but not surprised. So was Miriam."

"Miriam Bender. Your wife."

Hoffman nodded, with the first sign of genuine feeling. "She died the following week." He shook his head. "You never know what lays down that final straw, until one day a guy picks up a gun, kills a half dozen people and then kills himself."

Victor felt the words insinuate themselves around Cat's desperate question, whether there might have been some 'why' to Chris Austen's murder. "But he didn't though, did he?" he heard himself asking.

"Didn't what?"

"Kill a half dozen others. He only killed one."

CHAPTER TWENTY-FOUR: Present Day

Cat and Jackie let the kids play on the beach until after five, then herded them to the boardwalk's open air promenade for pizzas and sodas, gave in to the pleas for one round of miniature golf and finally shepherded them back to Cat's house.

It was after nine before Cat got Jane and Mats to bed. She rinsed bathing suits and draped them over the railing outside the back door, clapped sand from their rubber thongs and set them on the back steps, upended the children's overnight bags into the laundry room hamper, then indulged in a leisurely shower, pulled on cotton drawstring pants and a sleeveless T shirt, poured a glass of iced tea and went to check her phone messages. The first and last were Ritchie's familiar "Cat! Cat! Cat! Cat!" with a "Freddy, are you there?" from Ellice and an "Ellice around?" from Freddy sandwiched between.

Cat took her iced tea up to her room, crawled onto the bed, picked up her phone and dialed Ritchie's number.

"Where the hell you been all day?" he demanded.

"It's Sunday. The day of rest," she reminded him.

"Rest when you're dead. You wanna know what's been gettin' to me?"

"I want to know what would get you to sign my pay check."

"I *said* I'm gonna cut you your check, right after Memorial Day." Ritchie whined. "Meanwhile, think on this, Austen. In less than a year, Rocap goes from copygal to weathergal to anchorgal 'cause she knew how to buff other people's stuff and smile for the camera. But hard news? Name me one piece she did that wasn't fluff. You can't, right? Not until she did that infertility support group segment last week. And, where does she smash up? Down the road from a fertility *clinic*! See the connection?"

Cat sighed. "The clinic's legit, Ritchie, if that's what you're getting at. Of course, the same can't be said for everyone who works on the premises. Their security guards come from some outfit called Pro Patrol. Some of them have records. And one of them went AWOL."

"See! What did I tell you?"

"What did you tell me?"

"That all you gotta do is soften up Loverboy."

"It wasn't a matter of softening up, Ritchie. This guard was the one who *roughed* me up over at Whitney's."

"You got a name?"

"Everybody has a name."

"Don't be funny."

"Robert Borch. Maybe thirty or so, dark hair, six feet, two hundred, two twenty and most of that muscle."

"Hey, maybe this Pro Patrol's running some kinda stud service in the off hours outta the clinic."

"I hardly think there's a premium on the DNA of muscle-bound dimwits who've done time."

"Y'never know. I'm gonna check out Pro Patrol. Get me the scrapple copy by Tuesday, so's I run it before it goes stale."

"I think 'go bad', would be more accurate, although with scrapple, I'm not sure how you would know."

"Hey, how 'bout this. 'Scrapple: It's the squeal deal.' For the slogan contest. Whaddayou think?"

"Don't count your chitlins before they hatch." Cat hung up.

The phone rang almost immediately. "Hello?"

"Is this Mrs. Austen?"

"Yes."

"This is Leon Geller, you get my message?"

Geller? "Oh, yes, my brother told me you called back."

"Holiday's keepin' me busy. Is there a problem with your husband's site? I checked it out, I didn't see no damage."

"No, it was something else. I was wondering if you've noticed anyone visiting the site. When I was there on Friday, it appeared that someone had left flowers, I'd like to be able to thank them, but I don't know who it was."

"I don't know either. She leaves 'em all the time."

"She?"

"Yeah. Comes by just about every week. Plus your Memorial Day, Christmas, Easter, rain or shine. Most folks, they keep that up a year or so, then they start to slack off."

Cat felt a flush of guilt. Before Friday, the last time she had visited Chris's grave had been after Kevin Keller's funeral.

"I b'lieve she's got someone else buried here, out by the potter zone. Unclaimed or the ones don't get embalmed, or gotta get planted on the cheap. She goes back there first, then stops by the Austen marker and leaves a couple flowers. Stops a few minutes, like she's prayin' or something."

"And she's been doing this all year?"

"All year? More like three years. Three years this past spring, I b'lieve."

Cat felt her breath catch in her chest. "Oh. Oh, I see. Well perhaps I'll run into her next time I'm there." She thanked Geller and hung up.

Three years? Not one of her sisters-in-law, not Chris's sister, Charlotte. Daria Chavez?

I b'lieve she's got someone else buried here.

Someone she buried three years ago.

Cat got up and walked to the closet, moving with the unconscious deliberation of a sleepwalker. She tugged the boxed mementos into the light and began probing until her fingers detected the square of folded newsprint. She drew it into the light, a three-year-old obituary page from the local paper.

Alphabetically arranged, 'Austen, Christopher Michael' had been the first entry, a somewhat grainy picture of Chris above the copy. She scanned the column.

Austen, Christopher Michael, 36, Ocean City, of a gunshot wound. A native of Somers Point, Christopher had been a resident of Ocean City for the past fourteen years. Christopher was a decorated member of the New Jersey State Police. Survivors include his wife, Allegrezza (Fortunati) Austen, one daughter, Jane Cassandra, age seven, one son, Matthew Christopher, age two, all of Ocean City, one sister, Charlotte Maria Austen, of New York City. Visitation will be held on Tuesday evening from 6:30 to 8:30 PM at Morosco's Funeral Home and one hour prior to the services Wednesday morning. High Requiem Mass will be at St. Agnes Roman Catholic Church, Atlantic City.

Cat's index finger skated the surface of the paper, down to the 'C's. *I b'lieve she's got someone else buried here.* No 'Chavez'. Her finger moved on.

Stites, Raymond John.

Cat held the paper to the light. She could hear her heartbeat pulsing in her ears.

Stites, Raymond John, age 36, Somers Point, of a self-inflicted gunshot wound. Raymond had been employed by Twenty-Four Seven Convenience Mart, and most recently by Pro Patrol Manned Security-

Cat felt her chest constrict. Pro Patrol?

Raymond is predeceased by his son, Raymond Stites, Junior and is survived by his wife, Kathleen (Petrone) Stites of Somers Point. Visitation and services will be held at Morosco's Funeral Home, Wednesday Morning at 8 AM.

The paper slipped from Cat's fingers.

Lieutenant, there's something I need to discuss with you concerning Kathy Petrone...

And if he does, and whatever you find out, no matter how bad it is? Promise you won't keep it from me?

I won't keep things from you.

Except that Kathy Petrone was Mrs. Raymond Stites.

CHAPTER TWENTY-FIVE:
Three Years Ago

Kathleen held her smile in place while Raymond walked her to the car. She backed out of the driveway, raised her hand to wave, the gesture drawing sunlight to the thin gold band, the chip of a diamond. She had offered to pawn them once when Raymond had a bad run. It had been the only time he had ever raised his voice to her, the only time she had ever done anything to make him angry.

He stood on the concrete walk, cupped his hands, cried out, "Kathleen! Kathy! I love you!"

She realized later that she should have known something was wrong then. Raymond was never demonstrative, not in public. The car's irritable engine muffled her, "I love you!" She glanced at Raymond in the rear view mirror, saw that he hadn't heard her. It didn't matter. She would tell him first thing when he got home from work.

Chris donned his hat in front of the foyer mirror. Jane came running from the den. "Daddy, don't forget we're doing the Easter eggs!" Chris swept her up into his arms, kissed her throat, making her giggle. "You're my favorite girl, how could I forget?"

"What about Mom?"

"She's my other favorite girl."

Cat followed Chris as far as the porch, said, "Promise you won't be late", and Chris had replied, "I promise" as he sprinted down the porch steps. The morning had begun overcast, but the sun was taking over, burning off the early mist. A few of its rays spilled light over Chris as he turned on the sidewalk and flashed a smile, called out, "I love you three! I'll see you to-night!"

'Four', Cat thought. There are four of us.

And that was the last time she saw him.

CHAPTER TWENTY-SIX: Present Day

Cat threaded through the maze of four-wheeled surreys, bikes, skateboards, pedestrians clogging the boardwalk, half-listening to Sonny at Sunrise emanating from the headset planted over her brimmed cap. Ordinarily, Sonny would have taken the Monday holiday, but news of Whitney Rocap's suspicious crash had not circulated until after Sonny had signed off on Friday. The prospect of a three-day interval before Sonny had the opportunity to broadcast his analysis was unendurable. Monday morning, he hustled into the station and canned the compilation "Best Of Sonny" tape. "I spent two weeks observing the training procedures at the police academy and I've interviewed various of the highly-placed officials in the department and I can personally attest that there is something we are not being disclosed about this so-called hit and run. I define the DA's office to tell us why homicide investigators with the Major Crimes Bureau were sent to the scene of what everyone is intimidating is an accident. And why was it essential to close such a large apportionment of Mays Landing-Somers Point Road to traffic on a holiday weekend? My sources tell me that a crowd gathered at the parameters of the site and got so enlarged that there was talk of calling out the TAC team to assist the paramedics and crime scene analysts in successfully evacuating at the scene. Our lines are open."

Ordinarily, that would have gotten a laugh from Cat. Now, it caused barely a ripple in the frown of concentration.

What about a 'Kathy', the office manager?

Lieutenant, there's something I need to discuss with you concerning Kathy Petrone...

Kathleen (Petrone) Stites of Somers Point.

A slap between her shoulder blades snapped her to consciousness. Cat saw Joel Kaminsky jogging on her left. "C'mon, let's have a go at it." He was short, compact, a sprinter, but Cat had a longer stride. They raced to the point where the boardwalk narrowed and doglegged north, then pulled up, panting.

Joel went right in to his hustle. "You know, it's not too late to get you in a nice rancher just over the bridge, rent out your place for the season, twenty-four grand, I can get it leased by June first."

"My brother's getting married June first."

"What about the downstairs apartment?"

"I'm renting it to him and Ellice. Try the Nixon ladies across the street, they've got an unoccupied ground floor unit."

"I heard about the sweet arrangement Ellice and John got going. I'd be jealous of Home Stead, but I don't do commercial."

Cat could only nod, mutely. *What's Home Stead? Who's John?*

"You change your mind, let me know." Joel waved, headed back down the boardwalk while Cat trotted the last few blocks to her home. She rounded the house and let herself in the back door, pried off her running shoes in the pantry.

"Ellice?"

"In here!"

Ellice was sitting at the kitchen table, writing something on a notepad, lists of figures that put a troubled frown on her normally serene face. She tucked the papers in her purse. "How're the boards?"

"Crowded. Only Memorial Day and already I wish everybody'd just go home. Anybody call?"

"No."

Cat bit her lip. It wouldn't have made any difference if Victor had called, it was too late to redeem his promise of absolute candor. "Is Freddy going to be around after work?"

"I don't know. I'm going to stop by the bookstore downtown," Ellice said. "I'll bring Jane and Mats if you want."

"I thought maybe I'd take them visit Chris's grave. If you can hold off until I get back you can have the car. The kids might like to go downtown instead of to the beach."

Cat trekked upstairs, hearing the echo of her Aunt Cat's wisdom. *Sometimes, a secret, it drives you crazy. Then when you find it out, what happens? You're crazy and miserable. That's why they don't say 'curiosity, it makes the cat happy'.*

"Curiosity kills," Cat whispered.

But at least when curiosity killed, it killed quick. It wasn't the slow, burdensome death of not knowing, that dragged the future down with it.

Cat took a shower, changed into a straight black sundress and was pinning her wet hair into a chignon when the phone rang. Cat, anticipating Victor, kept her "Hello" somewhat frosty, but it was Cherry Wein, Ritchie's secretary. "Cat, look, I'm doing the payroll, your check's ready."

"Ritchie hasn't got you working on Memorial Day!"

"I come in a lot when I know he's taking off, it's the only time I can get anything done. Besides, it's easier for me to cut the checks when I don't have to hear him howling about money in the background."

"Doesn't he howl when he signs them?"

"I just slipped it in with some papers he had to sign when he ran in yesterday, I'll write in the amount and he'll never know it's gone until it's too late. I'll be here until about one if you want to run in. If not, I'll keep it under lock and key."

"I don't know if I want to deal with Atlantic City traffic today. I'll come in tomorrow. Wednesday at the latest."

"No prob."

"Cherry, do you have a minute?"

"Sure, what's up?"

“Ritchie told me you met Whitney Rocap for drinks, she started asking you about my husband’s murder investigation.”

“I was gonna mention it, Cat, I just didn’t know if it was okay to bring up, you know?”

“I didn’t know the two of you were friendly.”

There was a long silence.

“Cherry?”

“Look, we’re not. We ran into each other last week.”

“At that infertility support group.”

Another silence.

“It’s none of my business, Cherry,” Cat said at last.

“It’s a touchy subject. I mean, believe it or not, I do date, and a couple times, it almost got serious.”

“And she wanted to meet with you to talk about Chris?”

“Yes. She asked why he was at the ER that day, who were the investigating officers, who was the shooter. Did I think it was weird that Miriam Bender killed herself a few days later.”

“Why would she be asking you about Miriam Bender?”

“She was the founder of the support group, and we’d gotten a little friendly. We had something in common, you see. I mean there were women in the group that had treatable conditions, a few went on to actually get pregnant, but Miriam and I both had hysterectomies, the result of trauma. Car accidents. She didn’t wind up in a wheelchair, though.”

“Who’s been running the sessions since she died?”

“Different local doctors and nurses volunteer. Some people from State of the ART.”

“Any of them named Santucci?”

“No.”

“Does Randall Hoffman ever volunteer?”

“No.”

Cat’s brow furrowed. “You know, Cherry, I was talking to someone about Miriam Bender just the other day. They said she had a sister who insisted her death wasn’t suicide.”

“Well, it was strange. Miriam thought it was wrong to take a life. Totally against suicide, euthanasia, even abortion. But maybe all of us have something that can push us to the brink.”

“But we don’t all jump,” Cat concluded.

“No.”

“Maybe there were problems with the marriage? Or work, they were getting sued? I know liability premiums for ob/gyn have gotten exorbitant, a lot of them are dropping out all together.’

“That’s funny. Whitney brought that up. I wondered if she was doing something on malpractice suits, except I couldn’t figure out what your husband’s death would have to do with that.”

"No," Cat murmured. "I mean, he was- " she swallowed. "He died in a hospital, but there was never an issue of suing anyone."

"I thought when I had a few minutes, I might dig around, see if anything's been filed, civil or criminal."

"Oh, I doubt that there would be anything criminal."

"You'd be surprised. That detective from Major Crimes, you said he likes Sherlock Holmes?"

"Yes."

"Ask him what Holmes said about doctors."

ꙮ

You know your father, he was never much of a talker.

As Cat coasted into the cemetery, an explosion launched a spray of nesting birds into flight. She recognized the sound, the salute signaling a fallen officer. She had steeled herself at Chris's funeral, but blasts made her flinch and she saw, in the rear view mirror, Mats clapping his hands over his ears.

"It's just firecrackers," Cat reassured him.

She walked them over to Chris's headstone, laid her flowers at the base. Mats studied the marker, curiously, ran his finger along the letters engraved in the stone. "What does it say?"

"It's your father's name. Christopher Michael Austen. And the numbers are the year he was born and the year he died." Cat kissed her fingertips and pressed them to the stone.

"Do you wish he didn't died?"

Cat wondered how the past few months - Jerry Dudek's murder, the Phoenix conspiracy, the St. Agnes killings, the movie shoot that led her to Tommi Ann Butler's dark secret - would have played out if Chris were still alive. "Yes, I wish he hadn't died. Put your flowers next to mine."

"Do we have to *pray*?" Jane inquired.

"Not if you don't want to. Let's walk a little."

"It's hot," Jane said.

"If we walk down the path, we'll be in the shade."

"Ashley Kriesberg said when her grandfather died, they put him in a jar. A mayon*naise* jar," Jane informed them.

"How does he fit?" Mats inquired.

"And Andy Chu said his uncle planted their dog in the back yard and put a cross over it just like he was a *person*."

Cat thought of ten-year-old Kevin Keller solemnly officiating at the rites for this pet or that. *In the name of the Father, and of the Son, and into the hole he goes.*

"Don't you wish people didn't die?" Mats asked.

"They *have* to," Jane informed him. "Otherwise they just keep getting older until they're *ancient*."

"What's ancient?"

"Like Nonna."

"Please don't tell Nonna that she's ancient," Cat advised. "It might hurt her feelings."

"Why's that lady cryin'?"

Cat looked up and saw a slender figure rise, brush the grass from her skirts. Fresh roses had been laid before the modest markers embedded in the ground, and she held a few long-stemmed roses in one hand.

Cat shepherded Jane and Mats to a little wrought iron bench under a maple, watched as the woman made her way to Chris's grave. The sight of the newly-laid flowers startled her and she looked up. Still, she might not have spotted them if Jane had not demanded, in a tone loud enough to bridge the distance, "Why is that lady putting flowers on *our* Dad's grave?"

Their eyes met.

Cat recognized the dark hair neatly pinned away from the pale oval face, the inexpensive clothing, the thin frame. The woman turned and hurried off. Cat rose to call out her name, but felt her throat thicken and the exclamation, "Kathy! Kathy Petrone!" echoed only in her head.

CHAPTER TWENTY-SEVEN: Present Day

One of the yellow brick roads that lured the hopeful to the "World's Famous Playground" cut through an area known as West Atlantic City. Four lanes bordered by car dealerships, low-end motels, modest businesses, unkempt open space and older homes. Victor glimpsed the house number's four digits painted onto a metal mailbox staked against the shoulder of the road. He slowed, backed onto the unpaved shoulder and got out, slipped on his sunshades and discreetly adjusted the 9 mm at his waistband.

The small property was surrounded by chain link fence, a sign, 'Beware of Dog', hung from the metal gate. The lawn inside was even green sod bordered with small American flags for the holiday. A light colored sedan was in the open garage.

A woman knelt at a small patch of tomato plants staked on a quadrangle of soil below the porch railing. A man lounged in a worn metal rocker on the porch, smoking his pipe and watching the brisk pace of the casino-bound traffic. The screen door offered a glimpse of a narrow corridor leading straight to the screen door in the back.

At Victor's approach, the woman turned, wiped powdery earth on the hem of her cotton shift. She had a leathery complexion with high cheekbones and obsidian eyes. "*Qué quieres*?"

Victor stopped at the gate. "*Una mujer, se llama Daria Chavez*."

The creaking rocker fell silent.

"*La Migra*?"

"*No, señora*." Victor presented his shield.

The man pushed himself up from the rocker, tugged his belt high over his sleeveless T shirt and walked over to the gate. Victor looked into the face that had been seared brown by the sun, with creases scored deeply into flesh as taut and thick as hide. The man studied Victor's identification."The dog, he died las' month," he told Victor and turned to his wife. "*Traiganos limonada, por favor*."

She nodded silently and went into the Victor heard the clink of ice in glasses, the refrigerator door opening, closing.

The man ushered Victor to the porch, gestured to a plastic deck chair. "Daria, she's my daughter. She's in trouble, *sí*?"

"Why do you think that?"

"She run off again. People looking for her."

Again? "When did she run off?"

"Wednesday night. After dinner, someone comes by, we hear the car horn honking and she runs out, doesn' come back."

"Did you notify the police?"

Victor saw distrust infiltrate the man's dark gaze. "What could they do? They would jus' ask, did she do this before."

"And she had?"

The flimsy screen door flapped against the jamb, and the woman appeared, holding two glasses of lemonade.

Victor rose, took the glass with a quiet, "*Gracias, señora*." He leaned against the porch railing cautiously and the woman took the hint, sat in the chair he had occupied.

"Three years ago. Aroun' Easter time, *verdad*?" The looked to his wife for confirmation."*A pasqua, sí? Cuándo fui Daria* ?"

"*Sí*."

"*Qué pasó*?" Victor asked.

"It's the night before Easter, my wife an' I are at Mass. We come in an' we hear screamin'. I yell 'I got a gun' an' I hear someone run out the back door, I get just a little look at him. Big man. Daria, she's cryin', her dress, it's torn. There are marks." He stroked his bare throat. "Then, I did want to call the police, but Daria, she says no. She begs me jus' drive her to the airport. So that's what we do."

"Where did she go?"

"We got her on a plane to Florida. The next day her mother, she lives in San Juan? She calls to say Daria is there. Scared and cryin', don' wanna come out of her room."

"Scared of what?"

The man shrugged.

"Had she been in trouble with the law?" Victor asked.

The man shook his head.

"Trouble at work?"

"I don' know. I don' think so."

"She worked as a typist, didn't she?"

The man nodded. "She has an office inside her bedroom. She does typing for doctors and lawyers, at night, she works in a bar in Atlantic City. Worked all the time. She liked money," he added. "Everything was money."

"Who were her friends?"

"She don' bring friends here."

"What about men?"

"No men. No one."

"How long did she remain in San Juan?"

"Until she came back las' month. Just about a month ago."

Victor frowned. This account concurred with Eve Bellamy's recollection that Daria had left the area three years ago. But Detective Long had said Daria's name had turned up on the job application Borch had submitted to Pro Patrol *two* years ago. "She wasn't in the area two years ago?"

The man shook his head.

"She ever mention a man named Robert Borch? Bobby?"

"No."

"You said she seemed upset and afraid when she left for San Juan. Was she still afraid when she came back last month?"

His expression took on the worried, slightly bewildered expression that Victor's sister Remy often put on their mother's face. "Not afraid. She is more sad."

"Did she go back to work?"

The man shook his head. "She sits in her room. She don' talk to no one, except a phone call now an' then."

"You know who she talked to?"

The man shook his head.

"May I see her room?"

The man handed his glass to his wife, rose and opened the screen door. Victor followed him into the house. The door opened directly into the kitchen, a small utility room to the left. Victor laid his glass of lemonade on the counter as they crossed the room and diverted down a short corridor to a closed door.

Daria Chavez's room was large, painted in a soft eggshell white with a matching carpet. The furniture was pale bleached oak with a sheen that glowed like the satin of the bedspread. The only touches of color were the cinnamon red throw pillows on the bed. There was an oblong desk with file drawers, a computer workstation with a fax, a color printer/scanner a phone with two phone lines, all several years old; obsolete in an age of high-speed innovation. There was a small shelf with a row of volumes, medical and legal dictionaries, paperback volumes on editing, grammar, technical writing. A Roll-o-dex.

Victor flipped through it, saw the names, addresses, phone numbers of law firms, medical offices, State of the ART. "You call any of these to see if they had heard from Daria?"

The man shook his head. "Those files, they are old. He took everything else."

"Who did?"

"*La Migra*."

"When was *La Migra* here?"

"Friday night."

"How many of them?"

"One man. Big. Mean eyes. Maybe thirty. He took her papers. He took her computer things."

Damn! "Do you have a picture of Daria?" Victor asked.

"In the hall."

Victor followed the man out of the room. There were pictures hung along the wall of the short corridor. Victor studied one of them, a young girl in a cap and gown holding up her diploma with pride. There was something in the mascaraed eyes, some hardness and determination that robbed the face of its sweetness and optimism. Around her neck she wore a heavy gold chain with a pendant in the shape of a 'D'.

"Do you have a more recent picture of her?"

"*Sí.*"

The man went into the living room, retrieved a framed photograph of a woman in her late twenties, the same look of determination in her dark eyes, a bit more cynical perhaps. The off-white blouse radiated a soft silken sheen, it was expertly tailored. The hair was pulled away from her face, revealing flat gold disks in her earlobes. The makeup was more tasteful, the jewelry less ostentatious, except for the chain and pendant.

"She liked this necklace," Victor remarked.

"She bought it for herself after graduation. It was real espensive. Eighteen karat gold. She liked money even back then. That was taken about three years ago. She's thirty now."

"You said your daughter received telephone calls. Who here knew she was back from San Juan?"

"I don't know. Nobody."

"Did she say anything to you that would suggest why she ran off. Or what made her decide to come back?"

Chavez pondered the question. "Only once. She says to me, is it ever too late to make a bad thing right. You know, like she used to ask when she was a little girl, after the divorce, was it too late for her mother and me to get back together. What could I say?" He shrugged. "That sometimes, *sí*, there is no forgiveness. Sometimes, it is too late."

Victor walked outside. The woman resumed weeding her patch of tomatoes. "*Son primosos, señora*," he said, politely.

"*Sí, gracias*."

Victor turned back to the man. "Did Daria ever mention a woman named Whitney Rocap?"

"The news lady who got killed?" The man shook his head.

"Doctor Hoffman? Doctor Randall Hoffman?"

"No."

Victor slipped on his sunshades. "Kathy Petrone?"

Again, a shake of the head.

Victor hesitated. *Why not?* "What about a woman named Austen. Cat Austen?"

The black brows lifted, etching creases into the leathery forehead. "Mrs. Christopher Austen? She lives in Ocean City?"

"Yes."

"Daria, when she wen' out Wednesday night, she has this envelope. It wouldn't fit in her purse. Fat, like there were papers in it. A lot of stamps on it. The address is printed in black. It is made out to that lady, Mrs. Christopher Austen."

CHAPTER TWENTY-EIGHT: Present Day

Victor sensed, in his detectives' "Morning, Lieutenant", the uneasy sympathy one gives to the poor sap who's the last to know. Three years ago, Cardenas had been working undercover, had only been assigned to Major Crimes two years before. And now he was dating the widow of the guy Raymond Stites had gunned down.

They were not surprised that he could say, "I'm sure Adane has filled you in on the fact that Mrs. Petrone had been married to Raymond Stites," in a voice devoid of inflection, passion. There was something cold about Cardenas, something completely self-contained which made the notion that he was carrying on a romantic life inconceivable.

He pushed his chair away from his desk, crossed one leg over the other. "Robert Borch, first. He hung around to clean out the Rocap and Chavez files. He here or gone?"

Phil shrugged. "He's here, he needs cash and a place to crash. We canvassed all the pawnshops including the Gabors, so far, Rocap's jewelry didn't make the books. Which doesn't mean someone didn't take it in under the table. But," Long added, "Jeannie turned up something interesting."

"'Gabor' is short for Gaborchevsky," Adane told Victor. "They never changed it legally, just shortened it for the sign over the door. But Robert Borch's family did go to court to have their name abbreviated, from Gaborchevsky to Borch."

"They're family?" Victor asked.

Adane nodded.

"The Gabors own real estate, correct? Get the locations of any vacant properties among their holdings, they may be harboring him. Also, the clinic's daytime guard told Mrs. Austen that it appeared Borch had been meeting women at his work site."

"'Meeting' as in-"

"I don't think the euphemism requires clarification, Sergeant."

"Them's close quarters," Stan chuckled.

"So you'll also want to make a note of any renters who are single women. Did you locate the woman Borch's neighbor spotted leaving his house?"

Stan shook his head.

"Mrs. Petrone – Mrs. Stites lives in Somers Point," Adane spoke with the quiet resignation of one ready to accept the consequences for raising an unpleasant subject.

"Who's been following on her?"

Stan raised his hand. "I showed her neighbor Borch's photo. She says she's never seen him. Told me Petrone's been up in Philly all weekend, hadda take the kid to the hospital. Neighbor says she'll be back today, early tomorrow. According to her, Kathy Petrone's a sweet kid, devoted to her boy."

"Did she say anything else about the boy?"

"Like what?"

"Doctor Hoffman's fiancée mentioned that the child was two years of age. Stites died three years ago. Were you as diligent in freshman math as you were in freshman biology, Sergeant?"

"Oh. You want, I'll go stake out her place until she shows up, bring her in." Stan made the offer reluctantly.

Victor understood. Stan had a soft core that homicide hadn't calloused. "Just call and ask her to come in for an interview. Tomorrow will be soon enough. What about her husband, did the neighbor know him?"

Stan nodded. "Nice guy, quiet, never heard him raise his voice, never saw him touch a drop. The last day she saw him, she said she shoulda known something wasn't right because his wife's going to work, right? And Stites's there on the sidewalk yelling, 'Kathy, I love you, I love you!' so you could hear him all the way down the block."

"Okay," Victor said, evenly. "Let's talk about Stites."

Stan shifted, uncomfortably. "Model prisoner, got out ten years ago, took a job at the Twenty-Four/Seven down the road from the State of the ART. Married Kathleen Petrone, got hired by Pro Patrol. He had a thing for gambling. They lost a kid about a year before he died. The day he died, the wife worked seven to one, he worked eight to four."

Victor ran his finger along the razor crease in his trousers. "Stites was clean for ten years?"

"Except for the gambling. Not even a parking ticket."

"He and Borch got references from Daria Chavez. Pro Patrol has no proscription against hiring ex-cons. It's a long shot, guy who attacked Daria Chavez in her home three years ago fits their profile."

"Couldn't've been Borch, he was behind bars," Long said.

"Find out who it could have been. And," Victor added, "I'd like copies of the witness statements taken at the time of Christopher Austen's death."

"What for?" Stan blurted.

"I'm going to ask the DA to re-open the investigation." He rose, signaling the end of the conference. "Unless there is a question?"

They remained motionless. Finally, Phil rose, gave Adane a nudge. They headed for the door.

Stan hung behind.

"Sergeant?"

"Look, Lieutenant, I'm not what you'd call a scholar, but even I know about Pandora's Box. Open that box, you may not like what flies out."

"Thank you, Sergeant."

Victor waited until Stan closed the door before he picked up the phone and dialed Cat's number. Got her machine. "Call me as soon as you get this, it's important," he said.

ཀྵ

Cat was twisting the doorknob, when the phone started to ring, heard Victor's "Call me as soon as you get this, it's important" just as she yanked it open.

"Mrs. Austen," said the woman on her doorstep.

"Mrs. Petrone," Cat replied. *Stites*.

CHAPTER TWENTY-NINE: Present Day

Kathy Petrone hadn't changed much in three years, except for the faint lines etched along the corners of her mouth, the dark crescents under her eyes. "We can talk here on the porch if you don't want me in your house," she said.

Mrs. Raymond Stites, Mrs. Raymond Stites, Mrs. Raymond Stites. "It's cooler inside," Cat said. She waved Kathy inside, shoved the door closed and gestured toward the living room. "Would you like to sit down?"

Kathy hesitated, her eyes traveling over the wall of bookcases, the comfortable furnishings. "I can't stay. I have to get back. My neighbor's watching my son. He's been sick."

Mrs. Raymond Stites, Mrs. Raymond Stites, Mrs. Raymond Stites. "I'm sorry, truly. I hope he's going to be all right."

"Those were your children? At the cemetery?"

Cat nodded. "Jane and Mats. Matthew. A friend took them downtown."

"Look, Mrs. Austen, I always meant..." She closed her eyes. "I don't know what to say. How to apologize for someone else. Especially when that someone has shattered your life in a way that will always leave a few pieces missing, no matter how hard you try to put your life back together. All you can do is..."

"Put flowers on a grave," Cat concluded.

Kathy nodded. "But I swear to you – I *swear* to you – I don't know why Raymond did what he did. I knew he was under a lot of stress. But the 'why'? You only seem to be able to answer that when it happens to someone else. When it happens to you..."

"You're in shock," Cat said. "And when shock subsides..."

"The 'why' gets put on hold. Because it's all you can do just to get through the day," Kathy concluded. "You know I always expected – it sounds awful, I know, but I expected after it happened? To hear from your lawyer, maybe. And then, I realized with Randy's one-big-happy-family policy, you might not have even known that my last name had been Stites."

Cat gestured toward one of the overstuffed chairs and sat, to encourage Kathy to do the same. "Not until recently." *Yesterday.* "I didn't realize you were married to-" *Raymond Stites, Raymond Stites, Raymond Stites* "- Raymond Stites." There. She had said the name aloud, pronounced it as she pronounced any other name. Raymond Stites. It hurt, but not as much as she thought it would. "But if that's why you're here, to apologize or to ask why I didn't take legal action, it wouldn't have taken you three years. I think you're here because of something connected to Whitney Rocap's car accident."

Kathy looked up at her, a trace of fear in her melancholy gaze. "She called me. The last time was the afternoon before she died in that car wreck."

Her hand went to her throat, the fingers toying with the gold crucifix suspended from a fine chain. "I thought that I was done with it. The calls? You have no idea what sort of people come out of the woodwork after a tragedy. I took my phone off the hook for a week after – ward."

Cat knew exactly what sort of people came out of the woodwork. Even the well-meaning ones were intolerable; the cranks were odious and frightening. "What did she want?"

"She asked if I had ever figured out why Raymond would do something like that. To someone he knew. I just hung up on her. I have my son to think about now."

"What's the matter with your boy?"

"He has leukemia. His doctors want to try a bone marrow transplant. We went ahead with some of the pre-screening while they try to come up with a match. Find a donor. It's only a blood test." She shut her eyes, exhaled, shakily. "How obvious was that? I'm starting to sound like a ghoul, asking total strangers. I've even gone on the internet. God. For a moment, just the briefest moment before I hung up? I was ready to ask her. Whitney Rocap."

"I can't remember when I had my last blood test. I'll have one, that's not problem. When Whitney called you, did she mention a woman named Daria Chavez?"

"Daria? I haven't heard from her for years. She moved away. Why?"

"Because I'd been getting phone calls, too. From a woman who said she knew something about why my husband died. I wrote her off as a crank, but last Wednesday, Whitney Rocap called me and said I should hear this woman out, tried to get me to meet with both of them. I didn't go, but she was seen with a woman who answers Daria Chavez's description, and the police think when she was run off the road, this woman was in the car with her."

Kathy swallowed. "'Run off the road'?"

Cat nodded.

"What happened to the woman they think was Daria?"

"They don't know. But they believe foul play was involved. They even have a suspect, a man named Robert Borch."

"Bobby!" Kathy was incredulous. "*That's* why the police were asking my neighbor if she'd seen him around! I just got back from Philadelphia this morning, I haven't had time to go through my mail or check my phone messages."

Just got back, and the first thing she had done was to put flowers on her husband's grave, her child's, Chris's. Cat felt another warm tide of guilt. "I guess you haven't had time to read the newspapers, either."

"Not for the past few days. Nothing but the outdated magazines in hospital waiting rooms."

"Well, Friday morning, I decided to confront Whitney. I'd known her slightly, I just couldn't go on without finding out what she knew, or thought she knew, about my husband. So I went over to her place. I had no idea she was lying dead in her car, it hadn't made the news yet. I walked in on Robert Borch looting her house. He'd rounded up her paperwork, files. He even went to her office and posed as her brother, got her notes and files. It wasn't until I reported the encounter to the police that I found out Whitney'd been killed."

"Encounter?"

"He roughed me up. I was lucky to get away." Cat paused. "You don't look surprised."

"Well it's – it's not a stretch. To see Bobby doing something violent. He'd known Raymond from prison. Bobby was doing time for an assault."

"And they were still friendly?"

"No, Bobby never turned up until after Raymond's death. He'd finished another sentence, for theft or something, and one day he just showed up at my door. He told me he knew Raymond, that he'd known him in prison, saw his obituary in the papers. It mentioned Pro Patrol, and Bobby asked how hard it was to get hired by them. I told him he'd have to get a physical, a drug screen and provide three references."

"And you gave him a reference?"

"I know I shouldn't have, but I did. I think that's what Raymond would have wanted. I don't know where he came up with the other two references, but Pro Patrol did hire him."

"You sound like you didn't like him very much."

"I didn't like him at all. He was crude. A hustler. A – what do people call a gigolo?"

Cat recalled a few of her brothers' synonyms, none of which seemed suitable to mention, not even to the wife of a murderer.

"He acted like he thought I'd be – you know – lonely. For a man. Sort of came on to me, and I let him know I wasn't interested. He backed off after he got assigned to work at a condo in Margate. I heard it was a pretty upscale building, maybe a few of them were more susceptible than I was. God knows the ones at the clinic were."

"Susceptible? Romantically?"

"Well, I don't know how much romance had to do with it. You live at the shore, you know the type. The women who spend their summers at the beach house? The husbands work up in Philly, only make it down on the weekends, that makes five days of the week their wives have to amuse themselves. And at the clinic? They were desperate, and vulnerable, not feeling like real women. Maybe the uniform carries some sort of a mystique, I don't know. Anyway, once he started working, he left me alone."

"Why did you leave your job at the clinic?"

"I had to take some time off, to take my son up to Philadelphia for tests and check-ups. Eve had been good about covering for me, and one time she asked how much notice I would be able to give if a match was found, and I had to take time off for the procedure. I guessed that she was asking for Randy, and that he was worried I might just leave them flat. Eve told me that if I needed a long leave of absence, she could talk to Randy about picking up our medical coverage for a year or so. I thought that was generous, but I didn't want to take a leave unless I knew when and if I would be able to come back to work. Anyway, it was arranged that Randy would continue to cover me for a year regardless, so I resigned."

"Didn't Doctor Hoffman at least ask you to stay on to train a replacement?"

"I offered, but Eve said she knew the drill and Randy figured that she could fill in until they hired someone, and bring her up to speed. And I was only a phone call away if they hit a snag." She checked her watch and rose. "I have to get back to my son."

"Look, Kathy. There's one more thing. When Daria – assuming it was Daria – called me, she said she knew *why* my husband was killed. And you just said that Whitney implied she knew why Raymond did what he did. Everyone wrote it off as a random act, and with random acts, there's no motive. No'why'."

"Not unless...Raymond was under so much stress. I'll never forgive myself for not being able to see how bad it was for him."

Cat felt a tug that she told herself was *no*t sympathy. Not for her husband's killer. Not for the wife of her husband's killer. Still, she heard herself saying, "Are you going to be all right? Can you look out for yourself?"

"What do you mean?"

"Well... do you have a lawyer?"

"I don't understand."

"Kathy, you said the police were questioning your neighbors. They're going to want to interview you. Maybe you should find someone who can advise you before you talk to them."

"I don't know a lawyer. I couldn't afford one if I did."

Cat observed that she didn't say she didn't *need* a lawyer. A kernel of intuition told her that Kathy Petrone was not telling all she knew, or suspected.

Still, the sense of resentment that piqued Cat, was directed at Victor, not Kathy. He'd had all day yesterday to tell her that Kathy Petrone was Kathy Stites. "I do happen to know a lawyer," she said. "An old friend, and I'm sure he'd be willing to help you out as a favor to me." She took a notepad and pen from the end table, scribbled Steve's name and handed it to Kathy. "I don't know if I can get a hold of him today, because of the holiday, but I'll talk to him tomorrow, and have him call you. So maybe you should just lie low until you hear from him."

Kathy pocketed the paper. "I'm not entitled to your help. I'm not even entitled to civility, Mrs. Austen."

Chris had ushered a women in distress to the ER, and Raymond Stites had pulled a gun and shot him in cold blood. And now, here she was playing White Knight to the wife of Chris's murderer. No, said the inner voice, Mrs. Raymond Stites wasn't entitled to anything. But Cat heard herself saying, "'Cat'. All my friends just call me 'Cat'."

CHAPTER THIRTY:
Three Years Before

Most of the staff had left by the time Daria ran in to deliver the paperwork and pick up the following week's transcription tapes. Kathy offered a polite "Happy Easter" and a smile, but Daria scurried out without a nod. Doctor Hoffman left the signed correspondence on Kathleen's desk, the "termination notices", that never failed to evoke a chill. Kathleen had tried to tell herself that these little clusters of cells were not yet life, far less than little Raymond who had come into the world fully formed, quite perfect, quite still.

Perhaps tomorrow, after a good dinner, after her mother had left, Kathleen would talk to Raymond again about another baby. Surely Raymond understood how important it was to have someone to love. People who didn't need someone to love, they might as well be dead. Or they were monsters.

Cat remembered that wave of panic a few days before Mats was born. She had spent all of her love on Jane; how could there be anything left for another baby? "How did you have enough love for all of us?" little Cat had asked her mother once. "Weren't you afraid it would run out?" Jennie had only laughed and said that each baby brought its own bundle of love with it, so no matter how many children you had, you never ran out of love. There was no panic now, only the sense of wonder and a bit of self-satisfaction that she and Chris had finally managed this miracle without Doctor Hoffman's intervention. In her elation, she forgot that Nicholas or Charlotte had already been conceived and was stored, suspended and still waiting.

If Chris had not been murdered, she might have remembered sooner.

CHAPTER THIRTY-ONE: Present Day

Cat took the children to a matinee, sat back and replayed the conversation with Kathy Petrone in her head. Afterward, she took them for burgers and fries, and put them on a few rides. It was dark before they strolled home, and Cat pushed aside the messages to call Victor, helped Jane settle on a wardrobe choice that would best exhibit a three-day tan (pale pink sundress with a cotton crocheted sweater) and put them to bed early, turned off her phone and went to bed herself.

The next morning, she took a quick run then made breakfast for Jane, packed her lunch, watched her sprint across the street to the bus stop. How pretty she was! How Chris had adored her. Her brothers couldn't quite understand how Chris could be so delighted that his firstborn was a girl. They had all done the right thing and produced males first – even Carlo's son Michael had arrived two minutes before his twin, Carla. "You get your boy first, then you can have as many girls as you want," Carlo had advised, and on his first visit after Cat got home from the hospital, he grumbled, "So, you don't know how to listen, or what?" But the posture was phony, Cat and Chris knew it. They left Carlo alone beside the bassinet while Chris helped Cat to bed; Chris returned and found Carlo holding a swaddled Jane in his massive hands, crooning "Un-cle Car-lo, Un-cle Car-lo".

Ellice was gone when Cat emerged from the shower. Cat dressed Mats, then called the pediatrician, asked if he could fax an order for her to have blood drawn at the local lab Kathy Petrone had named, hung up and got dressed.

Mats was marching across the floor, holding a pillow at arm's length when the phone rang. He dropped the pillow and scrambled for it. "It's Vi'tor. He says are you here."

Cat dabbed on lipstick. "Tell him I'm on my way out, I have a doctor's appointment, then I have to see Uncle Steve."

"She says we're goin' to the do'tors, then we gotta see Uncle Stebe." Pause. "He says how come?" Mats asked.

"Tell him it's none of his beeswax."

"Mom says it's none of your beeswax," Mats informed him. There was a pause, then Mats said, "We was at the movies, and then we to get hamburgers and then we went on the rides."

Cat's eyes narrowed. Grilling a five-year-old!

"Uncle Carlo took us on diff'rent rides Sat'rday. He didn't' go on the bumper boats with us and Mark said it was because Uncle Carlo might sink 'em." Pause. "Mark says it's prob'ly 'cause Uncle Carlo gots a steel prick like Superman."

"Mats!" Cat snatched a tissue to rub away a lipstick smear.

"He says he wants you to come to the phone."

"Tell him I'm running late and you have to hang up."

"Mom says I gotta hang up." He listened for a minute, said "Okay", and hung up. "He says you better call him or else but he didn't say or else what."

Cat stopped at the lab, told Mats he could come in with her, but he should turn his face away because they had to stick her with a little needle, smiled to show him it wasn't going to hurt. She got two lollipops for her bravery.

Steve Delareto's latest receptionist had orange-yellow hair sprouting from dark brown roots, narrow silver rings on each finger, thumbs included, a series of silver studs outlining one ear lobe. She greeted Cat with "Knyelpyoo?"

It was only after a bemused Cat said, "I wanted to see Mr. Delareto if he's free. My name's Mrs. Austen", that she realized the woman had asked, "Can I help you?"

"Goweddonin."

Cat severed the syllables, came up with 'Go ahead on in' and knocked softly on Steve's door. She turned the handle, poked her head in. "Your, um, secretary? Said I could-" She did her best to mimic the girl's accent, "'Goweddonin'."

Steve pushed his chair away from his desk. His suit jacket was draped over the back of his chair. He wore a pale blue shirt and navy tie with a fraternity tie pin, dull gold cufflinks.

"Say hello to Uncle Steve," Cat instructed Mats.

"Hi."

Steve ruffled Mats' hair. "Mats, that little refrigerator in the corner, there are some juices and canned sodas in there."

Mats dropped his coloring book on a couch and went over to the mini-fridge. "Did you know there's Snickers bars in here, too?" Mats inquired.

"Take a couple, bring one to your sister."

"It's still morning."

"I've had a Snickers bar for breakfast."

Mats looked at him with worship.

"I got clients stuck for child care," Steve told Cat. "So I try to be kid friendly. Want a Pepsi? I'd offer to send Tambi for coffee but I send her out, she forgets how to find her way back."

Cat sat on the couch. "Tambi?"

"First eight days of her life she was officially 'Baby Girl' because her mom couldn't decide between Tammy and Bambi."

"She does everything but snap gum."

"She snaps plenty. Long as she confines it to the privacy of her desk, gotta be grateful for small favors. I interviewed thirteen applicants and you don't wanna know from the rejects." He dropped into a leather chair opposite her. "I'm lookin' to snatch the woman who works for Cardenas. Adane."

"Maybe I should mention it to Ellice."

"What's Ellice been up to? Freddy said he hasn't seen her for the past week, he's startin' to sound like he's wondering if she's gonna show up at the altar."

"She subs every day. And Freddy's been working a lot of doubles. I think he's planning on buying her a car for a wedding present." Cat turned to Mats. "Baby, go sit over at that little table with the coloring book," Cat suggested.

Steve threw his hands behind his head, laced his fingers. "I talked to Mary Grace Keller this morning. APBs on Borch, he hasn't surfaced. Not armed are you?"

"Not today."

"Well, watch your back. So what's up?"

"Two things. A request for information, and a favor."

"Let's do the information first, that may be tough. Favors are yours for the asking, you know that."

"I'm going to do a piece on that clinic, State of the ART."

Steve frowned. "How come?"

"Borch was a guard there. An ex-con. And I started thinking it was a good angle, how secure can a place be if the people who're supposed to be guarding it are ex-cons." Cat tugged at the tip of her ponytail, absently. "Are you buying any of this?"

"What's that on your arm?"

"Nothing. I had to have some blood drawn."

"I don't like the sound of that."

"It's nothing, Steve. Not relevant."

Steve hesitated. "We've known each other, what, thirty years? You need for me to tell you what you say to me is in confidence?"

"I need for you to tell me the truth. When I said I was doing a write-up on the clinic, you didn't say, 'Oh?' or 'That's interesting', you asked how come. As though you didn't like the idea."

He shrugged. "I just wondered why you'd take up another story that's obviously going to involve a lot of research. You've got a lot on your plate with the wedding and all."

"Steve, you're not nearly as good a liar as you need to be in order to be as good a lawyer as you are."

Steve glanced at Mats, who was coloring a picture of a large Easter egg, his upper lip rimmed with grape juice. "He's the image of Chris, I guess you know that."

"Steve," Cat sounded like she was pleading. "If someone said to Chris, 'I know something about how your wife died', he'd check it out. I asked Victor, and now I'm asking you: is it possible there's something about Chris's death I wasn't told?"

"I don't know, Cat. That's the truth. But..."

"What?"

"I knew that Hoffman was your doctor. Chris told me."

"When?"

"You guys went to New York, remember? Chris worked a couple doubles to get the time off."

Cat nodded.

"Day before you went up to the city, Chris was at a pile-up. Young couple. Chris recognized them from some kind of orientation session the two of you had to attend before you entered the program. They went through the same procedure you did. Had a kid, around the same time you guys had Jane. Anyway, Chris came to me with a legal question, said I wasn't to bother you with it, you'd only get upset."

"What question?"

"He wanted to know what happens if both parents die? To the embryos. I mean, it's not like they got assigned godparents. He told me he was asking because you two still had, you know-"

Nicholas or Charlotte. Cat pushed a strand of hair behind her ear. "Why didn't you ever mention this to me?"

"After Chris got killed and you had the miscarriage? I figured you guys had gone ahead with the last procedure and it wasn't relevant."

Because he assumed her pregnancy was the result of that remaining embryo. "It's.. .it's relevant, Steve."

Steve got up from his chair, dropped onto the couch beside her. "You know, the best thing about growing up with someone, there's not a lot they can tell you's gonna surprise you."

She twisted the rings on her right hand. "The New York trip? I got pregnant."

"You mean without assistance."

"Steven."

Steve grinned, reddened slightly. "Without medical intervention," he amended.

Cat nodded. "At the time, we were given the informed consent forms, to, you know, arrange for the disposition – disposal – eventually..." Cat covered her face with her hands. "Oh, God, what a mess. I never thought...I just wanted children so desperately."

Steven leaned forward, took her hand, pressed it between his. "Look, the only reason I know anything about this is because Chris came to me and asked. I don't handle a lot of divorces and weird as it sounds, that's where a lot of this wound up. You come to blows over the pots and pans. Get down to the kids and the dog, you bring out the big guns, but the embryos, it goes nuclear. Plus, the latest legislation's added another layer of complication. Corruption, possibly."

"Corruption?"

"Any time something new comes down the pike, people figure out how to exploit it for corrupt purposes way before we figure out how to use it for good or make it secure. The bio ethics, the legal ethics?" He shrugged. "And if you tell me 'legal ethics' is an oxymoron- "

"I would be willing to grant that you're the exception."

"The one that proves the rule, right? I know of a case, couple in New Jersey, had embryos in a storage facility – not State of the ART - and then they get divorced. So whaddayou do? You can't go 'You got weekdays and Christmas, summers and weekends, he's with me'. They both want custody."

"What did they do?"

"Well, the old wife, the bio donor, wants them destroyed, the bio husband wants them implanted in the brand new wife."

"Good heavens. What did they decide?"

"That basically, what the husband was asking was to force Wife Number One, to become a biological parent against her will. So they ruled in favor of termination."

Cat shuddered. "What if...well, what would happen if there had been no divorce, but when the couple went to arrange for the implantation procedure, they found that the facility had destroyed them?"

"Intentionally or accidentally?"

"Good heavens, I don't know.'

"It makes a difference. I mean, you have a better chance of an award if you could prove intent. Either way, it would be a tough case to win because it would be difficult to demonstrate how you'd been damaged."

"Put a dollar amount on your embryos, you mean?"

"No, I mean how do you prove you've been harmed by the action." Steve glanced toward Mats. "For instance, say you kept your embryo in storage, five, ten years before you say, 'Okay, let's do it', and you go to the clinic and find out that through some error, the embryo'd been destroyed."

Cat nodded.

"Now, I'm representing the defense, I'm gonna ask whaddayou been doing the past ten years? You bought yourself a nice condo? You been taking vacations? You got a promotion? You got a boyfriend? You get married? How're you going to prove this mistake kept you from living a full, productive life?"

Cat bit her lip, blinked back tears.

"You can prove that, I get an expert in embryology to prove the embryo wasn't viable anyway, you waited too long, put off getting pregnant 'cause you put the job and the boyfriend and the condo ahead of having a baby." He paused. "Can you tell me why this is an issue now, Cat?"

She looked into his eyes and saw sympathy and something else that had been there since they were kids, had adapted, but not extinguished, when she had married, started a family of her own. Why hadn't some smart, kind woman snapped him up? "The forms we signed, before Jane was born, were for a ten-year storage – unless we used them before that, which we totally meant to do. And if there were any left in storage at the end of the ten-year contract, we were to be notified by certified mail. So that if we changed our minds about disposal, or wanted the embryos donated or transferred, we could do it. Otherwise…"

"They automatically terminate the remaining embryos?"

Cat nodded. "Embryo. Singular. I should have gotten a letter from the clinic months ago."

"You think they destroyed your embryo without notifying you?"

"I don't know. I tell myself that maybe it was just some mail I overlooked, and then I tell myself that I would never have overlooked something that important, and then..."

"You remind yourself that life's moved on," he said simply. "Look, the clear-cut solution is to just ask 'em to provide you with your medical file, that should include copies of the original contract and a copy of any correspondence. Give them a call, and if they try to stonewall you, I'll take over. How's that?"

Cat wiped her eyes with the back of her hand. "That's fine."

"Okay, so what's the favor?"

"You may not want to do this." She paused. "There's this woman, she lives in Somers Point. She's a widow, has a sick child and she may need a lawyer."

"And she doesn't have any money."

"Not a lot. Do you mind giving her a hand?"

"Do I look like I'm gonna turn down a widow with a kid? What's she need a lawyer for? Estate problem?"

"No, the police may want to question her in connection with Whitney Rocap's accident. I think she may be more comfortable if an attorney could hold her hand. And you were so effective with Linwood, I thought you might like to go another round."

"With who? Cardenas?" Steve's mouth curved, wickedly.

"I thought that might appeal to you."

"Why'd you think I wouldn't wanna do it?"

"Well, the thing is, her name's Kathy Petrone."

"Yeah, so?"

"That's her maiden name. After her husband died, she resumed it. Her married name was Stites."

"Whoa. *Whoa!* We are *not* talking about *Raymond* Stites?"

Cat winced, nodded.

Steve pushed himself off the couch. "*JE*-sus Christ, Cat-!"

"Uncle Stebe," Mats said, tentatively, his small hand closing over the remainder of the Snickers Bar.

"What?"

"You're not asposed to say 'Jesus Christ'. Unless you're prayin'."

Steve nodded, ruefully. "You're absolutely right. Thanks for reminding me."

"That's okay." Mats resumed coloring.

"Okay. Mrs. Raymond Stites. And this better be good."

Cat sighed. "Sorry, I knew it was out of line to ask. I've got work to do, I'd better go."

"Hey, did I say 'no'? I said I'd do it, I'll do it. Where'd you meet her?"

"At the cemetery. Stites is buried in the same cemetery as Chris. Every week she goes to put flowers on their graves."

"Both of them?"

Cat nodded. "Can I ask one more thing?"

"Let's have it."

"Did Chris say what else he was going to do? If he was going to get another opinion about abandoned embryos?"

"He did say he was going to talk it over with Doctor Hoffman's wife and that he would get back to me.'

"Then what?"

Steve looked away. "It was the day before he died. And then, after his funeral, I heard from someone that she'd killed herself. But back then, I wasn't thinking about her, I was thinking about you." He looked at her. "Cat look. I'll take this as far as you want, but be honest with yourself. I know it's not easy to deal with, someone getting killed at random, like Chris was. Sometimes, it's a little easier if you can at least come up with a reason.

I hate admitting it, but these days, people kill for nothing. Just to kill. Victor had said that to her on their first date.

"It's not easier, Steve," she said.

CHAPTER THIRTY-TWO: Present Day

Victor pulled up to the kiosk and presented his shield to the blonde guard, who said, "Park wherever."

Inside, air conditioning and Muzak snuffed out the May heat and whirr of shore-bound traffic. The pale mauve of the walls was a soothing contrast to the sun's glare. Framed watercolors, and fresh plants in brass-bound pots, upholstered chairs flanking end tables with copies of *House Beautiful*, *Parenting* and the morning papers, the small nook furnished with a miniature table and chairs, books and toys mitigated the clinical air.

Victor's gaze panned down from the row of closed doors on the second floor to the keypad-protected doors on either side of the reception area. These opened onto glassed-in corridors that linked the labs to the main building. One door was marked 'Cryo', Embryology/Andrology, the other marked 'Laboratory Testing'.

The receptionist inquired, with awkward courtesy of a temp. "Sperm count or a donor consult?"

It took a minute for Victor to realize the import of her question. He presented his ID, said, "I made an appointment with Dr. Aquino."

The receptionist picked up the receiver and pushed a button. "Doctor Aquino, there's a Lieutenant Cardenas to see you," she said in a low voice, listened a minute and hung up. "Upstairs to your right, second door."

Paul Aquino's office was windowless, small and boxy, the furniture sleek and new, the diplomas in glossy walnut frames. The doctor appeared to be in his late thirties, with a narrow face, olive complexion, dark hair that was thinning on top, gathered at the nape of his neck in a nub of ponytail. "Lieutenant?" He extended his hand.

Victor shook hands. "Thanks for giving me some time."

Aquino sat behind his desk and gestured toward a chair. His fingers began to skip along the edge of his desk, as though executing a concerto heard only in his head. "I have to ask. Did you clear this with Randy Hoffman?"

"Why do you have to ask?" Victor inquired, calmly.

Aquino's fingers ran some imaginary scale. "He's the boss."

"I thought you were equal partners."

"Well, you remember your George Orwell. Some are more equal than others."

Victor came directly to the point. "Whitney Rocap. I understand she came by last week, spoke to you and Miss Bellamy about some sort of feature article."

"Yes. I'm surprised she didn't bring it up the night before, I would have told her she'd have to clear something like that with Randy. Maybe that would have saved her the trip, saved her..."

"The night before?"

"She shot a segment at a women's support group that meets in Atlantic City. Infertility. Miriam – Miriam Bender – founded it. Several of us in the field take turns acting as unofficial moderator. Tuesday was my turn. If she had asked about it then, I would have referred her to Randy."

"And Wednesday night?"

Aquino ran another scale to the corner of his desk. "When she showed up, Eve took her aside and explained that any sort of press had to go through Randy. She – Miss Rocap – asked if she could wait around and speak to Eve after the session. Eve suspected that Miss Rocap was trying to identify the attendees, perhaps, intending to contact them individually. It's against our policy to release the names of people who attend our sessions, even the ones who decide not to use our services. Certainly not to the press."

Victor nodded. So far it didn't contradict what Eve Bellamy had told him. "Did Miss Bellamy mention Daria Chavez?"

"Who?"

"She'd been a typist here. She took off a few years back."

"There was some home office worker who just stopped showing up. What, three years ago?"

Victor nodded. "She was seen with Miss Rocap Wednesday night."

"Miss Rocap came on her own, I didn't see anyone with her."

Victor slipped a notebook out of his breast pocket. "How did you come to succeed Miriam Bender?"

"Miriam was my – my mentor, I believe is the current term. We'd done public health work together. I liked her a lot."

"Her suicide must have been a shock."

The drumming fingers paused. "Yes. She was a bright, sensitive woman. Perhaps too sensitive and it got to her."

"What did?"

"The clinic's success. Miriam had a hysterectomy in her twenties. She could never have children."

"Odd choice of a profession, then?"

Aquino shrugged. "You can love life, even if you don't have the ability to create it."

"If you love life, you don't commit suicide."

Aquino shrugged again, continued drumming on his desk top.

"I conclude it wasn't the result of marital problems. Infidelity."

"What, you mean Randy and Eve? No, good Lord, no. Nothing took root there until about a year or so ago."

"I might have meant Doctor Bender."

Aquino's brows lifted, incredulously. "Miriam. Unfaithful? Out of the question."

"What about Doctor Hoffman's first marriage?"

"I never met her or his children. Two, I believe. I got the impression it was the usual story. Young med student – or law student or grad student –

marries the comfort of bed and board to mitigate the grind, and she marries the prospect of being Mrs. Doctor or Mrs. Professor down the line. He graduates, ditches her and moves on. He certainly didn't leave the first Mrs. Hoffman for Miriam Bender, he'd been divorced for years when they met."

Victor shifted topics. "You heard about the disappearance of the security guard? Robert Borch?"

Aquino's fingers began skating up and down the edge of the desk. Victor wondered whether he really played the piano. "Eve told me she had to call for a replacement, he simply didn't show up a few nights ago. So much the better."

"And why is that?"

"Let's just say that putting him in proximity of so many vulnerable women wouldn't have been my choice."

"He had a problem with women?"

"He had no problem with women, that was his problem."

"What about Kathy Petrone, did the two of them get along?"

"I assume so. I don't know anyone who didn't get along with Kathy."

"Tell me about her."

The fingers launched another scale. "Bright, competent, a sweet girl. Hardly missed a day of work. I heard that even after her husband's death, she cut short her time off to help stabilize things, because of Miriam's suicide. Considering the way she'd been widowed, I thought that was pretty amazing."

"Were you surprised that she was let go?"

"Very." He shrugged. "I know a little of the situation, the boy's condition. I gather, from what Eve told me, that Randy anticipated that the boy would have to go somewhere out of the area for treatment, that Kathy might start to need a significant amount of time off, and as much as Randy wanted to accommodate, it would really undermine the operation."

"Have you found a replacement yet?"

Aquino shook his head. "We've had a couple temps on the desk, general reception work, some filing but the more complex paperwork, scheduling, billing, Eve's taken that on until we get someone else."

"How many people have you interviewed for the position?"

"I – why, no one, to my knowledge."

"It's odd that Mrs. Petrone wasn't asked to stay on at least until a replacement could be found."

Aquino shrugged.

"Mrs. Petrone's child. You have any idea who the father is?"

Aquino blinked. "Why – no. I never thought about it. But I don't have to tell you that marriage is no longer a prerequisite to childbearing. It's not flattering to think how superfluous we men have become."

"Any chance it could be Hoffman's?"

Dr. Aquino seemed genuinely shocked. "There was never any indication that Randy treated Kathy Petrone like anything more than a valuable assistant. In any case, the pregnancy would have occurred around the time The Hoffman went into production."

"Meaning a relationship, a child would have interfered with his preoccupation?"

"Well, to be frank, yes. Randy – I don't know how to put this, and it's going to sound more cold-hearted than I mean for it to, but Randy doesn't – attach himself – to people who don't serve him in some way."

"And what function does Miss Bellamy serve?"

"Lieutenant."

"Okay," Victor conceded. "Other than the obvious."

"Eve's worked here for years, she can fill in for just about anyone. Which may be why Randy's been in no hurry to replace Kathy. Why add to the payroll if you don't have to?"

Victor laid his notebook on his lap. "Can I ask you a few general questions. About the profession?"

"Of course. What, specifically?"

"Safeguards against error, for example."

"Embryos getting mixed up?" Aquino smiled. "There weren't a lot to mix up ten years ago, when the clinic was founded. A woman undergoes the hormonal protocol and oocytes are extracted, immediately labeled with the date, her chart number and name. After they're united with sperm, the vials are coded and dated and these labels are checked and double-checked at the time of implantation and if there are any remaining embryos that the patient wants to preserve, the vials – they're called straws – they're labeled again before the transfer. Everything is witnessed, so that there's a traceable – I believe you'd call it, 'chain of evidence'."

"It's not possible for a patient to get the wrong embryo? Of embryos being unintentionally destroyed?"

"Well, in the case of a donation, through our OvaShare program, there really is no 'wrong' embryo as long as the donor relinquishes all claim to the material. As to unintentional error?" He shrugged. "The problem with this specialty – all medicine, perhaps - is that it puts science and human nature in direct conflict. Medicine can't guarantee results, which is why it isn't a good profession for a con artist. Ultimately nature will expose the truth. But the people who come to us often do try to con us, and frequently succeed. They lie about their histories, about the first wife they've abandoned, about the other kids they've fathered, where they're from. So think about it: a guy fathers a child in New Jersey, a few years later, donates sperm in California, and the offspring wind up as college sweethearts. It's what started bothering Miriam so much, I think. She used to read a lot, and often quoted the line, 'the resources of science are far from being exhausted'. Except that when she said 'exhausted', I think she meant 'corrupted'."

"Conan Doyle," Victor nodded, gravely. "How long can you keep an embryo in cryo?"

"Current science estimates ten years. Most people who store their embryos use them in a ten year span or sign for disposal."

"And that's the clinic's option? To dispose of them?"

"Oh, no. Embryos are the property of the patient, not the clinic. Most of the time, embryos are utilized or donated or disposed of prior to the ten-year termination cut-off. If that date approaches, and there are still embryos in storage, the patient is notified by certified mail with a request that they contact us regarding their wishes. Whether they want to continue storing them or transfer them or dispose of them."

"What if you notify someone and they don't respond?"

"We follow up. Attempt to locate a forwarding address, a change in the phone number But most of the time, in cases like that? They've abandoned the embryos."

"Have you ever had someone claim that you disposed of embryos without proper notification?"

"Never."

"Not possible that they might be stolen?"

"Stolen?" He looked amused. "They're stored in liquid nitrogen in a restricted area. It's not like stealing a candy bar from the Twenty-Four/Seven."

Victor rose, thanked Aquino for his time. When he descended the stairs, saw that the receptionist had been replaced by Eve Bellamy who cradled the phone to her ear with one shoulder while she typed something on the keyboard, nodded as a woman in a nurse's uniform held up a sheet.

Victor walked up to the reception window. Eve looked up, saw Victor. Her smile widened a bit, no trace of surprise in her glance. "No, Mrs. Austen, I'll put it together this afternoon."

She punched a button on the console. "Randy, Mrs. Copeland was delayed in traffic, she's running fifteen minutes late. Lieutenant Cardenas is here." She listened for a moment, hung up and turned to the temp who had greeted Victor. "Pull the file on Austen, A-u-s-t-e-n, will you. First name- oh, dear, I don't recall Mrs. Austen's first name? I know she went by her nickname. It was Mrs. Christopher Austen, I think her first name began with an 'A'."

Allegrezza, Victor thought.

"Now," Eve smiled. "What can I do for you, Lieutenant?"

"Robert Borch. Have you heard from him?"

She shook her head. "I don't expect to. I just went ahead and asked Pro Patrol to replace him permanently."

Victor thanked her and walked to his car. *What did Cat want with her medical file?*

He pulled up to the kiosk, rapped on the glass.

The guard leaned down. "Help you?"

"Robert Borch. Heard from him?"

"No. Jerk. They plugged someone else into his spot."

"I would think that would be the hardest slot to fill, midnight to morning."

"Yeah, well Bobby wasn't married, and I'm guessin' the kind of relationships he had goin' liked the late shift."

Victor glanced over his shoulder. His gaze settled on the open fields behind the curtain of closely planted arborvitae. There were a few mounds that had been turned over recently, but the darkness that was moisture had already been sapped from them, the earth was an even, parched brown. "They ever grow anything out in those fields?"

"Not that I've ever seen. They turn it over every once in a while so it doesn't go to weeds, I guess. Clinic's leasing it, I heard some talk they're gonna expand, but nothin' ever happens."

"How long have you worked here?"

"Three years. That practically makes me an old-timer around this place."

"You around when Doctor Hoffman's wife died?"

"I got transferred right around then because they lost two guys in the same week."

"One of them would be Stites?"

The guard nodded. "Kathy? His wife? Go figure. She's the type, cold days, she comes out with coffee, ninety degrees, she's bringing me a lemonade. She's takin' the lunch order, she always made a point of buzzing me, asking if I want something."

"You said they lost two guards. Who was the other one?"

He lifted his brimmed cap, ran his hand over his blonde hair. "I forget his name. Turnover's huge, you know. Santino? Fanucci? Or am I thinkin' about *The Godfather*?"

"Santucci?" Victor asked.

The guard snapped his fingers. "That's it."

CHAPTER THIRTY-THREE: Present Day

Cat took Mats to lunch at McDonald's, sat uneasily on a playground bench that was a sun baked disk of hard vinyl, watched Mats squirm through a chute made of suspended netting. He wriggled through the obstacle, impervious to the heat, his face flushed with pleasure. Cat wondered if Kathy Petrone ever took her son to McDonalds, to the beach, to the rides, realized how much more had been left to her than to Kathy, with no family and an invalid child in addition to the loss of her husband.

Cat tied Mats's shoes and asked him if he wanted her to take him to the lady's bathroom or go into the men's room by himself. Mats considered this, soberly, opted to allow his mother to take him into the ladies' room.

Her next stop was the library. She settled Mats on a bean bag chair with a picture book and stationed herself at the Microfiche.

Chris was at a pile-up...State of the ART...That's where he knew these people from. They went through the same procedure you did. Had a kid, around the same time you guys had Jane.

Cat and Chris had gone to New York the Valentine's Day before he died. So the pile-up that killed this young couple would have been in February. Cat scanned the obits for a husband and wife fatality, an obituary that mentioned a child. She was able to narrow it down rapidly to two: Warren and Joan Chin from Atlantic City, who had died on an ice-covered road three years before, left two children ages six and eight. The second couple were Richard and Myra Asher, who had died three days before Valentine's Day. Left a six-year-old boy, Richard Randall Asher, and Mrs. Asher's married sister, Carolyn Coleman of Ventnor.

A ping of recollection sounded. Asher. There had been a check-in sheet at the clinic's orientation sessions, alphabetical order. Asher had been directly above Austen.

Cat scribbled the name, turned to Mats. He had fallen asleep in the chair. She carried him to the car and settled him in his car seat without waking him, coasted into her driveway a few minutes before Jane's school bus was due to arrive. She saw the elder Miss Nixon waving, as she eased Mats into her arms.

Miss Althea met her at the curb. "Well, it looks like somebody's had too much fun," Miss Althea smiled, giving Mats a little pat. She fished a packet of mail from her pocket. "Here's what the postman left. I don't like to see it lying around, in case someone sends Ellice and Freddy money. And there was a messenger, delivering a package. I saw him knocking on your door, and then he went down and knocked on the downstairs. I thought he looked suspicious, so I just went over and told him I'd take the package and give it to your brother, and I let it drop that your brother was with the state police? And didn't he high-tail it out of here fast."

"You shouldn't have confronted him, Miss Nixon."

"Oh, I wasn't worried. My sister had my back. She's cleaning the Model Seven today, with the nice eighteen inch barrel. Even with them in the cabinet, you have to mind the salt air. It would be nothing for her to put a pill in that young man's hindquarters."

Cat felt a smile working its way to her lips. "What did he look like?"

"Big fellow and didn't he just resemble that man in the paper, the one the police are looking for? I do like a well-built man, but this too much time in the gym can't be a good thing. They start taking the steroids and they say that affects..." she lowered her voice prudently. "-other functions. I got the first two letters on his plate, and called it in. They're going to have a police car come by now and then. There, look, here's another one driving by." She squinted toward the driver. "That's Jack MacCready's boy. I certainly hope he'll turn out better than his father. Would you like some tomatoes?"

Cat knew better than to refuse. This was one of Jersey's summer rituals, cultivating and then divesting oneself of tomatoes. Cat had half-decided to fertilize a small patch in the corner of her back yard and let the kids put in a few plants, as soon as she could list potential recipients for the crop.

Cat crossed the street. The cop at the wheel rolled down the window. She leaned down, shifting Mats onto her hip.

"Never had a call from the Nixon ladies yet that didn't pan out, they got the old man's genes. Women were allowed on the force in their day, both woulda made captain," the cop greeted. "It's this guy Borch, he's too dumb to stay at large much longer. Any fugitive worth his salt knows you don't come onto the island where all we gotta do is open the drawbridge to yank your egress out from behind."

Cat heard the rumble of the school bus. She thanked the officer, offered him some tomatoes, which he declined with a chuckle. She tucked the mail under her arm and waited on the sidewalk until Jane got off the bus and crossed the street.

She worked the key in the lock, called "Ellice?" as she dropped the mail on the dining room table. No answer.

Cat set Mats on the couch, pushed the 'Play' button on her phone. Victor, asking her to call him as soon as possible, telling her he wanted to see her that evening. Louie Cicciolini telling her he was going to do Andrea's and Meryl's hair Saturday before noon, and then would drive directly to Ocean City to do Ellice, Cat, Jane, and Jennie, who was staying over the night before the wedding. Freddy, asking if Ellice was home yet. Her mother, asking if seven dozen rolls was going to be enough, she was going to call the bakery and get another three dozen rolls just to be on the safe side. Someone named 'John', asking Ellice if Friday afternoon was at all possible. Eve Bellamy calling from the clinic, asking Cat if she wanted her medical file mailed out or would she come and pick it up?

Cat poured iced tea for herself and Jane. Could it really have been Borch, poking around her mailbox? What on earth for? "Wanna help me cook?"

"What are you *making*?"

"Chicken acey-ducey. *Acitu duci*, sweet and sour. Unless you'd rather have scrapple acey-ducey."

"Ashley Kreisberg says only *hacks* write about scrapple."

"Really?"

"Ashley's mom says *anyone* can write articles. She's writing a *book*."

"Well, I wrote a poem. Wanna hear it?"

"Okay."

Cat took a pack of chicken breasts from the refrigerator, rinsed them and laid them in a Pyrex casserole. "Scrapple is made from leftovers; we fed some to Ashley's dog Rover; it turned him bright red, and then he fell dead; now Rover is pushing up clover."

Jane's grudging laugh had a shade of admiration.

Cat began to peel and chop an onion.

"John says *he's* going to write a book, too. He said he always wanted to and now he's going to retire and really do it."

"Who's John?"

"At the *book*store. Where we went with *Ellice* yesterday. John gave us each a book," Jane assessed her mother's expression. "He *gave* it to us, we didn't ask Ellice to *buy* it."

"Well, I thought I told you about taking things from *strangers*," Cat replied.

"He *owns* the book store. He and Ellice are *good friends*."

"Did John give Ellice a free book, too?"

"I don't know. Most of the time, they were in his back room talking. Can I try on my wedding dress after dinner?"

Cat recalled how devastated Freddy had been when Fawn Caprio had broken their engagement, the wedding preparations already underway. *Please don't hurt Freddy*, Cat prayed silently. She put butter and oil in a skillet, turned the heat on low.

The phone rang. Jane sprang into the booth, grabbed the receiver from the wall phone and said, "Austen residence." She looked at Cat. "She says it's Cherry."

Cat began to sauté the chopped onion, gestured for Jane to untangle the long phone cord, hand her the receiver. She wedged it to her ear with her shoulder, opened a bottle of Chianti, poured some over the sautéing onions "Go keep an eye on Mats for me, sweetie."

"He's just *sleeping*."

"Do you want to try on your dress after dinner?"

Jane grumbled and stalked off to the living room.

Cat added a few tablespoons of sugar and reduced the heat. "Hi, Cherry, I got backed up today, I'll be by tomorrow to pick up my check, after I drop off my son at nursery school."

"No prob. Any day Ritchie doesn't have to part with money is a good day. Look, I found out a little on the Mrs. Randall Hoffmans, if you're interested."

"What'd you find out?"

"He married Wife Number One, Harianne, a little more than twenty-eight years ago. Two kids while he did his internship and residency and she worked two clerical jobs, one at a lab, one at a real estate office. The latter got her first dibs on the starter house in Cherry Hill. He finished with his training and his marriage around the same time, 'round twenty years ago. Back to Philly for a fellowship in fertility medicine, came with the first wave of doctors staking out the shore, started off just practicing ob/gyn, moved into high risk and then infertility, that's what hooked him up with Miriam Bender."

Cat took the pan off the stove, poured the sweet and sour mixture over the chicken breasts, covered them with foil, wiped her hands on a dish towel. She sat at the kitchen booth and took down the notepad tacked next to the phone, penciled notes while Cherry spoke.

"Miriam'd taken another track. Parents dead, one sister. Scholarships and loans put the two of them through medical school. She came down here, opened her practice, did a lot of volunteer counseling. She and Hoffman met through mutual patients, women who needed counseling during the course of fertility treatments. When they started dating, she was in her mid-thirties, never married, her debts here paid up, she was making good money. The ideal partner."

Cat thought about what Jackie had said, that dating Hoffman had felt like an audition. "How's that?"

"Well, if he was looking for a founding partner for the clinic, she wasn't going to get pulled off the career track with kids, and her credit was good."

"Meaning his credit wasn't so hot? What, he was paying out a lot in alimony and child support?"

"No, he was doing good. He didn't take a real hit with the divorce, the first support order was two eighty a month, until the kids were eighteen, and I wasn't able to come up with any amendments or increases. Medical coverage, extras, like birthday presents, class trips, gym shoes, as far as I can see, if they came to more than two hundred eighty dollars a month, the ex-wife had to pick it up, or they did without."

"I've got two kids and our food bills come to more than two eighty a month."

"Well, what goes around, comes around."

"Meaning?"

"Hoffman's scoping out the area, right? Planning to build the clinic. And he goes gabbing to the press about how great his clinic was going to be for the area, how it was going to be a state of the art facility, how he thinks he may have found the perfect site out Somers Point-Mays Landing Road, yadda, yadda."

"I think I saw some of the copy at the time."

"You're not the only one. Apparently, he spent more time tooting his own horn than paying the piper. Somebody went and bought up the site before Hoffman made his bid."

"But Hoffman did build there. What, did this buyer turn it over to him for a profit?"

"No, it was a little more complicated than that. The buyer went and got the property re-zoned. Subdivided into three parcels, then he only went and put one of them on the market."

Cat closed her eyes, called up an image of the clinic flanked by open field. "That's why there's that open land on either side of the clinic?"

"Yup."

"Why didn't he build somewhere else?"

"Because it really was the best location for what he had in mind. Besides, the broker contacted Hoffman with an offer, the owner agreed to lease him those lots on either side of the clinic and give him first refusal when they went on the market. The expectation, I guess, was that Hoffman would want to expand somewhere down the line. And that the buyer would eventually sell."

"And neither happened?" Cat asked.

"Well, I don't know if Hoffman wanted to expand, but he hasn't been able to yet because the owner's never put the land on the market. He's been leasing those two empty lots for around ten years now, to the tune of eight grand a month."

"*Eight thousand*!" She scribbled '8,000', underlined it. "Who owns the land?"

"I'm still trying to find that out. The checks are processed through Home Stead Realty. They handle a lot of commercial properties in the area."

Cat wrote 'Home Stead Realty'. "Sounds familiar."

"Cat, look, there's a couple more things I may not get to bring up when you come by tomorrow, because Ritchie'll be hanging around. He's got me checking out this outfit Pro Patrol, and it looks like they're not real particular who they hire."

"So I gather."

"Anyway, their office gal and I get to chatting and she told me the cops had her pull records on Robert Borch and a guy named Santucci. Didn't you ask me about someone by that name?"

"Whitney had made a note of it. What about him?"

"A Charles Santucci'd been on their payroll, working at State of the ART until three years ago. One day, he flat-out doesn't show up for work, nobody ever heard from him again. They mailed out his last check, it came back, return to sender. Anyway, this gal told me what's weird? Is that this guy Santucci went missing the same day... well... the same day they lost another one of their guards."

"Raymond Stites," Cat said. "It's okay, Cherry. What did she say about Santucci?"

"Nothing, except they called this afternoon and asked her to fax his file. And Ritchie's getting the notion that this Borch is somehow involved with some shady pawnshop, Gabors? They're right down the street. The gal at Pro Patrol told me she didn't know them, that Borch had never worked security there or anything. So anyway, one thing leads to another, and I'm digging around in their medical workups- "

"You can't access medical records without a subpoena."

"You can access anything you can hack into."

"Silly me. You found something in Borch's medical records? I know they have to have drug screens."

"It wasn't that, and it wasn't Borch. It was..."

"Raymond Stites?"

"Yeah."

"You can say the name. What about him?"

"He had some tests run, not long before he, well, died. More than the usual. Blood work, chemistry profile, chest X-rays, there was a cranial X-ray, brain scan. They don't usually do that as part of a routine physical, the HMOs won't pony up."

"Maybe it wasn't usual. Maybe they were looking for something in particular."

"That's what I thought. But I read the reports and they were all negative. He was fit as a fiddle."

"Did you actually see his X-rays?"

"Nope, I can't read CT scans and X-rays, you could show me a blotch where a fly got in the crosshairs, tell me it was cancer and I'd believe you. The other thing is, the doc Pro Patrol uses for employee physicals? He didn't write the orders for these tests. They were ordered by Randall Hoffman."

ꙮ

Victor looked up, saw Adane usher Mary Grace Keller into his office. He put one hand over the phone, rose, motioned for them enter. He wrote something on a note pad and held it up. 'Daria's mother. San Juan.' "*Por qué estaba asustada*?" he said into the phone.

Adane and Mary Grace took the chairs in front of Victor's desk.

"*Por qué ella volvió a New Jersey*?" His mouth was turned down in a pensive frown as his listened to the woman's response."*Y qué había hecho*?"

He listened a few seconds more. "*Cuánto*?"

After another few moments, Victor thanked her politely, and promised to inform her as soon as Daria was located.

Victor sat and repeated his conversation with Daria's mother. "It corresponds with her father's statement. When she arrived in San Juan, she was terrified. For the past three years, she's been sticking close to her mother's home, helping her with some volunteer work at the church. Last month, she told her mother she had to come back here to make something right. Called her mother a few times, the last time was over a week ago. She never said what it was she had to rectify, she never mentioned Whitney Rocap. The only other item of interest is that Daria's mother found an envelope tucked in an inner pocket of the heavy coat Daria had been wearing when she arrived. Her mother opened it. It had a lot of money. Hundred dollar bills. She didn't count it."

"I took the liberty of checking Miss Chavez's bank records," Adane said. "The last transactions were three years ago. There were no large withdrawals around the time she fled."

"Her father said she'd do anything for money," Victor mused.

"I don't believe anyone short of a psychopath would do anything for money," Mary Grace commented. "There's always a threshold, it's just higher for some of us than others. Perhaps it tripped Miss Chavez up and that's why she fled to San Juan." Mary Grace was quiet, professional. Her porcelain complexion and delicate bone structure bore a close similarity to Kevin Keller. Perhaps that was an additional reason for the estrangement between Mary Grace and Maggie Keller. Sister Maggie looked at Mary Grace and saw Kevin.

"Any luck getting warrants on the Gabor properties?"

"The warrants aren't the problem, Victor. Jean's affidavits made a reasonable case for the probability that they might be harboring Robert Borch. It's the manpower to execute warrants simultaneously on the Gabors' twenty properties in eight separate municipalities at a time when most departments have their resources stretched by the onset of the season."

Victor nodded, grimly. "Mrs. Austen saw a notation written by Miss Rocap. 'Santucci'. He was a Pro Patrol guard, who disappeared around the time of Christopher Austen's murder."

"Victor." Mary Grace's smile was a bit impish. "You want to know what's harder than finding a needle in a haystack?"

"Finding a Santucci in New Jersey."

"If he is in New Jersey."

Long rapped on the door jamb and leaned into the room. "Hey, Mary Grace, what's shakin'?"

"Nothing that ought to be securely anchored," she smiled.

Phil chuckled. "Lieutenant, good news is Mrs. Petrone's agreed to an interview, she's here. The bad news is she's got her lawyer."

"It's not Lauren Robinson, is it?" Victor wasn't sure he was up to sparring with Robinson.

"No such luck. Steven Delareto."

Then she knows. Victor's eyes locked with Mary Grace's. "I'm sure you'll want to stay to say hello to an old friend."

CHAPTER THIRTY-FOUR: Present Day

Victor glanced through the two-way glass at a slender figure standing with her back toward him, dark hair gathered into a loose knot at the nape of her neck. Steve Delareto stood with his hand on her elbow, talking to her intently.

"She your idea of a cop killer's wife?" Long asked Victor.

"Sherlock Holmes once said the most winning woman he ever knew was hanged for poisoning three small children."

Victor entered the room, closed the door. "Counselor."

"Lieutenant."

Adane had set up a tape recorder. Victor walked around to adjust the volume, got a good look at Kathy Petrone. She was slim, with a long oval face that accentuated her air of melancholy. Dark circles were visible beneath the translucent flesh under her brown eyes, and the slender hands clasped and unclasped nervously. The skirt was simple, inexpensive, as was the short-sleeved white blouse. The shoes were creased imitation leather that had been buffed to a clear shine. She wore a thin chain around her neck, a crucifix.

"Mrs. Petrone – is it 'Mrs'?"

She looked up at him. "Whatever you like." The voice was low, precise without inflection. Her mouth was a long, narrow bow that tilted up at the corners in an ironic smile, for there was no mirth in her expression.

"I'm Lieutenant Cardenas. I'm taping this interview, for your attorney. I'm sure he has gone over the consent form."

"Yes. I'm accustomed to reading forms."

"Because of your job. Your former job."

"Yes."

"Are you employed now?"

"I do a little work from home. Word processing."

Victor saw Steve raise an eyebrow at that.

Steve held out a chair for her. "You see how it works, Kathy, is the Lieutenant's not gonna sit down until you sit down. King of the *caballeros*. And the last."

"That must be very lonely." She said it seriously, without any suggestion of flirtation or humor. She looked like someone who had been lonely all her life.

Victor waited for Kathy to sit before he took a chair at the end of the table. "How did you come to represent Mrs. Petrone, if you don't mind my asking?" he asked Delareto.

"Surprised to know we do a little *pro bono* now and then?"

"A little? Now and then? No, that wouldn't surprise me."

"A mutual friend of ours set it up, Cardenas."

"That does surprise me."

"I would've thought you'd be used to it by now."

Victor turned on the tape, announced the date and time, the names of the people present. "Mrs. Petrone, do you know a woman named Daria Chavez?"

Kathy licked her lips, her eyes cast down on her lap. "She did home office work. She did most of the clinic's typing until about three years ago."

"Then what happened?"

"She quit."

"Just quit? No notice?"

"Yes."

"Have you communicated with her in the past three years?"

Kathy shook her head.

"Mrs. Petrone, it would be helpful if you could verbalize your answers for the tape."

"No. No I haven't heard from her."

"When did you see her last?"

"It was ... the last I remember? Three years ago, the day before Easter. Daria came in to drop off some dictation. I never saw her after that."

"Did you speak to her that day?"

"I don't remember."

"Did she speak to anyone else?"

"I don't know."

"Did she seem agitated at all? Upset? Crying?"

"No, just a bit rushed, perhaps she had other stops, she worked for several professionals in the area."

"Who was at the security post that day?"

The hands twisted in her lap.

"Your husband. Raymond Stites." He glanced at Steve. The lawyer revealed no surprise.

"Yes. Raymond had switched with one of the other guards to take days. So that he could get off by four on Easter and have dinner with Mother and me."

"You worked a half day, you said. But your husband worked a full shift. You drive home separately?"

"I took the car. Raymond took a cab to work. I offered to take a cab home and leave him the car Raymond said he might get a lift, he would call me if he needed me to pick him up."

"Get a lift from whom?"

"I don't know. One of the lab workers, maybe."

"Or Daria Chavez?"

Kathy looked up at him, puzzled. "She'd already left."

"Did they have a relationship?"

"She used to stop in the Twenty-Four/Seven when he worked there. And they probably saw each other if Raymond was on duty when she dropped by the clinic."

"I meant a personal relationship."

"The Lieutenant means a sexual relationship," Delareto clarified.

The pause was longer this time. Kathy Petrone's gaze reproached him. "Raymond was never unfaithful to me." Said with the sort of certainty few women had, none of those undeserved.

"Based on what you describe as a casual relationship, she provided a personal reference for your husband."

Kathy sighed. "I think she thought that if she gave Raymond a referral, he might get a line on any Pro Patrol clients that were in the market for typist."

"Quid pro quo?"

"Yes."

"And Hoffman, he provided a reference as a favor to you?"

"Yes."

"What was she like?"

Kathy blinked. "Daria? Hard working. Driven. A bit – no, extremely – money hungry."

"We all are, to some degree."

Kathy shook her head. "Not to that degree. She didn't have her own home, or a husband or children, the things people want money for. It was just money for its own sake. There are some people who will do anything for money, even if they don't really know what they're going to do with it when they get it."

"And what would you do anything for?"

"My – husband. My son."

"How long were you and Raymond Stites married?"

"Almost five years."

"He'd been paroled a few years before that?"

"Yes."

"Stayed out of trouble?"

"Yes."

"Except for the gambling."

"Aren't we getting a little off the track?" Delareto asked.

"Not if the track is Chris Austen's murder investigation. I've asked the DA's office to reopen it."

Delareto stared at him. "You are one crazy sonofabitch," he said, slowly.

"Would you like that deleted from the tape, Counselor?"

"No. Leave it in."

Victor began to pace. "Doctor Hoffman thinks that your husband snapped under pressure. What sort of pressure was he under?"

"I'd lost a baby. I'd been trying to get pregnant again. We had some money problems. Raymond...he started gambling again." She sighed. "It was a – a compulsion. Some people call it a sickness, but it's not, just a terrible compulsion."

"Like Daria Chavez's drive for money?"

"Yes. Yes, exactly."

"Why don't you call it a sickness?"

"I have a son who's been hospitalized for a great deal of the past two years. I know what sickness looks like."

"How old is your son, Mrs. Petrone?"

"Two."

"When will he be three?"

"Not for – " She looked up, understood the import of his question.

"Who's his father, Mrs. Petrone?"

"His father was Joe None-of-your-business," Steve declared.

"Was it Robert Borch?"

"No," she said, quietly emphatic.

Victor studied her. Kathy Petrone looked to be in her mid-thirties. worn down, but there was something that kept her from having that 'seen-it-all' expression. How had she hooked up with Stites? Was it possible that Stites had been something other than a stone killer, or was Kathy was concealing a darker heart? "Your son. What's the matter with him?"

"He has leukemia. It's called CML. He's already had drug therapy and we're in a database for a bone marrow transplant."

"And incidentally, if you're up to taking a blood test, we're in the market for a match," Steve informed him.

"I'll mention it to my unit."

"You can skip Stan. He ran by the lab on his lunch break."

Victor's mustache arced in a rueful smile. A kid he didn't know two days ago. If he heard the boy needed a kidney, Stan would be on the operating table right now.

"This leukemia – is that how your first child died?"

Kathy looked down at her hands. "Raymond – little Ray – was stillborn."

"Your husband was in debt when he died?"

"Yes."

"You pay it back?"

"Yes."

"How?"

Kathy's hands clenched so tightly that her fingernails blanched.

"Where did you get the money?"

"You don't have to answer that, Kathy," Delareto said.

"No problem, Counselor. The DA can subpoena her bank statements." He glanced at Kathy, saw her exhale a bit. Relief? "And any safety deposit box in her name."

She tensed.

"Why did your husband kill Christopher Austen?"

"I don't know."

"Let's speak hypothetically, Mrs. Petrone. A man who has managed to stay straight for ten years, a man with a wife, a home, a job, for no conceivable reason this man walks into a crowded emergency room, pulls out a gun, kills a cop, then kills himself. What kind of man would do that?" Victor thought of how his father would berate him for bullying a woman like this.

"Cut it out, Lieutenant, you're losin' your manners," Delareto warned.

"You say he owed money. Enough that if someone said, 'Do this job and I'll tear up your markers', he would consider it?"

Kathy shook her head. "No."

"Why, then? What would Raymond Stites do anything for?"

"I don't know why he did it." Kathy was close to tears. "Don't you think I've thought about it just about every day for the past three years? Why is everyone bringing this up now? *I don't know*!"

"Who else is bringing it up?"

She bit her lip. "Whitney Rocap. She called me. Asked me if I had figured out why Raymond did what he did."

There was no 'why'. Victor plunged his hands in his pockets, started to pace. "Christopher Austen and his wife were clinic patients, correct?"

"Yes."

"So your husband would have seen them when they arrived for appointments?"

"Occasionally."

"Did he ever mention them to you?"

"No, never."

"Did he ever speak in a more general way about Austen, or harbor an animosity for cops, that might him to target someone in a uniform?"

"No."

"Did you ask Miss Rocap why she was asking this, three years after the event?"

"No."

"Did she bring up Daria Chavez at all?"

"No."

Victor flipped open a folder, withdrew a photograph printed from the videotape. It was grainy but caught Daria Chavez full face. He slid it in front of Kathy Petrone. "This is Daria Chavez, correct?"

Kathy studied the picture. "It looks like her."

"It's printed from the surveillance tape they run at the Twenty-Four/Seven. Whitney Rocap and Miss Chavez were seen there Wednesday night. She'd been at the clinic earlier, trying to land an interview. Why would they be hanging around the clinic?"

"I don't know."

"Daria Chavez may have been with Miss Rocap when she died."

"Yes, Mrs. Austen told me you suspected as much."

Steve regarded Victor with grudging admiration. Not a muscle in his face moved, nothing surprised the bastard. "And when did you speak with Mrs. Austen?"

"Yesterday."

"Where?"

"At her house."

"What did you talk about?"

"Whether Whitney Rocap had contacted me. Whether I had spoken to Daria Chavez lately. If I'd heard from Bobby Borch."

"And have you?"

"No."

"And he's not your son's father?"

Delareto moved his chair closer to Kathy's, leaned toward her as though to barricade his client from Victor's ambush.

"No," she repeated, firmly. "Bobby is not Chris's father."

"What did you say?"

"He's not my son's father." She paused. "My son's name is Christopher. Chris."

Victor's gaze met Steve's. He turned away, saw his ghost of a reflection in the grimy window glass. *Chris. Christopher Stites. No, Petrone. Christopher Petrone.*

"A few more questions. A man named Santucci. You remember him?"

"Chuck Santucci? There was a guard by that name."

"What about him?" Delareto asked.

"What about him, Mrs. Petrone?"

Kathy shrugged, her expression baffled. "I took several days off after Raymond died and when I returned to work, they told me he'd left."

"You never spoke to him after your husband's death?"

"I hardly spoke to him at all. Ever."

"You said the last time you saw Miss Chavez was the day your husband died, correct?"

"Yes."

"That afternoon, someone assaulted her in her home. You see any connection between that and what your husband did?"

Kathy shuddered. "You're not saying Raymond attacked her?"

"Certainly, he was capable of it." Victor noticed that her clasped hands were trembling in her lap. "He was capable of murder."

"You don't know anything about Raymond!"

"Well, I'll tell you what I know," Victor resumed, coldly. "I know that Daria Chavez was with Whitney Rocap. I know that the two of them were intercepted at the Twenty-Four/Seven, pursued and run off the road. I know that if the crash hadn't killed Whitney Rocap, she'd be dead all the same and I know that Daria Chavez has disappeared. I'm not sure I want to know what happened to her, but I've worked homicide long enough to have the sort of ideas that make one lose sleep." Victor leaned across the table, bracing himself on his palms. "I know that Robert Borch attacked Mrs. Austen and I know that he's still at large and that he's violent and that you, Mrs. Petrone, you're living on your own with an invalid child. So if you know anything that you're not telling me-"

Kathy Petrone sprang out of her chair so forcefully that it shot against the opposite wall. "Nobody's going to hurt my son!"

For the first time, she faced Victor eye to eye. "He's all I have left in this world. Nobody's going to hurt my son!"

Steve took her by the shoulders and guided her toward the door, opened it. "Hey, Adane, you around."

Adane had been observing from the glass. "Mr. Delareto?"

"Take Mrs. Petrone somewhere she can sit down, get her a glass of water, okay. I'll be right with you," he assured Kathy. "And Detective Adane's a nice person and all, but she tries to ask you anything, don't answer, okay?"

Kathy wiped her eyes, nodded.

Steve slammed the door, turned to Victor. "Why'n'cha just drag your club out and whack her over the head?"

Victor hit the 'Stop' button on the tape recorder. "I left it back at the cave. Why are you acting as her counsel?"

"Why d'you think? Cat asked me, and she asks me something, I don't say 'no', even when it's against my better judgment."

"Were you there when the two of them got together?"

"No. Jesus. Her and Mrs. Raymond Stites. Is there a point where that woman's gonna stop surprising me?"

Victor knew he wasn't talking about Kathy Petrone. "I suspect not."

"You think it's just coincidence that this Chavez woman and Borch and Stites and Kathy all worked for State of the ART?"

"I try not to fall back upon coincidence as an explanation when I can come up with another. How about yourself, Counselor?"

"Look, Cardenas. You were the one needed bone marrow, I'm not sure I'd kick in."

"But?"

Steve nodded toward the glass. "Who's out there, Raab?"

"ADA Keller."

"No kiddin'?" He rapped the glass. "Come join the party."

Mary Grace entered. Steve kissed her cheek. "How you doin', hon?" He had know Mary Grace since childhood.

"I'm fine, Steve. You look well."

"We just a threesome, here?"

Victor nodded.

"Okay, look. I'm here because Cat asked me to hold Kathy's hand if she's questioned and I said okay because Cat asked me to hop the space shuttle, I'd say where do I gotta go to get my ticket punched. But just between us, Cat's been asking questions. And the questions she's askin', I don't like."

"Why?" Victor asked.

Steve ran his hand over his jaw, looked around, as though he were afraid of being overheard. "Little while before he died, Chris came around askin' me some questions about certain issues. The same questions Cat's asking now."

"What sort of questions?"

"Bio-legal issues."

"I had no idea Cat and Chris had been patients at State of the ART, until Mrs. Petrone mentioned it, did you?" Mary Grace asked him.

"Yeah. Chris told me some years back."

"You saw her this morning?" Victor asked.

"Yeah, before lunch time, why?"

Victor began to pace, a shade of concentration fixing his features in an ominous mask. "Did she mention a letter she got from this Daria Chavez?"

Steve shook his head.

"What letter, Victor?" Mary Grace asked.

"According to Daria's father, she had a large manila envelope when she left the house Wednesday night, stamped, addressed to Mrs. Christopher Austen in Ocean City. And the counter clerk at the convenience store said she asked him where there was a mailbox, took something out to mailed it. Holiday weekend, it's conceivable it wasn't delivered until today." Victor's long legs crossed the room in three strides. He turned and continued to pace.

"You think she wrote to Kathy, too, and Kathy's not being up front about it?"

"No. That's not what I was thinking." Victor's expression was mask like. "I wasn't around three years ago, Counselor. Tell me what happened the day Chris Austen died."

"You know what happened."

"Humor me."

"Chris is on his way home- "

"He traveled the same route from the barracks every day?"

"Like clockwork. So, you know, if he was running late or anything, Cat would have some idea where he was. He sees a pregnant woman on the roadside, car's stalled out and she's having contractions, he offers to run her to the ER. He walks her in, he's looking for a wheelchair, Stites is there with his arm in a sling, he pulls out a piece and fires. Chris goes down, Stites fires off a couple more rounds, couple injuries, nothing serious. Some guy waiting to have a cut stitched had a coronary, kids start throwing up, people are screaming it's chaos. Two staff go to take him down, he turns the gun on himself."

"What happened to the pregnant woman?"

Delareto looked at Mary Grace. "She took off. Gunfire, people who can run, run, labor or no labor. The cops kept tabs on maternity the next week or so. They got a description, circulated sketches around the departments, the ERs. She never came forward."

"Did you see any of these sketches?"

"Yeah, years back. Why?"

Victor removed, from his pocket, the three-year-old photo Daria's father had given him. "Maybe the pregnant woman was an impostor. Maybe she fled because she'd been hired to play a role, maybe whoever hired her had intended for her to be killed as well, and when she escaped, someone was sent after her to finish her off. She got lucky again and left the country. I suspect her luck ran out Wednesday night."

Steve and Mary Grace looked at each other, dazed. Steve laid his palm over the photograph as though it pained him to look at it. “I can’t tell Cat,” he said. “I don’t know how to tell Cat.”

I don’t either, Victor thought.

CHAPTER THIRTY-FIVE: Three Years Ago

Cat dipped the last of her eggs into the dye, wiped her stained fingers on one of Chris's old flannel work shirts that she had thrown over her sweater. Jane was kneeling on a chair, the tip of one braid immersed in green dye, carefully applying miniature stickers to a canary yellow egg.

The knock on the door sent a wave of release through Cat's ribcage; only then did she realize the accumulation of tension as the afternoon crept toward evening. "Silly Daddy, forgot his key," she said, and hurried to open the door, yanked it so hard she stumbled, looked up and saw Carlo and Vinnie on the porch.

She knew. She threw her hands over her ears a beat before Carlo said, "Babe, he's gone". She only saw his lips moving. But she heard herself screaming.

Kathleen turned the oven down to warm, picked up the phone for the third time, but she didn't know whom to call. Raymond had left work more than an hour ago. Perhaps he had gotten a holiday bonus, stopped to pick up some little surprise or other. Or perhaps he had taken it to Atlantic City.

"Anything but that," Kathy whispered. "Anything."

Her phone started to ring.

CHAPTER THIRTY-SIX:
Present Day

Idling at a drawbridge opening, Cat entertained Mats by reciting "Get Up And Shut The Door", the fable of a husband and wife waging an escalating campaign of silence. She had avoided Victor for three days, not returned his calls. He hadn't immediately told her that Kathy Petrone was Mrs. Raymond Stites, she reminded herself, but it wasn't as easy to work herself into a state of umbrage as it had been three days ago. Now, she felt only a residual sense that she *ought* to be angry, but even that was waning, and she was feeling like the foolish pair in the fairy tale who allow themselves to be undone by their own obstinacy.

She resolved that as soon as she dropped Mats at preschool, stopped by the office to drop off her articles and pick up her paycheck, stopped at the bank and the dressmaker's, ordered more rolls for the wedding, she would call Victor. But driving along Atlantic Avenue, she noticed 'Gabors Cash For Gold' painted onto the rear of a narrow brick building, an arrow pointed toward the business's Pacific Avenue entrance.

Gabors.

Cat convinced herself that the subject of pawnshops might generate an interesting feature or two.

She stopped at a branch of her bank, deposited her check, withheld about a third of it to pay Miss Yolanda the balance on her gown and Jane's, pay the bakery for the additional rolls (though Jennie would tell her that she was only supposed to order them, not pay for them and would try to reimburse Cat, Cat would refuse, whereupon Jennie would give twenty dollars each to Jane and Mats) and compensate Louie for doing their hair on Saturday, (which Louie would decline because what kind of person would he be if he couldn't do a favor for an old friend from the neighborhood, whereupon Cat would slip the money in his jacket pocket when he was doing Ellice or Jane). Then she parked the car at a meter that jammed when she tried to put in a few quarters and headed around the corner to Gabors.

Cat read the *No one under the age of 18 permitted in store,* taped onto the entrance, pushed open the door, heard a cowbell clang, entered a stifling tunnel flanked by glass display cases. Ceiling fans slowly showered a trickle of grime from above, raised a scent of mold, salt and warmed-over dust.

Cat scanned the cases: jewelry, watches, silver mesh purses, money clips and cigarette cases engraved with initials of the pledger who had no intention of returning to claim them. Enamel hair combs, jeweled stick pins, silver baby spoons and cups, silver picture frames with the date of a birth, graduation, wedding engraved. Larger items had been suspended from the ceiling: gilt-edged mirrors, crystal chandeliers, door panes of intricate leaded glass in carved wooden frames. Cat tried to imagine hauling such stuff in to be pawned.

There was a counter at the back of the store, set behind a sliding Plexiglas panel. Mounted high on the wall behind it was a video camera, aimed at the shop.

"I can help you?" The speaker was stationed behind the sliding glass, a stout, iron-haired woman in a simple cotton wrapper. Her short fingers were busy squeezing toothpaste onto a soft-bristled toothbrush, rubbing a cocktail ring with a large purple stone. The door to the back room was open and Cat glanced past her and saw a man perched in front of a wooden table in the back room. He had unshaven jowls and wore a grimy T-shirt and jeans. He glanced up from his work at a mounted monitor, one hand reaching automatically for the shotgun leaning against his stool, decided that Cat was no threat and went back to his work.

His work was polishing a heavy gold neck chain that he held draped over his palm, its pendant dangling at the back of his hand. The pendant was large enough for Cat to identify the letter 'D'. The sight triggered memory, a slight twinge in Cat's chest. She recalled Borch, bumping and grinding, a pendant swinging against his chest. And somewhere else. She had seen that pendant, or one very much like it, somewhere else.

"You looking for something?" the woman asked.

Cat couldn't place the accent. Russian or Eastern European.

She tried to draw on her conversation with Vinnie. "A, uh, sort of birthday gift. For my boyfriend. I went by Clevingers but it's a little more than I can afford. Maybe something with his initial. A tie pin or something." The dim, stuffy interior was kindling claustrophobia. Cat wanted to get out into the sun.

"You look what we have in the cases."

Had she mentioned the neck chain and pendant in her report to the Linwood detective? She couldn't recall. Perhaps she had assumed it was something Whitney had bought for Jerry Dudek.

"Everything at Clevingers was at least a thousand dollars," Cat stammered, as she pretended to study the items in the case. "I don't think I see anything. And his birthday's this week. His name's- " *D,D,D*! "Danny."

"How much you looking to spend?"

There were people who cruised flea markets, second hand shops for a living. There had to be some sort of tone they assumed. Cat tried to approximate it. "Three..." she saw the woman's eyes narrow. "Fi...six hundred?"

"Lemme see what I got in back."

The woman waddled into the back room and exchanged a few words with the man, returned with the pendant. "He likes neck chains like this?"

"What is it, fourteen carat?"

"Eighteen."

Cat lifted it in her palm. "How much?"

"Seven fifty."

"I'm sorry, I think I can only go six fifty, tops."

The woman turned, said something in what sounded like Russian to the man in the back room. The man looked up; his baleful glance sent a trickle of moisture along her spine.

Trying to catch a whiff of ‘cop’ on her. Cat wondered if the scent of five brothers in law enforcement had rubbed off. He uttered three short syllables and the woman turned back to Cat. “Hokay,” she said.

There was no escape now. Cat took the bank envelope from her purse, her inner voice raging while she forked over seamstress, hairdresser, grocery expenses. *Are you out of your – five, five fifty, six, six twenty five – MIND! – six-fifty.*

“Six fifty.” She slapped it down on the counter.

The woman grabbed the bills through the Plexiglas divider, licked her index finger and recounted them. She glanced greedily at the envelope Cat slipped back into her purse. “See, look how nice this is going to look.” She held the chain up to her breast, the pendant settling over the faded cotton of her wrapper.

You recognize this woman?

That’s where she had seen it! The photographs Victor had shown her. Daria Chavez had been wearing it!

CHAPTER THIRTY-SEVEN: Present Day

Victor found the witness statements from Chris Austen's file on his desk when he arrived at 8 AM, Wednesday morning. Adane had slipped them into clear plastic sheaths, arranged them in a binder. Post-It's were affixed to several, where she thought an additional notation was required for clarification. There were thirty-three of them, not counting the hospital personnel.

... the cop walked in with the pregnant woman, and went over to where there was a wheelchair and the dark-haired man in the brown shirt got up and pulls his piece and he shoots the cop. I got myself under a chair, and then I heard the second shot and people started screaming and running for the exits, but I stayed put. I looked up, the floor's covered with blood and the cop and the guy in the brown uniform are both lying in it. There were a couple people bleeding that I think were hit.

Victor flipped to several diagrams, with X's above a handwritten caption, marking the name and position of witnesses, two miniature outlines of where Chris Austen and Raymond Stites lay dead. He went on to the statements from Kathy Petrone, from the employees of the clinic and Pro Patrol. Taken as a matter of form because there was no perpetrator to hunt down, no trial to prepare. Two memos, stapled together were the last documents. The first recorded a phone call made to the Somers Point Police Department two days after Austen's death. It was from Dr. Miriam Bender. *Doctor Bender phoned to state that the victim, Christopher Austen, called her the day prior to the incident and asked to meet with her today (Monday). She said that Mr. Austen did not state the nature of the proposed meeting.*

The second was a terse notation, was dated the following day. *Report from Atlantic City, Doctor Miriam Bender, suicide. Complete report pending.*

There was a knock on his door jamb. Phil Long leaned in.

"Raab's got the locals and the Fugitive Apps in place, ready to move on the Gabor rentals. And Stan got a call from one of his CIs, the good news is he swears he saw a guy looked to be Borch hangin' around Gabors Saturday night, the bad news is he stayed over Saturday night in detox, so his say-so's not enough to get us a warrant on the pawnshop."

Victor bit back an expletive. "So we can move on the sites in which we only suspect Borch may be hiding, but can't get a warrant on the place of business where he was actually spotted."

"You got it."

Victor rose. "Call AC and tell them I want a unit on the corner of Atlantic and Sovereign in fifteen minutes."

"Lieutenant, you don't have a warrant."

"I don't need one to pawn my wrist watch, do I?"

"You want me to do anything?"

"Don't tell my sister. She gave it to me for my birthday."

༄

Victor and Adane saw the black and white idling on the corner, when they rounded the corner. Adane rolled down her window, the cop at the wheel did the same.

"We got here five minutes ago, nobody's been in or out," he reported. "Cruised past, can't see into the shop from the front, the windows're grubby. They got a back entrance on Atlantic, you can see through the screen door. The son's in the back room polishing some goods at a work table. I saw what looked to be a twelve gauge, brought it up, it's licensed. They live in the apartment above, so there are no tenants to worry about. Whaddayou want us to do?"

Victor turned off the ignition, left his car double parked, got out, surveying the back of the pawn shop from the corner. He walked around to open the car door for Adane, who had conditioned herself to wait until the Lieutenant performed what he considered to be the obligatory procedure, though she did note that the uniforms observed the formality with ill-disguised astonishment.

"This is Detective Adane. Do you have a spare vest?"

The uniform nodded to Jean. "In the trunk."

"Give it to her."

"Lieutenant-"

"Put it on. I'm going in the front, I'm going to have a talk with the proprietor. All I plan to do is ask Mrs. Gaborchevsky a few questions, and I would prefer that her son didn't intervene."

"We got the back, don't worry."

Victor headed down a Sovereign, rounded the corner, drew glances from a the few lethargic pedestrians who could not understand why anyone would wear a suit and tie in eighty-five moisture-laden degrees.

He entered Gabor's, removed his sunshades. It took his eyes a few seconds to adjust to the dimness. He saw the iron-haired proprietress behind the counter, handing something wrapped in dingy tissue paper to a woman who had her back to him.

The shopkeeper looked past her customer. "I can help you?" Victor noted the shifty glance that did not match the perfunctory smile, the furtive closing of the door behind her. She'd made him.

Cat tucked the wrapped neck chain in her purse and turned. She looked at him, shouldered her purse, and made her way along the narrow aisle to the door.

Victor edged aside to let her pass, didn't look at her, waited until he heard the door's cowbell clang. He approached the counter, laid a copy of Borch's most recent mug shot down, laid his shield beside it.

The woman's lips coiled, indecisively. "He is cousin."

"I know that. I know you gave him the use of a house in Somers Point, I know he's wanted, I know he's missing. If you're concealing Mr. Borch, the

DA will talk to the state district attorney about your failure to comply with the state pawnbroking regulations and request confiscation of all of those properties. Including this one."

"He's not here."

"But he was here Saturday." He said it with assurance, though all he had was the word of Stan's none-too-reliable CI.

She swallowed. "He asks for money. We are busy Saturday, I give him money and he goes."

"How much?"

"Few hundred dollars. Four."

"In exchange for what?"

"He is cousin."

In exchange for what?" Victor repeated, patiently.

The woman shrugged. "He has piece of jewelry he doesn't want. My son and I do flea markets, we buy and sell."

"What sort of jewelry?"

"Gold chain, with pendant. Pendant in shape of letter 'D'."

"So you didn't put this item in the book?"

"He doesn't want to pawn it, he wants to sell."

"Where is it now?"

"I sell it."

"To whom?"

She pointed at the door. "That woman. She says she is looking for birthday gift for boyfriend."

The door to the back room opened. A hefty man walked out, a shotgun at his side, one finger coiled around the trigger.

Victor's gaze was steady, unblinking. "Tell your son to lay his weapon aside."

"Gun is registered," she told Victor.

The back door was old, the hinges rusted, the screens buckling. The three people in the shop never heard it creak.

"I don't care if it's registered to vote," Victor replied, calmly. "If he doesn't lay it down, I'll instruct my detective, who has her weapon trained on his head, to fire."

The woman looked over her shoulder, her eyes widening in astonishment. She gestured for the man to lay aside his weapon. He leaned the gun against the door jamb took a step to his left; Adane was three feet behind him, her weapon drawn. She withdrew one hand from her grip, grabbed the weapon by the stock and slid it to the floor, kicking it behind her.

"Officer?"

The uniform had his weapon drawn as well. "You got him?"

"Yes." Adane responded.

Adane kept her weapon leveled at the man's head while the officers cuffed him, recited Miranda.

"What about her?" one of them asked Victor.

Victor glanced at the woman, saw her mouth turn up in a smug little crescent, as though certain she was going to have the last laugh. "Get her out of here." He walked to the front of the shop, reversed the sign in her window from 'Open' to 'Closed'. "You can holster your weapon, Adane."

She lowered her weapon. "I can take care of this if you would like to follow up on a lead, Lieutenant." She discreetly didn't mention that the lead in question was the woman who had bought the neck chain.

"Are you okay?"

"I've never drawn my weapon before," she said.

CHAPTER THIRTY-EIGHT: Present Day

Cat pulled up to the clinic's security gate and Tony leaned down, flashed his 'I'm-ripe-for-prime time' smile. She dug out the card April Steinmetz, the *CopWatch* line producer had given her, handed it to him. "I found this. If you get any ideas for programming, you may want to send a proposal to her, she's producing the *Auletta* series."

"Wow! Thanks." He looked at it as if Cat had handed him a hundred dollar bill.

"So, I heard on the news something about your co-worker, Bobby, the police want him for questioning or something?"

"Yeah. I told 'em, I don't know where he is, the jerk."

"Told the police?"

"Yeah, they were out here yesterday, some county badge."

"Major Crimes?" Cat asked.

"Yeah. You can park it anywhere."

Cat parked in the Visitor's area. She realized that she was shaking as she approached the clinic's door, chided her 'imagination resolved on alarm'. Victor was right. Jane Austen was so pithy.

The beauty at the desk, reciting instructions with self-assured competence, looked both foreign and familiar. It took the voice, the efficient, "Put one copy on my desk and one on Paul's, then call the names to confirm, remind them that the orientation starts promptly at seven. And don't forget that Randy has to be out of here by five tomorrow for a business dinner" for her to realize that this was 'Little' Eve Bellamy.

The woman looked up and smiled with genuine pleasure. "Cat Austen?" Eve rose and held out her arms and gave Cat a brief hug. "I would ask how you're doing, but I read every single *CopWatch* piece. What fun that must have been!"

The two syllables, *CopWatch*, snagged the attention of the women glancing over magazines, the wide-eyed office temp, the scrub-suited technician emerging from the laboratory wing.

Cat returned the smile a little sheepishly, but Eve was sympathetic. She drew Cat into the office manager's cubicle that had a broad Plexiglas view of the reception area. "You didn't have to make the trip, I would have dropped your papers in the mail when I got them rounded up. Actually," she added, with a glance at the temp on the other side of the glass, "-I haven't had time to pull all of your paperwork, we're shorthanded, in the process of replacing the office manager."

Eve punched a button on the console. Cat's glance traveled to the left hand. The ring on her third finger was a full two carats. "Randy, come out here, see who's here." She looked up at Cat. "He'd kill me if I let you out of here without saying hello."

"I wouldn't want to interrupt him if he's with a patient."

"No, Randy's just finished his procedures for the day."

"When's the wedding?"

Eve smiled. "Friday."

"*This* Friday?"

Eve nodded. "Very small civil ceremony. Just us and the witnesses, because Randy's been married before, and I don't have any family to make a fuss."

Randall Hoffman swung into the doorway. "Cat Austen." His mouth formed the smile seconds before the eyes warmed up and Cat sensed that he wasn't really happy to see her. He took both of her hands, kissed her cheek. Cat felt awkward; Hoffman had always been so formal, never offered more than a handshake. "Come, let's go up to my office and chat, shall we?"

"I don't mean to interrupt you if you're busy."

"Go get caught up," Eve urged. "It'll give me a little time to pull your records."

Hoffman took her arm as they mounted the stairs. "A detective with the county was here. He told us that one of the Pro Patrol staff molested you." He gestured toward a chair. "You weren't seriously hurt, I hope?"

Cat sat. "No, just a scare."

Hoffman's office hadn't changed. The three-foot high glass front bookshelves still lined the wall. The room ran the width of the second floor, with windows overlooking the open fields on both sides, the sheer curtains closed to filter the sunlight. The dark blue upholstered chairs, the watercolors and framed diplomas and commendations covered nearly all of the dark, striped wallpaper. The only addition that Cat could see was that the small framed picture of Miriam Bender, once prominently displayed on his desk, was now tucked into a corner of one of the bookshelves.

"Well, I trust the police to pick him up." He leaned forward, propping his elbows on the desk. "You're not arranging an appointment, are you? Some news I should know about?"

Cat felt herself blush, shook her head. "Actually, I'm here to pick up a copy of my initial contract. Jane – my daughter – was ten last month. And a copy of the letter I should have received regarding the- " she swallowed. "Termination."

"'Should have received'? I believe I recall signing it, and Kathy was very conscientious about sending them out."

"Eve said she would round up a copy for me. But while I'm here, I was wondering if you'd be available for an interview sometime? My editor's been talking about a piece on IVF."

The crow's feet dug deep as Hoffman made an effort to keep the smile in place. "Of course. But I'm afraid we're not half as lively as *CopWatch.* What sort of article was he talking about?"

"Something that hasn't been covered a half dozen times. I've been going over the notes that Whitney Rocap sent me just before-" Cat hoped that the pause, the shake of her head didn't convey the hypocrisy she felt in feigning sorrow over the death of a woman who had hated her, and for whom she felt nothing.

"I didn't realize, when she proposed some feature to Eve that the two of you had collaborated."

"Oh, yes. I've known her for months." She couldn't decide whether she was proud or ashamed of becoming such a glib liar.

"Awful, what happened to her. Though I suppose there is some comfort to be taken."

"Comfort?"

"I understand her fiancé was the radio personality who was shot last fall. At least they're together now."

"That's not always a comfort for the people left behind."

"True. I know there were times when I felt lost without Miriam. Just as I'm sure you must have felt lost without Christopher."

"I have children. That's always a reason to keep going. I'm sure you feel the same, I understand you have children yourself."

Hoffman waved his hand, as if swatting mosquitoes. "They're grown."

Cat felt her throat go dry. This was not the empathetic Randall Hoffman who had given her Jane and Mats. Or perhaps it was, perhaps in her desperation, she had overlooked the cold-blooded vanity.

There was a light tap on the door and Eve Bellamy entered, handed a paper to Cat. "Here's the copy of your original agreement, and the termination notice. It's dated July first, last year. If you're absolutely certain you never received it, I'll have to go back and confirm that the other terminations issued around that time made it through the mail."

"Do you file the return receipt cards and the certified mail slips?"

"In the miscellaneous file. Would you like me to check?"

Cat checked her watch. "No, I've got to run. My brother's getting married on Saturday and my place is like Grand Central. Next week will be soon enough."

Hoffman rose. "I'll walk you down."

Cat wondered if he wanted to make sure she didn't hang around, try to chat up the patients in the waiting area.

A couple approached the reception desk, holding hands. Cat saw the last-chance desperation behind their counterfeit smiles.

I wouldn't have Jane and Mats if it weren't for Doctor Hoffman.

Cat felt a hand grip her elbow, heard Hoffman's genial voice in her ear. "Be careful driving back to Ocean City. This time of year, these back roads are murder."

CHAPTER THIRTY-NINE: Present Day

"No sign of Borch, Lieutenant, not in any of the properties the Gabors own, unless we missed one." Stan hit a bad cell in western Atlantic County. "My CI pan out?"

"He was there Saturday. That's five days ago."

"You talk to Raab?"

"Not today, why?"

"He said he got a report that a guy who fits Borch's description was spotted hanging around Cat's neighborhood yesterday. Her neighbors spotted him, the Nixon gals?"

Victor felt a ripple of annoyance. "If it happened yesterday, why wasn't this reported to us yesterday?"

"Lieutenant, you know how it gets in season."

"Lean on the Gabors."

"Uh...that's the other thing. They sort of walked."

What! The shout was only an echo in his head. When he uttered, "What?" his voice was level, cold. "The son approached an officer with a loaded weapon."

"Kenny Levine drew Gabor, jammed Raab up on Miranda."

"Levine can't claim Gabor wasn't read his rights, Adane and I both heard it."

"Yeah, but did you hear it in Russian?"

"I beg your pardon?"

"The son say anything to you?"

"No. Why?"

"What I heard is AC brings in the Gabor guy and start questioning him and he's giving them the silent treatment. So they call the PD's and Kenny draws the case, comes over, has a heart to heart with the guy, comes out and tells us that Tibor Gabor, I am not kidding about the name, incidentally, only understands minimal English, says he's gonna need a Russian translator and asks, by the way, if we Mirandized him in the mother tongue."

Victor muttered a curse in Spanish.

"Wait, it gets better. So they start calling around for a translator, try all the seasonal and fast food places, a lotta Russian kids work those, but these kids work eighteen hours a day, three, four jobs, they can't find one will take time off. So Kenny remembers that out past Vineland, you got the Sisters of the Holy Name convent and Mother Marya Polina is from the Ukraine. So we send out a car and escort the Reverend Mother to the interview room, eighty-five years old and her hearing's on the fritz. So they tell her what to ask him, and tell them what he says, right? Tibor starts goin' off on them and Mother Marya's translating, trying to clean it up some, but Kenny tells her she's gotta translate it verbatim or it doesn't count. So, she says they should all pray on it.

Raab says don't tell his rabbi he hadda ask Jesus for guidance, rabbi might take a dim view. Anyway, it gets the celestial okay, but they hit a snag on some of your scatology and whatnot, because the Reverend Mum can't bring herself to say 'em out loud, but she agrees to write 'em down. An' that takes a little back and forth because some of the words, she's not sure how to spell, never having come across them in the religious life, so to speak. Once we get the translation, disregard the four-, ten-, and twelve-letter words, the nut is that Tibor's in the back room cleaning up and he hears his mother arguing with someone and he picks up the shotgun, which is licensed, and goes out because there's been a couple smash and grabs down Pacific and his poor mom's gettin' up in years, what kinda son would he be if he can't defend his dear old mother."

"I ordered him to drop it, he didn't."

"In *English*," Rice reminded him.

"*Dios me salve*."

"So on that, he walks and that's the bad news. The good news is that if you can get your hands on that pendant and Chavez can authenticate it, Raab can re-arrest on receiving stolen merch, conspiracy to commit, accessory after the fact."

"I'll call Mrs. Austen."

"I been calling, there's no answer. She hasn't been picking up for the past couple hours."

Victor frowned. It had been more than two hours since they had crossed paths at Gabors. Where could she be?

ꕥ

When Cat pulled up to Kathy Petrone's house, she saw Steve's sedan parked in the driveway.

It was Steve who answered her knock. "I stopped by to go over a few things with Kathy. It's easier than having her come to the office. Because of her son. And she's been a little wary of answering her door, what with that creep Borch still at large. You okay?"

Cat nodded, puzzled. "Why?"

"Just a question. What've you been up to?"

"Picking up my paycheck. Errands. Is something wrong?"

Steve shook his head vaguely and waved her through the small living room. The inexpensive pine furniture contrasted with a costly grandfather clock that looked like an antique. A large stuffed rabbit was tucked into the corner of a chair and a small stack of Golden Books lay under one end table.

Kathy Petrone was standing at the kitchen table. Places had been set, with partially eaten sandwiches, tumblers of lemonade. Between them was a high chair, where a toddler with a mop of unruly hair and large brown eyes wriggled impatiently.

The little boy looked up. His complexion was milky pale, faint blue tinting the flesh under the eyes. Except for the pallor, he didn't resemble his mother. "'at oo name?"

Kathy lifted him out of the chair. "Say 'Mrs. Austen'," she prompted, tickling his chin.

He burrowed his head in his mother's neck, shyly, his thumb creeping toward his mouth.

"What's his name?" Cat asked.

Kathy stroked his hair. "His name is Christopher," she said, quietly. "Chris." She looked up at Cat. "I'm sorry."

"It's a good name," Cat said, flatly.

Steve held out a chair. "Why don't you sit down?"

"Can I get you some lemonade?" Kathy asked.

Cat dropped into a chair and shook her head. She dug into her purse and took out the copy of the letter and slid it across the table to Kathy. "Do you remember mailing this out to me?"

Kathy picked it up. The paper began to tremble in her hand. She put it down. "I didn't type correspondence, Daria did. She'd give us the originals and a disk with about thirty to forty typed pages, and Randy would sign what needed to be signed. I just made out the certified mail receipts and put them in the outgoing mail."

"So you don't remember mailing this one, specifically?"

"There was so much correspondence."

"Did you routinely file copies?"

Kathy shook her head. "The clinic had started to get away from paper because of space limitations. We'd keep the disks and print out additional copies from that if we needed to."

"The text on a disk can be altered to change information, dates. You could even add a bogus letter to the disk, letters that hadn't been transcribed, that never went out."

"Cat, what's going on?" Steve asked.

"I'm saying I have the copy of a letter here that I honestly don't remember receiving. Now, maybe I've just been preoccupied and scrapped it. Or maybe it got lost in the mail. Or maybe it was never typed up, or never sent out and when I asked for my file, someone at the clinic produced one."

Kathy lurched to her feet. "Excuse me a minute. I have to see if I can put him down for a nap."

"You need a hand?" Steve asked.

Kathy shook her head, carried the boy off to his bedroom. Cat and Steve heard her murmuring something to the child.

"You saying *Kathy* made the mistake?" Steve kept his voice down. "That she never mailed this notice to you, maybe had a hand in falsifying a document?"

Cat shrugged, helplessly. "I don't know what I'm saying, but I think she knows more than she's telling."

"Maybe so," Steve conceded. "But I'm not sure it's gonna help if you try to press the point right now, what with everything she's got on her plate."

"I'm not going to wait around for people to decide whether or not they're going to tell me anything."

"I don't like the sound of that."

"I'm not going to pressure Kathy, not when she's got her boy to think about. But I've got another lead I'm going to follow up on."

"What lead?"

"Remember that couple Chris said died in a car crash? Their name was Asher. I found out that Mrs. Asher's sister lives in Ventnor. I'm going to find out if Chris talked to her."

"You tell this to the lieutenant?"

"I haven't talked to Victor for days."

"He didn't tell you about...well, about how the interview with Kathy went?"

Cat shook her head. "Did something come out that I'm supposed to know about?"

"Kathy's my client now," Steve replied, evasively. "If there's something that you need to know, I think at this point it has to come from the lieutenant."

"*Steve*!"

"Look, Cat. I'm in a really awkward spot here."

"Well, I would trade my spot for *awkward* any day!"

Steve sighed, and reached across the table to pat her hand. "Okay, look. The police heard about a letter that may have been sent to you. You get anything odd in the mail lately?"

"There was no mail Monday because of the holiday. What sort of letter are the police talking about?"

"What letter?" The question came from Kathy, who stood on the threshold, her face paper white?

"Kathy, you okay?" Steve rose from his chair.

Kathy nodded, sank into a chair.

"I was about to tell Cat. When Daria Chavez went out Wednesday night, she had an envelope addressed to her. The store clerk saw her mail it."

"Oh. Oh."

Cat studied Kathy's expression. "You look almost relieved," she said. "You didn't get a letter from Daria, did you? You said you hadn't heard from her since she disappeared."

"I didn't!"

"Then why does the mention of a letter upset you so much?" Cat asked, quietly.

Unaccountably, Kathy started to sob, the convulsions wracking her thin frame, her hands pressed to her mouth to keep from crying aloud, waking her child.

Steve nudged his chair next to hers. "Kathy, look. I already figured out that you're holding back. I can't make you trust the two of us, but how long can you go on without trusting anyone?"

"I'll be in trouble. Because I didn't bring it up in the interview yesterday."

"Bring what up?"

The grandfather clock began to chime. "Raymond's letter."

Steve's head shot up. "What letter?"

"It came in the mail two days after he died."

"Where is it now, Kathy?"

"I kept it." Her tone was one of mild surprise, at the implication that she would have discarded anything that Raymond had left her.

"Can I see it?"

Kathy got up and went into her bedroom, returned with a faded envelope, addressed to her, slit at the top. Steve took out the sheet of folded paper, opened it, ran his eyes over it.

"You can read it out loud," Kathy said.

Steve glanced at Cat, back at the letter. "'Dear Kathy. I love you. I wish that counted for something. I made a list of what I owe. The money will be in our deposit box, but maybe you better move it to a new one. People think that once you been inside, and had all your time taken over, it doesn't mean anything to you anymore, but it does. I'd give anything if I had more than I got, but at least I can use what I got to leave you something to start over on. Start over, Kathy.' My God," Steve exhaled. "What money are we talking about here, Kathy?"

"The sixty thousand dollars."

"Sixty- " Steve choked. "Stites left you sixty grand? Where is it now?"

"It's almost gone. Not all of Chris's bills were covered on my plan, and the bone marrow transplant will take up the rest of it, and whatever I can make by selling the house."

"Why didn't you give it to the police?"

"I don't know. I was so confused. I wanted to confide in someone, but my mother had been so upset by what Raymond had done that I didn't want to add to her worry. And then Miriam died, so I couldn't burden Randy any more than I had."

"Did you tell anyone?"

Kathy nodded. "Eve had come to me and asked if I could give them a few hours a day, because things got so chaotic after Miriam's suicide. She was so ashamed of having to ask and I felt so bad for her. We started talking and I just found myself confiding in her."

"What did she tell you to do?"

"All she said was that when you didn't know what to do, it was best to do nothing, until you can think more clearly. That if I felt I couldn't keep the money, I could always give it to charity, which would be better than having it sit in a police evidence room. So I kept it. And then...I needed it for Chris."

"Okay, Kathy, look," Steve said. "I'm gonna put in a call to Kurt Raab and we're gonna go over this with him."

"No..." Kathy started to sob again. "He'll take my baby away from me. If it was just the money, but there's...I can't."

"Kathy," Steve's tone was firm, reassuring. "You think I'm gonna let them take Chris away from you? There's no way that's gonna happen. You have to trust me. You want to come clean don't you? So you can do what your husband said? Start over?"

Cat gasped, snatched the letter from Steve's hand, ran her eyes over it, murmuring, "'People think that once you been inside, and had all your time taken over, it doesn't mean anything to you anymore, but it does. *I'd give anything if I had more than I got.*' Do you know what he meant by that?"

"I thought he just meant how you lose a lot of your life when you're in prison."

Cat shook her head. "Not your *life*. 'Had all your *time* taken over'. 'I'd give anything if I had more than I got'. More *time*. He thought he didn't have any time left."

"Cat, what are you talking about?" Steve demanded.

"What if Raymond Stites somehow got the idea he didn't have long to live. And someone said to him, you're dying, but you can leave with sixty grand if you do this one thing."

"Where the hell would Stites get the idea he was dying? Excuse my language, ladies."

"He had a physical a few weeks before he died. Scans, chemistry profiles, blood work."

"Raymond didn't have a physical. He would have told me."

"Maybe he didn't want to worry you. Or maybe he got bad news and didn't know how to break it to you."

Kathy shook her head. "Even if Raymond did keep something like that from me, there was an autopsy. It didn't mention anything other than the - the obvious cause of death."

"I didn't say he *was* terminal. In fact, the tests were negative. I said what if he'd been *told* that he was."

"If he hadn't passed Pro Patrol's physical, they wouldn't have allowed him to continue working," Kathy protested.

"I didn't say Pro Patrol ordered them. In fact, they were ordered by Randall Hoffman."

"Randy! Why would he do that?"

"Maybe as a favor. Maybe your husband mentioned his insomnia, his headaches and Doctor Hoffman said, 'let's order some tests'."

"But Hoffman would know the tests came back negative," Steve objected.

"That's right," Cat agreed. "I guess I didn't think of that." She had, though. And she had also thought that Hoffman would have sixty thousand dollars in disposable cash.

CHAPTER FORTY:
Present Day

Incoming thunderclouds were moving in from the west, only a few faint rays of sun sifted though the purpling sky. Before Victor hit the Ninth Street Bridge, fat raindrops splotched his windshield. He turned onto Asbury Avenue, Ocean City's commercial district. Shopkeepers, who had put out sidewalk merchandise, were scrutinizing the sky, dismantling their open air displays. Victor saw a familiar figure, in a slim dark skirt and white blouse, help a silver-haired man lift a long table of books, edge it through the doorway. Ellice was laughing, her expression relaxed, her eyes dancing, unlike the tense, preoccupied look she had worn for the past week.

He turned onto Morningside and saw Cat's Maxima ease into her driveway just as the downpour hit. He pulled up in back of her, reached for an umbrella under his seat and hurried over to her car. He opened the driver's door, leaned down and handed her the umbrella. "You get Jane, I'll bring Mats," he said.

He removed his jacket and draped it over the Mats's head, lifted him and carried him to the porch.

Cat worked the key in the lock, shouldered the door open. She propped the umbrella in the corner of the foyer. "Jane, get Mats a glass of milk. And you can each have three Oreos."

"Ashley Kreisberg says they have trans fatty *acids*."

"Then just have two." Cat dropped onto the arm of the chair and hit the 'Play' button to listen to her phone messages.

Victor set Mats down and draped his rain-spattered jacket over a dining room chair. He saw the corner of a fat manila envelope poking from the mound of mail and packages on the table. He nudged it to the surface, saw Cat's name and address printed in large letters, black marker. He looked at Cat, who was concentrating on the answering machine.

Jennie: "I hope you didn't pay for those rolls. Can you bring two, three pounds of butter to the church tomorrow?"

Ritchie: "I heard the cops raided a couple dozen rentals in Atlantic County, what's up with that?"

Ellice: "Don't wait anything for me, I'm running so late, I'm into tomorrow."

Two hang-ups.

The phone rang and Cat reached for the receiver. It was Freddy. "Cat, Ellice there?"

"No, she left a message, she's running late."

"Jeez, I know the drill, how you're not supposed to see the bride before the wedding, but I always thought that meant *right* before the wedding, not the whole week before the wedding."

"You've never been married, Freddy. This is normal."

"Yeah, but I been engaged, and left standing. Look, you see Victor, tell him we're going over to Bud 'N' Lou's for a couple drinks after the rehearsal dinner, he's invited to come along."

"Nobody's popping out of a cake or anything, are they?"

"You nuts? Mom'd Jersey smack me up good, I went in for anything like that. Whaddayou think of this? 'Friends, Romans, Countrymen, lend me your steers.' For the scrapple thing'."

"I come to curry scrapple not to braise it?"

"I'm gonna go write that down. Tell Ellice to call me when she gets in, okay?"

Cat hung up, laid her head against the back of the chair. "You're invited out for drinks with the guys on Friday night after the rehearsal dinner."

Victor walked into the living room, sat on the ottoman facing her, took her hands.

"'Promise you won't keep things from me'. What, was that too vague? If I thought I could plea down to community service or something, I'd serious consider assault and battery on a police officer."

"Mrs. Austen. Don't tease me."

Cat raised an eyebrow. "I'm not teasing, Victor, I'm just too tired to be fighting mad right this minute." Cat drew her purse onto her lap. Victor noticed that her movements were sluggish with fatigue. She took out the necklace wrapped in dingy tissue paper. "You can consider it a birthday present."

Victor drew a pen out of his pocket, pushed the folds of paper aside, lifted the item by the chain. He rotated the links, thoughtfully. They looked cold, their luster gone. As with any object of greed, only the heat of avarice gave it a glow. He allowed the links to drop back into the paper. "Not my style."

"No, I hardly think you and Robert Borch have the same taste. Tell Kurt Raab that this hunk of evidence cost me six hundred fifty dollars."

"I beg your pardon? You saw this in Borch's possession?"

"Last Friday. He was wearing it, I thought it belonged to him." Cat pushed herself off the chair. "I have to get dinner."

She left Victor dialing the phone and went into the kitchen to decide what she could throw together for dinner. Jane and Mats were sitting at the kitchen booth, Jane relating her school day while she showed Mats how to precisely pry an Oreo apart so as to leave a flawless disk of white cream. "And Jason Morton left a note in the boys' room that there was a bomb in the school, except he's dyslexic and he can't spell so he writes 'dom' d-o-m, like Uncle Dom? There's a *dom* in the school. But they made us have a fire drill anyway."

Cat began studying the contents of her cupboards. "That's not anything that happens on a regular basis, I hope."

"Uncle Carlo told Aunt Annie that real bombers don't leave notes, people only do that when they're trying to ha*rass* you."

Mats twisted open an Oreo. “What’s harass mean?”

“Tease,” Cat replied. “Like when some big sisters tell their little brothers that being the ring bearer means they have to wear a bear suit in front of everybody.”

Jane rolled her eyes at the ignorant parent who didn’t understand that if five-year-olds who were going to kindergarten in the coming fall couldn’t figure out when they were being teased, they were just about *doomed.*

“Cat you look beat.” Victor stood in the archway. “Why don’t you go lie down, I’ll fix something to eat.”

Cat surrendered the kitchen without protest. She laid on the couch and pulled an Afghan down over her, stuffed a cushion under her head. The quiet chatter of Victor and the kids merged with the steady patter of the rain, and slowly evaporated. She drifted into a dreamy scenario, saw Chris walking down the porch steps, a few threads of sunlight penetrating the overcast sky, turning his pale brown hair golden. She was trying to tell him something, but he only smiled, the vague smile of someone who couldn’t hear her, and she tried to cry out louder, but he only smiled, and said something she couldn’t hear. She tried to walk down the porch steps, but she was carrying Mats, he was weighing her down, though she couldn’t understand why he was so heavy, he was only two years old. The weight of him anchored her to the top of the porch and Cat heard herself calling Chris’s name, crying it, screaming it, but Chris just waved his hand, held up his palm and the single ray of sun hit the gold band on his finger, the glare rebounded and Cat closed her eyes and when she opened them, he was gone, and she was standing alone on the porch steps with Mats clinging to her neck and Jane clutching at the folds of her bathrobe.

“Mommy?”

Cat opened her eyes. She saw Mats standing over her, his eyes wide and frightened, heard the sound of rain merging with the rhythm of the surf, gulls calling to each other. She felt the slick sweat gluing the bodice of her sundress to her skin.

“Mommy, what’s the matter?”

“Mommy just had a bad dream,” Victor assured the boy. “Sometimes big people get bad dreams.”

“Like kids do?” Mats inquired.

Cat noticed that he sidled close to Victor. Victor put his arm around the boy.

“Yes.”

“Was it monsters?”

Cat tried to shake off the dream-locked leadenness. “Yes, it was just a silly monster.”

“Monsters are just pretend,” he reminded her.

“I know.” They weren’t though. They just came disguised, in human form.

"Why don't you get a book, and I'll read to you until dinner's ready?" Cat sat up, pushed her hair away from her face. "What about Peter Rabbit, you like that."

"Jane says in Peter Rabbit, the sister rabbits were good, but Peter was bad."

"How about Hansel and Gretel?"

"She says Gretel was smarter."

"What does Jane say about Pokey Little Puppy?"

"You're asposed to share desserts with your famb'ly."

This was not an insurmountable objection, so Cat read until dinner was ready. By the meal's end, the thunder had rolled off and the rain had receded to a shower of light mist.

Cat pushed Mats' new bike out of the shed and launched him on a wobbling course down the sidewalk. Jane spied a trio of girls chalking a hopscotch grid on the wet sidewalk, stared conspicuously until she was invited to join in the game.

Afterward, they sat on the floor of the den, played Scrabble in teams, Cat and Mats against Jane and Victor. Then while Jane took her shower in Cat's bathroom, Cat bathed Mats and got him into bed with two short fables that she had devised, starring a heroic five-year-old named "Mats". The most recent, "Mats Goes to School", related how Mats triumphed over his apprehension and realized that kindergarten was nothing to be afraid of, after all.

Cat left a covered plate for Ellice and then sat in the living room with Victor.

Victor saw her expression relax from the troubled tenseness brought on by her dream, to a somewhat weary tranquility. He was reluctant to disturb it by mentioning the envelope from Daria Chavez, which had obviously been overlooked in the accumulation of mail piled on the dining room table.

"What was it you've been doing today that's got you so worn out, Cat?" Victor asked at last. "Wedding preparations?"

She shook her head. "No. I had to run out to the clinic, and then I stopped by Kathy Petrone's."

"What for?"

"Just...something I needed to ask her, about some paperwork she might have remembered from when I was a clinic patient. And then, one discussion led to another and she showed us something pretty startling."

"Us?"

"Steve was over there."

"What did she show you?"

"Stites wrote her a letter, probably mailed it right before..." She bit her lip. "It arrived a few days after he died. There was money enclosed in it. Sixty thousand dollars."

Victor scowled, reflectively. "It seems that Mrs. Petrone didn't know her husband as well as she thought she did. She insisted he would never have murdered someone for money."

"I'm not sure he did. Not just for the money, anyway."

"Come again?"

She shifted to look at him. "Cherry – Ritchie's secretary? She found out that Raymond Stites had a complete physical shortly before he died. Much more extensive than his routine annual. Kathy said that her husband had been suffering from worry, headaches and insomnia, but these tests were a lot more extensive. The sort you do when you suspect something is really wrong."

"I saw Stites's autopsy report. There was no underlying pathology, he died of a self-inflicted gunshot wound."

"That's what Kathy said. But think about it, Victor. Maybe we're posing the question the wrong way. The question had been 'why would Stites kill Chris and himself?' Answer: because he's crazy. And he wasn't. But if you ask, why would Stites kill *himself* and Chris, too? He committed suicide because he was convinced he was going to die anyway, and whoever knew that, and wanted Chris dead, offered Stites enough money to leave his wife comfortably off after he was gone."

Victor's memory called up a cat that had adopted them, a mottled calico quilt of a creature who grew fat and lame, and one day its familiar mew hit a shrill, minor key. Victor's father had taken the creature away in his car and come back without it, then picked up the little plastic feeding dishes, washed them and put them away.

You killed it! You killed it! I hate you! Remy had screamed at him, ran to her room and slammed the door.

Papi. Remy doesn't hate you, Victor had told his father.

Creatures like that can't put themselves out of their own misery. It would hurt your sister worse to watch it die slow.

Victor hadn't understood his father's words, not for years. Not until he looked at Marisol's pleading eyes as she lay dying, with no voice left, no movement, nothing but eyes that begged, *I want you to help me end it*. There were still times when he wondered if she had ever forgiven him for condemning her to live those last immobile, undignified weeks.

"What's the matter, Victor?"

"Nothing."

Cat looked at him for a minute. She remembered what his CI had called him, *El Desconocido*. The unknown. Yet, he had always been frank with her, told her anything about himself she had wanted to know. It was she who had kept secrets.

"Who ordered these tests?"

"Cherry said it was Randall Hoffman."

"Not Mrs. Hoffman? Miriam Bender?"

"That's not what Cherry told me. Why?"

"Well, I imagine either one could have signed an order in the other's name and no one would be the wiser. And either one could have come up with sixty thousand, certainly."

Cat twisted the rings on her right hand, absently. "That still doesn't answer one question. How could Chris be..." She pressed her eyes shut until the well of tears subsided. "How could he be set up? It was pure chance that he wound up in the ER that afternoon."

Victor took her hands in his and kissed them, then rose and went into the dining room. He picked the fat brown envelope from among the litter of envelopes and gifts covering the table and brought it back to her, sat beside her once more.

"What's this?" Cat looked at her name printed in black.

"Wednesday night, Daria Chavez's father saw her carry this out of the house when she drove off with Whitney Rocap. The clerk at the Twenty-Four/Seven saw her mail it. She wanted you to have it and probably realized you weren't going to show up."

"Steve said there was talk of a letter." Cat probed the envelope. "It feels like papers." She tore at the top of the envelope, pulled out a white sheet of paper wrapped around a wad of money. She began counting the bills, her fingers shaking. "Victor, there's ten thousand dollars here! And a note... 'Dear Mrs. Austen,'" she read. "'I'm sorry. I never knew until it was too late. I never spent any of the money. Daria Chavez.' Never knew what?"

"Listen carefully, love. You have a shooter who can be convinced to kill Chris and then kill himself. But where? It would be difficult to lure a seasoned cop to an isolated place where there would be no witnesses, so you do the next best thing. You lure him to a chaotic place, where the witness testimony is sure to be unreliable. An overburdened emergency room on a holiday weekend."

Victor pulled out a chair and sat, facing her, laid a hand over hers. "Cat, when I showed you the picture of Chavez, that she looked a little familiar."

She nodded. "Maybe I got a glimpse of her at Doctor Hoffman's office..."

"Or saw an artist's sketch. Done after Chris was killed."

Cat looked up from the wad of bills in her hand, her dark eyes dazed. "That woman was pregnant," she whispered.

"Maybe. Or maybe she appeared so in order to get Chris to take pity on her."

Cat felt her stomach reel. *No, no, no, no!* She lurched to her feet and dashed up the stairs, into her room, sagged against her bedroom door, panting. *No!* She staggered across the room, around her workstation and jerked open the French windows and stumbled onto the deck, a lump in her clenched fist, looked down at the wad of bills. *I'm sorry. I never spent any of the money.*

She stepped out onto the deck, into the falling rain, drew her arm back and flung the cash into the night.

Victor saw, through the dining room window, the bills weaving through the rain, falling like tears.

CHAPTER FORTY-ONE: Three Years Ago

Cat became a walking shadow with her face. It paced the house in the pre-dawn dark, tucking the Easter eggs in corners, behind furniture. It poured coffee for Trina Morosco who came to make the arrangements, sobbing as though it were she who had been widowed, when she carried off one of Chris's uniforms, just in case she was able to make Chris whole enough to have an open casket. It explained to Jane and Mats that Daddy was in heaven, but they were going to be all right, and Jane was to understand that if Mats didn't comprehend what was going on, Jane was to help look after him because he was only a baby. It donned a black dress and covered its face with a veil and walked down the porch steps to the waiting car.

Whenever it closed its eyes, Chris appeared, bounding down the porch steps, waving. So it did not close its eyes, not for days.

At Morosco's Funeral Home, it faltered as it approached the parlor, stumbled into another black-garbed woman whose 'Excuse me," had the tenor of grief. It didn't look up. It didn't recognize the 'Kathy' who had worked for Doctor Hoffman.

Kathy's 'Excuse me' was perfunctory. Her mother had taught her that good manners counted, even in difficult times. Her mother stuck by her and never said a word against Raymond, made all the arrangements because Kathy didn't know what to do. Kathy kept one hand over the folded letter in her pocket, the one that had arrived two days after Raymond's death.

Kathy and her mother were the only two people at Raymond's viewing, except for a priest who stepped in and spoke to her for a few minutes, asked her to call him if she ever wanted to talk about anything. Should I forgive Raymond? She asked.

Of course, he said. I have.

Kathy didn't understand. She thought the name Father Fortunati sounded familiar, though she couldn't figure out why.

CHAPTER FORTY-TWO: Present Day

Thursday morning, Cat's jog pounded out an incessant *turn a-way, turn a-way* as she ran along rain-slicked boards, the air dense with brackish moisture of an overnight rain. From her headset, Sonny at Sunrise, ridiculed a caller's "I seen it with my own eyes" by declaring that it was "just far too incredulous to believe that authetical one hundred dollar bills would just be tossed out a window without someone claiming to know which direction it was where they came from". Sonny could not quite stifle last night's echo of tires braking on wet asphalt, metal colliding with metal, shouts, sirens. The miracle of money raining from the sky caused drivers to collide, drew people from their porches and patios. It had taken a dozen police officers to keep the commotion from escalating into a riot.

Cat trotted down the boardwalk ramp and made her way home. As she rounded the corner, she saw lawns deeply gouged, the sod scattered on the sidewalk and street, a few bits of headlight and tail light glass on the asphalt, flower beds trampled, a slight dent in a car that had been parked along the curb.

Cat collected the five bills adhering to her porch steps, one stuck to the side of her car, another plastered to the small shed. She made her way up the back stairs and pried her running shoes off in the pantry, tugged off her canvas cap and padded into the kitchen.

Ellice was seated at the table arranging papers in her briefcase. "Victor called. He was pretty close-mouthed about whatever it is went on last night." She held up the newspaper to display the headline: *Cash Crop Dusts OC Neighborhood*. "I didn't get in until eleven. What did I miss?"

Cat told herself it was none of her business what Ellice had been doing until eleven. She turned on the tap and rinsed the dirt- and grass-caked bills in the sink, laid them out on a sheet of paper toweling. "Freddy called last night."

"It was too late to call him back, I went straight to bed. I'll try to get a hold of him today. I've got a fitting I have to squeeze in at noon. Miss Yolanda said if I'm on time, she can have the dress hemmed by four. I don't suppose you could pick it up for me, could you?"

At least that didn't sound like she was planning to leave Freddy at the altar. "No problem. I'm keeping Jane out of school so that she and Mats can go over to St. Agnes to help bake the wedding cookies. Mamma'll bring them back, so she can make up the apartment. She's staying over tonight and tomorrow. That won't mess up your schedule will it?"

"Are you kidding? Half the reason I'm marrying Freddy is to get her for a mother-in-law."

A car horn honked outside. Ellice bustled to her feet. "That's my cab, I've gotta run. If Freddy comes by, hide the dress and don't let him bribe Jane into getting a sneak peak."

Cat grabbed a Pepsi from the refrigerator, leafed through the paper, scanning the lead story, tossed the paper aside and glanced at the counter. Seven bills. Blood money. Even the rain could not wash it clean.

The phone rang. Cat hesitated before she picked it up.

The "How are you?" was Kurt Raab. "I heard what went down in Ocean City last night. Victor should've clarified that that was evidence before you pitched it streetside."

"I didn't give him the opportunity. And afterward, he was too busy helping with traffic control. I did find seven one hundred dollar bills this morning, you want me to turn it in?"

"It's probably about what you shelled out to the Gabors, so I didn't hear what you just said, fair enough?" He paused. "You know the story about King Solomon?"

"Which one?"

"Solomon gets to be King, right? And the Lord comes to him in a dream and asks him what he wants. And Solomon says he wants wisdom. And God's so pleased Solomon didn't ask for stuff like fame and wealth, He makes him the wisest guy in the world."

"I don't blame you for not being Solomon."

"I shouldn't have closed then investigation."

"It was a public place, there were witnesses. The killer committed suicide. You had every reason to close the file."

"Well, it's reopened. That's why I called. Delareto's gonna bring Mrs. Petrone here for an interview, over that money situation, the sixty K? Anyway, they're gonna be here around two, I figure you're entitled to sit in. Oh, and I picked up the Chronicle this morning I read your Scrappalooza stuff. I tell you, I needed a laugh. It was supposed to be funny, right?"

"If you laughed, then yes, it was supposed to be funny."

"So, look there's something I want to run by you, since you're a writer and all."

Cat sighed. "Groats and shoats?"

"No."

"Belly of the beast?"

"Nope."

"Another swine mess?"

"Damn it! Sorry."

"Marco beat you to it. You'll have to work fast, I think it's got to be postmarked by midnight tonight."

Cat peeked into Jane's room. Jane lay asleep, clutching her pillow with an expression of thoughtful concentration, as though analyzing all the angles of a puzzling dream.

Without Randall Hoffman, there would have been no Jane.

"What's the matter, Mom?" Jane's eyes were open, still analyzing.

Cat blinked. "Nothing, sweetie. Get dressed. Put on something you can get messy, you'll be helping Nonna make cookies."

"Mom, are you not marrying Victor because you're not done thinking about Dad?"

Cat brushed a long strand of hair away from Jane's face. "I'll always think about your father, Jane. Are your aunts and uncles talking about Victor and me getting married?"

"They're *betting* on it," Jane yawned.

"What about you, do you wonder about it?"

"I remember stuff, like birthdays and when Dad took me on the Ferris wheel, and when we took a boat ride once. But I don't think Mats has anything to remember about having a Dad."

"And you think he needs a father."

"Uncle Carlo says all boys need a father whether they like it or not. I heard him tell Uncle Vinnie that when Uncle Vinnie said how come Uncle Carlo let Mark move in."

"It's very good the way you look out for your brother, Jane. I think he's very lucky to have a sister like you."

"But who looks out for you?" Jane queried.

"I look out for myself. Don't you think I do a good enough job?"

"I heard Aunt Nancy tell Aunt Annie that there's some things you just need a man to do for you, and then they started whispering and Aunt Lorraine said they shouldn't talk dirty."

"They probably meant it's nice to have a man to do the dirty work like taking out the trash and cleaning up the garage."

"No," Jane clambered out of bed and pulled open a drawer. "Meryl said they meant sex."

During the drive to Atlantic City, Jane discoursed further upon the meaning of her aunts' conversation, which prompted a few ingenuous queries from Mats. Cat realized that this was another consequence of the decision she and Chris had made so many years ago: the response to 'where did I come from?' would have to be creatively ambiguous, or sidestepped all together.

The Daughters of Sicily had decorated the formal meeting room for the reception and were busy rolling out cookie dough, stirring a vat of tomato sauce and preparing party favors in the adjacent kitchen. Cat handed her mother the three pounds of butter she had picked up, refused to take money for it and reminded Jennie that if the conversation took the turn it had been known to take after Dottie Cicciolini took a quick look out for Monsignor Greg, determined that the coast was clear and produced a bottle of anisette, her mother was to remember how little it took to provoke Jane's inquisitive nature.

"They hear worse from your brothers," Jennie reminded her.

Cat shook her head, gave each child a kiss and told them to promise to be good for their Nonna. She nearly collided with Dominic in the stairwell. He was wearing a black T shirt and jeans, a leather bag slung over one shoulder. Clerical garb tended to camouflage his narrow waist, the definition of his biceps. He had continued to study ballet for the love of the discipline, though the local dance troupes, short a Rat King or Coppelius were not above calling the rectory to see if Father Fortunati would take pity on them and suit up.

"Smells like when we were kids," he greeted. "I heard about the miracle of money falling from the skies. Attendance at seven AM Mass was better than Christmas Eve. You okay? You look like you didn't get much sleep."

"Did you talk to Victor?"

"A bit. About the Chavez girl. And Miriam Bender."

Not about Hoffman? "Why was he asking about Doctor Bender?"

"I knew her, slightly. Miriam and I had some interesting discussions on childbirth issues, she was quite a philosopher. Ellice would have liked her."

Cat sank onto one of the steps and Dominic wedged beside her. "You wanna tell me what else is going on?" he asked.

"Jane informed me this morning that she thinks Mats needs a father."

"Victor going to be able to make it to the wedding?"

"Why? The parish chip in to the tune of a C note?"

"Bingo gets old after awhile."

Cat's gaze settled on the narrow bandage taped inside his forearm. "Steve talked to you about Mrs. Petrone's boy?"

"He said you were the one who got him to help her out."

Cat rested her chin on her fist with a sigh. "I hated Raymond Stites. It was easy, hating him, I didn't have to work on it, didn't even have to think about it. And then, life went on, and I had to remind myself to hate him, and it took a little more effort, and a little more, and then I met Kathy and I realized that I hadn't been the only one who- " She squeezed back tears, shook her head. "You know. Had emptied her husband's clothes out of the hamper the day after his funeral, or found a few strands of his hair threaded around the teeth of a comb or wondered if she should throw out an unopened can of shaving cream. What to do with his shoes. And then, hating Stites? It just got too hard to keep up."

"That's natural."

"And the past few days? I keep thinking about how at least I wasn't left alone, I had all of you. How my – my damn family - kept looking out for me and loving and putting up with me and saved me from being completely abandoned. Stop *smiling*!"

Dominic's eyes twinkled. "Cat. That's what damn families are for." He pushed himself off the step. "Gotta go rehearse the homily. I think I hit on a pretty good hook. Even though it's the first marriage for both of them, Freddy and Ellice aren't my typical starry-eyed twenty-year-olds, they've each been through a bad break-up, so I got to thinking about what Aunt Caterina used to say. About how you can't go back and fix the past, you can only go forward and make the best of what's left. Only thing I gotta worry about is the Daughters of Sicily. They put me on the clock. From the time Ellice leaves the starting gate to the 'I do's can't go more than forty minutes, tops. They've got to get the lasagnas out of the oven."

Driving home, Cat thought about it. Turning your back on the past and making the best of what was left was fine for Aunt Cat, for Dominic, for Freddy and Ellice, but her future would be nothing but skeletons and dark echoes until she could bring the entire truth about Chris's murder to light. She owed him that.

Cat ignored her answering machine and went straight up to her work station, brought up the Word page - "What I Know/Need to Know" – composed in last night's bout of insomnia.

1.Chris talked to Steve about infertility law.

2. Chris talked to Steve after the Ashers had died in a car crash.

3. Chris remembered that the Ashers had embryos in storage, just as we did.

4. Chris had planned to talk to Miriam Bender. (About the embryos they had in storage?)

5. Chris had died before he could meet with Miriam Bender. (To prevent him from asking Miriam questions?)

Cat's gaze became unfocused and the text in front of her dissolved into a hypnotic screen saver. *Think like Chris*, she told herself.

Chris had been very methodical. He would have done his homework before he talked to Miriam.

Cat logged on, brought up a search engine. *Always start with a specific topic, then work outward to the general.* One of her nephews had told her that. She entered 'in vitro fertilization' watched the links queue up:

Dictionaries, Medical: Pregnancy; pseudocyesis; childbirth issues; fertility medicine.

AskIt!: 'Eggs in an AskIt: Ovulation, fertility, embryonic and stem cell research, IVF.

CyberSwap: Category: FS: oocytes, embryos.

CyberSwap? Vinnie had mentioned a CyberSwap, but that had been an online auction site. She wondered what 'FS' meant, clicked on the link:

Twenty-four year old Caucasian, 5'10", auburn hair, blue eyes, genetically screened, HIV negative, single cycle, 8-12.

Healthy, negative STD white/Asian, 5'5", black hair, brown eyes, IQ 154, law student, single retrieval for adoption.

Healthy, twenty-one year old Caucasian, 5'8', 125 lbs, negative for HIV, STD, one pregnancy, single retrieval, surrogacy option will be considered.

Eight to twelve? Single retrieval? Of...what? Eggs?

'FS' couldn't mean 'For Sale', could it?

Okay, it wasn't exactly a new concept. Even State of the ART's OvaShare program allowed patients to donate surplus embryos in exchange for a fee reduction. And there were sperm donors, weren't there? Supply and demand. And clearly there was a demand, if these woman were offering their eggs on the open market with bids ranging from $3,500 to $23,000.

So what did that tell her?

Embryos were merchandise. Merchandise had value.

What happened to unclaimed merchandise?

Who might have a claim on unclaimed merchandise?

Cat checked her watch. Noon. She picked up the phone and dialed Kurt Raab's office, told his secretary – that is, administrative assistant – Lizette, that she would try to make it by two, but if she was late for the interview, they could start without her.

CHAPTER FORTY-THREE: Present Day

"Victor, look." Raab sat behind his desk. "I'll take the heat for this. But you went through any of those statements, you can't deny that the witnesses in the ER give a consistent story. Random shooting, murder-suicide. We go to interview the wife and she tells us about the money problems, how they lost a kid, how he's having headaches, they're classic stressors. It all fit the profile. We were thanking our lucky stars that Stites didn't take out the wife and the mother-in-law before he shot up the ER, which is the way these things usually go down."

Victor's somber gaze scanned the cluster of trees below Raab's window. The rain had coated the sun-blanched leaves so that they looked like wax, natural and unreal. "Then it didn't fit the profile, did it?"

Raab sighed. "You weren't at the funeral, Victor. And she lost a baby not long after that. God forgive me for saying this, but it was a lucky break that Stites did himself in, I don't think Mrs. Austen could have made it through a trial."

"I think you underestimate her."

Lizette knocked on the door, entered. "Mr. Raab, Mr. Delareto and Mrs. Petrone are here."

Raab stood up. "Mrs. Austen arrive yet?"

"No, sir, she called, said she was running late, and that you were free to start without her." She held the door, while Steve and Kathy entered, closed it, soundlessly.

"We can get started then, if it's okay with you and your client." Raab gestured to a pair of upholstered chairs in front of his desk.

Victor turned and perched on the sill, his back to the large window. The harsh backlight obscured his features.

"Kathy – Mrs. Petrone – knows you're gonna tape this, and she knows her rights," Steve said. "But first we want to hear that there won't be any charges filed, and you're not gonna dime into DYFUS to put the squeeze on her."

"I wouldn't use youth and family services to put pressure on her, you know me better than to suggest that, Delareto. Why don't we just hear what she's got to say."

"I don't hear we've got an deal, all either of us has got to say is '*adiós*'."

"Okay, look. I don't connect her to Rocap's death, or to Chris Austen's for that matter. But I think we can all agree that Mrs. Austen is owed a little piece of mind. If we can find out what went down the day her husband was killed, we can put it to rest once and for all."

Steve looked over at Kathy. She nodded.

"Look, I'll go first." Steve began. "Chris Austen came to me a little while before he died, asking about fertility law. Specifically about what might happen to embryos that were in the storage facility if both parents died."

"What prompted that?" Raab asked.

"An automobile fatality, a couple named Asher died, Chris was at the scene. They'd been patients of State of the ART, same time as Cat and Chris. The accident got Chris thinking about what could happen to any remaining embryos if a couple died. He said he was going to talk to Doctor Bender about it."

Raab glanced at Victor, could not detect any indication of whether this was news to him. "Did he?"

"I don't know."

"So, fill us in, Mrs. Petrone. If patients die. Or flat out don't want their embryos anymore. What happens?"

"If they're orphaned?" she asked.

"'Orphaned'? That's what they call it?"

"It was Miriam – Doctor Bender's - term."

"Go on."

"If a couple had provided for the unused embryos in their wills, it would be the responsibility of their executor to inform us of the particular provisions. That situation never occurred. In fact, most couples never acted on the termination notices by making any provisions or requests, they simply abandoned the embryos. In that case, the embryos were scheduled for disposal."

"Why didn't you just keep the embryos around?" Raab inquired. "They can't take up all that much room."

Sadness and cynicism mingled in Kathy's dark gaze. "No, but they did take up more room than anticipated, and they do require special equipment and conditions for storage. Doctor Hoffman and Miriam Bender founded a medical clinic. It wasn't meant to be a storage facility, both Randy and Miriam believed that the storage option would be secondary, minimal, and that, in any case, they would be able to expand their facility to accommodate any future needs."

"But?"

"But the land they expected to buy for an expansion still hasn't become available. And nobody did the projections regarding the embryos. Most procedures produce a dozen or so embryos. But most of the clients only wanted two or three children. Even if you have more than a single embryo implanted for each procedure, there was almost always a surplus. Some patients would have the surplus disposed of right off, but the rest would place them in storage."

"Sort of hedging their bets."

Kathy nodded, gravely. "And then life would go on. You have no idea how many times someone would be contacted that their storage contract was up for renewal and they would call us with, 'I forgot all about it'." She paused. "To answer your question - before the first year was out, the clinic had three dozen abandoned embryos. After five years, there were nine hundred. When I left, there were about seven thousand."

"Simply abandoned?" Raab was incredulous.

"Living children are abandoned or neglected or warehoused in orphanages," Kathy's tone was mildly reproachful. "Why do you imagine that something the size of a period at the end of a sentence would stake a greater claim on someone's conscience?"

"Okay. Point taken." Raab conceded. He glanced at Victor who remained leaning against the window sill, as immobile as stone. "How were relations between Hoffman and Bender?"

"Fine. The practice was growing, they seemed happy."

"Nothing changed around three years ago around the time Doctor Bender died?"

Kathy frowned, thoughtfully. "That would have been around the time The Hoffman went on the market. There was a dramatic increase in their income. But that was a good thing."

"It wasn't Bender's design and he took the credit?"

"No. Miriam was a psychiatrist, she didn't have the background in ob/gyn. Her spare time was spent working with support groups or in the free clinic."

"Hoffman ever get sued?"

"No."

"I had your husband's autopsy report faxed over. There was no underlying pathology, brain tumor, chemical imbalance, drugs to account for erratic behavior."

"I know." It hadn't been uttered as a reproach, but Raab felt it all the same. It should have come to his attention three years ago.

"So I'm wondering what prompted that batch of medical tests Doctor Hoffman ordered. Those kind of tests, you only get a work-up like that when you think something's really wrong."

"I never knew anything about that."

"Hoffman never mentioned it?"

Kathy shook her head.

Raab leaned across his desk. "Look, Mrs. Petrone, help me out here. Say your husband's told he's dying. And someone says, 'I can arrange it so your wife is left with a few bucks, so she won't be stuck with debts and the cost of a burial, and all you gotta do is- '"

Kathy shook her head, adamantly. "No."

"Mrs. Petrone. He left you sixty grand. Where'd you think he got it? And what was he doin' in the ER that day? He was there to take out Chris Austen and the woman who was paid ten grand to get Austen into that ER. Daria Chavez."

"Daria...?" Kathy was stunned.

"It looks like your husband was supposed to take her out, too. He missed. There was another attempt on her life that same day. Another former Pro Patrol guard named Chuck Santucci was the assailant. Mrs. Austen saw the name Santucci written on a paper in Whitney Rocap's home. Rocap was piecing together this whole deal, trying to get an interview with Santucci, who's doing time down at South Woods Correctional, and assisted by Daria Chavez who seems to have gotten a terminal case of scruples."

Kathy's head shook from side to side, in disbelief. Her trembling hands crept upward to cover her ears.

"Chris Austen's set up by Chavez." Raab's sharp tone penetrated Kathy's muffled ears. "Your husband finishes him off and kills himself. Santucci's sent to take out Chavez. Get it? No witnesses. But even though Chavez and your husband weren't gonna live to spend a dime, they'd want some money up front. Chavez because she didn't know she was on the hit list, and your husband because he didn't want to leave you in debt."

"*Raymond was not like that*!" Kathy screamed.

"Then what was he like, Mrs. Petrone? What, other than money, would Raymond Stites do something like that for?"

The question hit her like a blow. Her dazed expression froze all three of them, none moved fast enough to catch her before she toppled off the chair onto the carpet.

Steve got down beside her, lifted her in his arms and carried her to the tufted leather couch. "You maybe oughta call nine one one, she's white as a sheet."

Victor bent over her, lifted her wrist, felt her pulse. "Have Lizette get her some water," he suggested.

Lizette, Raab's secretary, nudged Steve aside and broke a small capsule under Kathy's nose. "Ammonium sulfate," she said. "I keep stocked on account of the Grand Inquisitor here."

"Cut me a break, Lizette," Raab was defensive.

Steve couldn't resist. "You want out," he said to Lizette, "You can come work for me."

"You go to hell, Delareto," Raab ordered.

Kathy's head jerked away from the capsule.

"I have a blood pressure cuff and a stethoscope," Lizette offered. "You want me to check her?"

"Perhaps she should be taken to the ER," Victor suggested.

Kathy's eyelids fluttered and her eyes opened. She groped for the back of the couch, tried to sit up. Steve slipped his arm under Kathy's shoulders, helped her into a sitting position.

"The room spinning? How 'bout we run by the ER on the way home?"

"No...I'll be all right. I want to get it over with."

"It is over with," Steve said, looking up at Raab. "And don't call us, we'll call you, okay? Torquemada?"

Kurt rolled his eyes. "You okay to walk, Mrs. Petrone?"

"I'm fine." She didn't look it.

"Lizette, give 'em a hand. Victor, stick around." Raab held the door for them, closed it and went back to his desk, dropped into his chair. "My mother found out I'd be poking around the ins and outs of fertility law, she'd wish I become a librarian."

"I have a high regard for librarians," Victor replied, evenly. "They're the custodians of the culture."

Raab sighed. "Victor, look. I been around a long time, I never heard a bad word against the clinic or Miriam Bender or Randall Hoffman. Other than he's closing on his third marriage."

"Hoffman abandons his first wife, his second wife commits suicide, he's marrying a woman half his age. If that doesn't inspire a bad word, it at least ought to raise questions about his judgment. As for Bender, I've put in a call to her sister. I heard there was talk she thought Bender'd been murdered."

"She had barbiturates in her system. We considered that she might have been doped and pushed, but nobody heard anything suspicious, no shouting, no struggle. No sign of forced entry." Raab shook his head. "Who's interviewing Santucci?"

"Adane."

"Okay. Keep me posted. For now, keep your distance from Hoffman. He gets nervous, he'll lawyer up, and if he can afford Marty Bevilacqua, he can afford to outspend this office. And there's something else we gotta consider." Raab hesitated. "Say Hoffman or Bender were up to something shady. So what're we talking about? Negligence? Nobody filed suit. Disposing of embryos without proper authorization? Doesn't sound like we're gonna even get the owner-donors behind us on that, they've abandoned them. The state treats them like property, not people. You want a conviction? You have to put a human face on it."

"Maybe. But something shook up Mrs. Petrone."

Raab nodded. "Hoffman lied to Stites about the test results."

"Then she ought to be angry. She's not, she's scared."

"Scared of Borch, maybe? He's still at large, knows where she lives."

Victor shook his head. "I think it's more than that. I think this is going to turn out to be more than a matter of sixty grand."

"Six, sixty, six hundred?" Raab shrugged. "What would your price be?"

"I'd like to think that I don't have one. But how much do any of us know about ourselves? Anyone who can't be bought would have to be the noblest person on earth, or the last."

CHAPTER FORTY-FOUR: Present Day

Of the four towns on Absecon Island, Ventnor outranked only Atlantic City in desirability. But by the freshly painted porch railings, the well-tended lawn and bubbles of hot pink azaleas beneath the picture windows, Cat concluded that the Colemans were reasonably well off.

Cat drove past the house, around the block, past the house again. *I have to know. I have to do this for Chris. For Chris.*

Cat's knock was answered by a "We're out back!" She followed the slate walk to the back yard. A child's pool had been set up in the center of the lawn, and three toddlers were splashing in two inches of water.

Beneath the 'Happy Birthday' banner suspended above the back yard deck, a woman was taping a blue paper table cloth to the underside of a picnic table. She wore white drawstring pants rolled to the knee, a black and white polka dot top, sunglasses with silver frames.

"Help you?"

"Carolyn Coleman?"

"That's me."

Cat estimated the woman's age somewhere in her mid-forties. She had a short dark bob, liberally threaded with silver, a complexion that suggested too many hours spent in the sun. "My name is Cat Austen. I'm a reporter from South Jersey Magazine, and I also write for the Chronicle."

"Wait-!" The woman pointed a finger. "Scrappalooza! I read those pieces just this morning! God, they were funny! Just open the latch on the gate."

"Ma!" one of the little boys cried out. "See me!" The boy leaned forward, touched the tip of his nose to the surface of the water, bobbed up, grinning.

His mother beamed.

Cat let herself into the yard. "They all yours?"

"No, just the one. The other two are kids from his play group. I'm babysitting them while their mother runs errands, she's going to reciprocate by picking up the cake. The party's for my ten-year-old nephew. Probably the last one before parties cease to be- " She rolled her eyes. "Cool."

Cat saw the bulk of diapers under the miniature bathing trunks. "How old is your boy, two, two and a half?"

"He was two last Valentine's Day." She gestured toward a pair of white wrought iron chairs. "I just started reading the Chronicle when they covered that movie shoot in Atlantic City. It must really have been a thrill, meeting Tommi Ann Butler. Scary, too, what happened on the set."

Cat sat. "I need the lull of something a bit frivolous like the Scrappalooza every once in a while, before I swing back to something serious. Right now, I'm researching a story about State of the ART. It's a fertility clinic."

"I know what it is." Apprehension cooled her tone by a few degrees. "That's quite a change from the Scrappalooza."

"Yes, but I was a patient, so I had a head start."

"A patient? Of Randy Hoffman's?"

"That's right. At the same time your sister and her husband were patients. Myra and Richard, wasn't it?"

"Dick. My husband's Richard, Myra's was Dick." She paused. "That would have been ten years ago."

"Yes. My daughter just turned ten last month. Doctor Hoffman – well, he was our last resort."

"Well..." She toyed with the hem of her shirt. "I know what that's like to be at the end of your rope. Myra tried everything. Monitoring, endoscopic surgery, herbs, even acupuncture. Hoffman was God-" she smiled, apologetically. "I meant to say 'a godsend'. Smart. Smart like people who came up with cell phones and PCs and take-out coffee. They see what people need before the people know it themselves. Or realize what they're willing to do for it. Myra and Dick were killed in a car accident. We took custody of their boy, Ricky."

"I know about their accident," Cat replied. "You see, my husband was one of the state troopers on the scene at the time."

Carolyn nodded, studying her. "Perhaps you should tell me exactly what you want to know, Mrs. Austen."

"I want to know if my husband spoke to you."

Carolyn Coleman got up from her chair and took a towel that had been draped over the fence. "Out of the pool, kids! Ricky will be home soon and we have to get ready for his party."

"Not *now*!"

"Yes, *now*. This isn't research, is it, Mrs. Austen? It's personal. Is it a custody issue? Are you and your husband divorcing?"

"My husband died, Mrs. Coleman. He was murdered shortly after he started asking questions."

"About...Myra's car accident?"

"No. About what happened to her embryos. You see, we had embryos in cryo, too, and when my husband saw who the victims were, it got him thinking about that. About what would happen to ours if we both died suddenly. I don't think that's uppermost in the minds of many couples in an IVF program."

Cat heard the faint rhythm of rubber soles on slate, turned and saw a lanky boy of ten unlatch the gate. He was pale, with a spray of freckles on his nose, wavy reddish hair above darker lashes.

"Aunt Carolyn, is the cake here?"

"Not yet. Go put your books inside, Ricky."

Ricky Asher. Myra and Dick Asher's child.

"I have to get things ready for the party. Ricky's friends will be here in half an hour."

"What did you tell my husband, Mrs. Coleman?"

"I told him that he should talk to Miriam Bender."

The Coleman boy trotted across the lawn, smiled up at Cat. She returned the smile, and her gaze snagged on the hazel eyes fringed with darker lashes, the pallor, flushed with exertion, spattered with freckles, the wavy, reddish hair.

Cat did not realize she was staring until she heard Mrs. Coleman say, "I think you had better go."

"You said '*I* know what it's like to be at the end of your rope'. How would you know that, Mrs. Coleman? Did my husband ask what had happened to your sister's embryos? Or had he already figured it out?"

Carolyn picked her toddler up, hugged him close. "Figured what out?"

"That your nephew and your son are biological brothers."

CHAPTER FORTY-FIVE: Present Day

Victor rested his head against the back of the chair, closed his eyes and mulled over the ironies of the situation. Investigating the death of a man who's wife he wanted to marry. Kathy Petrone's blood money exhausted in caring for her child, Daria's blood money showering the street.

He heard a knock on his doorframe, opened his eyes. "Come."

Stan Rice opened the door, stood on the threshold. "How'd it go over Raab's?"

"Not well. Have you heard from Adane?"

"Yeah, they got her waiting around until Santucci's mouthpiece got outta court to sit in on the chat. You had two calls. Doctor Rachel Bender, she said you can reach her this afternoon at her office, her number's on your pad. And get this. Hoffman's nurse, Bellamy? Called right before you got in, she said if she can get away from the office, can she meet you somewhere, she has something she wants to talk to you about."

"What?"

Stan shrugged. "She didn't say. You're busy, I'll have a chat with her. I heard she's a knockout."

Victor decided that Raab's injunction to stay away from Hoffman didn't prevent him from talking to the man's fiancee.

"Tell her I can't get away from the office, she wants to talk, she can come here."

"What if she doesn't want to meet on our turf."

"'The fair sex is your department'," Victor quoted. "Persuade her."

When Stan closed the door, Victor reached for the phone, dialed Cat's number, got her machine. He dialed Raab's office, asked Lizette if Mrs. Austen had ever come by or called back and got the anticipated, "No, Lieutenant". He felt a kernel of concern that threatened to blossom into full-fledged alarm. Victor wondered if he should try calling St. Agnes. She had said something about taking the kids there for the day. He decided against it, he didn't want to worry Jennie.

He checked his notepad, dialed Rachel Bender's number.

A gentle "Rachel Bender, here," answered on the first ring.

"Doctor Bender, this is Lieutenant Cardenas."

"Yes. How can I help you, Lieutenant?"

"We're re-opening an investigation into the shooting death of a state trooper. It occurred a week or so before your sister died."

"The one that took place in an emergency room? That upset Miriam terribly."

"Really? And why was that?"

"Odd as it may seem, she knew them both. The victim and the murderer. One had been a security guard posted to the clinic, the other had been a client. She told me that she had talked to him on the phone just the day before. The police officer."

"Did she repeat any of their conversation? I know it's been three years since her suicide, but anything you might recall would be helpful."

"Miriam didn't commit suicide."

"How can you know that, Doctor?"

"I knew my sister. We were twins, and what they say about the rapport is quite true. I would have felt it."

"You wouldn't say she was despondent, then?"

"No. Troubled about something, not despondent."

"Her colleague, Doctor Aquino, told me that she was unable to have children. Perhaps that had started to weigh upon her? Perhaps her husband decided he wanted a family?"

"A child, you mean?" That prompted a cynical chuckle. "That clinic was his child. He would refer to it as 'my baby'. Note the singular pronoun, Lieutenant. It was the only baby that gave him any sense of pride, the only one he ever walked the floors worrying about. The only one he'd grieve for if it were gone."

"Then, to your knowledge, the marriage was going well?"

She hesitated. "To my knowledge, yes. But something was troubling Miriam. In fact, she planned to come to Baltimore the week after we talked. She said she had a problem she wanted to talk over."

"What problem?"

"I don't know. But she did say something odd. She said 'I've got to get out of this. I wasn't thinking straight.'"

"Get out of what?"

"I imagine that's what she intended to discuss."

"Well, if the marriage was going well, what else could it have been? Had either she or Doctor Hoffman had done something that might expose them to criminal or civil charges? Scandal?"

There was a long pause.

"Doctor?"

Finally, Rachel Bender spoke. "People don't read any more, do they? I don't suppose you're familiar with Conan Doyle? Sherlock Holmes?"

"As a matter of fact, I am."

"Then perhaps you'll know what to read into it. I suspected that my sister's remark had to do with something she'd done that was giving her some moral qualms. When I pressed her about it, she just reminded me of one of the Holmes stories, I forget which. Where he professed a conviction that certain actions were illegal, but morally justifiable."

"Did your sister suggest that she or her husband had been involved in something illegal?"

"Miriam never did anything that wasn't morally justifiable in her eyes. As for the rest of us in the profession? Well, Holmes did calculate our potential as criminals. Do you recall what he concluded, Lieutenant?"

Victor recalled the quote. "That when a doctor turns to crime, he's the first of criminals."

"Because he has both nerve and knowledge," she added. "Is Randy implicated in something criminal?"

Victor heard a rap on his door, muffled the receiver with his palm. "Come in."

Stan entered, held the door for Eve Bellamy.

Victor rose. "I really can't say with any certainty at this time," he said into the phone. "But I will keep you updated. And if there's anything you can remember about that last conversation, please don't hesitate to call."

Victor returned Doctor Bender's 'Good-bye' and hung up, ignoring Stan's raised brow, a tacit plea to sit in. Victor couldn't blame him; Miss Bellamy, even in the simple white uniform that indicated she had come from work, her subdued makeup and pinned up hair, was stunning.

"Please close the door on your way out, Sergeant," Victor said, quietly.

Stan withdrew, closing the door.

Victor held out a chair. "How can I help you, Miss Bellamy?"

"I don't know who else to ask. Is Randy under investigation for something?"

"That's a question you may want to take to the DA. Why do you ask?"

"He's not his usual self. Not since the Rocap woman's accident, and all of the questions."

"He didn't seem upset when I visited your home."

"He wasn't. Not initially. But then a former patient of Randy's came by, a Mrs. Austen, asking for some paperwork from her file. I think Randy suspected that she didn't really want it, that she was using it as an excuse to pry some information from Randy about Whitney Rocap."

"Why would Doctor Hoffman have reason to believe that?"

"She told him so. At least, she told him that she and Whitney Rocap had been collaborating on something at the time of Miss Rocap's death. Something that had to do with the clinic."

Oh she did, did she? "And it concerns him that Mrs. Austen intends to take up where Miss Rocap left off?"

"Oh, Lieutenant." Eve buried her face in her hands. "I've always been able to turn to Randy when I didn't know what to do. Now I don't know where to turn."

Victor lifted and eyebrow, waited. She wouldn't have come here if she hadn't been ready to talk.

"You have to understand. Randy, and the clinic? They've been my whole world since I was a part-time file clerk working my way through nursing school. Everybody around him, well they just think he's God. And God doesn't make mistakes. The right thing to do? Well, it's always been whatever Randy said to do."

Because he's God?

"We're getting married tomorrow."

"Indeed? Then whatever Doctor Hoffman's concerns are – or yours – they're not serious enough to postpone the wedding."

A slight flush colored her cheeks. "Well, it's going to be a very small ceremony. And we wouldn't want to put things off indefinitely because...well, frankly, Lieutenant, I'm pregnant."

Victor offered a perfunctory, "Congratulations, then. Tell me, what sort of paperwork was Mrs. Austen asking for?"

"A letter from her file. She had been a patient, years ago. There was some routine correspondence that should have gone out some months ago, and she said she had never received it. A copy of it should have been in her file."

"And it wasn't?"

Eve shook her head. "Of course, we have been a bit disorganized since Kathy left, but the procedure is the same. All of the work is done on a Word file that's transferred to disk. Two paper copies are printed, one is sent to the patient and one goes in the file. When I went to Mrs. Austen's file, the letter wasn't there."

Victor ran his thumb along his mustache. "What did you do?"

"I told Randy. He asked me to get him the disk, the one her letter would have been on."

"He didn't ask you to just look on the disk yourself?"

Eve bit her lip. "He took it to his office. I was in the lab for most of the morning, and when I got back to the desk, the temp said he had brought the disk back."

"And then what?"

"Well, Mrs. Austen came, and she and Randy went into his office and talked for a bit while I checked the disk."

"And the letter was there. And you printed it out and gave it to her."

She nodded.

"And you wondered whether Doctor Hoffman altered the disk?"

She hesitated.

"Did you confront him?"

"Yes. And Randy insists he didn't do it, that I must have overlooked the letter. There are hundreds of pages on a disk and as I said, we've been a bit short-handed since Kathy left."

"But you don't think you overlooked it?"

Eve sighed. "No."

"What do you think?"

"I think *if* Randy fabricated a letter that had never been sent out, he was probably covering for Kathy. She's had such a run of bad luck, she would have been superhuman if she hadn't gotten careless once in a while."

"And Doctor Hoffman is concerned that her carelessness may have compromised the clinic? Did he think that's what Miss Rocap was really investigating?"

"I don't know. I took Whitney Rocap at her word, that she was just doing a story on IVF."

"But you're not taking Mrs. Austen at her word."

"Well, she's got more of a personal stake. If the clinic really was in error, it could result in a suit."

"Then this must have been an important letter."

"It was a standard termination notice, a letter stating when her remaining embryo was scheduled for disposal. When we make a good-faith attempt to notify the parties, and receive no response in a reasonable time, we are permitted according to the contract to conclude that the embryos have been abandoned, and to schedule them for disposal."

Remaining embryo? But hadn't Cat gotten pregnant with that last embryo, miscarried after Chris's death?

He realized that Cat had never said so, that he had violated his own cardinal rule, 'never assume'.

CHAPTER FORTY-SIX:
Present Day

The perfect Old Tyme Scrapple slogan did not come to Cat at two AM; it came as she cruised Atlantic Avenue in Ventnor, scanning the street corners for a pay phone.

She spotted one and pulled up to the curb, called Kurt Raab's office first, and was informed by Lizette that the meeting had broken up well over an hour ago and that Raab had left for the day. Cat thanked her, called Victor's extension, got a busy signal, hung up, retrieved her change and dialed the South Jersey office.

"Cat! I've been trying to reach you all morning!" Cherry exclaimed. "You need to get a cell phone, girl."

"It's on the 'to do' list. I'm at a pay phone. Look, do you have the info there on where to send those Olde Tyme slogan entries. And try not to imply how low I've sunk by asking."

"Are you kidding? Ritchie sent in fifty-four."

"I asked you not to imply how demeaning it is."

Cherry chuckled and read off the address.

Cat read it back while she scribbled it on the back of a deposit slip. "What did you want to talk to me about?"

"You remember what I told you about the property where the clinic is located? How they're leasing all that empty land?"

"Eight thousand a month, and Hoffman gets first refusal when it goes on the market."

"The whole transaction went through Home Stead Realty, and it was handled by their local office in Ventnor. But the queen bee of the firm is the woman who runs the outfit outta their Cherry Hill office, and guess who that is?"

"Sherlock Holmes says that guessing is destructive to the logical faculty."

"Harianne Feldman."

"Who's Harianne Feldman?" Cat asked.

"Harianne Feldman Hoffman."

Cat felt her heart swing toward her throat, stopped. "Hoffman's first wife?"

"Really sweet way of getting what's due you. Every check written to Home Stead Realty, a nice percentage goes to the broker. And the owner of that land? It's under a corporation papered in Delaware, so I peeled back some paper and not to strain your logical faculty, but guess who turned up?"

"Harianne Feldman."

"He should have held off all that thumping until he put some money down on the land. I bet she caught a vibration and yanked it out from under him."

"So as broker, she gets a percentage of the lease- "

"And as owner, she gets most of the rest."

"Is that ethical? Or legal?"

"Who knows? But if you'd been dumped, left to raise two kids on two hundred eighty dollars a month while he's making six figures *before* the millions he's pulling in from The Hoffman see how ethical you feel."

"I'm in Ventnor now. Where's Home Stead's local office?"

"Got a pencil?" Cherry read it off while Cat copied it awkwardly on a bit of bare space on the deposit slip.

Cat thanked her and headed for the post office a half block down the street. She printed out her Olde Tyme Scrapple slogan on the form she had tucked in her purse, bought and envelope and stamp and mailed it.

She spotted Home Stead's conspicuous orange and white striped awnings half a block off. Cat parked in front of the modest stucco building and pumped the last of her change into the meter.

Inside, the logo's brazen orange and white had been tempered to a cool cream and apricot that had been chosen for the vertical blinds, the upholstered chairs and textured walls. There was a nook with a glass coffee table bearing bound copies of the multiple listing book and brochures fanned into a perfect semicircle. The two office doors were closed.

The "Can I help you?" was uttered by an immaculately groomed young man, stationed behind a glossy walnut desk. He rose immediately and stepped forward to shake her hand. Cat made a mental note to tell Steve that he might want to think about raiding Home Stead's Ventnor office if Tambi wasn't working out.

Cat shook hands, and introduced herself. "I'm not in the market, really, I'm doing a feature for the Cape Atlantic Chronicle- "

The young man's professional demeanor cracked. "Austen! Scrapple! Try this on, 'A sty for a sty'." He walked back around the desk, started rummaging through a drawer. "I've got one of those entry forms, I think I'm going to go ahead and send that one in." He found the sheet of paper, slapped it on his desk and gestured to a chair. "So, what can I do for you?"

"I'm doing a piece on summer rentals. The commercial market. You know, comparing the different communities, what businesses are leaving, who's moving in, seasonal versus year round, how many properties are still available after Memorial Day. What your average week is like." *How easy it was to lie!*

"Well, when we started out, we located here because it was cheaper to rent than in Margate or OC. Harry pretty much got a lock on the PABA princesses. You know, they come down to the summer house year after year, they get bored with the beach or the kids get older and they decide to dabble in trade, trinkets and raffia, maybe open a café."

Cat observed that he hadn't lowered his voice, glanced toward the closed doors. She concluded that "Harry" wasn't in.

She took out a notebook and pencil and began to write. Who knows, she thought, perhaps it hadn't been a lie. There might actually be something she could turn into a story. "So they lease a storefront?"

"Or buy. They've got the cash."

"It sounds like a good market share to have a lock on. How did he manage to corral the market?"

"He?"

"Harry?" Cat was surprised at the note of ingenuity she was able to infuse upon the two syllables.

"Oh, Harry's not a man. Harianne. Feldman. The boss. She works out of our Camden County office, but she spends at least half the week down here in season. She's coming down for a closing tomorrow."

"Real estate seems to be attracting a lot of women. I guess because the schedule's flexible."

"Maybe- " He lowered his voice. "But she's not."

"Not juggling home and family with the job?"

He shook his head. "She's divorced. Long divorced. Her kids are grown."

"Then she's not one of the PABA princesses?"

He rolled his eyes. "But at least she's hands-on. A lot of them send us out to do the scut work, then skim off their three percent of our sweat."

"And that's where she is now, doing some of the, um, scut work?"

He nodded. "Kind of. When she comes down, she always runs by any properties between here and the shore, especially ones that've been vacated, off the beaten path. They're magnets for squatters.

Or fugitives? Cat scribbled a few notes in order to look busy. "Can you give me an example?"

He reached toward a stack of brochures on the corner of his desk, unfolded one and held it up to Cat. "Here- " He tapped the corner of the paper. "This one's out Gravelly Run Road."

Cat glanced at the picture of a ramshackle building that had once been white, the dingy exterior hemmed in three feet of creeping mold or dirt. The planks of the wooden porch were buckling, the bottom steps were boosted in place with bricks. An arc of swept dirt in front for a driveway. The description read: Handyman Special. 'Roadside market with living quarters above, two BR, single ba., pantry, eat-in kitchen. Renovate or build to suit on this busy seasonal location, zoned commercial. A great buy for the right party. Priced right at $54,500.'

"Good for a six pack and a tube of SPF fifteen if you were headed down the shore," he said. "The owner died last year, and the executor doesn't give a hoot."

"It says there's some kind of upstairs apartment, bathroom, bedroom. You leave the utilities on in a place like that?"

"Not gas or electric. I don't know about the water. Why?"

"No reason." Cat rose. "When will Harry be in?"

"Not for a few hours. And she's got a closing tomorrow."

"I've got a family wedding on Saturday. Maybe I'll give her a call and try to set up something for next week."

"I'll mention it to Harry when she checks in. You got a card I can leave for her?"

Cat handed him one of her cards and thanked him for his time. She almost made it to the door.

"Hey – I just thought up another one!"

Cat manufactured a smile.

" 'Greased lightening'. Whaddayou think? A hundred grand would make me my own boss."

CHAPTER FORTY-SEVEN:
Present Day

"Austen residence."

Victor checked his watch. Four PM. "Jane, it's Victor. Is your mom there?"

"No, she's still out somewhere. Nonna's here."

"May I speak to her, please?"

"Are you coming to the wedding?"

"I'll try to make it if you promise to save me a dance."

He heard Jane's giggle, a muffled, "*Non*na, it's *Vic*tor!"

"I went ahead and brought the kids home, I'm gonna get dinner started so Cat won't have to fuss. I don't know what's keeping her."

"Has Ellice talked to her?"

"Ellice, she's not home, either. And Freddy's on the road somewhere. Too much running around. The whole week before I got married, I didn't leave the house. You wanna know what I think? I think this is why they got those test tube babies. Two people can't find a couple hours to spend together, where you think the babies are gonna come from? Outer space?"

"Jennie."

"What?"

"A couple hours?"

"You mind your manners."

"Jennie, did Cat leave a note anywhere, something that might let you know what her agenda was?"

"Lemme take a look." He heard Jennie muttering. "I just see something she wrote down here on the pad by the phone. Lemme see if I can read her writing. It looks like it says, Home Stead Real Estate." Jennie sighed. "I hope she's not renting out this place, they try to talk you into that, you know, renting out to total strangers for the summer."

"Had she been thinking about that?"

"I don't think so. Freddy and Ellice, they're gonna move in downstairs after the wedding. Maybe you should try that idiot she works for."

"I will. I'll be in my office another hour or so, would you ask her to call me as soon as she gets in?"

"You come by, I'll fix you a bite."

Victor thanked her and hung up, his preoccupied frown deepening. He tried Delareto's office, got a young woman who told him, "I don't know where he's at because he just left about fifteen minutes ago, but you can try his beeper, lemme see if I can find where I left the number at."

She kept him holding so long he thought she had hung up. Finally, she came back on the line with "You still there?" and read out the number.

Delareto returned Victor's call within minutes. Victor thought he heard a child gabbling in the background. "You're at Mrs. Petrone's?" Victor inquired.

"Yeah." Steven lowered his voice. "What's up?"

"Have you spoken to Cat at all today?"

"No, why?"

"She's been incommunicado since she dropped the kids off at church this morning. She'd written something on a note pad, Home Stead Real Estate. Does that ring a bell?"

"I got my office space through Home Stead, their branch office in Ventnor. Main office is up in Camden County. Hold on."

Victor heard a muffled exchange.

"Kathy says the clinic bought their property through Home Stead, and that's who handles their lease on the adjacent land. Kathy says State of the ART's been optioning the land until it goes on the market. So they'll be able to expand. You want me to call over there, see if Cat's dropped by?"

"I'll do it. Meanwhile, if you hear from her, tell her to call me."

He got Raab on his cell. "Well, we re-arrested the Gabors, got them Mirandized in the mother tongue, but we didn't turn up Borch in any of their properties, unless there's one we missed. Or unless they've got some holdings under another name."

Victor told him about Cat's notation. "Could Home Stead be the firm that manages the Gabors' properties?"

"I don't think so. The Gabors own mostly residential and Home Stead's mostly commercial. How'd Adane make out with Santucci?"

"She's not back yet. There was a hold-up because Santucci wouldn't talk to her without his attorney present and his attorney was in court. One thing more." Victor repeated his conversation with Eve Bellamy."

Faking documentation?" Raab was incredulous. "Hoffman?"

"And if she's telling the truth, there's the matter of a forged signature as well."

"It's almost five. Gonna be hard to get a subpoena until tomorrow."

"He gets wind of this, he could disappear them before tomorrow."

"Hoffman's giving some speech tonight, so he'll have to cut out of work early. Put Stan or Phil on him. Discreetly. I want to know when he gets home, if he slips back over to the clinic any time tonight. In the meantime, tell Mrs. A. we'll probably want a sample of her signature. Her husband's, too, if he signed this paper as well, have a graphologist go over it."

Victor frowned. "Mrs. Austen hasn't been seen or heard from since this morning."

"What do you mean?"

"After she dropped her children off with her mother and called your office, she took off. Nobody knows where she is."

༄

Cat nearly missed the crumbling structure set back behind an arc of level dirt that served as a parking lot. She hit the brakes and spotted a weather-bleached sign with a barely decipherable 'Gravelly Run Quik Stop' propped against a tree, and turned into the drive, parked in the shade of a tree near the rear of the building.

The building itself was a decomposing structure of warped wooden siding on a concrete base, once white, now weathered to a blotchy dun hue. The awnings had been blue but were sun-bleached to near white, the window screens had eroded and torn away from the dilapidated wooden frames. A few of the glass windows had been shattered, filled in with newspaper, the rest were boarded up.

Cat got out of her car and circled toward the back of the building. She found a Home Stead Realty sign propped against a slanting cellar door. Several feet of level earth separated the rear of the building from a dense thicket of parched foliage.

She noticed that the rusted latch on the cellar's door had been thrown open, saw a padlock lying in the dirt. Cat lifted one door, saw a half dozen wide concrete stairs descending toward an earthen floor. Cat went back to her car and got a small flashlight, directed the beam to the stairs. She thought she saw the vague outline of a shoe's tread in the dry earth. A footprint? Of course, it could be weeks – years – old. Cat lifted the other half of the door, hunkered down and gazed into the cellar, saw the corner of a cardboard box, smelled moldy paper mingled with dank earth. Another scent infiltrated the odors of mildew and grime, a trace of charred meat, a whiff of grease. Not the staleness of rotting garbage, the smell was acrid but recent.

Cat rose, just as a strong arm circled her waist, thick fingers bored into the side of her throat. The blackness of the cellar infiltrated everything around it and the ground dropped away from her feet.

CHAPTER FORTY-EIGHT: Present Day

Somehow, the surface beneath her had converted from the warmth of dry earth to the chill of slick linoleum. Consciousness lagged behind sensation, and it took several seconds for Cat to realize that her eyes had opened.

She realized that the block of dull silver before her was a metal cabinet, that the misshapen blur was her own reflection. Her brain told her that the low-slung corkscrew was something familiar, but she could not remember what it was called.

Her limbs were liquid, without sensation, but the paralysis didn't cause her to panic. In fact, the cool linoleum under her cheek felt good, comforting, which was odd, because she hated the cold. She would think it all through when she was wide awake, but for now, she just wanted to sleep. She wondered, idly, if she could move. She moved one knee which shifted her weight and she rolled on her back. Facing upward, she saw the high curving spigot of a sink above her. A wall phone. That's what that flaccid corkscrew was, the cord of a wall phone!

That resolved, Cat was inclined to slip back into a comfortable unconsciousness when her drifting gaze halted on a wall clock. Something about the set of the hands wasn't right. The angle would make the time to be six-forty. But that couldn't be correct. She had told her mother she would pick up Jane and Mats before four. *I have to be dreaming*, she decided.

Wake up!

She waited for the dream to dissipate. Nothing changed.

I have to go get them.

No, too late, if it really was six-forty, they wouldn't still be at the church. She had to call someone.

She rolled onto her stomach and tried to pull up her knees. She began to propel herself, pushing her knees against the cold floor, inching toward the wall. She rolled on her side and worked her back against the wall, until she managed to brace herself against it in a sitting position. The long loop of the phone's cord hung down beside her.

It's almost seven o'clock.

She pushed her feet against the floor, and groped for the countertop above her. She tried to pull herself upward, her arms watery and numb. At last, she saw the phone's console next to her face. *Now all I have to do is get my hands moving.*

She slumped against the countertop and fumbled blindly for the receiver. It fell off the hook, dropped to the floor. Cat looked down at the receiver. Her sluggish brain struggled with the dilemma. *Dial nine one one*. Yes, that was it. She was satisfied, now that she knew what to do, she could rest.

Seven o'clock!

Her fingers lurched toward the keypad and she pressed the nine. There. She slid her index finger toward the top row and pressed the one, pressed it once again.

Her knees gave out and she slipped to the floor, and slid onto her side, her mouth a foot from the receiver. She heard, “Nine one one, what’s the nature of your emergency?”

Cat thought “I need help”, but heard, “Iee *ep*” in a voice that sounded like hers. “I eed ep”, she repeated.

“Ma’am, did you say you need help?”

“Stay of ee art.”

“Ma’am, did you say there’s a stake through your heart?”

Cat heard the soft whoosh of a door, felt a heavy tread vibrate the floor. That was fast. “’ey’re here,” she mumbled.

“Ma’am, is there someone there with you?”

The receiver floated into the air and something sharp pricked Cat’s bare arm.

CHAPTER FORTY-NINE: Present Day

The ring of the phone no longer touched off a hope that it would be Cat. Victor felt a grim certainty, the cop's instinctive knowledge that something had gone wrong.

It was Phil Long. "Look, Lieut, I'm hangin' here as long as a black man can cruise a seven-figure neighborhood without wearin' overalls from the Crystal Clean Pool Service. He finally pulls in almost a half hour ago. Whaddayou want me to do?"

"Give it another half hour." Victor hung up and the phone rang again, immediately. This time it was Freddy.

"I'm here with Ma and the kids, I'm starting to get antsy."

"Where's Ellice?"

"I don't know. There was a message from her on the machine, saying that she was gonna be late, then another one that her business got cancelled at the last minute, so she'd pick up her dress, tell Cat not to bother."

"Then they're not together."

"No."

"Look, Freddy, I'm following a few leads, and I'll have her license number put over the wire. Tell Jennie not to worry."

"That what works with your ma?"

"Point taken."

Victor was off the phone scarcely a minute when Phil Long called back. "His car just pulled out."

"Stay on him. Let me know if he makes any detours on the way to his dinner engagement." His console began to flash with another incoming call. He signed off with a quick, "Keep me posted" and punched the flashing button. It was Adane.

"Lieutenant, I'm on my way back, I'm sorry it took so long. When Mr. Santucci's attorney finally arrived, they wouldn't talk unless the Cumberland County DA would guarantee a sentence reduction. The prosecutor refused to deal until they talked. So I suggested that perhaps if Mr. Santucci told us a portion of his story, and if it sounded credible, Kurt Raab might persuade their DA to deal."

"What did Santucci give up?"

"He admitted that he had been paid to kill Chavez. His story was that he was hired at the last minute, that Raymond Stites was supposed to kill Daria Chavez, too, when he shot Christopher Austen. Santucci doesn't know why it didn't go down as planned, but he was paid to kill her and make it look like a home invasion. Daria's father came in unexpectedly and Santucci fled. He called his contact for further instructions and a meet was set up, but on his way there, Santucci started thinking that he just might be as expendable as Chavez, and he decided to disappear. He heard some time later that Chavez had left the country."

"And he wouldn't reveal the name of his contact?"

"Not without a deal for a sentence reduction."

"All right. We had a report that Hoffman may have tampered with clinic records. Raab wants to get them subpoenaed. Phil's tailing Hoffman now."

"I'm on Route Forty, I can divert to Mays Landing Somers Point Road and run by the clinic, to see if anything appears to be amiss."

"Okay, but just make a pass, let me know if there are any cars there, if there looks to be any unusual activity. Anything's out of the ordinary, call me before you act."

ଚ୍ଚ

Cat felt a warm, fluid torpor infiltrate her brain. A rough male, "You settle things with Rod?" kindled an ember of consciousness. She had heard that voice before, at Whitney's.

The response was inaudible, a background rhythm with a familiar cadence.

"I don't plant her soon, she'll need another shot. You said the stuff was short-acting. You got my bonus, right?"

"Don't worry. I said I'd take care of you, and I will. We'd better wait another ten minutes, it's still light. *Damn* summer."

A phone began to trill, stopped. Cat heard "No, I'm sorry you must be mistaken, but I really appreciate the call."

Recognition threaded through soothing semi-consciousness. She knew the other voice. Cat felt herself swept upward, carried from the cool quiet into a warm, humidity. She was laid on a soft surface, heard the chirruping of crickets, smelled the dry, dusky scent of parched earth, and felt something billow above her on a gust of tepid air, then settle over her face.

Where am I? Back in the cellar?

"That's only a couple feet. It's too shallow. I told you, what I gave her is short acting."

"It's as deep as I did for Chavez, and she didn't surface, did she? Just keep Rod busy and let me do my job."

"Well hurry up. That was a police dispatcher on the phone, she must have had time to punch in nine one one."

Cat felt herself rolling downward, landed cradled in earth. She tried to open her eyes and saw white fabric tented several inches above her. She inhaled warm, dusty air and the spasm of a languid cough constrict her ribs. She felt a tingling in her palms, the ebbing of a pins-and-needles numbness infused with a current of adrenaline. She inhaled again, found it a bit more difficult this time; when she exhaled, the tent billowed above her face then settled back. Something spattering over her, something that tickled her sandaled feet protruding from the bottom of the tent. Rain? No, it wasn't wet, it was a steady, dry shower and that wasn't absorbed by the earth around her, but accumulated in a slow, uneven weight. Dirt. Earth.

She opened her mouth to scream and felt the cloth sucked between her parted lips. The air that she inhaled was thin, with a mist of fine, dry soil. She swallowed, gagged, forced herself to swallow again. She tried to open her eyes. She felt the loose folds of a sheet being slowly weighted in place from above.

What's happening to me! What's happening to me!

Don't worry, I planted...Chavez!

He's burying me!

CHAPTER FIFTY:
Present Day

Victor had just decided that he may as well sign out when his phone rang. He checked his watch as he reached for the receiver. Seven. *Cat?*

It was Stan Rice.

"Lieutenant, we located Cat's car."

"Where is she?"

"No sign of her, but here's the thing. The car'd been pulled round the back of an old teardown out Gravelly Run Road."

"Any sign of a struggle?"

"Nope. But get this. I found one of Home Stead's signs out back. So I call their local office, in Ventnor? Get the manager, who tells me that Cat was there this afternoon, she's asking questions like maybe she's going to do some article or something. And he mentions this place, tells her how it's a pain to have to check up on these places're shut up, but they gotta be checked out because they're bait for the bottom feeders. So I figured it wouldn't hurt to drive out here."

"When was the last time someone from the office went out to the place?"

"He said the boss might make a run by, she's got a closing down the shore. I didn't see any sign of her."

"Sign of any activity at all?"

"Yeah. Place's been secured pretty well except for the cellar door. That'd been opened. I let myself in and right off I can smell someone's been cooking, so I pull out and call for backup. When they get here, we go in. Water's turned on, there's a few cans of chili and soup in one of the cupboards, not much dust on them, so I figure they haven't been around here long. It ain't first class, but it's livable, if you're not too particular. Squatter maybe, but I still put in a call to the print lab. See if any of Borch's prints can be raised."

Victor ran one hand over his jaw. He felt the roughness of late day beard. "Good work, Sergeant. Give me the location."

"That's another weird thing. The road runs off Somers Point-Mays Landing Road. It's only about a mile from the clinic. You wanna hang by the phone, I can handle this end."

"All right. If I leave the office, I'll be on my cell." He hung up and dialed Raab's cell phone number. Raab called back immediately, his tone hushed. "I'm out at the country club, slow dancing with Marty Bevilacqua while Hoffman gives his speech. Reproductive technologies – plural - for the twenty-first century. I never knew there was more than one, the one I knew about didn't involve a lotta technology, if you get my meaning."

"I do." Victor repeated Stan's report. "I'm going to take a ride out there. When you get to talk to Hoffman, ask him about the real estate agency that handles his lease. Home Stead. They've got the listing on the place where Cat's car turned up."

"You think Hoffman got his realty to harbor Borch?"

"I don't know. Wait, let me put you on hold a minute, I've got another call coming in."

It was Phil Long, he was hyperventilating, yelling. "Lieutenant! I'm at the clinic! Adane's down! Adane's down! We got two more, one of them looks to be Borch!"

Who was the other one?

"Other one's wearing a guard's uniform. Both gone. I got two more units here, state. I can hear the paramedics."

Victor exhaled, slowly. "What's Adane's status?"

"She took three rounds, two caught her in the vest, but she took one on the shoulder."

"Listen up. Rice is about a mile down the road. Get him to take point, you stay with Adane. I'll meet you at the ER."

He hung up and punched the other line. "Adane was shot out at the clinic," he told Raab. "I don't have any of the details, but it doesn't appear to be critical. I'm going to the hospital. And you can cancel the APB on Borch, there were two more down at the scene, he was one of them."

"I'll have to get someone to bring Mary Grace over to the ER."

"Any sign of Mrs. Austen?"

He didn't add, 'dead or alive'.

CHAPTER FIFTY-ONE:
Present Day

Turn away.

Chris's hand was raised, palm outward. Cat moved toward the porch steps to approach, because she couldn't hear what he was saying. He shook his head, waving her back.

I can't hear you.

Turn away.

Chris! Wait, I'll come down. I'll come to you.

He turned and smiled, the sun raising a gold aura on his light hair, like a halo.

The clouds closed in and there was a distant rumble.

Wait! Cat called. I'll come with you.

He shook his head, slowly, as if to say, "Turn away."

Wait! Cat called, but Chris was gone.

Panic kindled consciousness once more and the image of Chris dissipated. She was alone in the dark, loosely shrouded and under the earth. If she called out to Chris again, the limp weight would constrict around her ribs and she would not be able to inhale. She strained to keep her lungs expanded while she took in shallow breaths, while the tiny pocket of air tented within the loose covering grew increasingly hot and thin.

Think! Think! Think! Think!

The words were echoed by the shallow panting that jabbed at her dilated ribs. Cat had a brief flash of two little faces, shut her eyes. She felt a tug at her breast, staved off a sob of hysteria, afraid that if she allowed her ribcage to compress, she would not be able to expand it. She wondered how many breaths she would be able to take before there was no more oxygen to inhale. Not many.

Think! Think! Think! Think!

There are damn few quandaries you can't think your way out of.

Chris's sister Charlotte had said that, telling Cat and Chris about the time she had been trapped in an avalanche. How suffocation was a more immediate problem than the cold. "I remembered that the drawstring on my jacket was a hollow cord, only a little more than a quarter inch in diameter. I could barely move my arms, but I squirmed my hand toward it, pulled it free and worked it up through the snow, put the other end in my mouth. I had to concentrate on sucking in the air really slowly, so that I wouldn't collapse the cord when I breathed in. That's how they found me, they saw the cord poking out of the snow. There are damn few quandaries you can't think your way out of."

Charlotte was like Chris, resourceful and unafraid. She had outrun a lava flow, an earthquake, hostile insurgents. She had been caught in mudslides, rock slides, and an avalanche, wrecked eight cars and been stranded in the desert.

Think! Think like Charlotte! Think like Chris!

That's only a couple feet. It's too shallow.

If there hadn't been time to dig a deep grave, perhaps it wasn't very far to the surface, no farther than the snow tide that had washed over Charlotte. And it wasn't compact snow, was it?

I'm not wearing a parka with a drawstring, though. What have I got that I can use?

Cat wriggled her arms and discovered that she was able to work them down her torso, up toward her throat. She inched her hands over her skirt, felt something beneath her fingertips, the stiff paper of Home Stead's brochure.

Cat felt the sheet tamping down on her forehead. Each breath seemed to take in no more than a teaspoon of air, thin, hot air saturated with grit. She slid the paper over her ribcage, worked at it with her fingertips until she was able to unfold it. Unfolded, it was eleven by eighteen inches of thick, glossy paper. She began working at it with her thumbs and index fingers, gritty perspiration pooling at the corners of her eyelids, stinging her eyes. It was excellent paper stock, rolled easily into a firm, eighteen inch straw. She would have to pull the sheet away from her face, the sandy dirt would fall all over her, in her eyes, her nostrils. She would have to hope she could push it high enough to break the surface. She would have to hope someone would come by and see her before she lost consciousness. She would have to hope.

She worked the slender cylinder toward her lips and wondered whether it would be Victor or Chris who found her.

CHAPTER FIFTY-TWO: Present Day

Carlo Fortunati had caught the news and picked up Mary Grace Keller, drove her to the ER. Victor found him hovering over Mary Grace outside the treatment area. The door was ajar and Victor could hear Phil Long at Adane's side, babbling, "So Shamu, she stashes me in the closet right before Big Ben charges into the room, and the two of 'em start going at it, each wantin' a piece of my street action, so which one of them is gonna take out Joey Fortunati, he's playin' my pimp, right? And I tell you, I was something to fight over, I got on a red satin sheath with spaghetti straps, hump-me pumps, I got the eye shadow, wig's the Jane Fonda, seventies shag. Then I hear this *Boom!*, al'mos' like an earthquake and I try the door, and it's wedged tight because all four hundred pounds of Shamu went and had herself a heart attack and drops right on the other side. Lemme tell you, when they sprang me, if that don't put a whole new spin on comin' outta the closet, I don't know what does."

Victor heard Adane's pallid laugh. He squatted down in front of Mary Grace. "You okay?"

She nodded, her face paper white. "What happened?"

"I don't have the story yet. Adane was on her way back from conducting an interview at South Woods, I asked her to swing by the clinic. Phil said he was going to connect with her there." He rose, looked at Carlo.

"I don't think it's too bad." Carlo rubbed his hand over his broad jaw. "She took one clean hit in the shoulder, two in the vest, those'll bruise up some." He jerked his chin and he and Victor took a few steps away from Mary Grace. "So where's my sister? We run outta stuff to tell Ma and the kids."

The large rotating door whooshed open and Dominic appeared, escorting Sister Maggie, who was adjusting her habit, her square face pale. Carlo cuffed his brother on the shoulder.

Sister Maggie tolerated Carlo's hug, looked down at her younger sister. "Mary Grace."

"Hello Maggie," Mary Grace said, wanly. They could not be more different. Maggie was nearly six feet tall, strong-boned and no more than handsome. Mary Grace was fragile and pale as porcelain, with aquamarine eyes and an almost ethereal beauty.

Maggie plopped down in a chair beside Mary Grace. "Well, it still wouldn't kill you to pray."

"No," Mary Grace said, evenly. "But if I started up again at this late date, *you* might die of shock."

"Did you have anything to eat today?"

"I'm not hungry."

"I'll go find you a sandwich."

Mary Grace laid a hand on her sister's sleeve. "Stay. We're never in the same place at the same time any more."

"That's not my fault. I stayed put."

"So did I."

A small woman wearing blue scrubs and a surgical cap emerged, shucked off Latex gloves.

Victor presented his shield. "How is she?"

"She'll be fine, the bullet missed the artery, but I want to keep the shoulder immobilized for now. I'd like to give her something for the pain, she declined initially. She said she had to report to her commanding officer with a clear head."

"Can I talk to her?"

The doctor nodded. "Keep it down to about five minutes, though, I want to get her to a room."

"I suppose you should go in, too," Sister Maggie said.

Mary Grace looked at her.

"Well, you are her – the county prosecutor."

Victor took Mary Grace's elbow. "Would you like a few minutes alone with her."

"No, the doctor said she can only talk for a few minutes."

They went into the cubicle. Adane was lying on a gurney, an IV running into her left arm. Phil gave Adane's hand a squeeze and said, "I'll wait outside."

Mary Grace walked around, took Jean's right hand, bent down and kissed her forehead. "Can you talk a few minutes?"

Adane nodded, turned her gaze toward Victor.

"Can you tell me what happened?"

She nodded, cleared her throat, spoke with effort, her voice a whisper. "I approached from the west. The gate was up and no one was at the guard post. My headlights hit someone out in the field, about twenty yards from the clinic." She winced.

"Take your time, Adane."

"It was Borch. I had a vest with me. I pulled it on and got out of my car and unholstered my weapon. I called out that I was a police officer, he was to drop what he was holdling and raise his hands."

"He had a weapon?"

"I don't know. It had a long barrel, like a shotgun, but it could have been the handle of a spade or a shovel?"

"Who fired first, you or Borch?"

"I never fired. Right after I called out, I heard gunfire to the left, one shot. I turned and that's when I was hit. Twice, and then there was another shot, and I tried to get up and was hit a third time. I wasn't able to return fire. Five shots in all."

"One shooter?"

"I think so. I can't be sure. I must have lost consciousness for a few minutes. The next thing I remember is Phil at my side. He said Borch was dead."

"Did you see anyone other than Robert Borch?"

"No. But when I first pulled into the driveway? I could see that there were two cars in the lot. An older model, maybe one Borch had been using. The other car was Doctor Hoffman's."

"You're sure?"

She winced again, nodded. "You said not to approach if I saw anything suspicious, to call it in. I didn't follow orders."

"What orders? I don't recall giving those orders, I believe I left it to your discretion. Mary Grace, why don't you stay with her until they arrange for a room. I want to have a word with Phil."

Victor included Carlo in the conference. It would have been too much to expect Carlo to stand on the sidelines, even if he had not had a personal stake in the events. "She says she saw Hoffman's car parked outside the clinic."

Phil sighed in frustration. "Hoffman pulls out 'round six. On the bridge, the bar starts coming down. He guns it, either he caught me tailing him or he didn't wanna be late for his gig. I got held up, put me about ten, fifteen minutes behind him. He coulda run out to the clinic and backtracked to the country club. I hadda decide which one to go to."

"It's lucky for Adane that you opted for the clinic." Victor turned to Carlo. "Look, can you stay with Mary Grace? I don't know when Raab's going to be able to come by for her."

Carlo had been a cop too long to be duped. "You don't have to keep me outta your hair. You get a line on my sister, you're gonna call right?"

Victor patted Carlo's burly arm and walked out to his car, thumbed Raab's number on his cell, as he pulled out of the lot.

"What's Adane's status?" Raab inquired, immediately.

"She'll be fine. But Borch and another guard are dead. You talk to Hoffman yet?"

"Wound up his speech a few minutes ago. NewsLineNinety's here to shoot some footage, I hope to the Almighty they don't have scanners, or they'll all be heading over to the ER."

"Don't worry, Carlo Fortunati there, he can handle them. Tell me, do you happen to know what time Hoffman got to the country club?"

"Little after six, him and the Bellamy woman both."

"Hoffman lost Phil on the Ninth Street Bridge and Adane says she saw Hoffman's car in the clinic's lot."

"There's self-park available and there's always a solid cocktail hour before these things kick in, be easy for him to lose himself forty-five minutes or so. Are there gonna be problems with Adane?"

"Not physically. Tactically, she says her weapon was never discharged. Five shots in all, the shooter was in the vicinity of the clinic's parking lot."

"Who's out at the clinic now?"

"State cops, CSU and Stan."

"You go out there. Get Adane's weapon bagged. Just pray Marty Bevilacqua doesn't get wind of this, or he won't let me within a mile of Hoffman."

Victor hung up and punched in Stan Rice's cell number.

"Got the ME here, he says the afternoon guard was shot at close range, we found him in the parking lot, near Hoffman's reserved space. Borch was shot from more of a distance, he was out in the field. I called Landis, he hasn't heard from Cat, told me to try his secretary at home. Name's Wein. W-e-i-n." Stan recited her number. "How's Jeannie?"

"She's going to be fine."

"Oh, and the ME said both of the guards, they died happy."

"I beg your pardon?"

"They both got it on not long before they got taken out."

"I presume you don't mean with each other."

"Jeez, I didn't ask."

"I think I can wait for the autopsy report. I'm on my way over. Stay there until I arrive." Victor hung up and dialed Cherry Wein's number.

She picked up on the first ring.

"Miss Wein, this is- "

"Lieutenant Cardenas, I know. I just got off with Ritchie."

"Did you speak to Mrs. Austen at all today?"

"Yeah. She was in a pay phone somewhere. I'd dug up some info on Home Stead Realty. Namely that Hoffman's first wife runs their Camden County office. It looks like she's turning a profit from the lease option State of the ART's got on that land around the clinic."

"Run that by me again?"

"She goes by her maiden name, Harianne Feldman. Don't know if she's trying to bury her connection to Hoffman or just wanted to cut all ties. I can keep digging."

dug up...buried...keep digging...

Someone out in the field...it was Borch...drop what he was holding...a spade or a shovel...

Victor broke the connection and floored the accelerator, drove one-handed while he thumbed nine one one. "I want a paramedic unit and any units that can be spared to the State of the ART clinic on Mays Landing-Somers Point Road."

"Can you state the nature of the emergency?"

"You'll be dead an hour from now if you don't do it!" He tossed the phone onto the passenger seat and sped down the narrow single lane, veered onto the shoulder and plowed through the line of arborvitae grazing the side of his car. He braked hard, grabbed a flashlight from his glove compartment and sprang out of the car.

"Rice!" Victor turned on the flashlight, swept it in an arc.

"Here!" Stan Rice jogged toward him. "What's up? You find Cat?"

God, don't let me be too late. Don't let me be too late. "She's here," he said.

CHAPTER FIFTY-THREE: Three Years Before

Freddy had brought her home from the hospital. Her mother had filled the refrigerator with food and taken the kids so that Cat could get some rest.

Cat walked upstairs and picked up the framed wedding portrait, sat on the bed, looked at the two figures, so very young. Until death, she thought. But death was supposed to come much later. She wanted to join him. Wanted to close her eyes and slip into darkness. But she couldn't, she had Jane and Mats. She held the picture to her breast, waited for the tears to come. She waited until the light waned, sat in the dark, waiting, fell asleep, woke, waiting. And waiting, she began to forget about Nicholas or Charlotte.

Kathy read Raymond's letter and did what he told her to do, moved the money to another safety deposit box, kept just enough out to pay the mortician in cash and pay Raymond's debts. She packed up his clothes and left them in the American Legion bin adjacent to the grocery store. She put the wedding picture in a drawer with the dried flowers, the remnants of the little nosegay Raymond had brought her.

Her mother told her that she had to go on, but she wanted to die. She thought about it every day, considered it quite calmly, wondered how it might be arranged so as not to inconvenience her mother.

And then someone knocked on her door, and changed her mind.

CHAPTER FIFTY-FOUR: Present Day

"Turn all the vehicles toward the field, and hit the headlights," Victor ordered. He shed his jacket and tossed it on the hood of his car. "Where'd they find Borch?"

Stan directed the eight headlights toward the mound where the smooth earth had been scored and puckered by a half dozen shoeprints. Victor approached the perimeter of the spot and dropped to his knees, then to his stomach, his gaze level with the ground.

"Lieutenant?"

Victor waved Stan back. Stan looked around at the other officers who were watching the erratic behavior of the usually self-contained lieutenant with alarm.

Victor reached up. "Flashlight!"

Stan handed it down to him, silently.

Victor rolled the flashlight's beam against the earth, his eyes scanning the expanse of rippling topsoil.

Something glistened white, a scant inch of glossy cylinder protruding from the ground. Victor moved his fingers forward, touched the object gently; it was a sheet of stiff, glossy paper, tightly rolled into a cylinder. He moved his fingers above it, thought that he felt a soft puff of warm air emerge.

He lurched back into a kneeling position and threw aside the flashlight, began to scoop the earth from around the object.

"Lieutenant, what's the- "

"Step back about three feet. Tell the uniforms to get over here and start digging."

"Victor- "

"*DO WHAT I TELL YOU*!"

Stan froze for a second, then threw off his jacket and whistled sharply, signaled toward the uniforms. He got down beside Victor and began digging up handfuls of the loose soil.

Victor took a fistful of the earth, compressed it in his palm. "Cool," he muttered. "There's a little more moisture in it. This ground's been dug up recently."

"You want me to find a shovel?" One of the officers asked.

Victor shook his head. "You may hit her."

"Her?" Stan gulped.

"*Keep digging!*"

They worked blindly, propelled by the somber lieutenant's inexplicable passion. Victor's hands circled the small protrusion of white, excavating carefully around it, while the others hollowed out a narrow trough in the loose earth.

"I feel something," Stan said. "It feels like fabric. A sheet or something.

"Don't stop!" Victor heard the whine of a siren.

An outline began to emerge, white with dirt nestled in its folds, the lower half of a face with something protruding from the lips. Victor's fingers worked more gently as he brushed earth away from the jaw, gently lifted a fold of white to expose the nose, eyelids, forehead. His abraded knuckles started to bleed. He heard Stan's panted "Jesus Christ, Jesus Christ, Jesus Christ" as he tunneled fiercely with cupped hands.

Victor dug his palms under her head and neck and lifted her, pulled the white paper tube from her lips. "Cat." He whispered her name aloud.

The siren rose to a shrill high and broke off.

"I got her knees," Stan said. "All of us lift together, we can get her out."

"Watch her neck." Victor kept one palm under her cheek, another hand under her ribs. The four of them lifted her, rolled her onto the ground. Two paramedics approached and one pried open one of Cat's eyelids, trained a beam of light at her pupil, felt her throat for a pulse. "She may be doped up, her breathing's shallow, but she's got a pulse." He slipped an oxygen mask over her face. "Move aside, Lieutenant."

Two paramedics lifted Cat onto a gurney. Victor followed them to the ambulance. They lifted Cat into the vehicle and climbed in. "I'm riding with you. Rice!" Victor tossed Stan his car keys. "Get my car."

One paramedic tried to prevent Victor from getting into the ambulance. "Why don't you get someone to drive you, Lieutenant? There's not enough room in here for all of us."

Victor reached up and grabbed the man by his shirt, yanked him to the ground. He jumped into the van and pounded the ceiling with his fist. "Get moving!" he yelled.

CHAPTER FIFTY-FIVE:
Present Day

Chris came for her, but he was not beckoning her, he was holding up his palm as if waving good-bye. His lips were forming something and she strained to hear the words. It sounded like he was telling her to get moving, but the voice didn't belong to Chris, and she began surging forward, not falling, not soaring, simply moving through space.

She felt herself surging forward, not falling, not soaring, simply moving through space. She opened her eyes and saw the white ceiling of the ambulance three feet above her and started to scream, flung her arms upward to push it away from her.

"Cat, Cat, it's all right. You're in the ambulance." Victor gripped her hands.

"Maybe you could hold her arm, Lieutenant, I'm going to try to put a line in."

Cat jerked her hands back, hugged her chest. "No!"

"Cat- "

"I don't want to be sedated! I won't wake up!"

"Mrs. Austen, let's calm down- "

Cat flung her arm, gave him a backhanded slap on the shoulder, tried to sit up. "No! I won't wake *up*!" she screamed.

"Mrs. Austen? Cat? I don't want to have to restrain-"

"I can't breathe! I can't *breathe* in here!"

"Pull over," Victor told him.

"Lieutenant- "

"Pull over. That's an order."

Victor's speech had resumed its normal monotone. Somehow, the paramedics found it less intimidating when he had shouted. The driver pulled over to the side of the road. Victor unlatched the back doors of the van, admitted the cool, moist air. Cat struggled to sit up, fending off the assistance of the paramedic. She leaned over, her forehead on her knees and allowed the fresh air to ease away the hyperventilating.

Victor hopped out, saw that they were in the parking lot of a liquor store at the base of the bridge that linked the Somers Point to Ocean City. He turned, and held out his hand to Cat. "Come on," he said. "Let's take a walk."

"Lieutenant, she could go into shock."

"I'm taking responsibility."

"Yo, Lieutenant, what gives?" Stan pulled up in Victor's Jag, got out of the car, handed Victor his jacket. Victor draped it around Cat's shoulders. She was shivering, her eyes glazed, the pupils dilated with panic.

She looks out of it, Stan mouthed to Victor. "Why don't I run you over the ER, hon?" Stan suggested to Cat. "Your Mom, Carlo, Freddy, they all went over there."

Cat felt her jaw quivering. "I w-want to go home."

"Lemme give you a lift, I'll call the ER from the car."

"I want to be out in the open."

"Hon, you can't walk over the bridge in this traffic."

"Says who?" Victor looked at him and Stan closed his mouth. "Call the ER and tell them I'm taking Cat home. Then follow us over the bridge. We'll keep to the right lane."

Stan shrugged and got back into Victor's Jag, waited until he saw Victor draw his coat tightly around Cat's shoulders and started the car. There was no pedestrian walkway, so Victor and Cat took the right eastbound land, Stan tailing them at a crawl.

Victor said nothing, allowed her to set the pace, to decide whether they spoke or remained silent. She stopped only once, as the causeway passed over the bay, removed her sandals and pitched them into the water, continued walking.

Stan called the emergency room. Within five minutes, a caravan formed behind the Jag: Carlo in his Volvo; Freddy in his Cherokee; Marco, Dominic and Jennie in Jennie's fire red Buick; Joey in his pampered Corvette; Vinnie in Vinnie, Jr's old hatchback, because VJ had a date, talked his dad into a loan of the new Lincoln.

In summer, vacationers got a jump on the weekend and started streaming across the barrier island bridges Thursday evening. It did not take long for Cat's languid pace, the line of family vehicles behind her, to dam up incoming traffic. Horns honked, and cars swerved into the passing lane. One driver veered around Cat and Victor and pulled to a halt in front of them. His car door shot open, obscenities emerging in advance of the speaker.

Victor tightened his grip on Cat's shoulder. "Stay here."

He stepped forward, his eyes locking on the irate glare of the driver. He did not produce his badge, did not raise his voice. He simply said, "Get out of our way."

The man lurched forward and locked eyes with Victor. Blinked. He pivoted and scuttled back to his car. The revving engine spat fumes as he pulled away. Victor put his arm around Cat's shoulder once more and the two of them continued walking.

Once over the bridge, Cat's family went on ahead. They were all home by the time she and Victor were spotted walking down Morningside.

Cat would never remember how she got home. The remainder of the reel was blurred and asynchronous, suspended between the image of a cellar door and the sight of her mother's silhouette standing on the porch.

Cat walked up the porch steps and felt two arms circle her. She didn't want to be confined, but something told her not to throw them off. She lowered her cheek to the soft waves of her mother's hair, inhaled her mother's favorite perfume.

She felt the arms fall away and crossed the room, the fingers groping for light switch, turned on the upstairs light and mounted the stairs.

Jennie looked up at Victor. There was a rosary suspended over one palm. "Maybe she should have something to eat?"

"Let her get her bearings, Jennie," he said, gently.

Cat eased open the door to Mats's room, backed out, leaving the door ajar. She looked in on Jane next. *My children. Mine and Chris's*. She walked to her room, reached around the door for the light switch, turned it on before she could bring herself to cross the threshold. She walked across the room and turned on the lamp on the night table, the desk lamp on her work station.

She reached around the door jamb to turn on the bathroom light and entered, looked into the mirror. She did not recognize her reflection. It was not the blotches of dirt that spattered her white face, the matted strands of hair falling over her brow, but the eyes. The eyes that stared into her own with fear and a dazed resignation. Chris was gone.

Cat felt particles of loose earth crawling over her ribcage and she remembered the earth falling on her, seeping into her sandals, her dress, her eyes and hair. She clutched the fabric of her sundress and tore it away from her, the buttons springing from the fabric, spilling onto the bathroom rug.

She reached into the shower and turned on the knobs, pulled off her dress and her underwear, left them on the floor and stepped into the shower, leaving the door open, stood for a long time watching the streaks of dirt slithering along her skin, pooling and vanishing down the drain. She pick up the shampoo and poured a thimbleful in her palm, inhaled its peach scent. The scent triggered a quiet rumble from her empty stomach.

I'm alive, she thought.

Downstairs, Victor washed his hands at the kitchen sink while he talked to Stan. Cat's brothers huddled in the dining room, trying not to look like they were eavesdropping. "I want you to track down Harianne Feldman," Victor said in a low voice.

"She manages Home Stead. Leave my car, Joey can give you a lift back to the clinic to pick up yours."

"You want me to pick her up?"

"Not yet. Just get a fix on her. I know she has a closing here some time tomorrow afternoon. Another thing," Victor added, grimly. "Call search and rescue, have them bring out the dogs."

Stan understood. "Chavez. You think she's buried there."

"I'm certain of it."

He found Cat sitting on her bed, wearing a pair of loose drawstring pants, a sleeveless T-shirt. Her hair hung in damp strands around her face.

"Why don't you try to lie down," he suggested.

She eased herself down on top of the bedspread. "Don't turn out the light."

Victor tried to throw a blanket over her. She flinched and pushed it away. "I don't want that on top of me."

Victor bent down, kissed a strand of her wet hair. "I'll be downstairs."

"No, stay here until I fall asleep."

Victor unbuttoned his grimy shirt, laid it over a chair, pried off his shoes and got onto the bed. Cat lay with her back to him, staring at the open door. Victor put his arm around her, laced his fingers through hers.

Cat's gaze shifted to the picture on her bureau, the skirt of her white dress pooling around Chris as though the two of them were drifting on a cloud. She fell asleep, looking at it.

CHAPTER FIFTY-SIX: Three Years Ago

She crept up to the attic one night and unzipped the plastic bag, took the wedding dress out. The whiteness had faded very slightly, the fabric wilted a bit. Cat threw off her clothes and put it on, pulling it over her head, roughly, pushing her arms into the sleeves.

It still fit. It would have been better if it hadn't, better if a pinch or a tug had announced that time flowed forward, that the past had loosened its hold. But the gown settled against her as comfortably as it had been fourteen years ago. She grabbed the bodice in both hands and pulled with all of her might, pulled until she heard the fabric rend like a sob tearing out of her throat.

Kathy looked at herself in the mirror. She saw nothing but the flush along her pale cheeks, a flush that was absurdly like the shame of a teenage girl who had gotten herself in trouble.

It was wrong. Wicked. People would know that it wasn't Raymond's and there would be questions. No, it wasn't wrong to take a little life that no one had wanted. What was wrong is not being loved. Not having anyone to love.

And Kathy needed to love someone so very much.

CHAPTER FIFTY-SEVEN: Present Day

Cat woke to the scent of strong caffe latte. She opened her eyes and saw Mats staring at her. "Vi'tor says I gotta keep a eye on you 'til he gets back."

Cat pushed away the blanket Victor had laid over her and put her arms around Mats.

"How come you're hugging me too tight." He squirmed back and studied his mother's face.

"I don't think I hugged you yesterday, so I have to get in two days' worth," Cat replied, solemnly.

"Nonna tol' Uncle Carlo an' Uncle Freddy to go out an' get us some doughnuts because they were getting in her hair."

"I bet Nonna looks silly with Uncle Carlo and Uncle Freddy in her hair."

"Not on her *head*," Mats giggled.

"You better go downstairs so that Jane doesn't get first pick of the chocolate ones," Cat suggested. "Ellice and Nonna can keep an eye on me."

Ellice was standing in the doorway. She placed a steaming mug of caffe latte on Cat's night table.

Cat looked into her eyes. "I'll be okay. I'll make it to the rehearsal tonight. You're not postponing the wedding."

Ellice sank onto the bed and sighed. "Freddy brought it up. It wouldn't kill us to wait."

"No. I can't – " Cat swallowed. "You start putting things off because the timing isn't right, you start to forget about it all together."

"A week or so."

Cat swallowed a wave of blind panic, blinked back tears. "Was Victor here all night?"

"He just left a few minutes ago." Ellice sat on the edge of the bed. "I'd better warn you, don't turn on the radio."

Sonny at Sunrise. Cat reached for the cup, took a sip of the caffe latte, was grateful that her mother had made it particularly strong. "How bad is it?"

"Thematically or grammatically?" Ellice mimicked Sonny's self-important tone. "'Whereas a virtual processional of a line of cars traversing the Ninth Street Bridge at a below the minimum limit had traffic in virtual bottle up beyond the Somers Point Circle which would ordinarily have been a sensible time for the local officials to intervene had not the causation of the crisis been the favorable treatment of one of their own.'"

"You're making that up."

"Honey, only Sonny could make that up. Landis called a half dozen times." She patted Cat's hand. "What say you go to the beach and lie out, away from the phone and the airwaves?"

Cat thought about soaking in the sun, surrounded by nothing but light and air. "There are parts of yesterday I don't remember clearly. And I don't think I want to know."

Ellice understood. She had put horrors of her own behind her. "Well, 'let us not burthen our remembrance with a heaviness that's gone'," Ellice quoted, calmly.

Jennie came into the room, her bright hair in pin curls. "*Figgiu mi'*." She kissed Cat's hair. "I'm gonna kill that Sonny at Sunrise."

"Is he still talking about the virtual bottle up on the bridge?" Ellice asked.

"No, he's goin' on to the detective who got shot."

"What detective?" Cat asked.

Jennie sat on the bed, patted Cat's hand. "She's gonna be okay, I don't want you to worry about it. That woman who lives with Mary Grace Keller. She got shot last night."

"Jean Adane? What happened?"

"I think Victor's going to explain everything, he just went to get changed and then he wants to check in at the office. Ellice you go run your errands so you get done."

Jennie waited for Ellice to leave. "You got all day to cry it out. What that man did to you, he wasn't dead already, Carlo'd kill him."

"Dead! Who – who's dead?"

"That big security guard the Nixon sisters saw hanging around here the other day."

Robert Borch? Fragments of echoes welled up.

Let's get it done with.

I said I'd take care of you, and I will.

That doesn't look much more than a couple feet.

It's as good as I did for Chavez, just take care of Rod and let me do my job...

Cat pressed her hands over her ears.

"You go lie out, like Ellice said. I gotta run over to the church, I'll take the kids with me."

"No, I want to keep them with me today." She looked up at her mother's troubled expression. "Mama, after Chris died, I wondered, sometimes, what it would have been like if I hadn't had them."

"Well, maybe that's why God saw to it you had them."

God, or Randall Hoffman. There had been a time when Cat couldn't tell the two apart.

"Some people want them and it doesn't...God doesn't seem to be helping out much," Cat said, tentatively.

Jennie cupped Cat's chin in her hand, just as she had done when Cat was a child. "I waited for people around here to tell me anything, I wouldn't know half what I know. Children are here for one reason. God wants them to be here. How he works out the here and there, that's none of my business. What I say is you live and let live and once in a while you light a candle."

"How'd you get so smart, Mama?"

"I didn't get smart waiting around to be told what's what, that's for sure. Now you drink your caffé, I gotta get something on the stove. Louie Cicciolini and his boyfriend are coming by, Louie wants to get a look at Ellice's headpiece so he knows how he's gonna do her hair."

"I think it's 'partner', Mama, not 'boyfriend'."

Jennie shrugged. "Partner, boyfriend, whatever. All I can say is, I'm gonna see he gets a good breakfast. I was Dottie Cicciolini I'd be ashamed to have a boy of mine that skinny."

Cat felt the sun's weight bear down on her, warming her down to that core of dread. She was fighting off the urge to doze when she heard Mats's voice. "Uncle Stebe!"

Cat looked over her shoulder and saw Steve Delareto clad in a bathing suit and short-sleeved shirt, balancing a backpack and beach chair on one arm, little Chris Petrone on the other.

He knelt and set the toddler on the sand, tugged a rolled-up beach towel from the backpack. "Can you stand some company?"

The little boy was wearing a long sleeved T-shirt, nylon trunks plumped by the diaper beneath, a brimmed cap, sneakers. Cat, with instinctive maternity, lifted him on her lap while Steve unpacked a thermos and a plastic bag with some grapes and Cheerios, opened his beach chair.

"Did Victor tell you to come keep an eye on me?"

Steve chuckled, ruefully. "Freddy. He'd do it himself, but I get the feeling he's going nuts trying to keep tabs on Ellice. I think he still half expects to be left at the altar. Besides, it's Kathy's day to visit the cemetery, then she got a call from Chris's doctor, he wants to see her in person later today."

"It's not bad news, is it?"

"I don't know if he said. Even if he did, Kathy's not the type to burden other people. I had to practically kidnap the kid to get her to let me baby-sit."

"Does she know about what happened last night?"

"Not that she let on. I'm pretty sure the cops're gonna want to question her again, though." He began rummaging in the backpack for sunscreen. "C'm'ere, Chris."

The little boy plopped down in front of Steve, obediently. Steve began rubbing sunscreen on his exposed legs and face.

Mats trotted up to them. "Is this your boy?"

"No, he's a friend. His name's Chris."

"Can he put his face in the water?" Mats was wary.

"No, Chris has never even been to the beach."

"In his *life?*"

Steve nodded. "I brought along a pail and shovel for him, I was hoping I could find some kids around here to show him how to make a sand castle, do beach stuff." Steve pretended to look around the beach for likely candidates.

"*I* know how," Mats stated.

Steve handed Chris a new red plastic pail and shovel. Mats led the boy to the edge of the blanket. "First," he told the toddler. "You gotta put sand in the pail up to the top."

"What with all the hospitalizations, he's used to have strangers pass him around." Steve settled in his beach chair. "You wanna talk, or just sit?"

"I can't talk about what I don't remember."

"You didn't witness any of the shootings, then?"

The plural made her shudder. "I heard about Jean Adane."

Steve nodded. "It looks like it's not serious. But Borch and another guard were fatally shot. It looks like getting rid of the guards was high priority, and Jean Adane got lucky because the shooter was on the clock."

The rhythm of the surf muffled the human sounds, synchronized with Cat's heartbeat. Cat closed her eyes and heard the pulsing in her ears, the sound that had penetrated that awful darkness, kept reminding her that she was alive. "Did Kathy ever mention Home Stead Realty to you?"

"Only when Victor called yesterday, looking for you. He asked about it. She said they brokered the deal on the clinic."

"Did she tell you that Home Stead is managed by the first Mrs. Hoffman?"

"Hoffman's ex?" Steve lifted the brim of his cap, ran his palm over his hair. "Kathy knew that, I'm sure she would've mentioned it when Cardenas called yesterday."

"Maybe she's holding out on you."

"No. I think she trusts me. As much as she can trust anyone right now."

"Well, she's holding *something* back," Cat insisted. "Look how long she went without ever mentioning her husband's letter."

"I think she would've come clean sooner or later."

"I don't know. Some secrets have to be dragged into the light. And some you trip over." She hesitated. "I went to see Mrs. Coleman yesterday."

"Mrs. Coleman?"

"Her sister and brother-in-law were the accident victims Chris had talked to you about. She's a few years older than I am. Forties. She's got a little boy around two, and they took in the nephew, he's ten. I saw the two boys together. That's when I tripped on the truth."

"What?"

Cat sighed, shakily. "I think the two boys are biological siblings."

"What?"

"The way she talked suggested that she'd had problems with fertility. Now she's in her forties, with a toddler who has the same hair coloring, eye coloring, facial features as her sister's son. They're not first cousins, Steve. They're brothers."

"You think she pled her case to Hoffman or Bender and they figured, what the heck, why waste the dead sister's embryos?"

"What would have happened to them otherwise? That's the question Chris was asking. That's what must have been tormenting Miriam Bender."

"Enough to commit suicide?" Steve asked, dubiously. "Look, weird as this sounds, if this Coleman woman was her sister's heir, she might have had a claim on them anyway."

"Maybe she didn't know that. Maybe she was made to think that the clinic could dispose of them after the donors died."

"So Hoffman or Bender offer to transfer them to her?"

"Or to sell them." Cat waited for him to protest. "I don't hear you saying that it's impossible, that it's too Aldous Huxley, and that I must be mistaken."

"I've read the new stem cell law. It made embryos a pretty valuable commodity. It's a brave new world, all right."

"Or a craven one. Remember you said that people figure out how to exploit things for corrupt purposes way before we figure out how to use it for good? What do you do with a commodity, Steve? You buy low and sell to the highest bidder." Cat pushed her sunglasses onto her forehead and looked at him. "Vinnie told me about this online auction site, CyberSwap. He brought them up when I was asking him about the Gabors. The pawnbrokers?"

"I know who they are. I'm not sure I see the connection."

"What happens if they have a piece of pawned merchandise that's unclaimed?"

"You have to notify the owner by certified mail, and after a certain period of time, you can declare it abandoned property. After that, you've got to advertise it publicly for auction- "

"Notify, advertise," Cat interrupted. "All of that takes time and money and they eat into profits. What if you've had something left on your hands that you know is valuable and you're certain the donor isn't going to retrieve it? Emeralds, embryos, if society regards them both like merchandise, then why shouldn't they be marketed like merchandise? Or black-marketed like contraband? Steve, I checked out that CyberSwap site, there were women putting their oocytes out to the highest bidder, with donor's age, race, educational level, health status, eye color."

"Back in the day, you said 'oocyte' outside of bio class, you'd get yourself smacked up. Yesterday, Kathy told Kurt Raab how Miriam Bender called them orphans."

Cat's gaze rested on Mats. Matthew Christopher. There had been no Matthew on either side of the family. That had been in honor of Miriam Bender's father. "I don't think I've ever met a more decent human being than Miriam Bender. I can't see her taking advantage of women who were desperate, women who couldn't afford an IVF program or were at the bottom of the OvaShare waiting list. I can see her setting these women up to take embryos that were abandoned. I can't see her selling them."

"Look, Cat, even if you're right, whether they were bought or donated, you're gonna have to have the buyers come forward and testify."

"They could order DNA testing."

"And who're you gonna test? Every kid born to one of Hoffman's patients in the last couple years? And how're you gonna go about locating them?"

How old is your boy, two, two and a half?

He was two last Valentine's Day

Cat's gaze settled on Chris, squatting in the sand, looking up at Mats as reverently as Mats looked up at Jane. "Steve, how old is Chris, exactly, did Kathy ever say?"

"His second birthday's comin' up, June..."

"Maybe there is one woman we can locate." Cat looked at him, her dark eyes sober. "You've seen pictures of Raymond Stites. The boy doesn't look anything like him, does he? He doesn't look anything like Kathy, either."

CHAPTER FIFTY-EIGHT: Present Day

When Victor arrived at Major Crimes, a shower, shave, fresh clothes and twenty ounces of strong coffee had eradicated all traces of the previous night's ordeal. Stan Rice appeared far less tranquil. He had gone back to the field, watched while they exhumed the body of Daria Chavez. He witnessed the autopsy, immune, for once, to the offhand levity of the ME.

Phil looked only marginally better, having spent the evening in a warped vinyl chair outside Jean Adane's room. "She's good to go," he told Victor. "But the PBA mouthpiece doesn't want her to talk unless she's got a rep."

"I don't want her to have to talk at all." Victor sat behind his desk and gestured for the two of them to sit. "Phil, have someone from Raab's office lean on Cumberland County's DA. I want Santucci to tell us who paid him off."

"Why don't we just haul in Hoffman?"

"Because unless we have enough to go up against Martin Bevilacqua, we won't be able to hold him. Let's wait until CSU finishes working the clinic. And Stan, I want to be up to date on Hoffman's phone records, calls that come into his service, home, cell. And Home Stead Realty's too, both offices. You can reach me on my cell."

"Where will you be?"

"I'm going to stop in on Adane. And then I'm going to have to notify Mr. Chavez that his daughter's been found."

It was mid-afternoon when Steve and Cat returned from the beach. Steve carried little Chris in one arm, Mats in the other. Jane shouldered Steve's beach chair, commenting to her mother that only *babies* needed to be carried.

Steve took the two boys in the outside shower while Cat went up to get showered and dressed for the wedding rehearsal.

When Cat went downstairs, she found Carlo sitting on the couch with Chris Petrone on one knee, Mats at his side. He had the narrow bifocals, which he hated to wear, perched on his nose and a copy of *Pokey Little Puppy* on his knee. In the course of Carlo's stint as a pediatric ward storyteller, sometime magician and annual Santa, he had committed a dozen or so Golden Books to memory, and often embellished the text extemporaneous commentary.

"Now you see the problem we got here with Pokey," he told the boys, "-is that he's too much out for himself. Goin' out into the world, wanting to see what's what, no problem, but you can't run home, eat all the pudding and leave none for your brothers and sisters. That's not right. There's always gonna be more shortcake down the pike, but you only got one family and with family, it's share and share alike, you get my point?"

Two-year-old Chris, his thumb firmly planted in his mouth, looked up, awestruck, at this genial giant.

Cat looked at Chris. One day, he would ask, 'Where did I come from?' What would Kathy tell him? What was the truth?

"I share, Uncle Carlo," Mats reminded him.

Jennie had Steve sitting at the kitchen table in front of a bowl of vermicelli. Steve looked up and shrugged, helplessly.

"Cat, what did you eat today?" Jennie inquired.

"We had lunch on the beach, Mama. I can wait until after the rehearsal. I need to run an errand."

"What errand?" Steve asked, warily.

"One that won't wait," she said, pointedly. "Mama, can you take the kids to church with you? I'm only running over to Somers Point, so I'll hook up with Ellice so we can drive to St. Agnes together. Steve, I'm going to need maybe an hour for my errand, why don't you and Chris hang around here. It will take at least that long for Carlo to get through *Pokey Little Puppy*."

Steve gave her a wry look. "Cat, do you think you have time for *errands* right now?"

"I think if you wait for the right time, you end up just waiting."

"That's right," Jennie nodded.

Steve walked her to her car. "One hour," he said, firmly. "And Cat, I don't know what the doctor wanted to talk to her about, but you get the sense that it's bad news, do the right thing and back off. It's waited this long, it'll keep."

It had waited this long, Cat mused as she drove to Somers Point. This long to realize that Raymond Stites had believed he was dying, and loving Kathy so much that he would agree to kill a cop; not for the sixty thousand dollars, but so that she wouldn't be left alone. Chris Petrone was alive because Chris Austen had died.

It wasn't Kathy who answered her knock, it was Eve Bellamy.

"Eve? Hi. Where's Kathy?"

Eve smiled her sunny smile. "I called earlier and she said she had an appointment, said she'd leave the door unlocked in case she was running late. C'mon in and wait with me."

"A doctor's appointment, I think." Cat stepped into the living room. She heard Eve close the door behind her. "Weren't you getting married today?"

Eve held up her left hand, wiggled her fingers to display a broad, ruby studded wedding band. "A small and simple. Randy's prepping the boat, we're taking it down to Virginia Beach for the weekend. That's all the honeymoon we can manage right now."

Cat tried to put some warmth into her "Congratulations".

"Is Kathy expecting you?"

Cat shook her head. "I probably should have called first, too. Maybe I should just leave her a note?"

"Why don't we just wait another ten minutes? She said she wouldn't be long."

We'd better wait another ten minutes.

The voice had been familiar. Cat had not recognized it because the words had usually been spoken in such a sweet, girlish tone.

Never with the coldness of a killer.

CHAPTER FIFTY-NINE: PRESENT DAY

Victor always tried to allot ample time when making a notification. Still, it was never enough, he could never quite anticipate the time one needed to cope with the screams, the tears, the shock, the hysterical disbelief.

As it turned out, he had rationed more than enough for Arturo Chavez, whose reaction was immediate comprehension and sorrowful resignation. "I always knew she coul' not live long. Greed, it eats you up fast." Then he made a few simple inquiries about where Daria's body would be taken, how soon he thought the medical examiner would release it, and let Victor go.

He bought flowers for Adane and slipped into the hospital room, found her asleep. Mary Grace Keller was sitting in a chair at the head of the bed, slumped over, her head resting on the pillow beside Adane's.

No tienes familia, Victor's father had said, '*no tienes nada.*' He laid the flowers at the foot of the bed and left.

Stan Rice was at his desk when Victor returned "Your mom called," he said.

"Give me a few minutes."

Victor called his mother and allowed her to remind him that he was to come to dinner that weekend, to wish him a happy birthday and remind him of the day he was born, how she was sitting there thinking about it and how it made her sad to think that he had no children of his own, and maybe he could bring the girl he was dating the one Milly had told him about?

"I'll ask her, *Mamí*. She has a family wedding this weekend."

He let the conversation run its course, then signaled for Stan to come in.

For once, Stan did not seem to mind that they were headed into a Friday evening and he was still at his desk. "Been a lot of phone activity. You sure Hoffman and his ex aren't on speaking terms?"

Victor cocked and eyebrow, sat behind his desk.

"'Cause there's calls between the doc's cell and Ms. Feldman's cell. And a lot of them weren't during business hours. Evenings, Sunday mornings."

"Really?"

"That's not all. You said Hoffman let the Petrone woman go and there hasn't been any contact? Well Petrone called the clinic this morning. Got the answering service because the clinic's closed. I called the service, they said the clinic was scheduled to close because the doc and the Bellamy woman are getting married. They went ahead with it, high noon, but not before Hoffman got back to Petrone. I been trying Petrone's number, all I get is her machine."

Victor wondered what had prompted Kathy Petrone to call Hoffman; more importantly, why would Hoffman call her back on his wedding day? "Call Steve Delareto, try his cell first. When I called Mrs. Austen's house this morning, her mother said Delareto had come by with the Petrone boy, all of them went down to the beach. What about Mrs. Feldman?"

"Phil's gonna go over to Ocean City to bring her in as soon as she's done with the closing. That should be another hour or so. Look, if I can get away from my desk once Phil gets back, I'd like to run over see how Jeannie's doin'."

"Go ahead."

Victor reached for the phone, dialed Hoffman's home number. He got the machine. He pulled up Doctor Aquino's number, got another answering machine, but in a few minutes, Aquino called him back.

"Lieutenant. Sorry. I'm screening my calls, it's been press, press, press all day since that shooting on the clinic's grounds last night."

Victor thought he heard the drumming of animated fingers on a table top. "Did you attend Randall Hoffman's wedding today?"

"Oh, no. As I understand it, there were only two witnesses, their attorney, and a friend. I called to congratulate them and to ask whether we're going to have office hours on Monday. Eve said it would be up to the police, whether or not we were allowed back on the site."

"You didn't talk to Hoffman?"

"No, I guess she was picking up for him, he was on the dock, getting the boat ready. He and Eve are sailing down to Virginia for the weekend."

"Thanks for your time, doctor."

Victor dug up Hoffman's cell phone number. It was picked up on the second ring by Eve Bellamy.

"This is Lieutenant Cardenas, Miss Bellamy. I'd like to speak to Doctor Hoffman."

"Randy's out on the dock, he's getting the boat ready, we're sailing to Virginia."

"It's important that I speak to him as quickly as possible."

"Why don't you give me a message and I'll have him call you back, oh, within the hour."

It was then that he heard something, a soft chiming sound in the background.

"It concerns the business we talked about, Miss Bellamy-"

He heard a short, trilling laugh. "It's Mrs. Hoffman."

The chiming stopped; it continued in Victor's brain. It was a clock. He called up an image of the Hoffman's foyer, hallway, living room. Of course, he had not seen the upstairs. She may have been on the second floor. Or she may have been anywhere else, using Hoffman's cell.

"Yes," he said, evenly. "Mrs. Hoffman. Please tell your husband to call me."

"Of course, Lieutenant."

Victor hung up and strode into the day room. Stan was standing, pulling on his jacket, the phone wedged to his ear. "Hang on," he said, and pressed his palm to the mouthpiece. "I got Delareto, he's still over Cat's. He said she ran over to have a talk with Kathy Petrone about something that couldn't wait. Sounds like he tried to talk her out of it."

"She's over there now?"

"Yeah."

"You said you tried to call over there, you only got the machine to pick up."

"Maybe she's screening her calls?"

"Maybe." Victor held out his hand for the receiver. Stan handed it to him. "Delareto, tell me something. You've been to Mrs. Petrone's house?"

"Yeah, why?"

"Tell me, has she got a mantle clock? One that chimes?"

"No. But she's got a grandfather clock, I think it's an antique. She said her mother left it to her. Why?"

"I'll have to get back to you on that."

Victor hung up. "I need to run over to Somers Point, and I'm going to need some backup. You can stop in on Adane after we're done."

CHAPTER SIXTY:
Present Day

Did 'you'll never get away with it' ever deter them, Cat wondered? Not the brazen ones, the ones who were too heartless, or too arrogant or too crazy to consider the possibility of capture and retribution. And when you were at the wrong end of a gun, it didn't much matter, anyway.

"You got Raymond Stites to kill Chris."

"Stites." Eve spoke the name as though it soured her tongue. "Bobby and Roddy and Chuck Santucci didn't need nearly as much persuading."

"Meaning Raymond Stites couldn't be seduced. But he could be deluded," Cat interpreted. "He really was stressed out. Is that what gave you the idea to order those tests?"

"I got Randy to. Of course, he did it because I told him it would ease Kathy's mind, and he would do anything to keep Kathy – functional. Randy only has use for people who take care of him, you see. He couldn't afford to lose her. But I was the one who gave Raymond the test results."

"The wrong results."

"Well, now, that all depends, doesn't it. On what they were meant to accomplish."

"Use him to silence my husband because Chris was close to the truth. Embryos that were to be destroyed were being sold."

They stood facing each other in the dining room. Eve was under the archway where she could keep an eye on both the front door and the dining room, where Cat stood with her back to the table. Cat's position was near enough the picture window to give her a peripheral glimpse of the street. A police cruiser exceeding the residential speed limit would not have aroused much notice, not in summer. The second gave her a bit of hope.

"So whose idea was that? Yours or Doctor Hoffman's?"

Eve laughed. "Oh, Randy had nothing to do with it. For him, it was pay top dollar or do without. Of course, there was the OvaShare option, but even at a discount, IVF isn't cheap."

"So, it was your idea?"

"No, actually, it was Miriam's."

"I don't believe that."

"Oh, not to sell them," Eve scoffed. "That wouldn't have been *humane*. She came upon so many women through her support group. A lot of them could be IVF candidates, if they had the money. Or if they hadn't gambled it all on a single procedure that failed. And there were more than enough embryos to go around, enough to drive Miriam to depression. If your husband hadn't started nosing around, she really *might* have hit bottom and killed herself."

Cat swallowed. "And, of course, she didn't."

"Randy was always going to need me sooner or later, I intended that. As a widower, he was a lot easier to work on."

"How did you find out what Miriam was doing?"

"Raymond. He mentioned it to me because Kathy and I had become so friendly. It was very useful, being nice to Kathy, she *appreciated* it so much. Raymond had seen Miriam meeting with people at the clinic. Very late at night. He was afraid she might be doing something illegal, and when something illegal is going on, the first one to catch blame is the ex-con. So I - not 'confronted' – I *befriended* Miriam. And she confessed that she had gone so far as to adjust the inventory orders, and alter records to cover the additional supplies of hormones. Of course, I never had to sink that low."

"You had The Hoffman," Cat said, hoarsely.

"I had both of them. I helped her, bided my time until I could figure out how to make use of it. That's the Hoffman influence, you see. Use people until they're used up."

Cat shuddered. Perhaps the police cars had not come for her. What if Steve called? What if he *didn't* call, just came over? What was going to happen if Kathy walked in? "And then the Ashers died in a car crash."

"Was that their name? You all run together after awhile. That's what started your husband off, wasn't it? He called Miriam, and of course Miriam couldn't go to Randy at this point. She went to the only one she could talk to." Eve smiled.

"So you killed her. And set my husband up and got rid of the witnesses, or thought you had. "Why didn't you kill Kathy?"

"Raymond and Kathy and Miriam *and* your husband dying? That would have been a bit extreme. Besides, I wasn't sure that I wouldn't need her. And I had something better than a bullet to keep her quiet, if she did become suspicious. And, of course, once she did get pregnant, she was a conspirator. I've never met anyone more intelligent and at the same time more naïve."

"And after Miriam died? How did you manage?"

"Quite nicely. There was still a willing clientele. All I had to do was to undercut the competition. Half what the clinic charges still allowed me to put aside a very nice nest egg. The overnight guards were well compensated for overlooking the fact that the facilities were used during the off hours. And I've assisted Randy and Paul and Mark hundreds of times. The implantation procedure isn't all that difficult. You don't need twelve years of postgraduate training to figure it out, all you need to know is where to point and when to fire."

"And were you going to keep this up until you married Doctor Hoffman? What if one of the women talked?"

"About what? Participating in a felony? Not after they had gotten pregnant, certainly. Because they were willing to do anything to have a child, anything at all. You remember how that felt, don't you?"

On the other side of the front door, Victor gripped his weapon. He motioned for the two officers to circle right and take the back door, gestured for Stan, crouching below the picture window, to keep his head down. He heard "Because they were willing to do anything to have a child, anything at all. You remember how that felt, don't you?"

"Yes. I remember what that felt like." He heard only the slightest tremor in Cat's voice. "What happens now?"

"Well, it will look like Kathy shot you and then killed herself. I mean the two of you certainly have your reasons to be at odds. But that lovely lieutenant of yours won't buy it, and the ballistics should match the bullets to Randy's weapon and at last I'll break down and tell them that Randy confessed it all to me, how he set up Raymond Stites, set up your husband. And every dollar, every phone call, every piece of paper will be traced back to Randy and then Randy will know what it means to be the used instead of the user."

Kathy had been intercepted, escorted to a neighbor's house. She had given a layout of the house, told him that she had left the door unlocked for Eve, reasoned that Eve would probably have left it unlocked.

She had reasoned correctly. He didn't have to kick in the door. He was able to slip into the foyer so silently that Eve never heard a thing until he ordered her to drop her weapon, until she turned and saw him standing there with his own weapon trained on the site where her heart ought to have been.

CHAPTER SIXTY-ONE: Present Day

Victor watched through the window as Stan escorted Eve to one of the patrol cars. Cat sank onto a dining room chair, propped her elbow on the table, her head resting on her palm.

"It wasn't Hoffman, it wasn't Miriam, it was Eve."

Victor pulled a chair away from the table and sat facing her. "Look, I sent Phil to pick up Harianne Feldman at her closing. Ellice was there."

Cat looked up, blinked. "Ellice?"

"She's not going into real estate, is she?"

"Ellice has been awfully secretive lately, and I know she wants to quit substitute teaching."

"Well, listen. When she gets here, I want the two of you to go on to the church. Let her drive. Give Freddy my apologies, I probably won't be able to make it over to Bud 'N' Lou's."

"I guess...you were waiting outside the door long enough to hear some of what was said."

Victor took her hand. "Nothing I didn't already know. Or suspect. Nothing that changes anything between us."

Cat squeezed his hand, looked into his eyes. "How is it that you always know where to find me?"

"How is it that you haven't given up trying to lose me?"

Cat and Ellice, an hour and fifteen minutes late for the wedding rehearsal, arrived at St. Agnes to find Freddy gone. He had gotten there a half hour early, decided at last that he had been jilted once more, stormed out to Bud 'N' Lou's. By the time his brothers located him and dragged him back to the altar, he was considerably over the legal limit.

Carlo lumbered back to the nave where Cat stood with Ellice, the attendants and Jennie and announced. "Freddy's plastered, and Dottie Cicciolini's been hittin' the anisette up at the piano. Whaddayou wanna do?"

"He didn't go do anything at Bud 'N' Lou's he can't take Communion," Jennie fretted. "He better not oversleep. Your father- " She made the Sign of the Cross "- the day we got married? He overslept, he's in a hurry, he runs down a dog on the way to the church, all through the ceremony he's crying harder than my mamma, rest in peace." She crossed herself again.

"He *hit* it?" Jane demanded. "Did he *kill* it?"

Dottie Cicciolini, idling at St. Agnes's ill-tuned Steinway, heard "Hit it" and began pounding out the Wedding March.

Cat looked at Ellice. The two of them began to shudder.

"No, he just nicked it, but it comes time for the Sacrament, and he won't take it- " Jennie mimicked her late husband's baritone. "'I almost killed a little dog! God forgive me I almost killed a little dog!'"

"Who's dog got killed?" Freddy yelled from the altar. "Somebody's dog got killed?"

"Tell Joey to shut your brother up," Jennie demanded of Carlo. "Anyway, we hadda cut the honeymoon short because we hadda use some of the money to pay the vet. And your father brought that dog soup bones from the restaurant until the day he died. So you gotta remember, Ellice, if you think everything's gonna go smooth- "

"- you're barking up the wrong family tree." Cat's shuddering erupted into a fit of hysterical giggles.

"See what your brother did?" Jennie demanded. "You go tell the girls and your brothers we're gonna get this done before Ellice changes her mind. Go give your brother a smack and then come back walk me down the aisle." Ellice's parents had died years before, so Jennie's entrance would signal the beginning of the ceremony.

"Stop, or I'm going to start laughing, too!" Ellice hissed as Carlo escorted Jennie to her place. "Cat, I'm so sorry I've been AWOL all week and I know you've needed someone to lean on."

Cat's giggles made an awkward transition to sobs. "I'm so tired of leaning. I'm so tired of being weak."

"Mom," Jane rolled her eyes. "You're em*barr*assing us."

"Yo," Carlo yelled. "Let's get this show on the road!"

"Good God, how drunk is Dottie!" Ellice pressed her fingertips over her ears to muffle the thunderous march.

"I'm the one who should have been there," Cat wept. She gave Jane a little nudge. The three bridesmaids strode down the altar, carrying invisible nosegays. "I mean, you're getting married, you're going into the real estate business...Mats, it's your turn to walk down the aisle now, do it just like we practiced."

"I'm scared."

"Did you say I'm going into real estate?" Ellice said, aloud.

"Go ahead, honey, I'll just be a couple steps behind you." She turned to Ellice. "Aren't you?"

Mats began a tentative walk down the aisle. Several paces along, he turned and whispered, loudly, "C'mon, Mom!"

Cat fell into step with the procession, shot Ellice a puzzled look over her shoulder.

"Yo, Maid of Honor, eyes front," Carlo boomed.

Cat looked ahead toward the altar and felt a tug of *deja vous*. She believed she could feel the pressure of her father's sleeve pressing her hand to his side. If she closed her eyes, she would see Chris at the altar, turning to her with a smile.

She felt her facial muscles tighten, felt the warm track of a tear sliding down her cheek. *I won't cry. I'll cry later. I have the rest of my life to cry.*

Dominic reached over gently, nudged her chin. Cat smiled and gave him an 'I'm okay' nod. He waited for Ellice to step in place. "Okay, I'm going to open with a prayer- "

"Ellish..." Freddy swayed toward her, unsteadily. Joey grabbed his sleeve to keep him from toppling over. "I'm glad you could make it."

Ellice looked from Freddy to Cat. "Freddy, I bought a store."

Freddy blinked.

"What'd she say?" Carlo demanded. He was at the end of the four brothers queued on Freddy's right.

"She said she bought a *store*, Uncle Carlo," Mats told him.

"That's why I was late, I was at the closing."

"I thought you weren' gonna show up."

Ellice sighed and shook her head. "Okay, time out. Freddy, listen up. Are you too drunk to listen?"

"I am practically completely sober."

"Freddy. John McKnight's retiring, he told me he was putting the book store on the market, the one downtown on Asbury. I know it's a risky venture, but it's something I've always wanted to try. And I bought it, so if it doesn't work out, the real estate will appreciate at least. And if it does work out, you can retire early and drive me nuts."

"Do we get *dis*counts?" Jane whispered, loudly.

"I heard these little book stores aren't doing good anymore, people aren't reading," Lorraine announced from her pew. Her sisters-in-law shushed her.

"You gonna take mail orders?" Carlo asked. "You don't wanna get killed by the onlines, you gotta at least take mail orders."

"Are you gonna change the name?" Jane inquired. "I don't like 'Sea Reads'. It sounds like 'seaweed'."

"Seaweed," Mats giggled.

"And get yourself a web site," Carlo added.

"Yeah, get Jason to do it, spends all his damn time at the damn computer anyway," Vinnie muttered.

"Don't say 'damn' in church!" his mother ordered.

"What about Quillfeathers?" Sherrie called from her seat.

"Sounds too much like one of those places they hold those wift poetry readings," Vinnie grumbled.

"You have a nice grand opening party, serve some cake, some cookies," Jennie advised.

"'Booked and Printed'," Joey suggested.

"'Run For Cover'," Marco proposed.

"Hey." Freddy was squinting toward the back of the church, swaying. "Whoosat?"

The wedding party turned.

A tall black man had slipped into the back pew. He rose and walked toward the altar.

Ellice froze. "Elon," she said.

"I thought I should come get a look at what you're marrying into."

He was tall, with Ellice's grave, wary expression, Ellice's dark, sloe eyes.

"Freddy," Ellice said. "Freddy, this is my brother, Elon Watson. Elon, my fiancé, Freddy Fortunati."

Watson found himself taken into a fierce embrace. But it was Freddy who threw his arms around the man, Freddy who gave him an audible kiss on the cheek and Freddy who keeled over at his feet.

Elon turned to his sister. “You sure know how to pick ‘em.”

“Welcome to the family tree,” Cat said.

CHAPTER SIXTY-TWO: Present Day

Harianne Feldman was the type of woman who was more attractive in her early fifties than she had been in her early twenties. Then, youth had been her predominant asset, but it was an asset that she had neither time nor money to augment. Two jobs, two children, one husband and then no husband left her little time for cultivating any sort of style. With security, she had blossomed into a sleek, self-possessed and very attractive woman.

Victor left his office door open, offered her a chair and reminded her again that she had the right to call an attorney.

"Why don't we see where this is going and then I'll decide if I need one."

"Ms. Feldman, you were married to Randall Hoffman."

The woman smoothed the short-waisted jacket of her business suit. "Many years ago."

"What sort of contact have you had over the years?"

"None. Randall moved on. So did I."

"No communication at all? No visits? Phone calls?"

"We have nothing to talk about."

"His corporation purchased and is leasing land through Home Stead Realty."

"Yes."

"And there's been no reason to communicate regarding that?"

"I didn't handle the transaction."

"No. Hoffman might not have gone through with it if you were the owner. You are the owner? That is, you're the one who receives the lease payments."

"Minus Home Stead's transaction fee."

"And you receive a percentage of that."

Harianne Feldman smiled.

"You and doctor Hoffman had children, correct? Boys? Girls?"

She hesitated, trying to calculate where he was going. She decided to answer. "Two girls. Rowena and Guinevere." She offered him a self-deprecating smile. "I was romantic. Expecting the protection of my white knight. I'm not romantic now."

I can see that. "You said he had no contact with you. Surely, he had visitation?"

"He could have. He chose not to. When Randy was done with us, he disposed of us with less thought, no doubt, than he gives to a batch of unclaimed embryos sitting in a Petri dish."

"But he paid support?"

She ran her carnelian fingertips through her gold waves. "Randy was ordered to pay us two hundred eighty dollars a month until Guinevere was eighteen. He never missed a check. He never missed his eight thousand dollar a month lease payment, either."

"Yes. I don't suppose you would have bought the land unless you were certain that he had settled on that particular site."

She smiled again, but her smile was a bit strained. "I don't see much point in continuing to discuss the past, Lieutenant. I thought we were here to discuss the fact that some fugitive was thought to be squatting in one of Home Stead's unoccupied properties."

"We're talking about both. The property Doctor Hoffman lost to a more timely buyer, and the property the fugitive used to hole up in, both of them came about because of information someone on the inside provided."

Feldman raised her eyebrows, waited.

"Eve Bellamy. When Randall Hoffman decided to buy land, Eve Bellamy had just started working as his file clerk, but Eve Bellamy had a talent for making herself indispensable. She kept you updated on Hoffman's plans and when she needed a place to hold Robert Borch until she decided whether or not she had no further use for him, you reciprocated by finding the location."

"I think I will call my attorney after all."

Voices from the hallway cut short his reply. Victor could barely identify the shrill, out-of-control, "I want to see her *now*! I demand to see her *immediately*!"

Victor looked up. Through the glass separating his office from the day room, he saw Hoffman charge into the bureau, followed by his attorney and Phil Long. Hoffman spotted Victor and strode into his office. "Lieutenant." Anger vibrated through his tone. "I want to see Eve right now."

Victor saw the ripple of surprise loosen the hold on Harianne Feldman's composure. It was not the sight of Hoffman that put her off balance. It was the realization that Eve Bellamy was in custody.

Victor said nothing, waited to let the scene play out.

Hoffman's tanned face had gone russet with fury. "Am I not making myself clear, I want to see her now."

Bevilacqua came up behind his client. "Okay, Cardenas, I don't know what game you're running, but it's done with. Mrs. Hoffman's my client. What's the hold-up?"

Victor said nothing.

At last, Ms. Feldman said, "I believe I'm the hold-up. I think the Lieutenant is waiting for your client to show some sign of recognition. Even that sort of vague 'how are you?' that you offer someone whose name and face you can't recall would be nice. Well, what? Twenty-six years? Is a long time."

Hoffman's jaw went slack. "Ha- Harianne?"

Victor spoke. "Mr. Bevilacqua, this is Ms. Harianne Feldman. She was the first Mrs. Randall Hoffman."

Bevilacqua looked at his client. "Randy?"

Hoffman nodded. "I – uh – what are you doing here, Harianne?"

Victor rose. "She's here because she's being questioned in connection with her part in harboring Robert Borch. Now, if you're certain you would like to see Miss Bellamy, she's in the conference room down the hall."

Victor led the group down the narrow corridor, nodded for Martin Bevilacqua to wait behind the glass. Eve Bellamy was sitting in a chair, toying with a strand of long hair as she chatted with Stan Rice, who had been stationed in the room to keep an eye on her. For the first time he could recall, Victor saw Stan uncomfortable in the presence of a woman.

Victor rested his hand on the knob. *God forgive me*, he said silently, and then he opened the door, and dismissed Stan with a nod. Stan looked relieved to get out of there. Victor allowed Harianne Feldman and Randall Hoffman to pass in front of him, enter the room.

Eve jumped to her feet. The shock, the knowledge that the game was utterly lost passed over her features so swiftly that Victor believed he only imagined a crack in the exquisite mask.

He did not imagine the scornful amusement in her voice when she went up to Ms. Feldman and kissed her cheek, slid an arm around her. “Hi, Mom,” she said, then turned to Hoffman.

“Hi, Dad.”

CHAPTER SIXTY-THREE: Sixteen Years Before

Cat Fortunati's mother and Aunt Caterina helped Cat lift the white skirts while she slipped on the low satin pumps. Then they tugged her train into place.

Carlo's booming voice ascended the stairs. "Yo! Let's get this show on the road!"

Jennie patted Cat's hand and said the most re-assuring words she could come up with on her only daughter's wedding day. "Don't worry, I'll make your brothers behave themselves."

Aunt Cat hung back until her sister left the room. "Allegrezza, I'm not one to give advice. Me, I never married. I made my choice. And I'm not saying a family wouldn't have been nice, but when I figured it wasn't gonna happen, I made the best of things. Because it's not just about what happens to you, it's about what you do with it, too. Things happen that set you back, but you don't let them pull you down. You go on from there and make the best of what's left."

Ten Years Before:

Kathleen Petrone waited in the small room behind the judge's chambers, toying with her short veil. There was a tentative knock on the door and Raymond poked his head into the room.

"Raymond! You can't come in here, it's bad luck!"

Raymond closed the door behind him and took her in his arms. "There's no bad luck from here on, Kathleen, and no bad times, either. Cross my heart." He criss-crossed his finger over the spot where, years hence, he would put the barrel of a gun.

CHAPTER SIXTY-FOUR:
Present Day

Brides are like babies: love makes all of them beautiful. But Ellice would have been beautiful by any measure.

The wedding went off smoothly. Freddy was sober, Mats had not dropped the ring and Dominic concluded his homily in time for the Daughters of Sicily to get the lasagnas out of the oven.

At the reception, Victor danced with the Nixon ladies, with Jennie, with Jane, with the bride. He even offered his hand to Sister Maggie, who told him to "Get along with your nonsense", but took a turn around the floor all the same.

He waited for Cat to fulfill her obligation to dance with her brothers and Mats, and then went up and took her hand. They didn't speak, simply moved with the music, and Victor recalled the morning he had gone swimming, slipping into an even tempo with the sea, hoping for that same rhythm with Cat.

He would never forget the shock on Hoffman's face.

He saw Steve Delareto walk into the room, realized he hadn't seen Delareto at the wedding, nor at the reception. Steve went straight up to Freddy and shook his hand, kissed Ellice on the cheek, exchanged a few words then headed straight for Cat.

"Sorry to cut in, Lieutenant, the two of you look good, but I need to talk to Cat."

"What's up?" Victor asked.

"Cat can tell you anything she wants, but I really need her for a few minutes."

Victor nodded and withdrew.

Steve took Cat's hand. "Let's go talk in the church."

"Steve, what's wrong? Has something happened to Kathy?"

"Come on."

Cat allowed him to lead her down to the sanctuary. They sat in the last pew. There were still garlands along the aisles, flowers on the altar.

"Steve, you're scaring me. I didn't see you at the wedding. Is it about what happened at Kathy's? Is she all right?"

"I'm glad she wasn't there. I'm not saying I'm glad you were, but Kathy's got all she can cope with now."

"I'm alive because she wasn't there. Eve was efficient. She wanted to kill both of us together."

"Well, the thing is, Kathy wasn't there because there was some news her doctor wanted to talk over. About the boy. It looks like they got their match."

"For the bone marrow transplant? That's wonderful."

"Yeah, well good and bad. It's gonna mean a lot of money. She's gonna probably have to sell her house, find some rental. Plus, the surgery'll be done in Philly, so there's the commuting, unless she can stay in a hospice up there. And this all hinges on notifying the donor, see if the donor agrees."

"I can't think anyone would begrudge that little boy his chance."

Steve laid his hand over hers. "I remember your wedding Cat. I wanted to hate Chris, but I couldn't. He was a hell of a guy. I mean, he wasn't one of us, but he was a great guy." He looked at her. "Excuse me, not supposed to say 'hell' in church."

Cat smiled.

"It's weird. This thing about bone marrow. The best matches are identical twins. Siblings are good, but biological parents aren't always. You'd think they'd be the best, wouldn't you? Because who wants a kid to live more than his parents? But statistically, a good match with your bio parent isn't all that common." He took her hand. Squeezed it hard. "But it happens."

She didn't understand, not for a minute or two. Then she saw little Chris Petrone, saw the mop of unruly brown hair, the fair complexion, the large, dark brown eyes.

You've seen pictures of Raymond Stites. The boy doesn't look anything like him, does he? He doesn't look anything like Kathy, either.

No. He looked like Mats. He looked like Chris.

CHAPTER SIXTY-FIVE:
Present Day

Cat was lying on a chaise on the front lawn, a cushion settled under the hip bone from which they had drawn the marrow. It was the last day of school, and she was waiting for the bus, watching Mats pedal his bike up and down the sidewalk. The Nixon ladies were weeding their tomato patch, and later they would come over with a bag of surplus tomatoes for Freddy and Ellice. Cars orbited the beach block streets looking for a place to park and unload blankets and hampers and sunscreen and family, head toward the shore.

Life went on. And on. And in the end, it hadn't been about Chris's premature death, or the devil's bargain that Raymond Stites had made, or even the selfishness of Randall Hoffman in abandoning his family. It had been about what she and Kathy and Eve had done with what had been dealt to them.

The mail truck pulled up and double-parked. Cat took the stack of junk-laden mail and began separating hers from those for Freddy and Ellice. The last was an envelope with the Olde Tyme Scrapple logo in one corner.

Cat slipped her thumb under the flap and opened it. There was a letter with a narrow paper stapled to one corner. Cat adjusted her sunglasses.

'*Dear Mrs. Austen,*

Congratulations! Your slogan has been chosen as the finalist in the Olde Tyme Scrapple and Varietal Meats competition. Look for your slogan to appear in our national advertising campaign and everywhere Olde Tyme Scrapple and Varietal Meats can be found.

Once again, congratulations, and remember, if it's Olde Tyme, it's "The Best Of What's Left!"

Cat looked at the check. One hundred thousand dollars. She had never held a check for one hundred thousand dollars in her hand.

"Vi'tor!"

Cat looked up. Victor pulled up and double-parked, got out. He ruffled Mats hair. "I just came to talk to Mom for a minute. Show me how you ride your bike."

Mats took off along the sidewalk.

Victor dropped onto the grass next to Cat's chaise, took her hand.

"Why aren't you at work?"

"I had some pressing business."

"What?"

"I've decided that if I have to wait, I want it to be because I'm waiting for an answer, not because I'm waiting to ask. Cat, will you marry me?"

Cat looked down at the paper in her hand. She folded the check back into the letter and slipped them into the envelope.

"What's the matter? Not bad news?"